The
Lost
Letters
from
Martha's
Vineyard

The Lost Letters from Martha's Vineyard

A Novel

MICHAEL CALLAHAN

MARINER BOOKS

New York   Boston

THE LOST LETTERS FROM MARTHA'S VINEYARD. Copyright © 2024 by Michael Callahan. All rights reserved. Printed in the United States of America. No part of this book may be used or reproduced in any manner whatsoever without written permission except in the case of brief quotations embodied in critical articles and reviews. For information, address HarperCollins Publishers, 195 Broadway, New York, NY 10007.

HarperCollins books may be purchased for educational, business, or sales promotional use. For information, please email the Special Markets Department at SPsales@harpercollins.com.

FIRST EDITION

Designed by Chloe Foster

Library of Congress Cataloging-in-Publication Data has been applied for.

ISBN 978-0-06-328260-5

24 25 26 27 28 LBC 5 4 3 2 1

CV 03 25 2024 1022

For Jackie Ward

Everyone has three lives: a public life, a private life, and a secret life.

—GABRIEL GARCÍA MÁRQUEZ

Prologue

She sits, shivering. The water had been black and surprisingly cold. Tap cold. She hadn't expected the shock of it. Icy trickles from the sopping hair tangled around her neck seep down her back. She spasms involuntarily, tries to will the bitter chill away.

How had she not *seen*?

She had been stupid. So incredibly stupid.

No time for all of that now. She inches closer to the wall, scurrying deeper into the shadows. The moon is full, luminous, enormous. Tonight it is her enemy, washing the meadow in soft lavender.

She rubs her arms vigorously, trying to get warm, thankful it is not November or, God forbid, February, when the combination of the plunge into the water and the New England frost might have already killed her. Still, it is too cool to try and wait out the night. Her teeth are chattering. She'll have to move at some point, figure out where to go and, more important, how to get there without getting caught. Because she knows he's still out there. Somewhere. Waiting to finish what he started.

What he'd planned all along.

A noise. Rustling. She whips her head side to side, paranoia and fear filling her quickly, like water into a jug.

No, she thinks. *I can't sit here, wait for him to find me. I'm not giving up like that. Not without a fight. I've come too far, found strength I didn't even know I had. I'm smart. I've figured out other things. I can figure this out, too.*

It is not lost on her that figuring out things is what has led her to this moment, trembling in the crisp night air, trying to survive.

She inhales, taking in a deep, steadying breath, and launches onto her feet. She places her hands on the wall behind her to steady her legs, still tired and weak from the swim through the dark water. She is not familiar with Chappaquiddick, knows it only from the small arrowed wooden signs planted around Martha's Vineyard that vaguely point in its general direction. There is a ferry that travels here, five minutes over, five minutes back, every day, though she has no idea where the terminus is, or even where on this small patch of sandy, scratchy island she is. She only remembers hitting the water, the electric force of it enveloping her body, the survival instinct kicking in and her legs kicking with it, until she was once again above the surface, swimming, tentatively, clumsily at first, then smoother, calmer, talking to herself, remembering, commanding her limbs to move, right arm forward, slicing into the water, then left, turning her head to breathe, the familiarity of the strokes slowly returning to her muscle memory.

Impulsively she bolts from the safety of the shadows and dashes through the meadow beyond, her clothes wet and heavy. It's like running underwater. *What time is it?* She almost laughs at the thought. *What possible difference could what time it is make in this moment? Is this how it is before you die—your mind crumbles into randomness to blunt the force of what's coming?*

She hears him.

He is behind her now, running, and she dares not look back. She can make out the tall grass whistling against his legs as he sprints, trying to catch up to her.

He's gaining.

She reaches a worn white wooden fence and lunges across it, awkwardly tumbling onto a gravel road on the other side. Hands braced on the ground, she scrambles back up, but as she lifts her head, it's already too late. He's standing in front of her, chest heaving, eyes wild, the moonlight behind him giving a sinister glint to the gun he holds in his right hand.

"All you had to do," he says, the anger raging in his low voice, "was leave it alone. But you didn't—"

No, she didn't.

She eyes him evenly. "I couldn't."

Her response seems to catch him by surprise. And for a moment it is just the two of them, standing alone on a godforsaken road on a tiny, deserted stretch of tiny, deserted Chappaquiddick, staring into each other's eyes in the dim light. She summons the courage to speak again. "I had to know."

He shakes his head, lifts the gun, and points it at her. "I hope it was worth it."

Then he pulls the trigger.

One

Lucinda Cross hates people who are late, a fact Kit knows all too well as she hustles up Sixth Avenue toward the network building, stealing a glance at the time on her phone, as if confirming how late she is will somehow make it all better.

Her phone vibrates in her pocket. Claire again. Claire's not much of a phone person, but circumstances being what they are, she has become one now. She's convinced that Kit cannot possibly handle all of the minutiae of emptying their grandmother's house alone. So tomorrow Claire is leaving Russell and the boys to fend for themselves for a few days in Maryland and coming up to help. Kit often jokes that while at Tulane, Claire may have majored in psychology, but she clearly minored in guilt. It might, Kit thinks, explain Claire's adult conversion to Catholicism.

"Hey," Kit says. "I've only got a minute. I'm late for work."

"Who was he this time?" her sister asks. Kit can almost see the smirk.

"Be nice."

"I'm always nice. Anyway, I'm sure the great Lucinda Cross will understand."

"I have clearly taught you nothing about the people who work in television."

Claire laughs. "Only that I'm glad I am not one of them."

Sometimes Kit wishes she wasn't, either. It was fun at first, right after college: the insane hours, the bad food, the rush of adrenaline from the breaking news or bubbling scandal, the shameless flirting with the occasional cute cameraman—and what sometimes came after. Five years later, pushing papers and coordinating and re-coordinating shoot schedules as a line producer, it doesn't all seem quite so fizzy. She's a junior producer of a generally well-regarded and, even more important, well-rated news program. She has a career most people would consider to be glamorous and interesting. But increasingly her heart isn't in it. She wishes she knew what it *would* be in.

Claire, on the other hand, is like Nan. As a teenager she had wanted nothing to do with the city, happy to hunker down in Nan's big roomy house in Rye with Jane Austen, NSYNC blaring in her bedroom. Kit was thirsty for the raw energy and creativity New York offered on every sidewalk, attacked it like a castaway finding food. She'd gone to NYU, moved to Soho right after college as Claire settled in a bucolic small town with her college sweetheart and drilled down roots as far as she could plant them. Maryland wasn't far, but Nan still hadn't been thrilled. Both girls reminded her regularly that she had begun her life in Nebraska and ended up in Rye. She could hardly complain about having to sometimes schlep to Manhattan and Maryland.

"How much do we have left to sell?" Kit asks, rounding onto Sixth Avenue.

"I'm going to start posting the remaining stuff online day after to-morrow. Then we'll just have to deal with the house. Are you sure there's nothing else you want?"

"No," Kit says emphatically. She stops on the street, catches her reflection in an office building window. She fingers the blue sap-phire necklace, pats it back into place. It was her grandmother's favorite piece of jewelry, the only one she wore every day. Claire is taking the Dinko Bjelan painting, the William and Mary buffet, and the pearl choker their father bought for Nan for her fiftieth birth-day. Twelve years later her mother and father would go out for din-ner and never return. Claire had been nine, Kit only four. Kit envies Claire's sharp memories of their parents. She has almost none. Just fading pictures of faces that vaguely resemble her own.

"Kit? You still there?"

"Yes, yes. Sorry. No, I have the necklace and the photo albums. That's all I want."

"Well, just so you know, that does not get you out of your pledge to tackle the attic."

"I'm crying foul. You caught me in a moment of weakness."

"As all good negotiations go."

Kit laughs as she pushes through the revolving door into the glossy lobby of network headquarters. "Look, I'm here. See you tomorrow."

*

Signature with Lucinda Cross is hardly the network's most popular program, but its PBS-y feel and lustrous, revolving guest list featuring some of the country's premier names in the arts, culture, academia, science, politics, and occasionally—and begrudgingly, because Lucinda loathes professional athletics—sports has made it a jewel, a bastion of prestige and Peabody Awards. The network largely leaves the show alone, though lately that has begun to change as ratings have turned softer. Even Kit has found herself growing weary of the show's faux gravitas, never better exemplified than in its closing, where at the end of each episode its immaculately tailored host declares, "I'm Lucinda Cross, with my signature," as her name in colonial-style script handwriting unfurls across the screen, the picture slowly fading to black. The irony, of course, is that the signature is not that of Lucinda Cross at all but a long-departed production assistant with baronial penmanship. Lucinda's real signature looks like that of a serial killer. It's why she never gives autographs. Can't break the mystique.

Kit drops her bag on her chair and wriggles out of her cropped denim jacket, softly moaning as she eyes the stack of memos, books, and folders strewn across her cubicle desk. She's been gone less than a week. At least she's been missed.

Out of the corner of her eye she catches the small paperweight, ironically now buried under a pile of paper. She picks it up, inspects it. A gift from Nan when she turned eighteen. Who gives an eighteen-year-old a paperweight as a birthday present? Claire got one, too. It's cut glass, with a simple three-word engraving: *Always Be Brave*.

As she's putting it back she feels a presence behind her, turns to see Priya, Lucinda's often-put-upon assistant, arms outstretched. "Welcome back," she says, folding Kit into a warm hug.

"Thanks for holding down the fort," Kit says, stepping back, "and . . . cute boots!"

"Thanks!" Priya preens, always happy to have her fashion choices noticed. Priya lives with a tabby named Ishkibibble on the Upper East Side in a studio paid for by her conservative Indian parents, who constantly fret about her being seduced by New York's earthier charms. She's cute and cherubic and overly accessorized, and either constantly complaining about her overbearing mother trying to marry her off or exclaiming how some inedible object is "delish," as in, "OMG, that Monica Vinader bangle is just delish!"

"She wants to see you when you can pop by," Priya says, nodding down the hall toward Lucinda's door. "Actually ASAP, though she took great pains to make sure she was not quoted as saying 'ASAP.'"

So Lucinda. She instructed everyone on the staff not to bother Kit during her bereavement leave, while sending endless text messages herself, all ending with the suitably passive-aggressive, "This can wait till you get back."

"Wish me luck." Kit heads down the hall toward the corner office, adjusting her blouse and suddenly wishing she hadn't worn her hair in a ponytail. Commenting on one's poor fashion choices is one of Lucinda's specialties. Christiane Amanpour meets Miranda Priestly.

Kit knocks on the glass wall. "Hi," she says, walking into not an office but a spread from *Elle Decor*. The glass tables are Phillips, the throw pillows abc carpet & home, the drapes—drapes! in a thirty-third-floor office!—from some workshop in Zurich, no doubt hand-sewn by Swiss nuns at spinning wheels. Kit used to wonder how Lucinda got any work done in here. She came to quickly realize that everyone else did the work.

Lucinda is standing behind her glass desk, flipping through a coffee table book, her black bob lustrous and severe as ever, a ponderous Bulgari necklace threatening to tip her over. She looks up, purses her lips into what for her passes for a smile. "So nice to see you," she says, walking over and placing a carefully manicured hand on Kit's forearm. Her version of a bear hug. "You know, I was serious. You could have taken a few more days."

Kit shakes her head. "Thanks. I'm fine. I am really grateful that I got to have her for such a long time. Lots of people lose their grandmothers much earlier."

"But not ones who raised them from toddlerhood," Lucinda says, waving Kit into an Eames chair. "You know, I studied the reverence for the elderly in the Korean culture for my senior thesis at Bryn Mawr."

Kit fights to stifle a laugh. She's never met anyone better at turning any situation or subject back to themselves. Lucinda takes the seat across from her, crossing her legs and balancing her monstrous Lucite reading glasses—Prada, naturally—in her right hand as she pierces Kit's gaze. "Tell me about her."

It's odd, really. Not just that she's getting the full-on Lucinda Cross interview treatment, but that she's being asked about Nan. Not many people know Kit's backstory, that Nan was her grandmother but actually had to step into the role of her mother, the one who braided her hair and hugged away the tears and clapped from the third row at the school pageants, and managed all the rituals, big and small, that followed. She feels a rush of emotion rise into her throat, her eyes moistening. How do you describe the person who, in the wake of unspeakable loss, stepped in and gave you your life?

She tries anyway. She talks about how Nan grew up on a farm in Nebraska, how she wanted a bigger life, left home at twenty-one and went to New York to secretarial school, and after a few years met her grandfather, the rakish young lawyer at the firm where she spent her days typing and filing. How she was a free spirit who ended up with a serious and conservative son she fought to understand, but whom she loved dearly, even when he married his high school girl-friend at twenty-two instead of going to explore the world as she'd hoped. How she loved the Guggenheim, and how she taught Kit how to make her legendary vanilla apple pie. And how, when the worst happened, she took on the awesome responsibility of raising her son's two girls to be independent, free-spirited women. *Don't take the easy road. Explore. Question. Fight,* she always said.

Always be brave.

Two

The house is a traditional center-hall colonial—beige clapboard, dark pine shutters, wood-framed fireplace, curving staircase. Her grandmother had a deep and abiding fondness for such architecture. She once said she had wanted the house to look like the kind of place a sailor would return to after a long voyage. Nan loved the ocean. She could spend hours just standing at the surf's edge, staring out at the water.

Kit finds Claire in the kitchen. Though they are sisters they look, at best, like distant cousins. Claire is shorter, in a constant battle with fifteen pounds that refuse to leave, with a mom blunt cut and a heart-shaped face that would be at home on pancake mix. She is the kind of person, when she is old, that no one will be able to picture as ever having been young. There is a calm, relentless kindness to Claire that Kit has always admired and envied. Her maternal instinct kicked in early, trying to shield Kit from the blunt force of the sudden loss of their parents. Kit sometimes wonders how much less pious, how much more carefree and spontaneous, her sister might have been if they'd lived. And if she herself would have been less of a hell-raising teenage rebel, and would have eventually mustered the ability to let someone get close. Instead, she's toyed with a conveyor belt of men who have been pretty, vacant, and easily dispatched. *Next.*

After the usual round of greeting/hug/inquiry about the drive up (or in Kit's case, train, then Uber up), Kit glances at the stacks of sparkling dishes and serving plates, surveying the chaos Claire has unleashed onto every counter surface. "I told you we should have just hired a clean-out company to do all of this."

"Nonsense," Claire replies. "It just feels wrong to let all of this go so easily, without a proper accounting." She sweeps her hand around the kitchen. "I mean, look at this beautiful delft china. We had some incredible holiday dinners on these dishes. You should keep it."

Kit hops onto the counter. "And where exactly am I going to store service for sixteen? I live in a one-bedroom apartment in downtown Manhattan. You're the one with the split-level. And you're the one who loves to cook. Take it—you can pass it to one of the boys when they get married."

"One passes china to one's daughters, not one's sons."

"That's incredibly sexist."

"Sure. Tell you what: the next time you pick up your nephews from soccer, ask them if they're pining for their great-grandmother's china. Let me know what they say."

"Maybe one of them will turn out to be gay."

"*Now* who's being sexist?"

Kit shrugs. "Not sexist. Stereotyping, perhaps, but not sexist."

"Enough jibber jabber," Claire says, organizing the china into tidy stacks. "Go. You have a date with the attic."

Kit slides off the counter, exhaling wearily. "OK, OK, I'm going. Please send a reconnaissance team if I'm not down in two hours."

*

Nan was not particularly sentimental. The drawings and craft projects she and Claire made as children were suitably ooh'd and aah'd over and displayed in the kitchen or sitting room for a respectable period, then promptly dispatched into the trash. The one exception was Christmas. At Christmas, Nan became a one-woman Hallmark store, with a big, fulsome tree (always real; *Fake trees are for fake Christmas,* she was fond of saying), lights, an imposing crèche, and reams of fresh greenery, holly, and ivy snaking around every window and up the bannister. Opening a trunk, Kit surveys the cornucopia of ornaments, glittering in row after row. *Oh, man, we forgot about these,* she thinks. *But Claire has to take them. She must. If she won't, I will. We can't let these go.*

That would be like letting go of Nan.

It washes over her in a wave, hard and unexpected and unforeseen and brutal in force, as it has every time these past weeks. In her everyday times, in her busy times, Kit thinks of her grandmother's passing and focuses on what needs to be done, the loose ends, the busywork of death. But it is when she is caught off guard—an old song piped into a restaurant, a rediscovered birthday card saved in a shoebox—that she finds herself emotionally assassinated, buckling under the sheer weight of the loss of the woman who raised her, comforted her, sacrificed for her, loved her. And so here she is, on her knees in the attic, sobbing, head bowed, her hands shaking as they clutch the open lid of the trunk. There will never be another Christmas where she will watch Nan hang these ornaments with the care of a museum curator. There will never be another Christmas in this house at all. Just one of many losses realized and absorbed, each a blow that sends her back reeling into herself.

Fifteen minutes later, after the storm has finally abated, Kit glances over toward the two small windows, dust particles dancing in their sunbeams, and gathers herself. She rises, wipes her eyes, surveys the mishmash of dusty boxes as she forms a plan of attack. She silently curses Claire for not just hiring the damn clean-out company and being done with it all.

Two hours pass. Two hours of foraging through piles of yellowed books and old scarves and empty picture frames, but the piles are dwindling, the trash bags bulging, a light at the end of the attic. She bows her head, ducks into the corner of the gabled eave, where an old wooden crate is covered by a pile of moving blankets, file boxes with long-ago utility bills, and old curtains. Kit removes a dust-covered hatbox—who keeps a hatbox?—then the file boxes and the curtains, throwing back the blankets and with them a volcanic eruption of dust that sends her into a sneezing fit. It takes two trips down to the garage and a few more mumbled curse words for Claire to find the right tools to pry open the lid of the crate.

Photo albums filled with pictures of people she doesn't recognize. The silver serving utensils from Nan's mother in Nebraska that they could never find, now tarnished into grubby blackness. Her father's high school diploma. Even more random, a moth-eaten fisherman's sweater. And then, at the top right corner, on the bottom, a small, rectangular, gray linen box, tied lovingly with a black felt ribbon.

Kit lifts out the box, then slides onto the floor next to the crate. She unties the ribbon, lifts the lid, and slowly extracts the contents, carefully preserved. First, a folded, yellowed playbill. Kit scans the wording.

THE MARTHA'S VINEYARD PLAYHOUSE PRESENTS
MERCY WELLES
IN
THE ROSE OF AQUINNAH
A NEW PLAY BY STANTON WILLIAMS
AUGUST 22–29, 1959

Martha's Vineyard? Odd. She'd never once heard Nan mention Martha's Vineyard, even in passing. Nineteen fifty-nine. That would have been before she'd met Pop, when she was living in the women's hotel in New York. Maybe she'd gone for a trip with some girlfriends?

A few more random items. Two matching clamshells, each with almost identical swirling. Kit extracts a faded yellow prize ribbon, the SECOND PRIZE in blue now barely visible.

Two more artifacts, tucked into the playbill. A black-and-white photo of her grandmother—looking slim and deliriously happy in a pale sundress, her arm around a striking, rugged-looking young man dressed in a white T-shirt and blue jeans. A blank envelope containing a notecard, with SYCAMORE in raised navy-blue letters across the top, with a handwritten message: *Nancy—Something to remember me by, or to stow away in the attic.* It is signed, simply, *R.*

Kit grins. *Oh, Nan. A secret summer romance on Martha's Vineyard. But who was R.? And why was the card addressed to Nancy?* Her grandmother's name is Edith. She runs her fingers across the back of the envelope, which feels slightly ticky-tacky. It's stained. Likely residue of some sort of glue. But none on the photograph. She scans the box again. Empty. Whatever the card was originally attached to isn't here.

She hears Claire yelling for her from the recesses of the house. She hurriedly places the items back into the box, tucks it under her arm, and scurries down the attic stairs.

*

Kit towels off her wet hair, thankful to have washed off the dust and grime of the attic. She's exhausted. Now: pajamas, water, bed.

She walks back into her old bedroom, gets into her soft, roomy Yankees T-shirt and yoga pants. She's about to slip under the covers when she spies the gray linen box on the dresser. She'd dropped it there on her way downstairs to see Claire, who is now at the other end of the hall, dead asleep after FaceTiming with Russell and the boys.

Kit retrieves the box, spreads the contents out on the bed, taking time to inspect them more thoroughly. She's sure she does not know the man in the photo, who is most definitely not her grandfather. She puts one of the shells to her ear, feels a prick of emotion as she remembers Nan telling her as a little girl, *Listen and you can hear the ocean.* Putting it back she picks up the playbill again, then reaches for her laptop. She plops down onto the bed in lotus position, flips it open.

The Rose of Aquinnah, she types into the search bar.

No results. At least none that are relevant.

New search. *Mercy Welles,* she types.

Her producer's instinct tingles as she scans the page. Two results down she spies an entry with the tantalizing title "The Strange and Curious Case of Mercy Welles." It's from a blog called *Long Lost Hollywood.* She clicks on it.

> Hollywood is littered with stories of promising young actresses who came to Tinseltown with big talent and big dreams, only to be vanquished by the soul-crushing workings of the show

business machine. One such nubile star was Mercy Welles, who was in the midst of a promising career when, for reasons never explained, she abandoned Hollywood, never to be heard from again.

A milky-skinned, innocent honey blonde from the Midwest, Mercy had done a few small parts, earning money as a model in advertisements for cigarettes and cars in the 1950s, when she came into her own with a standout performance in 1958's *The Lovely Dream*, which earned her an Oscar nomination as Best Supporting Actress. Critics swooned over her, tagging her as the next Audrey Hepburn or Lana Turner. Engaged to up-and-coming director Louis Flynn, who had made an impressive debut with his 1956 film *The Days of Waikiki*, they quickly became one of Hollywood's new "golden couples," a staple at industry parties and for a hot minute a regular presence in fan magazines. Studio executives were circling. Observers predicted big things.

Then, just as suddenly, it was all over. Breaking her engagement with Flynn, she vanished from Hollywood almost overnight in the summer of 1959, leaving behind a trail of rumor and innuendo—most of which never made it into print. Her flustered agent, the veteran Hollywood dealmaker Sy Sigmund, would only declare that, "She decided she'd had enough. That's all I can say," refusing to elaborate.

Mercy Welles was not the first, nor the last, willowy starlet to bolt the unforgiving glare of the Hollywood spotlight for safer ground, but she remains one of its most unique and mysterious. As the pictures below attest, she also remains one of its most alluring.

Kit scrolls down. Her eyes widen as she feels her blood freeze. She stares in disbelief as she looks at Mercy Welles—laughing in a booth at the Brown Derby, looking up into the drenched lighting of a studio headshot, cocking her head during a party to hear a whisper from Peter Lawford—and sees her grandmother staring back.

Three

B everly Hills didn't hold much interest. The Rodeo Drive shopping, the three-hour hair appointments, the McCarthy salad by the pool at the Beverly Hills Hotel—these were the pursuits of the rich, bored, thin (and sometimes not so thin) spouses of the studio executives and producers who ran Hollywood, all of them trying, each and every day, not to think about how utterly pointless their lives were.

Mercy lifted a champagne coupe off a passing tray and slowly retreated to a corner of the room, her preferred spot at any party: sometimes it was more fun to be the audience than the act. She was wearing a pale pink silk evening dress by Jacques Fath, which, given the fact that the designer was dead nearly five years now, she figured would clearly be interpreted as the sign of a promising career now stalled. She didn't care. She had adored Fath's amusing clothes, his whimsical floral skirts and hemp sacking. And his grandfather had been an acclaimed French playwright. What was fashion if not textile stagecraft?

She watched The Wives gliding through the space like well-appointed mannequins circling on intersecting lazy Susans. Their expressions certainly appeared just as blank.

Louis sidled up to her. "I know that look."

"What look?"

"You're dissecting The Wives."

She took a sip of the champagne. "Guilty. You've got to allow me *some* fun. Remind me why we're here again?"

He sighed. "For the same reason we're at every one of these. To make sure people see us and remember who we are. It's Hollywood. You're here today—"

"Gone tomorrow. I know, I know. You should have it printed on cards, you say it enough."

He took a slug of bourbon. "If only someone would ask for my card."

She glanced over at his profile. With his sandy hair and deep brown eyes, Louis Flynn looked more like a genial college professor than one of Hollywood's new up-and-coming directors. He wasn't tall—five-seven at best—but he carried himself with an air of affable gravity that made him more imposing than his physicality might suggest. He was, by far, the most charming man she'd ever met. Also the moodiest. She never knew which of several versions she was getting whenever he walked through the door. She hated that she found this unpredictability arresting.

"C'mon," he said, taking her by the elbow. "Time to mingle."

He led her through the throng, consisting of the two standard groups that populated every Hollywood party: those who had power and those trying to get it. Louis may have been a rising director and Mercy an ascending actress who, at twenty-six, had already been nominated for a supporting Oscar. But they had no real power. The difference was that Mercy didn't care. Louis cared about little else.

Don Rickles, his froggy face contorted from a particularly animated round of storytelling, held court in a corner, regaling several doughy men with observations that elicited the guffaws one expected from a Rickles routine. *Wasn't it exhausting,* Mercy wondered, *to have to entertain, to have the power switch on all the time?* She spied a few other boldface names—the Gabor sisters, Richard Basehart, the singer Frankie Avalon—scattered amid the industry folk, but for the most part the soiree seemed to be a largely studio executive–suite affair.

She and Louis drifted up to the perimeter of a group of five that included two producers (only one of them truly successful), the actress

Constance Baxter, clearly in denial about a recent weight gain—her polka-dot bell dress was too young a pattern and gripped her like a vise—and a silver-haired couple Mercy didn't recognize. Louis made an awkward, rather brazen attempt to infiltrate the circle.

"What are you doing?" Mercy whispered.

He shot her a glare. "Trying to land a picture," he hissed. "Constance Baxter is doing a big comeback vehicle for Paramount."

". . . Well, I have no interest," Constance was saying. "As it is, I try to stay out of New York as much as humanly possible. It's just gotten so dirty and overcrowded. Why would I ever leave all of this sunshine and palm trees?"

"But the museum is supposed to be spectacular," the silver-haired wife offered demurely. "I keep telling John we must wrangle an invitation to the opening."

The successful producer took note of the young couple's presence. "Ah! Our brash young director and his beautiful muse have joined our company. What say you, young Mr. Flynn?"

"I'm sorry. What are we discussing?"

"Whether the forthcoming opening of the new Guggenheim Museum warrants a trip across the country."

Louis laughed nervously. "I'm afraid I'm not much for art."

"Well, I think it sounds marvelous," the wife said. "I'd go for the Kandinskys alone."

"I'd have to agree with you," Mercy interjected. "It's going to be a very different kind of collection: Chagall, Klee, Fernand Léger. And the building itself. I'm fascinated by Frank Lloyd Wright."

Mercy noted the look of dull surprise that registered on the surrounding faces. You could almost hear their collective thought: *Wait—isn't she an actress from Idaho or somewhere? How does she know about art?*

"Well, I see you have snagged a real woman of culture there, Louis," quipped the other producer, who currently had two westerns, neither of them very good, on television. He raised his glass in toast. "To the women who make us better."

Constance snorted. "If only men would *let* us make them better."

Louis smiled at her. "Is it true that Robson's dropped out as director on *She's Nothing but Trouble*?" The script, written by an acclaimed novelist, had somehow been bought by Constance. Two studios were now fighting for the right to make it. Her shot at once again being a star.

Constance took an artful drag on her cigarette. "Alas, yes. But," she said, looking intently into his eyes, "I'm sure I'll find ample amusement auditioning replacements."

The producer's wife, showing her discomfort at this line of conversation, offered a new topic, about a restaurant opening in Bel Air. The talk turned to seafood. "Careful there," Mercy whispered, delicately raising her coupe to her lips.

Louis kept his eyes on the conversation. "What's that supposed to mean?" he muttered back.

"You know what it means."

"You're being ridiculous," he said. "Like I said, it's her big comeback vehicle. She could hold the key to my career."

A society photographer arrived and asked them to gather for a photo. Afterward, he dutifully scribbled down names from memory. He turned to Louis. "I'm sorry. You are . . . ?"

Louis stiffened. "Louis Flynn. I'm a director."

"Oh, we only do names, not jobs," the photographer said, jotting it down.

"It's not a 'job.' It's a profession."

The photographer looked up, his eyes steely. "Of course."

Louis waved toward Mercy. "And this is—"

"Oh, I know who she is. Mercy Welles." He delivered a broad smile in her direction. "Can I just say, I loved *Summer Sonata*."

Mercy smiled. "Thank you. That's very kind." She turned to say something to Louis, but, reading his stony expression, stopped herself.

The photographer looked at the ring on Mercy's finger. "When are you two getting hitched?" he asked.

"Well, we think—"

"We're in no rush," Louis interjected. He turned to her. "I think I spied Hal Wallis out by the pool. I'm going to try and get a word."

She was about to reply when he began walking away. The photographer arched a slight eyebrow, flipped his pad shut, and ambled off.

Mercy threaded her way through the chattering crowd, back to the front of the house. She passed out onto the front patio, with its four imposing Ionic columns and sweeping view of the carefully cultivated rose garden. Someone said that the owner had wanted it to look like Tara from *Gone with the Wind*.

"Lost your man?" came a voice from several feet away.

Constance Baxter was smoking what appeared to be a fresh cigarette. She extracted a silver cigarette case from her shiny black patent leather handbag, which swung on her forearm like a pendulum.

Mercy didn't smoke, hated how the practice infiltrated your hair and clothes until you couldn't smell anything else. But it somehow felt rude to decline. She nodded her head slightly and extracted a cigarette out of the case, leaning in as Constance lit it. She faked inhaling, blew smoke out over the roses.

"Your fiancé seems a little tense," Constance said.

"You know how directors are."

"I certainly do. I married two."

Mercy briefly studied her. There was still something compelling about Constance Baxter, even now, in her too-tight dress, looking like a weary Italian contessa longing for life before the war. She could remember going to the movies growing up, watching Constance spar with various dashing leading men. But then it seemed her fame had just slowly ebbed away. Evidently she had done some theater in New York, plays that closed as quickly as they'd opened. No wonder she had no interest in the Guggenheim. And now here she was, the great actress coating her bitterness in smoke at a party she clearly had no interest attending.

They stood side by side for a moment, looking out over the sweeping lawn, until Constance broke the quiet.

"Well, I should be going. I'm meeting some friends for the floor show at the Cocoanut Grove."

"That sounds like fun."

"It isn't," Constance said matter-of-factly. She looked at Mercy starkly. "My dear, would you mind terribly if I offered you two small pieces of advice?"

"Please."

"Stop feeling guilty that your career is going better than his. It's an odd thing our mothers gave us, this sense that our worlds should only be about him, what he needs, what he's feeling, whoever 'he' happens to be at any given moment in our lives." She took a final drag of the cigarette, stubbing it out in a garden urn. "You know I, too, saw *Summer Sonata*. You were marvelous. I have no idea if your Mr. Flynn is a good director. But you, my dear, you have the one thing all great actresses need most: presence. Take it and run with it. Don't make your life all about his. Seize your opportunities. Because trust me, they don't come forever." She patted Mercy lightly on the forearm as she passed to go back into the house.

"Wait," Mercy said, turning. "You said you wanted to give me two pieces of advice. What's the other?"

Constance spun back around. "Don't end up like me."

Then she turned, dissolving into the party.

*

Mercy put her key in the lock, shoving the entry door of their Poinsettia Place building open—she'd have to call the super again about how bad it was sticking—and hurried up the two flights. She called it "their" apartment although only Louis was on the lease, since proper young actresses were not supposed to be cohabitating with the men in their lives, even if they were engaged to said men. She'd had to tell her family that she didn't have a phone, that they had to call her agent if they needed to reach her. Her mother, still not over the day five years ago when her daughter had calmly announced she had purchased a one-way bus ticket to Los Angeles, would have disowned her if she'd known the truth. Every time her mother wrote she never failed to mention that Henry McCloskey, who ran his father's shoe store in their small Nebraska city and had the unfortunate nickname of Buckethead, was still single.

Mercy dropped her bag and keys on the hall table, unpinning her hat just as Louis was rounding the corner. "Oh, hi," he said. "I . . . I thought you were at an audition."

"Canceled," Mercy said, brushing his cheek with a kiss. "Evidently Sirk caught a cold. Not that he'd ever cast me anyway."

"You would be great in a Douglas Sirk film."

"I wasn't great enough for him to cast me in *Imitation of Life*."

"At least you're *getting* auditions."

Their eyes met briefly. She turned, placed her hat atop her bag, then took in his gabardine pants and blue blazer. "Well, you look nice. I thought you were staying in and writing tonight."

"I was. I mean, I am. I was just running out for a quick bite with Ted. Clear the cobwebs kind of thing. I can't seem to get the treatment right."

"That's what happens when you try to do too much," she said, walking past him into the kitchen. He followed her in as she popped open the refrigerator, hunting for something to nibble. "You're already a terrific director. I have no idea why you're now going to torture yourself by also being a writer."

"Probably because no one is actually letting me direct."

She shut the refrigerator door. "That's not true, Louis. You have directed."

"Yeah. A movie nobody saw and an episode of *The Rifleman*. Impressive. It's just like being nominated for an Oscar."

This again. She said nothing.

He forced a laugh. "I'm sorry. I'm just grouchy from writer's block." He looked at his watch. "I need to get going. I don't want to keep Ted waiting."

"Remember, we have dinner tomorrow at Kitty and Stewart's."

He closed his eyes. "That's tomorrow? Is there any way we can get out of it? I really need to hunker down with this treatment if it's ever going to actually materialize into a script."

She held her tongue for a minute, weighing her reply. He had been like this a lot lately: hair-trigger, prickly. She knew it was due to the pressure he was putting on himself, had tried to be patient. But the constant ego-stroking was growing tiresome. She lifted her chin. "I wish we could, but we can't. It's a dinner party for eight. Kitty's already prepared half the food. It would be terribly rude to cancel."

He exhaled, shrugged his shoulders. "OK." He walked over, kissed her perfunctorily on the temple, then walked out of the kitchen. She heard the front door close.

She'd opened the cupboard to extract a can of tuna fish, then reconsidered. She inhaled.

He'd been wearing his best shirt, the one she was always telling him brought out his eyes. And cologne.

She wasn't hungry anymore.

Four

Orson Welles was notorious for not wanting to be interrupted during lunch. The occasionally overexuberant producer or writer who was unaware of this quickly learned the error of his ways when he approached the booth as the star sat sipping an ice-cold martini and devouring a plate of grenadine of beef. Interlopers were quickly and brutally rebuffed, scurrying back to the safety of their tables.

Mercy walked through the front door of Musso & Frank, looking for any distraction from the memory of Louis's strange exit from their apartment the night before. She spied Welles at his normal table in the front, flipping through a copy of *Variety*. A piece of the restaurant's famous sourdough hung from his mouth, giving him the appearance of a ravenous, well-dressed Saint Bernard. While they shared a surname, only one of them had come to it by birth. As Mercy followed the maître d' down the row of booths in the Old Room, she consciously avoided even passing eye contact. In Hollywood, insouciance was the most important acting skill of all.

Approaching a scarlet leather banquette, Mercy scanned the rest of the lunch crowd. No one else famous, as far as she could tell, though her eyes narrowed as she got a glance of the grill counter, trying to discern if the mousy, bespectacled figure at the far end sipping snapper soup was Edith Head, engrossed in a paperback novel. Now *there* was someone for whom she might break the rules and introduce herself. Head's clothes were feminine, tailored works of art for which she'd already won six Academy Awards. Even if the rumor was that she'd stolen half of the designs.

She slid into the booth and opened her compact, fiddling aimlessly with her hair. She was twenty-six but feared she looked thirty. The industry did that to you. With her green eyes, pale skin, and wavy, honey-blond hair, she knew she was objectively pretty. It did little to assuage the paranoia.

"Sorry I'm late!" came the nasal greeting above her. Cass Goldman leaned down to graze her cheek with a peck.

"I wouldn't expect anything less," Mercy said. "It's when you're on time that I get nervous."

"Hey, I'm getting better," Cass retorted, scooting into the other side of the booth. "I swear, I don't know why you love coming to this place. They haven't changed the decor since the twenties. Or the menu, either, for that matter. There's much better people-watching at Chasen's."

"Those are all of the exact reasons I *adore* coming here," Mercy replied. Musso & Frank was positively draconian about enforcing a no-pictures policy, and equally forceful about policing diners so that the famous were not bothered by autograph-seekers. As a result, there was a certain sector of Hollywood that dined here frequently and happily, hungry for the delicious thing unofficially the star on its menu: privacy.

A waiter sidled up to their table, and before he could speak Cass blurted out, "Singapore sling with a twist, please."

Mercy ordered a coffee then leaned back in the booth. "It's barely noon!"

"If you'd had the morning I had, you'd be drinking, too." Cass was a script supervisor at Warner Brothers, but said her real title should be "Woman Who Puts Up With Everyone Else's Bullshit." She related a story about a particularly prickly encounter with Howard Hawks, who had scored a surprise hit with *Rio Bravo*—who knew the combination of John Wayne and Ricky Nelson would sell tickets? He had come up to Cass's desk, plopped down a pile of scripts, and drolly remarked, "The next time Jack Warner wants to send me a pile of horseshit, make sure he includes a shovel."

After they debated whether that *was* actually Edith Head at the end of the counter—Cass thought not, "but you never know with Edith, she always looks like a vampire"—Cass brought up the dreaded topic of the wedding.

"So, when are we finally going shopping for the dress?" Cass asked as she took a slug of her drink. "You know, I bet you could get Helen Rose to make it for you. She made Grace Kelly's."

"Grace Kelly was a famous leading lady who was marrying a European prince," Mercy said. "I am barely known by my own family."

"You are a fabulous actress who was nominated for an Academy Award this year."

"For a supporting role. Which I didn't win." She had sat in the back of the Pantages, convinced she couldn't win and wouldn't win but, deep deep deep deep down, still holding on to the glimmer that, well, maybe, you never know, and then had politely applauded as Harold Hecht had accepted on behalf of Wendy Hiller for *Separate Tables*.

"You're changing the subject. We were talking about your dress."

"No, *you* were talking about my dress."

Cass put the drink down. "You know, you're an odd duck sometimes. Why don't you ever want to talk about your own wedding?"

"Stop being silly."

"Stop being evasive."

Mercy looked at Cass appraisingly. Cass was short—she couldn't have been taller than five-two—and round at the hips, with an angular face and dark eyes that were slightly too large. She was the kind of woman Hollywood either cast as the nasty busybody or shoved into the production office. They'd met shortly after Mercy had arrived in town with a different name and a plainer appearance, as they both stood side by side, staring up at a bulletin board at the YWCA, scanning for places to live. They'd struck up a conversation that Mercy still remembered as one of the funniest she'd ever had. They'd lived together for two years.

Mercy knew Cass wasn't going to let it go.

"OK, so you're right," she said. "I *am* being evasive." She took in a deep breath. "The truth is that I'm not sure wedding plans are the best thing to be focused on right now. Things . . . aren't terrific with Louis."

Cass gulped down the last of her drink, waved the empty glass in the waiter's direction as she held up two fingers.

Mercy frowned. "Are you okay to have another?" she asked.

"Oh, you're having one, too." Cass leaned across the table, took Mercy's hand in hers. "You can always confide in me, honey. You know that. After all, I'm one of the only people in this town who knows your real name is—"

"Don't—"

"Edith Stoppelmoor, from Beatrice, Nebraska."

"You're positively evil."

"I'm positively your best pal. Now out with it. What's going on?"

Where to start? Louis had had one film produced. It was a splashy debut—some of the exteriors were actually filmed on the island of Hawaii, an unheard-of production expense for a first-time director. And while it hadn't lit the box office on fire, it had been critically well received. Mercy had been filming a bit part at the lot next door, and one day in the commissary their eyes had met and that had been that. They'd been engaged for three months now, following a romantic Valentine's Day dinner at Romanoff's and the floor show at the Mocambo. Louis had made sure the news was dropped in Hedda Hopper's column.

Then came the Oscars.

"The first month after we got engaged was everything: plans, flowers, kisses, the whole thing every girl dreams of when she's to be married," Mercy said. "And then we went to the Academy Awards, and I didn't win. And—I don't know—it seemed to affect him somehow. Like I was damaged goods."

Cass shook her head. "That's crazy."

"It's not crazy. He was different. He *is* different. A girl knows when her fella is acting different." She took in the pursed look on Cass's face and regretted her tone, its dismissive implication of *You burgeoning spinster, how would you know?*

"I mean, you know what I mean," Mercy continued. "You can tell when someone is acting differently."

Cass moved past the slight. "How has he been acting?"

"Tired all the time. Reserved, pulled back. He's always busy, but he's never really specific about what he's so busy *with*. He's working on a treatment that never seems to be materializing. And we never talk about the wedding anymore. It feels like—"

She was rescued by the waiter, who arrived with their meals and fresh drinks.

Cass picked up her knife and fork, began cutting into her sand dabs. "It just feels like what?" she said. She kept her gaze down at her plate. Mercy wondered if she was as afraid of hearing the answer as much as Mercy was to give it.

Mercy cleared her throat. "It feels like he doesn't love me anymore."

Cass slapped down her cutlery. "Do you love him?" Cass adored being blunt, "getting to the heart of things." As long as it wasn't about her own life.

"I . . . I, well . . . yes. Of course I love him. I wouldn't be upset if I didn't love him."

"Are you sure?"

Mercy felt a bolt of heat zip up the back of her neck. "What is that supposed to mean?"

"It's not supposed to mean anything," Cass said, retrieving the utensils and returning to her fish. "I'm merely trying to determine how you're feeling about the man you're engaged to marry."

"I know you don't like him, Cass."

"Don't turn this on me, chickie," Cass said, pointing the knife in her direction. "I'm simply trying to help you." Mercy downed a sip of her Singapore sling, fresh and fruity and bitter. "I think," Cass was saying, "you need to remind yourself why you fell for him in the first place. And why you agreed to marry him. In the process, maybe he'll remember why he asked."

"And how do you suggest I accomplish that?"

Cass shrugged. "Go away together. Maybe a long weekend in Palm Springs or somewhere. Just the two of you, away from Hollywood."

"And what if it doesn't work?"

She looked up from her lunch. "Then it doesn't. But at least you'll know." She waved her arm in Mercy's direction. "It's better than this bundle of nerves you are now."

It wasn't such a terrible idea. A getaway would provide clarity, a chance to rediscover their love. Mercy just needed to unearth it. "I don't like Palm Springs," she said absently. "It's just Hollywood in the desert. Besides, the reporters there can be even more intrusive than the ones here."

For the next ten minutes they bandied about other locales—Chicago, Key Largo, London—each one falling by the wayside from the darts Mercy flung.

"Wait. I've got it," Cass said.

Mercy's anticipation rose from the certainty in Cass's voice. "I'm listening."

"Martha's Vineyard."

"Martha's Vineyard? Is that near Sonoma?"

"Turn right and head about two thousand miles. It's not an actual vineyard. It's an island off the coast of Massachusetts. Near Cape Cod. I went there for a wedding a few years ago. We took a ferry over. Not a lot of tourists, mainly Boston folks with weekend places. Small and cozy, and absolutely no Hollywood or Broadway people." She gathered her napkin from her lap and dropped it on her plate. "I'm telling you, that's the ticket. You go, you eat some *chowdah*, take a sail, and after a week we'll be dress shopping like madwomen."

A week in New England in spring. Mercy could almost picture it: a fireplace, steaming mugs of cider, soft cashmere sweaters, a walk hand in hand by the water.

It felt right. Perhaps—just perhaps—she could find answers on Martha's Vineyard.

*

In most cases a gentleman would rise when a lady arrived at the table, but Sy Sigmund wasn't a gentleman, a fact Mercy knew all too well. But he had been a fantastic agent, taking a chance on a demure girl with little confidence and grooming her into an actress. As the maître d' deftly pulled out her chair, Sy slouched on the other side of the table holding a cigar aloft, his face wrinkled like a deflated balloon. He wore a cheap gray suit he'd no doubt purchased thirty years ago.

"I never understand why you always want to sit outside," he grumbled. "I sweat my *farshiltn* ass off every time I see you."

"Sunshine is good for your health." They were on the terrace of the Sunset Tower Hotel, which was already crowded, although no one seemed to actually eat anything. Drinking was another story.

Sy pointed the cigar in her direction. "You look nice."

"I should mark this date down. You never compliment my appearance."

"Not my job, cookie," he said, flicking an ash. "My job is to make you a star."

Mercy tried to look casual, bordering on disinterested. To Sy, eagerness was merely a pale copy of desperation. She window-shopped around the menu. "And what's the latest on that?"

"Joe Pasternak just bought the rights to an unpublished novel about four girls looking for love in Florida on their break from college. It's called *Unholy Spring. Fakakta* title. He's changing it to *Where the Boys Are.* He's using contract people, but he's signed Connie Francis, which is a bit of a stunt—I'd lay money she can't act to save her life—but she sells records, so she might sell tickets. He wants Natalie Wood for the lead."

Mercy put the menu down. "And?"

"No way Natalie Wood is doing this," Sy said, taking another puff. "She's Marjorie Fucking Morningstar, for Christ's sake. She thinks she's an *actress* now."

"Go on."

"Pasternak won't want to upstage Francis. I have a gut feeling about this picture. It feels fresh. The lead role is pretty meaty. It would show you could carry a picture on your own, but since it's about four girls it's still small enough that if the movie bombs it won't kill you. Could be a big deal for you, Edie."

Edie. It was the closest he ever came to a term of endearment. She looked over at his sagging face, as rumpled as his suit, and flashed back to that first interview in his cluttered office, when she'd sat on the opposite side of his desk, lace-gloved hands fidgeting nervously. He'd studied her for a good two minutes without saying a single word and then, out of nowhere, muttered, "Shipping."

"Shipping?" she'd replied.

"You got a look about you. Like you could be a shipping heiress from Maine. The hair, the pale skin. With Kelly retired, there could be an opening for someone like you." He'd picked up her headshot, eyes darting back and forth between the photo and the girl now in front of him. "Can you act?"

A memory had flooded her brain in the moment. An afternoon with her Grampa Tom, when she was about fifteen. She'd begged for acting lessons and rides to auditions from parents who thought the stage frivolous, vain, and a poor runner-up to the 4-H club as an acceptable leisure activity for a young girl. But Grampa Tom knew differently. He was the one who had encouraged her, believed in her. "The world needs storytellers, Edie," he'd said one day on the porch. "Don't let anyone discourage you. Go tell your story."

She knew the last thing Sy had wanted to hear about was the wisdom of Grampa Tom. So instead she'd poured open like a faucet, spewing roles she'd done in Omaha, the rave review from the critic from the *Beatrice Daily Sun* about her lead performance in the community production of *Saint Joan*, the ad she'd done for Camel cigarettes. He'd put his hand up, cutting her off.

"Yeah, yeah, that's all nice, kid. We'll get you a test." He'd picked up the photograph again. "But first we have to do something about this name: 'Edith Stoppelmoor.' The waitresses at Norms have better names than that."

She wasn't naive: she knew she couldn't expect a movie career as Edith Stoppelmoor. But changing her name, just like that? Right now? "Well, I have an aunt Lillian I'm fond of, so perhaps—"

"Too stuffy."

"Well, I can think about it some more."

"*You* don't have to." Taking in her panicked expression, he'd said,

"Don't worry. You get a vote." He'd begun leafing through some books on his desk for inspiration. "But you want me to represent you, I get the final vote."

It took a half hour before they'd landed on Mercy Welles. She certainly did sound like a shipping heiress from Maine. He'd been right about another thing, too: within three years she'd earn an Oscar nomination.

"So?" He waved the cigar at her, pulling her out of the memory.

"Sorry. I don't think I'm right for a fluffy picture like that. You know what I'm after. Something serious. Something meaningful, that I can sink my teeth into."

"Something dull," he cracked dismissively. "You been spending too much time with your moody director."

Sy didn't like Louis. She avoided discussing the relationship when at all possible. "Actually, Louis and I are taking a little break together," she said. "We're going away, just the two of us."

"Where?"

"Off the coast of Massachusetts. I haven't even told him yet. I want it to be a surprise. But it won't be long. A week, maybe two."

"Two weeks is two years in Hollywood."

"You'll survive."

"Will *you*?"

She shot him a look.

"You're young, you're a knockout, you got nominated for a goddamned Oscar," Sy said. "And now you're going to disappear for two weeks?" He raised his empty whiskey glass, shaking it at the waitress across the terrace, who slowly ambled over. "Another of these. And a Tom Collins for the lady."

The waitress left. "I don't drink in the middle of the day, Sy." *Liar.* Hadn't she just sat in the dining room at Musso's with Cass just a few days ago, enjoying the soothing effects of a Singapore sling?

"You clearly need a drink if you're going to do something this stupid when offers are finally coming in."

"I wouldn't call the chance to kiss strangers on the beach in the company of a jukebox singer an incredible offer." She sat back, letting out a deep breath. "I need to do this, Sy. And I need you to be all right with it and not berate me. Please."

He felt many things—protective of her, opportunistic about her, and definitely worldlier than her—but Mercy knew that above all he felt paternal toward her, in his own irascible, cranky-uncle manner.

"Fine," he said, throwing up his hands in defeat. "Go on your vacation. I'll try to keep your career warm."

Five

Faced with an empty afternoon after leaving Sy, Mercy stood in front of the hotel and pondered her options. She decided to take the short walk across Sunset Boulevard to the Chateau Marmont, where she could have a coffee and read a magazine. It was so rare to be able to walk anywhere in Los Angeles. And the Marmont was also a Hollywood hub—you never knew who you'd run into.

Fifteen minutes later, sitting on a striped director's chair under a roomy umbrella on the patio, she contemplated how to bring up the trip to Louis. He'd be reluctant to leave Hollywood at a time when he was aggressively seeking his next picture. She'd just have to convince him how important it was to their mutual future. Mercy decided she'd lobby for two weeks and settle for ten days. She'd stop at the market on the way home, buy a good bottle of wine and some cutlets to make chicken Française.

Then, just like that, there he was.

Louis, walking into the hotel. Through the front window she could see him popping by the check-in desk, making an inquiry. Had Hal Wallis finally agreed to a meeting? Why hadn't he told her? Perhaps he wanted to wait, surprise her with the news. She smiled, thinking of how hard he'd worked, how much he *needed* some good news. A picture coming through would mean putting off the trip, but it would be worth it.

She wrestled with what to do—run up, alert him to her presence, or let the meeting commence uninterrupted? She surveyed the patio, wondering if Wallis was already here. Nope. So like Louis to get to a meeting early.

Then *she* walked in.

Adrenaline and dread dripped into Mercy's veins. Constance Baxter wore a plain gray day suit and pearls, an Hermès scarf artfully draped over one shoulder. She barely acknowledged Louis as she passed him, but Mercy had witnessed enough assignations to know what one looked like. She flashed back to a few days before, finding Louis in the apartment, smelling of guilt and expensive aftershave.

The front desk clerk discreetly slipped a room key across the check-in desk. Louis scooped it up and fell in step behind Constance, keeping a few stealthy feet away. A minute later they disappeared together into an elevator.

She could hold the key to my career.

Now he was holding a key to their hotel room.

Adrenaline and dread gave way to anger. What a colossal fool she'd been. A caricature of the young Hollywood actress, airily hopscotching her way through parties as she was two-timed.

She couldn't risk a scene—she was paranoid about Hollywood gossip, the ravenous appetites of reporters for scandal. You never knew where they had eyes. She opened her purse, tossed some money on the table, and quickly rose, hurrying toward the exit.

She stopped.

No.

She wouldn't do this. She wouldn't play the role of the injured party, allow him the opportunity to explain it away. Two words she had never spoken aloud, that perhaps she had never even *thought*, ricocheted around her brain.

Fuck him.

Mercy turned back into the lobby and approached the front-desk clerk, now busy scribbling notes in a reservations book. He wore a crisp military-looking uniform and a metallic gold bar that said ALFRED. Sensing her presence, he looked up.

"Miss Welles," he said, slightly jarred. "How . . . how nice to see you."

He recognized her. And, from how nervous he now appeared, wasn't happy to see her. Good. This would make it all easier.

"Thank you, Alfred. I see that Mr. Flynn has just checked in. Can you tell me what room he's in, please?"

She had to give it to him—he managed to remain remarkably stoic. Aspiring actor, no doubt. He cocked his head slightly, issued a condescending Mona Lisa smile. "Unfortunately, it's firm hotel policy that we cannot release any information on our guests," he said politely. "I *am* sorry, Miss Welles."

Mercy leveled her gaze, barreling past the pity rising in his eyes. "I see. Well, Alfred, then I fear we have a small problem. Because I think you know that I need to see Mr. Flynn immediately, and I think you also understand why. Now, I know this puts you in a terribly awkward position, and for that I do apologize. Though in all candor I think we'd both agree it is nowhere near the awkward position I now find myself in. So I need you to recognize fully what decision you are being faced with. You can tell me, right now, which room Mr. Flynn is in, and I will tell no one how I obtained this information. Or you can hold to your policy, and I can walk over to the phone booth over there and call Robert Harrison at *Confidential*, and he'll have a reporter and a photographer dispatched to this hotel within the next ten minutes. I sincerely doubt Mr. Brettauer would welcome such publicity, particularly when it could have been so easily avoided." Erwin Brettauer, the Marmont's owner, was known as an easygoing man—odd for a native German—and one of the few upscale hoteliers who earnestly welcomed Negroes. But despite the hotel's reputation as a haven of indiscretion, he loathed scandal. "So," Mercy said, "I will ask one final time: The room number, please?"

Alfred stood behind the desk, paralyzed, eyes unblinking, skin now a chalky white. A trickle of sweat snaked down his left temple.

"Very well," Mercy said, opening her purse to extract a coin as she began walking toward the phone booth.

"Wait, please," Alfred called after her, looking around the lobby with paranoid eyes. Mercy sauntered back over to the desk. He flipped the reservations book around so it now faced her, then casually retreated out of sight. Cute. *"Did you tell her the room number?" "No, I did not."*

Mercy scanned the entries, spied Louis's signature.

502.

In the end, her emancipation took less than eight minutes. She had calmly walked up to the door, knocking lightly and saying, in her best high-school French, "*Service de chambre, compliments de l'hôtel,*" and Louis had promptly swung it open, shirt open and feet bare, holding an empty ice bucket. To his credit, he hadn't even flinched. He'd simply declared, loudly for Constance's benefit, "Hello, Mercy," and then stood there, the two of them staring at one another in silence.

She'd taken off her engagement ring, dropped it into the ice bucket, and retreated down the corridor.

*

Mercy put the teacup down on the coffee table and began massaging her temples. "I have no idea what to do."

Cass sat across from her in a club chair. "You'll figure it out, kiddo. You always do." Cass did neither sentimentality nor disingenuousness particularly well, and it showed. She took a sip from her own cup of tea.

Mercy stood up from the sofa, began slowly pacing around the living room. Cass's apartment, tucked away on a leafy side street in West Hollywood, was in one of the petite Spanish-style bungalows that the studios had set aside two decades earlier to lure the great writers of America—Hemingway, Benchley, Parker—out to the sunshine to write for the movies. The writers had spent most of the time drinking. Much like Cass herself, the cottage was small, tidy, efficient.

"How do I even go back there to get my things? I don't want to have to see him again. Ever."

"We can arrange to get your things."

"I just told Sy I was leaving for a while. Now I have to call him and tell him I'm not, and why." Mercy ran her fingers through her hair. "And never mind what I'm facing when the reporters hear about this. I'll be the laughingstock of Hollywood."

"Honey, I am trying very hard to be supportive here, but you're being overly dramatic," Cass said. "I know this hurts. But you're not the first girl to get jilted by her fella in this town, and you won't be the last. It's not a novel story."

"I know, I know." Mercy did another spin around the room before plopping back down onto the sofa. "I just wish I could ..." She trailed off, looking away.

"Do what?"

Mercy narrowed her eyes, as if she were trying to solve a math puzzle. "But I could, couldn't I? I mean, why not?"

Cass exhaled wearily. "For Christ's sake, honey, I'm not Ted Annemann! Spit it out!"

"I could still go," Mercy said quietly. "I could still go to Martha's Vineyard."

Cass began shaking her head. "Oh, I don't know about that, sweetie. I mean, it was one thing to go for a romantic getaway. But by yourself? Off-season? What would you do in the middle of a New England island alone? Won't you be even more depressed, thinking about what you were *supposed* to be doing there, with him?"

"No, I don't think so. The reasons the escape was so perfect are still there: it's a place I can go figure out what I want, what comes next. Maybe I was meant to go alone."

"And maybe I was meant to be Susan Hayward," Cass replied tartly. "You need to think about this. I worry you'll get there and be incredibly lonely. That's the last thing the doctor ordered."

"No, you're wrong, my dear friend. I can't stay here. The entire point of the trip was to clear my head, to get answers. They just won't be the answers I was hoping for. But it feels right. I have to go. Will you help me?"

Cass was quiet for a minute, but there was resignation in her skeptical eyes. She got up and riffled through a drawer, finally extracting a business card. "Here," she said, handing it to Mercy. "Call Hal. He's the travel agent who made the arrangements to go to Martha's Vineyard for the wedding. He's good people, a friend of my sister's. He'll get you all situated."

Mercy took the card, smiling. It felt good to smile again. To be taking action, rather than just reacting. Mercy took Cass into a warm hug. "Thank you for being my friend."

"Always, honey," Cass said, finally breaking the embrace. Hugging was another weak spot in her repertoire. "But you need to promise me something."

"What's that?"

"Promise me," Cass said, "that you'll write."

Six

Mercy walked out of the small door with the tiny gabled awning and the sign proclaiming HARBORSIDE INN, LUNCHEON * DINNER, stopping briefly to admire the dual green window boxes overflowing with tea roses, azaleas, and ivy. It was a week before Memorial Day, and Martha's Vineyard was sprucing up to welcome the tourists who would arrive to drink in the charms of the eighty-seven-square-mile island.

She had been lucky to get a reservation—another week and she'd have been forced to stay in Vineyard Haven, which Cass's travel agent had labeled "fine, but all of the good stuff is in Edgartown." Mercy needed to be where the good stuff was.

She slid her clutch under her arm and turned away from the wharf, making the left onto Main Street. The early afternoon air was brisk—it couldn't have been sixty degrees—and she reminded herself she'd need to buy a warmer coat. Summer may have been coming to New England, but it was clear that it was nowhere close.

She inhaled deeply, her body leaning into the rhythm of the stroll. Last night she'd collapsed into bed from the arduous three-plane trip. This morning she'd slept in, followed by a long, hot soak in the tub. Now, she was feeling the most like herself since her ill-fated visit to the Chateau Marmont a week ago.

Main Street was hardly bustling—a few people hither and thither, but otherwise what one might expect of a quiet seaside town on a weekday in shoulder season. A gust of chilly wind pierced the thin fabric of her raincoat, and Mercy decided perhaps a longer walk could wait until she'd purchased those warmer clothes. She was about to turn back for the hotel when she spied a weathered sign swinging in the breeze up ahead. It was in the shape of a whale, and its old colonial type declared THE WHITE WHALE.

A pub. Perfect.

She pulled open the heavy oak door and practically tumbled inside. A long, brightly burnished mahogany bar sat to the right. The wood floors were coated in a fine film of sawdust, curving into deep hunter-green walls with white wainscoting and the occasional blob of weathered ship's netting. There were a few tables and chairs scattered about; on the left a sizable fireplace snapped and crackled, providing warmth and a cozy ambiance. Three of the tables were occupied. A lone, grizzled-looking man sat at the far end of the bar, nursing a draft beer. Mercy shook out of her coat and flung it over a barstool, then hopped up on the next one.

A few minutes later a stocky, imposing man—she guessed mid-fifties, his body burly, solid—ambled to her end, a quizzical look on his face. His Irish brogue was thick. "We don't typically serve ladies alone at the bar, miss," he said. He sounded like Barry Fitzgerald in *Going My Way*.

She was about to reply when one was issued for her from the other end. "But we certainly should!" came a feminine voice. A wiry woman who was clearly related to the man—they shared the same mischievous eyes—walked down the length of the bar and joined him, smiling as she flung a towel over her shoulder. She wore a man's flannel shirt and blue jeans, and her brogue was even more pronounced than his. "Any woman's money is as good as any man's, and if she be dying of the thirst, then why should she be denied?" the woman asked incredulously.

"I don't mean to cause any trouble," Mercy said quietly. "If it's your policy, I'm happy to sit at a table."

"You most certainly will not!" the woman cried. "Dennis, give the woman a menu—you're going to eat, dearie, I think? You certainly look like you could use a decent meal—and see what she wants to drink."

Dennis silently slid over a menu, looked at her expectantly. "Hmmm," Mercy mused. "How about a nice glass of Cabernet?"

Dennis shot the woman next to him a look, but before he could open his mouth she quickly commanded, "See what we have in the back," and shooed him away. Mercy fought a chuckle; it was like stumbling into a Joyce story. "I'm afraid I've caused a ruckus," she told the barmaid. "First with the seating, now with my request of liquid refreshment."

"Oh, don't mind him," the woman said. "He's just cranky because he lost his bet on the Red Sox. Always gambling away money he doesn't have." She plopped her elbows onto the bar. "Anyway, where might you be visitin' us from, dearie?"

Mercy sat up a bit straighter. "Los Angeles. I just got here last night."

The woman was impressed, flamboyantly shaking her head of salt-and-pepper hair. "Los Angeles! Well, my, my, California folk! I have to say we don't get too many of you." She extended her hand. "I'm Bridie deCoursey. I run the pub with me cousin Dennis. A warm Gaelic welcome to Martha's Vineyard."

Mercy shook her hand. "It's so nice to meet you, Bridie. I'm—"

She stopped. No one had recognized her in the short time she'd been here, but that wasn't so unusual. She was hardly famous outside of Hollywood. More like someone vaguely familiar, a face people stared at and tried to place. Still, an Oscar-nominated young actress fleeing her cheating fiancé to hide on a distant New England island was a tabloid reporter's dream. One she didn't need to see printed. Oh, why had she said she was from L.A.? "I'm Edie."

Bridie pointed down at the menu. "Well, Miss Edie from California, you're a wee thing and I can see you shivering in that light sweater and so what you need is a nice, big bowl of seafood chowder. I made it just today. Highly recommended for anything that ails you."

Even a broken heart? Mercy wanted to ask. It sounded tempting, but she didn't want anything that heavy. She settled for a plate of oysters.

*

She slurped down another oyster, but now wished she'd ordered the chowder. She generally avoided creamy soups and sauces; the studios were fanatical about actresses' weight. Wasn't Judy Garland now a drug addict because of Louis B. Mayer's tyrannical obsession with her body when she was a teenager?

She felt a blush of cold wind at her back as the door swung open. A man came to stand by her at the bar, scanning the place.

"Bridie just went in the back, if that's who you're looking for," Mercy said. Look at her—already a local! "She'll be back out in a minute."

He looked to be around thirty, maybe even a bit younger—he had a slightly ruddy complexion that bore the effects of the sea. He was tall and broad and had the taut body of a man used to physical labor. He wore a thermal skull cap and a heavy tan jacket, and both his blue jeans and his boots needed a thorough cleaning. He was dark and handsome in a romance novel antihero kind of way, with a square jaw and facial hair that was more eight o'clock shadow than five. He quickly surveyed her meal on the bar, spied the bottle still on the bar. He met her gaze with brown eyes that flashed open mockery. She suddenly felt flustered, and quickly turned her attention back to her oysters.

"Is that a Cabernet you're drinking?" he asked.

She had expected a pronounced New England accent, but his smoky voice belied his appearance. He sounded manly but refined.

"Indeed. Not the finest vintage, but perfectly suitable for a chilly evening by the sea."

He shook his head. "Tourists."

Her eyes narrowed. "Excuse me?"

He exhaled wearily. "You're drinking a Cabernet while you're eating oysters. You couldn't have made a worse pairing if you'd tried. Texturally it's all wrong—fish turns to sand when paired with a wine with so much tannin. Second, oysters taste like tin cans with a wine like that. You'd be better off drinking motor oil."

She was taken aback at his rudeness. "You're a fisherman, are you?"

He scoffed again, louder this time.

"Every tourist thinks the only thing people who live on this island do is fish, eat chowder, and drink beer."

"The words of a man dressed in fishing attire who is bellying up to a bar and is about to order—what?—a glass of Chardonnay?" She internally cheered her retort. Anytime she had a fight with Louis she always managed to find the perfect comeback four hours later.

His eyebrows arched a bit in surprise. Whatever he'd expected, it wasn't . . . that. They held each other's gaze for a few seconds until Bridie's brogue intruded.

"Well, look who the cat drug in!" she said. "Ren, this is Miss Edie from Los Angeles, California."

Mercy threw her own arched eyebrow back at him then drolly uttered, "Charmed."

His dark eyes bored into hers for a few more seconds, his expression unreadable. Was he impressed with her moxie, or dismissing her as vacant?

Why did she care?

Ren turned back to Bridie. "Just wanted to pop in and let Dennis know we're on for Sunday morning at Gay Head. Tell him I'll pick him up at four."

Bridie shook her head as she wiped down the bar. "Why grown men spend their only days off gettin' up in the middle of the night, I'm sure I'll never understand."

"Wait—four in the *morning*?" Mercy heard her own voice asking the question, and immediately regretted it.

He turned back to her, his disdain now in full bloom. "It's fishing, darlin'. Because as you know, that's all we islanders do: fish, eat chowder—"

"And drink beer," she said. "And please don't forget the fourth thing they evidently do: be rude to the visitors who support their livelihoods."

He barked out a curt laugh, then fished into his pocket and dropped some cash on the bar. He nodded to Bridie. "Bridie, please get Miss

Los Angeles here a decent glass of champagne," he said. He turned back to her and winked. "Because *that's* what you drink with oysters."

He left as abruptly as he'd come in. "Is every man on this island as . . . welcoming as that?" Mercy asked.

Bridie laughed as she poured a flute of champagne. "Oh, don't mind Ren. He's actually a pretty nice fellow once you get to know him."

"I'll have to take your word for it." Mercy took a sip of the champagne. She had to admit: it was nice. "You know him well, then."

"Oh, since he was a little boy. He has quite the story."

Mercy found herself suddenly curious. "Story?"

"Oh, spend enough time on Martha's Vineyard, dearie," Bridie said, "and you'll quickly learn that everyone here has a story."

*

She spied it out of the corner of her eye on the way out. On the bulletin board by the door, with notices for a sale at the Country Store, a coupon for Duffer's Miniature Golf, and an ad for Tony Curtis and Janet Leigh in *Perfect Furlough* (soon to open at the Edgartown movie theater): a bright orange flyer that declared *Seasonal Cottage for Rent*.

> BEAUTIFUL AND COZY COTTAGE IN THE HEART
> OF EDGARTOWN AVAILABLE FOR RENT
> FOR SUMMER SEASON, EFFECTIVE IMMEDIATELY.
> OPEN PORCH, LIVING ROOM,
> KITCHEN, ROOMY BEDROOM AND BATH. $1800.
> ASK FOR FRED.

There was a local number at the bottom.

Impulsively, she plucked it off the board. She'd come for an escape. Who said it had to be short?

She folded the flyer, shoved it into her raincoat pocket, and headed out into the cool night air.

Postcard

May 20, 1959

Dearest Cass—Safely arrived and already feeling better. (Wine helps!) Lovely here. May be staying longer than I planned. More soon.

Oodles of love, Mercy

Seven

And you're *certain* it's her?"

Lucinda Cross is surveying the random assortment of photocopied publicity stills and newspaper clippings Priya has helped Kit pull together about Mercy Welles, vanished ingenue of the silver screen, now splayed about the desk. Lucinda takes a carefully manicured nail and idly flips through some of the pages, shaking her head in mild astonishment.

"I think so," Kit says from the couch.

Lucinda picks up a photograph of Nan, taken in the 1970s, that Kit extracted from an old photo album.

"She changed her hair drastically, and of course she's older here, and a few pounds heavier," Lucinda says. "But I can see it. Your grandmother and Mercy Welles were clearly the same person."

Kit had been reluctant to bring the tale to Lucinda, but she couldn't tell Claire. At least not until she knew more. At the funeral Kit was the one crying like a three-year-old, issuing tearful lamentations aloud as the casket was slowly lowered into the ground at Greenwood Union Cemetery. Claire had stood, matronly in a sack of black and Jackie O sunglasses, stoic and impenetrable, holding Kit's hand. But Kit knows Claire's still waters truly do run deep. She worries what this latest news will do to her sister's carefully ordered world, what will happen if Claire discovers that everything they thought they knew about the woman who raised them was a lie.

Lucinda, analytical and detached, will offer clear-eyed counsel, the thing Kit needs most in this moment.

Lucinda gathers some of the materials, walks over to where Kit is sitting on the sofa and sinks down next to her. "I can't imagine how you're feeling," she says, and for a moment Kit is taken aback, because maternal concern is not an armament Lucinda keeps in her quiver. But she's right—she can't imagine. Kit doesn't know what to feel.

"Well, I think you know what has to happen next," Lucinda continues, as if reading Kit's scrambled mind. She props an elbow on the back of the couch, rests her head on her fist. "You need to get to the bottom of the story."

The story. Of course that's how Lucinda sees it. But then, in fairness, isn't that so clearly what it is?

"I don't know," Kit says feebly. "I need to think about that. Perhaps it's better if I just leave it alone. Clearly Nan didn't want us to know."

Lucinda shakes her head. "If that were true, she wouldn't have saved a shred of evidence from her past life. But she did." She picks up the playbill for *The Rose of Aquinnah,* then the picture of Kit's grandmother, dewy and smiling, posing with the unidentified young man. "She had to know that after she died you'd find these."

"Unless she didn't realize she'd saved them."

"We all know the mementos we've saved," she says, "and where they are. If I asked you right now to get your hands on possessions that were once owned by your parents, could you tell me where they are?"

Kit thinks of her mother's simple brocade wedding gown, which Claire restored and wore and is now lovingly preserved in her cedar closet in Maryland, waiting for—what, exactly? And her father's pipe, sitting in his ashtray, both on a side table in her New York apartment like a history exhibit. "Yes."

"Exactly. We don't save the things that don't mean anything. Especially if we keep them hidden from everybody else."

"But maybe I don't want to know any more."

"If that were true, you would have never brought this to me,"

Lucinda says, a trace of steel creeping into her voice. "You may not admit it, but the truth is, Kit, that you're as much of a journalist as anyone here. You know there's a story here and you want to know what it is. It's instinctual. I think you'll regret it if you don't pursue it. And I think deep down you agree with me."

Kit does. Which is the worst part.

"Did you look up the play from the advertisement?"

"Yes," Kit says. "Nothing. If it was even produced, it never went farther than Martha's Vineyard. In the scattershot items about Mercy Welles that exist it's not even mentioned. I couldn't find anything on the playwright, either."

"I have something for you," Lucinda says. She walks back over to her desk, retrieves one of her heavy-stock notecards, and hands it over. In her awful scrawl is a name and a phone number.

Kit scans it. "Who's Alistair Clarkson?"

"Your grandmother only made three films before she vanished from public view. Clarkson directed one of them, *Summer Sonata*."

"He's still alive?"

"Indeed."

"My God, how old is he?"

"He was, like your grandmother's paramour Louis Flynn, one of a crop of young directors making noise back in the 1950s. He's British, and spent most of his career directing theater. He's now in his late eighties and, from what I gather, still quite sharp. Lives in a small apartment on the Upper East Side. And also, from what I am told, will never pass up a free lunch with a pretty young woman who wants to listen to him reflect on his august career. I got his number from a friend at *Vanity Fair*."

Panic floods Kit's veins. "You didn't—"

"Of course not," Lucinda says dismissively. "Give me a little credit for discretion, Kit." She tosses her reading glasses on top of the desk, the classic Lucinda-ism for indicating a meeting has ended. "Go have lunch with him. I'll even let you expense it. But keep your eye on the prize. Remember the question you're trying to answer. Which is not, Who was my grandmother?"

Kit's eyes constrict. "Then what is it?"

Lucinda sinks into her desk chair, folding her arms. "Who was Mercy Welles?"

*

Like La Grenouille, Alistair Clarkson is refined, a tad stuffy, and slightly overperfumed. He sports a silver barbershop mustache, a fluffy bow tie, and an elegant walking stick that Kit will later discover serves as both practical ambulatory aid and theatrical affectation. He was already ensconced in the booth when she arrived. "I do so love it here," he is saying in his clipped English accent, refined through an education at Oxford he never fails to mention in his occasional victory-lap interviews. "It's one of the few places where one can order a decent salade de pamplemousse."

Kit nods. She finds the "salade" on the menu, discovers it's comprised of grapefruit, prunes, and honey. *Hard pass.*

"So you want to discuss Mercy Welles," he says as he reaches for his reading glasses and begins scanning the menu. "What a curious topic to mine after all of these years. Whatever piqued your interest?"

In requesting the lunch date, Kit had not, of course, revealed the truth. She couldn't risk having it drift out into the Hollywood gossip ecosystem. She pictures some oily host on *Access Hollywood*, all spray tan and porcelain veneers, previewing the "shocking new developments" in the scandalous story of the Hollywood starlet who vanished almost sixty years ago. She cannot do that to Nan. If a narrative does emerge, it will be Kit who controls it.

"I'm always scouting about for story ideas. It's part of the job," Kit says airily. "Lucinda sometimes enjoys digging up little nuggets from the past. I found an item about Mercy Welles on a blog and thought it might make a cute feature to tie in for next year's Oscars coverage."

"Goodness, you do play ahead of the mark," Alistair replies. "That's six months away."

"There's one golden rule in television: ABT," Kit says. "'Always be taping.'"

The waiter takes their order and Alistair settles into his role of storyteller, a road paved with more than a little self-aggrandizement. "Well, I have to say, I simply adored Mercy Welles. She had such command of the camera. You cannot direct that in an actress; she must bring that to the role herself."

It feels odd to hear her grandmother described this way, in the body of a long-ago would-be leading lady. Kit had often pictured Nan toiling away in secretarial school. In reality she'd been sitting on movie sets, hobnobbing at parties with Cary Grant. She breaks off a piece of bread, reaches for the butter. Carbs be damned. If ever there was a time to eat one's feelings, it's now. "How did you come to direct her?" Kit asks.

Alistair squints, trying to recall the details. "I believe she had some sort of arrangement with Paramount, but I couldn't swear to that," he says. "Anyway, she'd been a fourth female lead in a picture about a group of young WACs during World War Two that almost nobody saw. But when they sent her in to audition for *Summer Sonata* she just stopped me dead. There was something angelic but also sensual about her appearance. She was the kind of woman you couldn't help but stare at."

Kit feels her composure starting to crack. It's just so difficult—the collision of hearing vivid memories of Nan from before her father was born, and from the feeling of—what? Betrayal? Silly, but that's how it feels—that Nan never brought herself to tell the granddaughters she raised the truth, never trusted them enough to reveal who she'd once been. She wonders if her grandfather or her father knew. She doubts it. You don't bury your secrets deep in the attic and then casually air them out along the way.

"Anyway, I insisted on casting her. The studio wanted Tina Louise. Can you imagine? The woman who would become famous for *Gilligan's Island*? Though I must say she was quite good in *God's Little Acre*. Anyway, Mercy was simply wonderful in the role, and the notices agreed. And then her next picture, boom: she lands an Oscar nomination. I don't think she ever really got the fame she deserved. She could have been up there with Kim Novak, Julie Christie. She had that kind of poise. I would have loved to have worked with her again. But . . ." He trails off.

"But?"

He shrugs. "You know the story." He makes a theatrical hand gesture. "She just . . . disappeared."

Their lunches arrive—Kit notes that Alistair has eschewed the much-lauded salade de pamplemousse in favor of veal Orloff—and the conversation veers from current cinema ("Rubbish, all of it," Alistair declares dismissively) to Kit's work for Lucinda Cross. Eventually Kit swings the chat back to Mercy, and Alistair waxes about her acting style, her ability to wear costumes, her professionalism. Still, it all feels very surface, like a Wikipedia entry. She's not getting any closer to the truth.

"You know, I hope you won't find this rather odd, but you remind me of her," Alistair says, putting his napkin to his lips as he finishes his veal. "You have that same sort of vitality, that independent spirit." He leans back a bit. "You even faintly resemble her. Perhaps that's the story!"

If you only knew. "Thank you, that's very nice of you to say," Kit manages. She has heard this a lot lately, how much she resembles the younger Nan, with their mutual ivory skin and clear green eyes. Claire is darker, more like their father, with chestnut hair and brown eyes. Kit had been approached by a modeling agent as a teenager, but Nan had quashed the idea; she thought the fashion industry viperous. Now it all made sense. Fashion, entertainment, it was all too intertwined. Nan didn't want her anywhere near her own past.

"I'm just curious," Kit says, "how much of her personal life did you know about? The blog mentioned she was engaged."

Alistair accepts his coffee from the waiter. "Oh my, we're really going back into the history books now, aren't we? I was trying to recall all of this after I received your lunch invitation. Yes, she was engaged to a young director."

"Louis Flynn."

"Yes, Louis Flynn. Bright young man. I recall meeting him once. He made a very big splash with some tropical picture and then quickly faded. There was a rumor he was in line for Constance Baxter's comeback vehicle, *She's Nothing but Trouble*. My, how fitting that title was for a Constance Baxter picture. *There's* a story for you. But he didn't end up directing it. I'm not sure why."

Kit has done some preliminary research on Flynn. His IMDb profile lists two dozen television episodes—medical dramas, cop shows—in the 1960s and '70s, and then he, too, disappears. Maybe that's just what happens in Hollywood. Either you make it big, or you vaporize into the ether.

"Did you ever hear what happened to him and Mercy? Why they never married?"

Alistair takes a sip of the coffee, shakes his head. "I confess I was not invested in the romantic foibles of Hollywood starlets. Perhaps there are some old gossip magazines archived somewhere that can help you. They were always writing about such things."

"And you have no idea why she suddenly left Hollywood?"

"There were rumors, of course. Mainly revolving around the nine-month variety."

Kit nods. It's crossed her mind, of course. At first blush she dismissed it: her grandmother looked positively waifish in the photograph with the unidentified man on Martha's Vineyard. Still, that doesn't mean she didn't get pregnant *on* Martha's Vineyard, which would certainly have explained why she never went back to California. But the theory had been quickly dispatched: Kit had combed the family photo albums and found several pictures of Nan in early 1960 looking slim, if a bit distracted. Perhaps a miscarriage? At this point anything was possible.

"The truth is young actresses come and go every day in show business," Alistair is saying. "Mercy Welles was hardly the first or the last to decide it wasn't for her."

He's right. But still. It's one thing for a Midwestern girl who couldn't get an audition for two years to board the bus back home. Mercy Welles—Nan—had been nominated for an Oscar just months earlier. The dream of a million girls, discarded like wastepaper. Why? *Why?*

As if reading her mind, Alistair says, "Though it is quite odd, isn't it? Both Hitchcock and Wilder were rumored to be interested in her. And if I'm remembering correctly, I believe Nancy White had also wanted to photograph her for *Bazaar*. But none of it came to pass."

"Well, I agree with you, it is certainly odd. But surely someone knows what happened. Where she went, why she left. She had to have confided in someone."

Alistair shrugs. "If she did, said person never betrayed her confidence. Or maybe nobody really pursued the story." He lifts his coffee cup in a toast. "Until now."

Eight

The Margaret Herrick Library sits inside a dust-colored, Spanish villa–style building in Los Angeles that houses the Academy of Motion Pictures Arts and Sciences on La Cienega Boulevard, right next to the tennis courts in Beverly Hills. Kit walks into the cool, expansive lobby, goes through the security sign-in and checks her bag in a locker, then hustles up the short staircase to the Special Collections desk.

"Ms. O'Neill," a fortysomething woman sporting a black cashmere turtleneck and a sloppy topknot says with brisk efficiency. "You're right on time. I'm Jennifer Kauffman, one of the research librarians here. I've pulled the files you requested, though I can't say there's a ton here."

She hands Kit a thin, crumbling paper folder marked *Welles, Mercy* that contains a few yellowed gossip column clippings, two cast lists, and a telegram from her agent congratulating her on her Oscar nomination. Kit fails to hide her disappointment. "This is it?"

"There are separate ones for the three films she was in, and I have those here," Jennifer says, sliding over a few other, slightly beefier folders. "But most of what's in these is budgets, memos about the early rushes, some notations from the censors, that sort of thing. Not really a lot about Mercy Welles, per se. It's funny. Until you called I hadn't known her story."

"Well, that appears to be the problem," Kit says. "Nobody does."

"I have another folder I can give you after you return these, which is the photographs folder. But you'll need to wear these"—she hands Kit a pair of dainty white cloth gloves—"to handle them." She points to her left. "In the general circulation room there are a ton of books about mid-century Hollywood that might have indexes with information about her."

Kit sighs. She's come three thousand miles on a wild-goose chase, and so far the goose is nowhere in sight.

Jennifer picks up Kit's research application form. "It says here you're researching a feature for *Signature with Lucinda Cross.*"

"Yes." Really, no. Kit has no intention of letting Lucinda splash Nan's story across the airwaves. But she needs Lucinda's name—and the time—to do the detective work. She'll figure out the rest later.

"That sounds like an interesting job," Jennifer says. "I'm curious: How did you come up with this idea?"

A secret in my dead grandmother's attic. Kit shrugs. "I've always been fascinated by old Hollywood. And mid-century seems like it was such a glamorous era. And hey—free trip to L.A." She laughs. "Though from the lack of archival material here it looks like getting to the bottom of her disappearance is going to take a bit more digging than I thought."

Jennifer crosses her arms, leans on the reference counter. "Well, don't despair just yet. You never know what will turn up in the most unexpected place."

*

Kit sits in one of the last rows of the vast art deco Vista Theatre in Los Feliz, stifling a yawn. It's not the movie but her sleep schedule that's the issue. At eleven last night—2 A.M. back east—she got a text from Josh, one of the members of what she fondly calls her "bullpen." He's a bassist in a band named Six Pins Dolores—they came up with the name one night when they were stoned, watching *Dolores Claiborne*—and his wiry body, long black hair, and tattoo of Josephine Baker have proved to be good company when she needs the occasional heroin hit of salacious affection. The text had been typically succinct: *R U Up?*, the standard code for *Wanna hook up?* She had to relay that while she was, in fact, up, she was also on the other side of the country, thus not available for casual middle-of-the-night entertaining. He issued a pithy *Cool. Talk Later* and then vanished back into cyberspace.

She knows Claire is right about this. She has to stop treating men like instruments occasionally to be played, coolly dispatching any who show any real interest in her as a human being. *Another day.*

For now she takes in the black-and-white image of her grand-mother, flickering across the giant screen. The Vista is one of the last theaters in Los Angeles that still shows vintage films, and tonight it is screening *Summer Sonata,* Alistair Clarkson's 1957 drama about a dashing young composer who, while on holiday, falls for a simple country girl, only to be forced to choose between her and his prom-ising career. In the end he chooses music, leaving the tragic hero-ine with sheet music and a composition he wrote to commemorate their magical summer together. The film's music rights are caught up in some sort of legal battle, so that unlike Mercy Welles's two other films, this one isn't available to stream or to be found on the occa-sional spin on Turner Classic Movies. Kit suspects Lucinda made a call to get it screened here.

Kit has already seen the other two: the WAC movie, in which Nan is merely part of the giggling ensemble, and *The Lovely Dream,* which earned her the Supporting Actress Oscar nod. But like the critics, she, too, feels the performance in this movie is the better one, the one that seems to have aged more gracefully. There is something lumi-nous about her grandmother on the big screen above her, smiling be-atifically through tears as she says goodbye to her great love. Maybe it's all of the weepy violins in the soundtrack, or the way the leading man looks at her, but there is something riveting about her. She re-calls Clarkson's words, feels her body once again seize with emotion.

Her day at the Herrick hasn't been a total loss. From what Kit has pieced together her grandmother had a very archetypal start: Edith Stoppelmoor from Nebraska takes a bus, arrives in town to become a star, takes odd jobs, then ends up in a romance with a hot young director. She appears in three pictures, is just beginning to make a name for herself, is on the cusp of real stardom. And then ... nothing.

For some unknown reason, Mercy Welles bolted Hollywood in 1959 and, from what she discovered in Nan's attic, ended up on Martha's Vineyard. She was clearly there for most of, if not all of, the summer—even a small stock production would have taken six weeks to rehearse and get off the ground. There is no record of Mercy Welles's post-Hollywood life anywhere in the Herrick materials. It's clear she went to Massachusetts and then never returned to California. Nan married Pop in 1961. Kit will have to check with Claire—that is, when she finally gets up the nerve to tell all of this to Claire—to see if she can nail down the date when Nan and Pop actually met in New York. Kit seems to vaguely remember they were together about a year before they married. Which then leaves roughly a year of Nan's life unaccounted for. And one nagging question.

What happened that summer on Martha's Vineyard?

The movie ends. Kit files out onto the sidewalk under the delightfully gaudy marquee, fishes out the phone now vibrating in her bag. Local area code. She clicks and finds Jennifer Kauffman on the other end.

"Hey," the librarian says. "I'm glad I caught you. I hope it isn't too late."

"No, no. I'm just out of the screening of *Summer Sonata* at the Vista."

"Nice. What did you think?"

"Really lovely. That scene outside the church—"

"I know, right? A double-hanky if ever there was one. But listen: I think I may have a break in the case."

Kit feels her pulse quicken. "Talk to me."

"A lot of girls who arrived during that period couldn't afford apartments, so they either stayed in women's hotels or cheap buildings that specifically catered to the newbies. Those residences kept meticulous records, many of which were then eventually donated to us when they closed. So I did some digging through the archives, and after a few false starts I hit pay dirt. And I do mean dirt. You owe me for the dry cleaning of this outfit. The dust was everywhere."

"Deal. And?"

"I found out that after Mercy Welles first arrived here in the mid-1950s, she was roommates with a Warner Brothers script supervisor named Cass Goldman at the Garden of Allah apartments on Sunset Boulevard."

Forget the pulse—Kit's heart is now beating like a tom-tom. "Please tell me Cass Goldman is still alive."

"Oh, better than that," Jennifer declares triumphantly. "I know where she is."

*

It takes Kit just under an hour the next morning to drive to the Motion Picture & Television Fund campus in Woodland Hills, a sprawling forty-eight-acre complex that houses cottages, apartments, and nursing facilities for those who worked in the trenches of the entertainment industry and are now taking their final bows. The place looks more like a 1970s college campus than a retirement community, all cement buildings and faux waterfalls and space-age architectural touches, as if the whole compound had been designed by George Jetson. She winds the car through the twisting enclave to a row of tidy bungalows until the GPS alerts her that she's here.

She should have called first, but something told her not to. She's dealt with enough reluctant sources to know that sometimes the element of surprise yields the best results. She has no idea what shape Cass, now ninety years old, might be in. Though the fact she is still living independently is a good sign.

Kit steps out of the car, flinging her bag over her shoulder, and instinctively tugs down the sides of her blue blazer, smoothing it out. She can't get over how nervous she is. She once confronted a suspected hit man on Tenth Avenue to get a quote for a segment, and feels more on edge now. She takes in the exterior of the beige cottage, lets out a deep exhale.

Here we go.

Three pushes of the doorbell yield nothing, and her spirits begin to deflate. Maybe Cass is at a doctor's appointment, or, God forbid, worse. She backs off from the door, takes a few tentative steps around the side, when she hears the faint sound of scraping. Moving toward the back, she spies her: on her knees, hunched over a flower bed, spade in hand. Cass Goldman wears a straw cartwheel hat festooned with a bright green band, and her gaze is intense as she dislodges some stones in the dark dirt to make room for her begonias, sitting in two clay pots.

"Excuse me!" Kit says a little too loud as she stealthily approaches. "Miss Goldman?"

Cass's face jerks up, the muddy palm of her gardening glove flying to her chest. "Oh, for Christ's sake!" the old woman says. "You scared me to death."

Kit can instantly see it, can imagine this wrinkled, bony woman roaming a studio lot armed with a pile of scripts, barking orders. The stories she must have. Though in this moment Kit only cares about one of them.

Kit inches closer, trying to calm the woman's nerves. "I am so very sorry," she says. "I tried ringing the bell and then just took a chance you might be outside. I didn't mean to startle you."

Cass squints up at her, palms resting on her knees in the soft earth. "No, no, that's fine. No harm done. Which at my age is not always a given. And you are . . . ?"

Kit squares her shoulders. "My name is Kit O'Neill. I'm from New York. I wanted to know if I could ask you some questions about my late grandmother. I believe you knew her as Mercy Welles."

Cass's eyes balloon wide in sudden surprise. Kit can't read her expression: Shock? Bemusement? Suspicion? Perhaps a combination of all of them. "Well, well, well," is all Cass says. She extends her arm out. "Help me up."

Once she's steadied, she removes her gardening gloves, beckoning Kit with a bony finger. "Come."

Fifteen minutes later they're settled inside the cozy cottage. Kit sits on a tufted settee and glances around, surveying some of the paintings on the wall, sipping one of the two cups of English breakfast tea Cass has poured. A small plate of Milano cookies sits on the table. Cass is studying her.

"You'll have to forgive an old woman's staring," she says. "But my, you look so like her."

"Thank you," Kit says. "I am so grateful for your kindness in spending some time with me."

Cass smiles. "It takes me back," she says quietly, "to an afternoon many, many years ago when I served your grandmother tea."

"That's what I'm counting on, those memories. I have so many questions."

Cass nods slightly. "I'm sure. Well, my memory is not what it once was, I'm afraid. But I'll try to help if I can. You say your grandmother never told you about her life as an actress?"

"No. And I have no idea why she would withhold that. Do you?"

Cass raises her eyebrows briefly. "Well, I suppose we all have things in our past we would rather leave in the past."

Kit smiles. "Do you?"

"Of course," Cass says. "Don't you?"

Kit thinks of her pyramid of empty men, the hell she put Nan and Pop through in her teenage years. But mainly she thinks of her grandmother and Cass, how fun it would have been to be a fly on the wall during their late-night gab sessions, two girls trying to make it in Hollywood in the glamorous 1950s. "Can you tell me about her?" Kit asks.

And so Cass does. About their fortuitous meeting at the YWCA, their years as roommates, Mercy's rise through show business and her ill-fated romance with Louis, which ended with infidelity in the spring of 1959.

"So that's why she went to Martha's Vineyard? To get over her breakup?"

"It's why she went," Cass says. "I'm not sure it's why she stayed."

"How long was she there?"

Cass shakes her head. "I can't recall, exactly. A few months, I think."

"Do you know what happened there? Something must have for her to have just never come back here." She looks at her plaintively, searching for clues, for anything, but Cass's expression has gone blank. Kit can almost feel a veil of inscrutability dropping over the old woman's face. She feels a door closing, and a desperation to stick her foot in it to keep it propped open.

"I found this picture," Kit says, extracting the photo of Nan and the mystery man. She hands it to Cass. "Do you know who he is?"

Cass lifts the reading glasses on the chain around her neck and puts them on, then spends a moment staring at the picture. Kit can see the corners of the old woman's mouth turning upward, ever so slightly. The look is warm. Like spying an old friend.

She knows, Kit thinks. *She knows.*

Cass slowly removes the glasses, hands the picture back. "I'm sorry," she says quietly. "I don't."

Kit tries to hide her crushing disappointment. She has interviewed enough recalcitrant sources to know that Cass is holding back. She clearly knows the identity of the mystery man, and probably exactly what happened that summer. She was ready to talk. Then, suddenly, she shut down. *Why?*

Time for a new approach. "Did Mercy ever write you that summer?"

Cass's eyes refocus on her. "Yes. She did."

"By any chance do you still have the letters?"

She shakes her head. "No, I'm afraid. When I moved here a decade ago my nephews went through my things and threw out all of my old boxes. I don't mind telling you I was very cross with them." She shrugs. "But what can you do? The past is the past."

Except when it changes everything in the present, Kit thinks. "Do you recall how you found out she wasn't coming back to Hollywood?"

Cass looks to the ceiling. "I believe in one of her last letters that summer she wrote to tell me she had decided to go to New York. But she didn't explain her reasoning, and I didn't press her."

"Did you keep in touch? After that?"

"Christmas cards, that kind of thing, for a while. But cross-country friendships were a bit more challenging to maintain then than they are now."

They talk a bit more, nibbling around the edges of Mercy Welles's life in Hollywood, but Kit senses the well has run dry. She leaves her card, asks Cass to call her if anything comes to mind that might help unlock what happened that summer. Cass is gracious if reserved, pledges to telephone if anything strikes her.

A few moments later, Cass watches at the window as Mercy's granddaughter climbs into her rental car and drives off. She hopes she's doing the right thing.

But I made a promise to you, my dear friend, she thinks. *I hope you intended me to keep it.*

May 25, 1959

Darling Cass—

Happy Memorial Day weekend!

I have done perhaps the second-most impulsive thing in my life after boarding the bus from Nebraska to California, though perhaps that doesn't really count as impulsive, since I began planning it after seeing Jennifer Jones in *The Song of Bernadette* when I was ten.

I have rented a cottage here on Martha's Vineyard for the entire summer.

I know, I know! It's mad. But I had dinner at a local pub a few nights ago, and after imbibing too much wine (which a very rude fisherman told me I had no business drinking), I spied a flyer for this cute little place to rent and something just struck me. I think being here could be really good for me, to get away from the business and The Director Whose Name Must Not Be Spoken and all of it. Sy will have a conniption, of course, but the more I think about it, the more I am convinced it's the right thing to do. I've been on the phone with the bank in L.A. non-stop trying to get money wired here (evidence, perhaps, I should have thought this through a bit more), but it seems like it's all settled now and I am feeling very relaxed and hopeful.

Perhaps I can entice you to visit? (Though we both know you won't.) After all, this is really all your fault. There is no telephone here, which I am also happy about, and so we'll have to communicate the old-fashioned way, via correspondence. How very Jane Austen it all will be!

Must run now, but more soon. You can write me back using the post office box on the return address, even though we both also know how terrible you are with writing. I will try to phone somehow, since I know you are no doubt sitting there with a thousand questions and being cranky about how irresponsible I'm being. But be happy for me, darling—I feel better than I have in weeks.

Love,
Mercy

Nine

What am I doing?

The question thundered in her brain as she continued pedaling, the cool breeze off the Atlantic a tonic on her clammy skin. She remembered the indulgence yesterday of the candies from Hilliard's Kitch-In-Vue and picked up the pace. "The camera adds pounds" was an omnipresent axiom in modeling, but also in Hollywood. When would she be before a camera again?

That question brought her back to the first. What was she doing? She was hiding out on an island off the coast of Massachusetts. She certainly wasn't the first—hadn't Agatha Christie disappeared for nearly two weeks back in 1926? Yet it was beginning to feel selfish and indulgent. Not even her family knew where she was. And yet she had no desire—none—to tell anyone. There was a delirious freedom of rebellion coursing through her that she didn't want to relinquish. Cass knew. That was enough.

She stopped and hopped off the bicycle, straddling it as she turned to look out at the churning blue water. Yes, it was madness to stay here. But this wasn't just wounded pride. She felt, somewhere deep inside, that there was some other reason she had decided to stay on Martha's Vineyard, some other purpose, even if she didn't know exactly what it was yet.

The wind gusted up, sending the hair swirling around her face. She saddled back onto the bike.

Twenty minutes later she coasted into Vineyard Haven, which was a lot like Edgartown and yet nothing at all like Edgartown. It seemed more open, its main street wider and airier, the pace just a bit slower. She spent the next few hours buying apples at Cronig Brothers and browsing summer dresses at Brickman's. She climbed up the forty-five-foot tower of the West Chop Lighthouse, which wasn't very tall for a lighthouse, but between the trek up and the miles of biking she knew her legs would be as stiff as starch tomorrow.

She stopped for iced tea and a sandwich on the second-floor deck of the Mansion House, a charming white and green hotel that dated back to 1794. Her penchant for people-watching kicked in—it wasn't The Wives, but it would do—and she began studying the waitress. The girl was around her age, with dark brown hair pulled back into a tight ponytail to display a wide, heart-shaped face. She kept tarrying at Mercy's table, seemingly inventing reasons to constantly come over and check on her. Mercy noticed her covertly looking past her, gazing through the window on Mercy's left, which showed the hotel dining room. The poor waitress might as well have had her face pressed up against it, cupping her hands at her temples to keep out the glare.

"Well, whatever is going on in there," Mercy casually remarked as the girl distractedly refreshed her iced tea, "I have to say it seems to have certainly captured your attention."

The girl's cheeks flushed pink. "Oh, ma'am, I am sorry," she said. The accent was pure New England. "I didn't mean to be rude."

Mercy laughed. "Don't worry. It's just that now you've got *me* curious as to what's going on inside."

The girl quickly glanced around, as if the boards of the deck were listening. "Well," she said almost conspiratorially, "it's just we don't see Mint out that much anymore. She rarely leaves Sycamore. So sightings of her have become something of an island pastime. It's like seeing a celebrity."

Mercy was confused. And intrigued. "I'm sorry, seeing . . . who?"

"Mint Sewards," the waitress whispered, pretending to wipe a wet spot from the table. "You could say Mint's the grande dame of the Vineyard. The Sewards go way back. Like, *all the way* back. I mean, they *are* Martha's Vineyard. She lives in the big house on the bluff in Edgartown."

Oh, you had to love a good town gossip. It was like being back in Hollywood. Mercy turned, leaning forward so she could catch her own glimpse of the mysterious island matriarch through the window.

"Oh God, don't look!" the waitress hissed in near panic. "They'll fire me if they find out I was yapping."

Stifling her amusement as the girl shuffled off to attend to another table, Mercy slowly inched her chair around the ornate white metal café table so she could gain a better view. Inside she spied a group of four middle-aged women sitting around a round table set for tea, chatting amiably. Thank God for sunglasses. She didn't want anyone to see *her* spying, either.

The women inside didn't appear particularly grand: all had the flat, ruddy, seafaring faces of women who would have looked at home on a widow's walk, waiting for their men to return from a long voyage. But there was one who seemed slightly different from the others. Her body was smaller, bonier, her clothes a touch more refined, her hair a bit more modernly styled.

Regal. That was the word that came to mind. That *had* to be Mint. She had a smooth, diamond-shaped face, and big, luminous eyes that said, *I have a story to tell, and I'll never tell you.* Mint. What an odd sobriquet. Then Mercy smiled as she remembered her own, whipped up in Sy Sigmund's office.

The jumpy waitress returned. She looked back into the window, where the quartet was readying to leave. "Mint and her ladies," the girl said. "Well, at least two of them are, anyway."

Mercy followed her sight line. "What do you mean?"

"The two to her left? Their blood is almost as blue as the Sewardses'. But the other one, Mrs. Chadwick? Not so much. She's sort of Mint's charity case. 'Least that's what everyone's always said. Though never to her face, of course."

Mercy watched the women slowly leave the table, the formidable Mint Sewards in the lead. It reminded her of Eulalie Mackecknie

Shinn, the stuffy mayor's wife leading her pick-a-little ladies in the play *The Music Man*. Didn't she hear that Jack Warner was doing a film version?

The waitress's shrill voice interrupted her tangent. "I'm so sorry," she said, slipping the check onto the table. "I shouldn't be gossiping. I don't mean to get the zorros on you, but this is a good job and I need to keep it. I shouldn't be telling tales out of school. I swear, sometimes I don't know what gets into me."

Mercy smiled up at her. "You're a girl who's curious about people. There are worse things."

The girl seemed to stiffen. "Not on this island."

Something about the delivery made the hairs on Mercy's arms stand up. Why did it feel like a warning?

Mercy studied her a bit further. She had a sturdy build, coated in a filmy veneer of femininity that was trying too hard. She was the kind of girl who pined for boys for whom she would always be background scenery, the one always living vicariously through her prettier, more sophisticated friends.

"What's your name?" Mercy asked.

"Vera," the girl said cheerily. "Vera Harding."

"And you live here year-round?"

She threw her arms out. "Born and raised. I've never been off island."

Mercy smiled. *My God.* To live your entire life on a chilly postage stamp of bramble and never venture beyond it. She suspected there were people far older than Vera here who could boast the same. "Well, it's nice to meet you, Vera. I'm Edie."

Vera smiled back, her expression slowly melting into what could only kindly be called a snigger. "No, you're not," she replied.

Mercy felt a stab of anxiety. *Oh, no.*

Vera took another covert look around the deck, then quietly sank down in the chair on the other side of the table. "So, I have to ask," she whispered urgently. "Why is Mercy Welles hiding out on Martha's Vineyard?"

*

Mercy sank wearily into the soapy water of the claw-foot tub in her cottage, turning the page of the Nancy Drew book she'd found in the living room bookcase. *The Secret in the Old Attic*. God, how she'd loved these stories growing up, dreaming herself out of the bland flatness of the plains and into a world of adventure. But despite immersing herself in Nancy's heroics trying to solve the mystery of an old song, all Mercy could think about was Vera Harding.

She closed the book, admonishing herself. How long had she expected she could wander around this island without anyone recognizing her? Damn her false modesty. Hadn't it been to her credit that she didn't think of herself as anyone famous enough to *be* recognized? No, just stupid. All it was going to take was one movie-crazy, *Modern Screen*–reading waitress to turn her hidden holiday upside down.

Because she was finally ready to answer the question she had posed to herself earlier on the bicycle. She had found peace here, an oasis of serenity she hadn't expected.

She stretched her body underneath the warm water, working to release the tension out of her shoulders as she replayed the last part of her conversation with Vera. There had been no point in denying who she was, so she had quickly shifted to playing defense. Her new bubble of tranquility had to be protected at any cost. She'd done the only thing she could think of.

"How clever of you, Vera," she'd told the girl, who predictably beamed from the compliment. "But I certainly cannot be the first actress to come here to get away from everything for a little while." She'd said it all very casually, as if remarking on the balmy weather.

Vera had taken the bait. "Of course," she'd said empathetically, quickly assuming local confidante status. "Katharine Cornell? She lives in a cute place called Chip Chop right by Lake Tashmoo, near the Sound. Do you know her? I see her all the time. We chat."

That was news. Cornell was one of the most accomplished stage actresses of the last half century; she'd been on the cover of *TIME*. She also, Mercy strongly suspected, had no idea who Vera Harding was.

"No, I can't say I know her," Mercy said. "But I am sure she's here for the same reason I am: to rest and relax." Time to strike a bargain. "And I want you to know how much I appreciate your discretion, Vera. Truly. I know you won't mention my visit to anyone. And I'd like to repay you for that kindness by taking you to dinner some-time. You know, I don't know anyone here. It would be lovely to have someone here for some fun girl talk."

Vera had gone saucer-eyed at the prospect of private access to a pipeline of bona fide Hollywood gossip. "Oh, I'd love that, Miss Welles."

Closing the deal, Mercy had reached her hand across the table, placing it gently on Vera's forearm. "Oh, please. We're friends now. You must call me Mercy."

Was it fair? Mercy wondered post-bath, cinching a belt around her yellow day dress as she padded barefoot from the bedroom to the living room. She tossed the book onto a side table, debating the eth-ics of using her acting ability to disarm Vera. But weren't they both getting what they wanted? Mercy got to be Edie awhile longer, and Vera got herself an identity, however temporary, as best pal of a not-so-famous actress. Mercy had made far more Faustian bargains.

A knock at the door interrupted her thoughts. She hoped it wasn't Vera, assuming they were now going to pal around daily. She glanced outside the front window and spied a dusty blue Chevy Apache parked outside. The cargo bed was filled with a hodge-podge of household and gardening tools, blankets, a hose, and a few fishing rods. *Ah.* Mercy headed toward the door. She'd bumped into the landlord on the street yesterday, asked if he could send a handyman over to address both the dripping faucet in the kitchen and a shutter that banged at every stiff breeze.

She opened the door, and there he was.

Cleaned up from his last ignominious appearance, now in a neat, red-checked cotton shirt, faded blue jeans, and boots, though the grizzly beard growth was still there, along with the dark, dismissive eyes. She felt a sensation inside herself she didn't immediately recog-nize and didn't care to. He stared at her intently, until one eyebrow arched slightly, and his mouth slowly edged into a cocksure grin.

"Well, well," he said. "Look who's playing house."

My God, he was rude. And arrogant. And, her mind briefly interjected unhelpfully, ruggedly good-looking. She wanted to slam the door—hard—right in his face, but the specter of another night of uninterrupted sleep lost to the creaky clanging of the shutter and the drip-drip-drip of the faucet prevailed.

"Not that your opinion matters in the least, but I'll have you know I am not 'playing' at anything," Mercy replied tartly. "I rented this cottage with money I earned myself."

Reflexively she shut her eyes. Why was she justifying herself to this lout?

"Well, Miss Hard-Earned Money, formerly known as Miss Los Angeles, I am here to fix your issues. That is if," he said, looking behind her in the doorway, "you actually let me in."

She stepped aside. Ren. That was his name. A fisherman. She recalled Bridie's verdict from that night two weeks ago. *He's actually a pretty nice fellow when you get to know him.*

She strongly doubted that.

Mercy followed him into the kitchen, where he retrieved a wrench from his back pocket and began fiddling with the faucet. "May I offer you something?" she said. His bad manners didn't mean she had to follow suit.

He laughed. "Have any good wine?"

She leaned against the kitchen counter, folding her arms as she watched him attack the faucet. "Sorry. As you know from experience, I clearly need to work on my wine selection. I wouldn't want to offend your clearly finely honed palette by offering something that doesn't pair properly with . . . handiwork."

He shot her a look that was almost admiring. "I appreciate the thoughtfulness." He looked down at the tiny steel oval now in his palm, extending it over to her. "Here's your problem. The O ring is corroded. I have another in the truck. Once we swap it in, should be good to go. Then I can take a look at the shutter."

"Well, that's good news. I'm glad it's not a complicated repair."

"Indeed. Because you need your water." He walked past her, and the wattage of his sudden smile unsteadied her. "After all," he said, his face now a bit too close to hers, "a girl can't live on cheap wine alone, right?"

She watched him walk out of the kitchen, heard the slam of the screen door as he headed to the Apache to retrieve the shiny new O ring. She fought to ignore the current of heat now rushing through her.

Ten

It was thirty minutes later and Mercy was ensconced in the cozy parlor, once again engrossed in Nancy's adventure—the girl detective, tied to a chair, was currently facing off with a deadly tarantula—when Ren casually strolled in from the kitchen, drying his hands on a tea towel and acting like he lived there. He eyed the book cover. "I hope I'm not interrupting your intellectual reading," he said. "I'm all finished. Faucet works, shutter nailed back."

If he expected her to be embarrassed, he was going to be sorely disappointed. It was her holiday and she'd read whatever she damn well pleased. She manifested her best carefree look. "Thank you," she said, trying to imbue it with a hint of royal dismissal.

"Nancy Drew," he said, nodding as he flung the towel over one shoulder. "Heavy stuff."

"She was a role model for me."

"I should have known."

She cocked her head. "And why is that?"

"She's a girl who knows how to stir up trouble."

"I beg your—"

He laughed—a deep, bellowing bell ring of a laugh. "Joke! Good God, woman, don't you ever relax? You're on the Vineyard now. You're on vacation, and from the looks of it it's one you desperately need. Embrace your surroundings."

She rose, smoothing down the front of her unwrinkled dress. "Well, thank you for coming out to make those repairs," she said. "I'll sleep better, that's for sure. As for my vacation, I will say to you that it's going very well indeed. Who knows? Maybe I'll have my own mysterious adventure."

"I suspect you will," he said. He gave her a broad smile, and reflexively she returned it. "So, you hungry?"

She hesitated for a moment. "I . . . Well, I . . ."

"Just a question about a meal, not a mystery in the attic," he said. "I was going to go get some seafood at one of my favorite joints. Care to join? I figure you're about due for a break from sitting at the bar at the White Whale eating oysters and listening to Bridie sing the greatest hits of Delia Murphy."

"I didn't know Bridie sang."

"She doesn't. That's the problem. So—you in?"

This is a bad idea, she thought.

"Um . . . OK," she offered meekly.

Even as she collected her jacket and purse, her mind insistently repeated the verdict.

This is a bad idea.

*

They took the coast road all the way around, the evening air rushing in through the open windows as the truck hugged every curve, past Sylvia Beach and the lighthouses, East Chop then West Chop, past Lambert's Cove and Paul's Point and Cape Higgins. Mercy turned to him, now relaxed behind the wheel, and asked, "Where *is* this restaurant, anyway? Canada?"

"Don't be in such a rush. That's the problem with all you city tourists. You're always in a hurry to *get* somewhere. That's not what life here is about. It's about the opposite. Slowing everything down." He nodded over to her. "Put your head out the window."

"What?"

"I want you to put your head out the window and take in a big, gulping breath." He nodded again toward the passenger side. "Go ahead."

It felt silly. But she'd come this far. She bent her head out the window, grabbing the frame with both hands, and inhaled.

"Ahh," she said.

"Ahhh!" he said, slapping the steering wheel. "Exactly! You cannot buy the feeling that delivers. Greatest smell on earth."

"Chanel No. 5 is the greatest smell on earth," she replied, ducking back inside the truck. "But I take your point. There is something . . . restorative about this place. I guess it's why I decided to stay for the season."

His eyebrows raised. "You rented Fred's cottage for the entire summer?"

She put an elbow on the window frame, feeling her body relax into the rumbling rhythm of the truck. "I sure did."

There was a question—actually, several—evident in his eyes as he glanced over at her. They went unasked. She turned her attention back to the shoreline, watching as the sky gradually began to darken into a swirling mélange of deep blue, pink, and orange.

Ten minutes later they pulled in at a tiny Shaker-style house with a screened-in porch and a pointed gable. A faded white sign declared THE HOME PORT, with little horizontal ones underneath that in hand-painted letters advertised seafood specialties, home cooking, and Sealtest ice cream. "Where are we?" Mercy asked.

"Menemsha," Ren said. "Little fishing village. One of the best parts of the whole island."

She raised an eyebrow. "Let me guess: because the tourists don't come here."

His eyes glittered with a mix of sarcasm and boyish excitement. "Exactly."

It wasn't true—clearly, some of the people imbibing giant lobsters and steaming bowls of hearty soup were tourists—but as she took the chair he held out for her at the old wooden table she saw what he meant. There was an off-the-beaten-path, ramshackle charm emanating from the checkered tablecloths and the smell of wet wood. She looked at the outline of the cove outside the window and made the decision right then to rent a car. He was correct: this island was pocked with hidden treasures to explore. A bicycle alone would be insufficient. She asked him for a recommendation on where to get a vehicle.

"Are you used to driving?" he asked after he'd ordered them beers. She didn't have the heart to tell him she hated beer. "The roads here can feel pretty twisty, especially at night."

"It's OK. I'm up for a little adventure. After all," she said, "I'm Nancy Drew."

They ate some delicious seafood, made all the better, she had to admit, by the acidic, vinegary taste of the ice-cold beer. She asked him about his upbringing on the island and he answered perfunctorily, describing "your standard New England family" and how he had fallen in love with oystering young and never looked back.

"Has your family been here a long time?" she asked.

"You could say that."

"So you must know Mint Sewards."

His eyes flicked up as a fresh round of beers arrived. There was a sudden, stony look in his gaze.

"I'm sorry," she said. "Sore subject?"

He shrugged, taking another gulp of beer. "Man, that's nice. I love that they serve the coldest beer on the island here. Don't tell Bridie I said that." He forced a laugh. "And Mint? No, not at all. I mean, she's sort of a legend here, I guess. People are always asking about her. Why do you ask?"

She shrugged, still curious about his reaction. "Just heard some folks talking about her and she seemed to be a big deal. And now that I'm a local, I want to be up on the who's who." She smiled, popped a battered shrimp into her mouth.

"Well, you've already met the two most important people: Bridie and Dennis."

"And you, of course. You needn't be so modest."

"Well, that goes without saying." He smiled and quickly pivoted, asking her about her background. She talked about Nebraska, about wanting a larger life, taking the bus to Los Angeles. After that, she became deliberately vague, talking about taking "odd jobs" and meeting interesting people. None of it untrue, almost all of it grossly misleading.

He forked a big piece of flounder and swooped it into some creamy tartar sauce. "You're being very humble," he said. "You didn't even mention the Oscar nomination."

She leaned back in the chair. It was quiet for a minute, the only sounds the boisterous taproom-like conviviality around them. She felt heat creeping up the back of her spine. She didn't mind that he knew who she was. But his smug revelation of the fact felt like a sneak attack. At least Vera had come out with it right away.

"How long have you been rehearsing that?" she asked, more pointedly than she'd intended.

He put down his fork. "I mean, that night at the White Whale—"

"When you were being a rude ass."

He paused. ". . . when I was being a rude ass, I thought you looked vaguely familiar. But I didn't put it together till later."

Had Vera blabbed? Did it matter? She was reminded yet again of her own fecklessness. If he knew, then clearly other people did, too. Maybe no one cared?

It had been nice, being anonymous, having people get to know her, not the image of her. She thought back to a few days ago, once again sitting in the White Whale. She had finally succumbed to the siren's song of its legendary chowder and discovered the raves had been justified. She was chatting with Dennis, whose crusty façade had slowly cracked; he seemed to have warmed to the idea of single women sitting at the bar. She'd discovered he'd come to the island from Boston in the late 1920s, not long after he'd first emigrated to the United States. He'd found work as a day laborer, then eventually became a policeman. Bridie, his cousin, followed from Ireland not long after, working as a housekeeper in one of the hotels. Later, they'd bought the White Whale.

Mercy had asked him about his adjustment to life here. "I felt at home immediately here," he'd said. "I think because the island then was so quiet, so damp and gloomy. It reminded me of Fanad." Eventually, Mercy steered the conversation to the only other interesting local she knew of: Mint Sewards.

"One of the finest women to ever step foot on this island," he'd answered without hesitation. "There's a reason she's so admired here."

"And why is that?" Mercy had asked.

He'd considered his answer for a moment. "Well, you know," he said, "she was widowed young, with three kids to raise on her own, and everyone lookin' at her because they think when you got money you got everything, and she had the name and that meant something to people and so she had to live up to it, to earn it, and she did all of it without a complaint. She was a real lady, I tell you. Still is."

"What happened to her husband? How did he die?"

An odd look had swept over Dennis's face. "Accident. It was all very sudden" is all he said. It was clear it was all he was going to say.

Mercy had looked over to Bridie, standing nearby, who shook her head slightly. Mercy wondered if Bridie's impression of Mint was a bit different.

"Where did you go?" Ren asked, pulling her out of the memory.

"Sorry," Mercy said. "I was just thinking back to something Dennis said at the pub the other night."

"Look, I didn't mean to spring it on you like that. I mean, that I knew who you were. I guess I thought I was being clever."

"It's fine."

He took a sip of his beer, looked down at the last of his flounder. "Boy, I am terrible at this."

She tilted her head slightly. "At what?"

He waved his finger back and forth between them. "This. Dinner. Small talk. Maybe that's why I spend all my time with oysters. They don't require so much conversation."

She felt herself smirking. "'So much'? So you talk to them?"

"I do if they don't behave."

"And how often does that happen?"

"Unfortunately, a lot."

They both looked at each other and began laughing. "Oh, I don't know," Mercy said finally. "I think you may be better at this than you think."

After dinner he drove her back to Edgartown. The ride was quiet, each of them lost in their own thoughts. When they got to the cottage he walked her to the door, and as she turned to thank him for dinner their eyes locked for a few lingering seconds. She buckled first.

"Well, thank you for dinner," she said. "That was . . . surprisingly nice."

"Of course." He nodded, shoved his hands into his pockets. "Well, good night, then."

She leaned against the porch railing and watched the truck pull away, and for the hundredth time asked herself what she was doing.

Eleven

June's warmer weather took firmer root and the Steamship Authority's summer schedule kicked in, bringing in eight ferry loads of people a day and a ninth at 10 P.M. on the weekends. Crowds swarmed into Farmer Greene's in West Tisbury for strawberries and produce, plucked live lobsters out of the tanks at Marshall's Fish Market in Oak Bluffs, treated their children to rounds of miniature golf in Vineyard Haven before invariably succumbing to the pleas for ice cream at the Dairy Maid. But as much as the whole tableau seemed to Mercy to be some windswept version of *Our Town*, she couldn't shake her own restlessness.

She'd gone out to Old Colony, located in a hangar at the airport, and rented a jeep, but her initial zoom around the island, the sun in her eyes and hair flying about her face, had left her feeling as if she was merely killing time. She made a pledge to dive more deeply into the history of the island, unearth the spots like Menemsha that the tourists didn't normally visit.

Or maybe she just needed to admit what was at the root of her feeling so out of sorts. The thing no amount of breezy driving was going to let her escape.

It had been two weeks since their dinner and there had been no sign of Ren. No pop-by, no message, nothing. After a few days Mercy had caught a movie and then wandered back into the White Whale, ordering a glass of dry white wine and casually inquiring if Bridie had seen him. She had not. Her eyes bored into Mercy's with a knowing look that said she knew the inquiry was anything but offhanded.

The sea air was clearly rusting her acting ability. She needed a diversion.

And so tonight she had put on a pale pink silk dress in a blouson silhouette, with a collared portrait neckline and a back kick pleat, grabbed her wrap, gloves, and bag, and headed out to the Boathouse Bar at the Harborside Inn to listen to some music.

But now, sitting alone at a corner table nursing a glass of champagne, Mercy felt anything but bubbly. For one thing, she was wildly overdressed: other than the three tuxedoed gentlemen of the Herb Kemp Trio and the bar's white-jacketed waiters, everyone else was casually attired, a sea of weathered patrons in loose cotton sweaters, pressed khaki pants, and tartan skirts imbibing chilled martinis and frosty beers. The woodsy room was dominated by knotty pine walls and rattan furniture, giving it the air of a plush Elks lodge. A small fire crackled in the oversized fireplace, there to mitigate the low chill of the night air now seeping in through the open windows.

It was hard to actually hear the music amid the din of carrying-on—a woman two tables over was telling a story about a disastrous sea bass meal she'd recently endured—but Mercy dutifully joined in the smattering of applause when the trio ended its set with a particularly bouncy rendition of the Mills Brothers' "Paper Doll."

A few minutes later, she was surprised to find the trio's pianist standing in front of her table, a glass of scotch in his hand.

"I hope I'm not intruding," he said. "I just wanted to come over and make a quick introduction. We're so honored to have Miss Mercy Welles here listening to us tonight." He extended his hand. "Stanton Williams. It's a pleasure to meet you."

Another dart to her anonymity. She took his hand, waved to the open chair across from her. "The pleasure is mine. Won't you join me?"

He nodded and sat, and as she took him in, it struck her how dramatically her life had changed in so little time. Growing up in Nebraska it would have been inconceivable for a white woman and a Negro man to sit together in public. Not that such a convention was ever tested—Mercy had not even seen a Negro in person until she'd arrived in Los Angeles. For all its supposed liberality, Hollywood was also segregated, though the powers that be took great pains to invite Black entertainers to the occasional studio party in a lukewarm effort to prove otherwise. She had a brief image of Sy throwing a fit, warning how a photograph of this moment could torpedo her career. Mercy glanced around the room. If anyone was startled at this turn of events, they didn't seem to be showing it. She took another sip of her champagne and surveyed her companion more closely.

Stanton Williams had a low, smoky baritone that contrasted with the softness and delicacy of his looks and bearing. He was striking, with a sharp, angular jawline and dewy skin. He was the kind of man people described as pretty.

"I really enjoyed your set, Mr. Williams," she said. "That arrangement of 'All the Things You Are' was lovely."

"Thank you, ma'am. But in a place like this, we're just the background noise for people to have another round," he said. "But I do appreciate that. Nice to know that somebody out here is actually listening to the music. And please—call me Staxx. Everybody does."

Staxx. It was jaunty, and suited him. They exchanged pleasantries for a few moments—how she'd come to be on Martha's Vineyard (she left out the part about Louis cheating on her), how he had (long family history), the weather, the best place to get a lobster roll, which she dutifully noted and promised to investigate now that she had her jeep.

He looked over his shoulder, spied his bandmates walking back in from their smoke break. They'd be sitting for the next set soon. He turned back to her. "It would be dishonorable if I represented to you that I only came over here to engage in casual conversation. In all honesty I have . . . a proposition for you."

She fought to conceal her knee-jerk reaction. If Sy would have torn the rest of what was left of his hair out over a casual photograph of her and Stanton Williams together, she imagined he would throw himself out into the Pacific if she accepted a date. What was more interesting to her was how, in the moment, the idea held more appeal than she might have imagined. Was it his engaging manner, his easygoing presence? Or a way to deflect thoughts of a cranky oysterman? Or was it, perhaps, simply that it would be so deliciously wicked and forbidden?

"Go on," she managed to say before hiding in another sip of her drink.

"I'm part of a group that's putting on a new play in Vineyard Haven," he said. "We can only afford to do one production a year. And it would make all the difference in the world if it had you in it. It's this incredible play, by a very talented new playwright who is going to be a major force in American theater."

"Really? What's his name?"

He smiled. "Stanton Williams."

So that was it. He wanted her for his play. Mercy blew past her own reaction—disappointment? relief?—so she could focus on addressing the question at hand.

She shook her head. "I don't think so, Staxx," she said. "I hate to disappoint you, but the entire reason I came here was to escape acting."

He cocked his head slightly. "Escape acting? Or escape Hollywood?"

"Same thing."

"I don't think they're the same thing at all. And I don't think you do, either."

She smiled. She had to give him one thing: he was charmingly persistent. "I'm only here for the summer."

"We premiere August twenty-second. Right after the fair closes. The island will be packed with tourists."

She nearly choked on her drink. "August! And you're still casting? It's mid-June! You should be knee-deep in rehearsals by now."

"I know. But we couldn't get all the money together. We've got a really great crew. It would mean a lot to all of us if you'd consider this. There aren't a lot of places where a Black playwright can have his work produced. We need financial support to expand, to keep it going. And we can get there, I know we can—*if* we have an Oscar-nominated actress to star in this year's production."

It was painfully obvious that her acting ability had little to do with any of this. The theater needed a "name" who could get people curious enough to buy tickets.

"Katharine Cornell lives here, does she not? Why not ask her?"

Staxx shook his head. "She's too old to play the lead. You, on the other hand . . ." That million-watt smile again. ". . . are perfect."

Mercy sighed. "Summarize the plot."

It was an opening, and he rushed to take it. "It's called *The Rose of Aquinnah*," he said. His words came in a torrent, laced with excitement and possibility. "It's about a local girl from the island who lives a sort of uninteresting life. Her family runs a small restaurant, and she works there as a waitress."

Mercy conjured an image of Vera Harding standing center stage. "Go on."

"Every day is the same, but she dreams of being a novelist, which her parents and her brother all dismiss as fantasy. And then one day a mysterious man comes into the restaurant, and she's instantly intrigued. He's very quiet, reserved, but each day he comes in for coffee and eggs, and they begin talking. And soon a romance blossoms. Only it turns out . . . he's dying."

Mercy recoiled. "Oh, good Lord. That's dark."

"Life is dark sometimes," he said. "But the darkness can be beautiful. It's actually a really poignant love story—about taking chances, of being an authentic person, of not being afraid to want love. And how even the briefest of great loves is still better than never having love at all."

"So an homage to Tennyson. Mixed with *Dark Victory*, with a dash of *Rebecca*."

He chuckled. "I wouldn't have thought to put it that way, but . . . sure." He was quiet for a few seconds. He looked away, catching the stares of his impatient trio mates. "At its heart, I think it's about feeling like you're different, and having the chance to feel like you belong somewhere. To someone. Even if only for a moment."

She studied his profile, the perfectly symmetrical outline of his face, the deep-set eyes, the strong chin. There was a singular charisma about him, but it was actually more than that. There was a quiet strength, a determination that drew you in. How bold a dream he carried. It was audacious enough to want to be a playwright or screenwriter. It was an incredibly brazen goal for a Black writer, no matter how talented. She had no idea if his play was any good. But she was curious enough to want to read it.

He looked back at her, flicked the blazing smile back on. "Admit it: you're intrigued."

"I'm . . . all right, yes, I'm intrigued. But I am making no promises. Other than to say I will read it." She exhaled wearily. "But with that said, even if I *were* to agree to it, and I'm not, putting on a theatrical production in what—nine weeks?—is insanity. It can't be done. Or at least not done well."

"You don't know these folks," he said. "Or me." He leaned a bit across the table. "I know it sounds foolish. But it's important to a lot of people. And we've already built some of the sets." He looked back over his shoulder, where one bandmate had already picked up his trumpet and the other was settling in behind his cello. Their combined stony look now said clearly, *Flirting time with the white lady is over.* "Look, I've got to get back," he said. "Just promise me you'll think about it."

"Honestly, I can't see—"

"Just think about it, OK? I'll get you the script and we'll talk again." He stood, delivered a gracious nod, then threaded his way back to his eye-rolling bandmates.

Five minutes later, sipping a fresh glass of sparkling goodness and listening to the trio's mellifluous version of "On Green Dolphin Street," Mercy sank back into her chair and tried to picture herself standing in the middle of a tiny playhouse stage. It would completely defeat the entire purpose of coming here. What anonymity she was still clinging to would disappear overnight. She would have to tell the winsome Staxx she couldn't do it.

But she'd read the script. Just to be polite.

*

Mercy glanced at the clock. Ten past nine in the morning. He was already late.

She'd arrived home from the Boathouse Bar after eleven, her mind swimming from both Staxx's proposition and one too many glasses of champagne, only to discover a note slipped under the door.

Breakfast tomorrow? I'll pop by around 9 to see if you're free. R.

Now here she was, dressed in a crisp white popover and pedal pushers, furtively glancing out the front window for a sign of his truck. But the truth was she'd been happy to get his invitation. A bit too happy, really. He'd basically given her the brush-off for two weeks, and now, at the snap of his fingers—or at least the stroke of his pen—here she was, waiting for him.

Then she heard his boots on the steps, the gentle rap at the door. He looked through the screen, let himself in. "I hope you're hungry."

"You're late," she blurted out. It felt petulant. She avoided eye contact, pretended to be inspecting her purse.

He looked at the clock, then back to her. "We need to get you on island time."

She met his eyes. "I'm just saying, it's polite to be on time, that's all."

He cocked his head, and she tried to ignore how handsome it made him appear. "OK, then," he said. "Are the forty lashes over? Or are there still a few more to give?"

She shoved her bag under her arm and walked by him, out the door. "You're impossible."

He laughed. "I was right off the shake. You're clearly hungry."

She made him make a pit stop first, at Ethel Roberts' Shop on Simpsons Lane, where she'd taken a bracelet with a broken clasp to be repaired. He'd waited outside but took in her longing expression after she came out, when she stopped to gaze adoringly in the shop window.

He strolled over from the truck. "Something catching your eye?" he said.

She sighed, still staring at the display. "Indeed. Look."

In the middle of the window sat an open, gray velvet-lined jewelry box, holding a simple but spectacular silver necklace. At its end lay a sparkling rectangular sapphire.

"It's just so beautiful," she said.

He nodded. "So buy it."

She laughed. "'Buy it'? Just like that? You're confusing me with Barbara Hutton."

They began walking back toward the truck. "Well, it's always nice to look." She opened the passenger side door. "Come on, I'm starving."

They ate pancakes at Stam's overlooking Vineyard Haven Harbor before heading into Oak Bluffs, where Ren insisted on buying two massive cake doughnuts at Walmsley's "for the road," as if they were about to drive to Philadelphia. She had resisted the temptation, mostly (OK, so she had a bite). He ate both.

"Keep eating like that and you're going to look like Jackie Gleason," she said as he flicked crumbs off of his lap.

"Do you *know* Jackie Gleason?"

She gave an offhand nod. "We say hello."

He laughed heartily, a good, rollicking belly laugh, and she liked that she could make him laugh. "So," he said, "beautiful day for sightseeing. I have some choice spots to show you."

"I'd like to make a request first."

He arched an eyebrow. "More errands?"

"More like research. I want to see Aquinnah."

As she was leaving the bar last night Staxx had hurriedly retrieved a copy of his play, *The Rose of Aquinnah,* from his bag and thrust it into her hands, and she'd spent the morning poring over its pages. The play concerned a girl who had been raised on the most remote part of Martha's Vineyard, Gay Head, which had originally been called Aquinnah when it had been settled by the original natives. In addition to finding the love story itself tender and absorbing—it was a testament to Staxx's talent that he could write characters so unlike himself—Mercy had been impressed at the amount of historical research he'd artfully sprinkled throughout his play, such as the legend of the Wampanoag settling the land after traveling to the island atop an ice floe. The town had been rechristened Gay Head by the locals in 1870, though Mercy understood why Staxx had gone with its original name instead. *The Rose of Gay Head* didn't have quite the same romantic pull.

Thirty minutes later they pulled up at the terminus of State Road, and as she alighted from the truck Mercy took a moment to catch her breath.

"My God," she whispered.

She couldn't remember the last time she'd seen anything so spectacular. A series of towering cliffs, ranging in color from dusky white to blue to gray and myriad shades of brown, thrust up from the churning cobalt sea below, frothing whitecaps dramatically crashing against their clay sides. In the distance stood a stately brick and sandstone lighthouse, topped by massive windows framed in black, jutting fifty feet into the sky.

He sidled up beside her. "I know. Impressive."

"Is it still operational?"

"Yup. It was automated a few years ago. But up until then Charlie Vanderhoop lived there as the lighthouse keeper for more than thirty years."

She shook her head. "Such colorful names: Vanderhoop, Mint. It makes Ren seem positively pedantic."

"I'd probably agree, if I knew what 'pedantic' meant."

"It means 'dull,' among other definitions. Which you are not."

A pleased look crossed his face. "I'll take that as a compliment."

They held each other's stare for a few seconds. Finally, he said, "Let's go."

It took some doing—the path down to the water was rocky and steep, and Mercy's espadrilles had definitely been the wrong choice for such an expedition—but it was worth it when they got to the bottom and the silky sand of Moshup Beach. A smattering of other people sauntered along the shoreline. In the distance, a young couple splashed in the water with their small children.

They spent an hour walking the water's edge. They talked about everything—where they'd traveled (she was stunned to learn he'd spent a season oystering in the Delta de l'Ebre, off the coast of Spain), what they loved to do most in their free time (he told a hilarious story about Bridie trying to teach him how to make proper ham and cabbage), her uneventful Nebraska childhood and turn into acting. She shared with him Staxx's proposal to star in his play, and he appeared slightly intrigued. His younger brother, it turned out, was a producer of the production and one of the locals trying to resurrect the old Martha's Vineyard Playhouse. She used the opening to ask a bit more about his family, and the conversation quickly turned as chilly as the water. She could almost see a curtain lowering in front of his face.

"Do you ever think of leaving?" she asked, as they stood for a moment, staring out at the horizon.

"Never."

"Why not?"

He shrugged. "I don't know anything else. And I like it here. It's my home. Island life, it's in your blood, I think."

She folded her arms. "Barbados is an island."

He smiled. "No oysters."

"So why are you not out there plucking oysters now?"

"Oystering is done in the colder months. So I work as a sort of jack-of-all-trades in the summer. Fixing the odd creaky shutter."

"And don't forget your side career as cheerful sommelier."

He winked at her. "That's me: always happy to help."

They walked on in silence for several minutes, taking in the sun and the waves and the towering cliffs. He reached down to pick something up, then ran into the shallow surf to wash it off. When he came back he handed her his treasure: two perfectly symmetrical gray clamshells, each etched with elegant swirled lines and splashed with aquamarine.

"Quahog," he said. "Delicious, but also quite beautiful. Wampanoag women have been making jewelry and crafts from these for centuries. They call them wampum."

"'Wampum,'" Mercy repeated. "They're exquisite."

"So are you," he said. His eyes betrayed momentary embarrassment, as if he'd been caught doing something he shouldn't. But her tender smile melted all of it away. He slowly brought his hand up and used the back of it to caress her cheek. Then he leaned in for a gentle, textured kiss.

That night, she placed the two shells on top of her dresser, sitting side by side.

*

Mercy was hardly in need of pound cake—she was already beginning to feel her clothes getting a tad tighter, a result of too much time spent in the jeep instead of on the bicycle. But it was thirty-three cents at First National, and she convinced herself that Sy would approve of this as responsible thrift. On this extended holiday she has been watching her healthy balance, deposited at the Edgartown National Bank, slowly begin to ebb, and it has begun to make her nervous. She would have to be more careful with what she was spending to avoid risking running out of money by the end of the summer.

She was putting the buttery loaf in her cart when she heard a small whimper behind her. "Oh, dear, is that the last one?" She turned to see an older woman with tight curls and a weathered complexion. She looked familiar. Then Mercy placed her. She had been one of the women having tea with Mint Sewards at the Mansion House Inn the eventful afternoon she'd met Vera. Mrs. Chadwick. The one Vera had labeled Mint's "charity case."

"Oh, here, you take it," Mercy said, transferring the pound cake into the woman's basket. When she began to protest, Mercy cut her off. "Believe me, you're doing me a favor. I should be buying fruit."

"Oh, that's very kind of you, dear. I've just been craving it. Thank you." The woman nodded warmly and walked off.

Mercy finished her rounds at the store, her cart filling with, among other things, Sunshine crackers and two packages of Downyflake frozen waffles (so much for the fruit), which she justified by reminding herself they were on sale, two for twenty-nine cents. Shouldn't her newfound economizing come before worries about her waistline?

She was loading her bags into the jeep when out of the corner of her eye she spied the woman again, this time standing idly with her groceries. Mercy walked over.

"Mrs. Chadwick, is it?" she asked.

The woman seemed astounded to have been recognized by name. "Yes, dear. I'm sorry, I've already forgotten your name."

"Oh, no, I don't think we've formally been introduced. I'm Mercy." *Edie!* she immediately screamed to herself. *Edie!* Too late now. "May I offer you a ride?"

Mrs. Chadwick smiled. "Your kindness knows no bounds! And after I purloined your pound cake! I was just going to call my son. He was supposed to be here by now. But if you wouldn't mind, that would be lovely. I don't live that far."

Her full name, Mercy discovered, was Grace Chadwick. She was a nervous sort of woman, the kind who in movies was always trying to soothe the leading lady's petulant moods. Mercy peppered her with questions, and discovered she'd come to Martha's Vineyard in the late 1920s, and that her late husband, John, had worked in the cranberry bogs until the great hurricane of 1938 flooded them with salt water. John had then scored a job with the WPA during the Depression to restore the bogs, before he eventually became a trader in cranberries himself, storing them in the barn until the people from Ocean Spray came onto the island to bid. The Chadwicks were Vineyarders whose lineage stretched back a century. Grace knew everybody: Dennis and Bridie at the White Whale, waitress Vera. Mercy kept her budding friendship with Ren out of the conversation. Ditto her interaction with Staxx.

They pulled up to a modest gray shingle-style house with a small red barn on a plot of land not far from the harbor. Mercy was carrying the groceries in when a man in his mid-thirties came charging out of the house to relieve her. "I'll take those," he said cordially. He turned to Grace. "Mom, I told you I would pick you up!"

"When?" she asked acidly as she passed. "Tomorrow?"

They bickered, the way mothers and sons do, for a few moments before Grace introduced him as her younger son, Jimmy. His eyes widened on hearing her name. "Wait a minute," he said, "you're

Mercy Welles, right? The actress? I heard a rumor you were here!" So much for Vera and her secret-keeping.

"Oh my!" Grace exclaimed. "I didn't even make that connection. Oh, I am losing my mind early, I'm afraid." She turned to Jimmy. "It must be the stress of unreliable children."

They all laughed and Jimmy hugged her, telling Mercy it had been nice to meet her before leaving to run his own errands.

Grace insisted she stay to enjoy a slice of the pound cake. As she poured them both some peach iced tea, Mercy wandered over to the kitchen windows, surveying the shimmering sunlit water in the distance. Over to the right, the road turned sharply up a steep hill that ended in a spectacular cliff overlooking sweeping Edgartown Harbor. Atop the cliff sat an imposing manor house, akin to Hawthorne's House of the Seven Gables, painted bright white, with black shutters and a wraparound portico with large windows. It had to be the house Vera had mentioned. "Who lives there?" Mercy asked.

Grace followed her sight line. "Oh, that's Sycamore," she said, gingerly setting the tray with the drinks and cake on the kitchen table. "The Sewards family mansion. The finest house on the Vineyard. Joseph Sewards built it for his wife, Thankful, not long after they settled here in the early sixteen hundreds. Joseph's son, Hezekiah, then added on, and over the years the house has been reconstructed after various storms and such. But parts of it go all the way back to the very beginning."

"It's stunning," Mercy said, her eyes still focused on the estate. She wondered what it must be like to carry the mantle of the first family of Martha's Vineyard. To be, in effect, local royalty. How many times had people asked her what it felt like to be a "movie star"? The truth was she didn't feel like a movie star at all. What people see on the outside is rarely what is.

She sat down, broke off a piece of cake. "You know, Mrs. Chadwick, I believe I saw you at the Mansion House Inn having tea with Mrs. Sewards a few weeks back. So you're friends?"

Grace remained quiet for a few seconds, as if carefully contemplating her answer. She took a genteel sip of her iced tea. "Yes. As much as one can be a friend of Mint's, I suppose."

Oh, Vera was right. There's a story here, Mercy thought, calibrating her next question. She felt her fascination with the island's ersatz first lady growing. "She's hard to get to know, is she?"

Grace shrugged. "She keeps to herself mostly, I suppose. We met a long time ago, when we were both young wives, though our lives went in very different directions. When I first met Mint she didn't know many people. She and Jasper had started a family in Boston and then he brought her here to raise the children. But I didn't really travel in those kind of circles. The founding families are a tight-knit group. Bloodlines are everything, and I was a washashore."

"A . . . what?"

"A washashore. I believe that term actually originated on Nantucket, or so I am told, but people often use it here. It's for people who aren't from the Vineyard. Recent transplants."

"You've been here for three decades and you're still considered a transplant?"

"Oh, my dear," Grace said, lifting a piece of the pound cake onto a small plate, "my late husband's family goes back to the mid–eighteen hundreds and *they're* still considered washashores."

Mercy cast her eyes back out the window toward the mansion. "And Mint's husband? I only hear people talk about her, not him."

"He died, oh, must be fifteen years now. It was all very tragic."

"What happened?"

Grace hesitated again, longer this time. She picked up a long spoon and began idly circling the bottom of her iced tea glass. She seemed to be arguing with herself over how much to disclose.

"I'm sorry," Mercy said. "I don't mean to pry. I'm sure it was very difficult for her to lose her husband so young."

Grace put the spoon down. "There was an accident. Jasper ended up falling from the cliff. They found his body near Gay Head."

"How awful."

Grace didn't speak for a moment, breaking her pound cake into small pieces. Finally she said, "It was terribly hard on Mint and the three children. But the island rallied around her. And she carried herself with enormous dignity through it all. That was around the time we became friends. I was happy to be there for her at a time when she needed people."

"Her children must have been quite young."

"They were," Grace said. "Patrick was barely seven. He's still with her in the house, at least in the summer. He's in law school at Dartmouth. The daughter, Ellenanne, left the island some years ago, when she was just eighteen. I don't believe she's been back since. No one talks about her anymore."

Yet another story, Mercy thought. "And the third child?"

"The eldest. A troubled boy. As a teenager he was an absolute beast," Grace said. "But he calmed down as he got older. Though he and Mint aren't close. I don't believe they even speak. But then, of course, it's really none of my business."

"The eldest son, he's here on the island?"

"Oh, yes," Grace said. She reached for the pitcher, refilling Mercy's glass. "He does a lot of handiwork for the landlords who own cottages and houses around the island in the summer. But most of the year he works as an oysterman. Perhaps you've seen him in his truck. His name is Warren. But he goes by Ren."

June 24, 1959

Dearest Cass—

Thanks for your last letter. I actually laughed out loud at the story about Mamie Van Doren. I wish I could have seen Susan Hayward's face when she showed up at the party in that outfit. Where is Cholly Knickerbocker when you need him?

I cannot believe I have been here a month already! I am all cozily ensconced in my little beach cottage, and having myself a little adventure. Interesting things afoot here—I have been approached to star in a local play—but it's all much too long a story to get into in a letter. I promise that despite my newfound budget restraint I will find a way to call you soon to do a proper catch-up and fill in all of the blanks.

I have had some interesting encounters here. I was having a glass of iced tea at a hotel and the waitress, of all people, recognized me. I panicked. I so needed to protect my privacy here, which has been key, I think, to escaping the ghost of Louis. Anyway, this waitress, Vera, now assumes we are best buddies. I hope the occasional girls' lunch will convince her to keep my secret, though at this point I don't know how much of a secret it is.

I also had an interesting visit the other day with a local woman who is a close friend and confidante of the island's matriarch, whose family goes back to the 1600s. The more I learn about this family the more intriguing they seem. (I can already picture you shaking your head at me across a table at the Brown Derby saying, "Not everything is a movie, sweetie.") But I think they actually might be.

I may or may not have been spending some time with a young man here who does repairs on a lot of the Vineyard properties (like I said, more on a phone call), but it turns out he is a son in this very family. It's funny—he took great pride in "unmasking" me as Mercy Welles, the actress, while conveniently keeping his own mask in place. I don't know why he never mentioned it, or why he seems to be estranged from them. Perhaps he's just an old-fashioned black sheep, the one who never tows the line? I don't know. But now I want to find out.

Leave it to me to escape to the other side of the country and then find myself in the middle of intrigue. But at the same time I am discovering more about myself while I am here, dashing about in my zippy little jeep. More soon.

Mad love and hugs,
Mercy

Twelve

The water in the shower turns on, rousing Kit out of sleep. Her eyes flutter open, adjust to the sunlight now streaming in through the window. She forgot to close the blinds last night. That tends to happen when you stumble backward, intoxicated and in the clutches of a ne'er-do-well bassist, onto your bed and it's past two in the morning.

She can hear him humming, and it irks her. She always wonders why he has to sleep over, why he can't be like every other guy and just leave with a sly comment and a kiss on the temple. She's one of the only women she knows who *wants* the guy to leave and has found the one who doesn't treat this as a gift. It's not like he wants a commitment any more than she does. But he likes the playacting part of the relationship thing, the faux snuggling and hair stroking and telling her how beautiful her eyes are. She finds it all ridiculous. Which is why her relationships, if she can even call them that, are measured in weeks, not months or years.

She has to pee, but she'll hold it. Kit's never enjoyed peeing in front of people, even other women, doesn't understand why producing bodily fluids in someone else's presence is seen as genuine intimacy. It's just gross. She'll wait till he gets out of the shower, though if he decides to blow-dry that curtain of shiny black hair, that could be a while.

His text hit her phone just after midnight. She'd barely heard from him since she got back from L.A. two weeks ago, but he caught her at the right moment—after two glasses of rosé—and she invited him over. He is a decent lover, a little quick on the draw, but has a long, lithe body that is smooth, almost feminine, and a pierced tongue that can work wonders. Best yet, he doesn't like to talk much. She feels this actually may be his best quality.

Her phone buzzes and she reaches out to pat the nightstand, searching. She picks it up, looks at the battery icon in the top right: 12 *percent. Damn. Forgot to charge it.* She clicks into the call. "Hello."

"Hey," Priya says. She's already at the studio—Kit can hear the bustle in the background. "Sorry to bother you so early, but I can't find the McMillan materials and Lucinda needs them for a breakfast meeting. I've searched your desk. You didn't take them home by any chance, did you?"

Kit fights to clear her head. "No, no," she says. "Wait—I think I gave them all to Larry Allen. He was looking for something to inform the graphics. Ask him."

"Gladly," Priya purrs. "Did you see that new P.A. he hired? He's *soooo* delish."

Kit rolls her eyes. "OK, I'll be in shortly."

Priya begins to say something, but Kit clicks off, plugging the phone in and then clambering out of bed as Josh walks into the bedroom, towel-drying his hair with another towel wrapped around his waist. Yet another thing that annoys her—he always uses several towels, as if he were visiting the Ramada.

"Morning, babe," he says. "I'll be out of your hair in a minute."

Kit smiles faintly, passes him on her way to the bathroom. At least she has him trained.

She closes the door and looks at herself in the mirror. Her hair is a wild, untamed mess, her skin ashy. She's still sporting smudged mascara, now congealed at the corners of her eyes, and clad only in a pajama top. The whole effect is that of a heavy metal band groupie from the nineties, stumbling into the sunlight for her walk of shame.

She sits on the toilet, runs her fingers through her hair. Ever since she's come back from L.A. she's been drinking too much. She's even started smoking occasionally. Just a bummed one every few days, but still. She's been late to work twice this week.

She flushes the toilet, returns to the mirror, runs the tap cold and splashes water on her face. The reflection staring back remains brutal, unforgiving. *What is wrong with me?* she mouths to her harrowed face.

But she knows what is wrong with her.

Cass Goldman had been her best lead, and then completely shut down. Kit knows that Cass is holding back, but she's old and Kit doesn't have enough time left to shake the truth out of her. Her nascent investigation into who her grandmother may have been has hit a wall. "Oh, Nan," Kit says in the hollowness of the bathroom, "what were you hiding?"

And then, out of nowhere, a memory. It is the turning point, the nadir of her teenage rebellion. Kit is sixteen going on thirty, and at the height of her defiance and acting out against Nan and Pop, against life itself. After their parents died, Claire had made a hard turn into religion, perfected the art of being "the good girl" to cope, to find solace and meaning. Kit had pivoted, gone in the complete opposite direction.

She has been thrown out of Rye Country Day School the year before for bad grades and worse behavior, and is now sleepwalking through Rye High. But at this moment she is sitting in an interview room at a police station, where her "sleepover" with her best friend, Jill Slovick, has quickly gone bad. Nan cannot stand Jill, has warned Kit repeatedly that the girl is "a bad influence," given too much freedom and too much money by wealthy parents who are buying her off with a flashy car and a closet full of shoes to justify ignoring her emotionally. This is probably true, but Kit doesn't care. Jill is wild, fun, wicked. She's Kit's role model. Or was. Until tonight.

It's two in the morning, and she's been sitting here for almost two hours after getting busted with Jill shoplifting booze at a late-night liquor store in Mount Vernon. How Jill thought two preppy girls from Rye would not be noticed trying to pilfer bottles of gin under their puffy jackets is beyond her, but that's Jill. They were accosted by a security guard, a scuffle ensued, Jill began to physically fight back, so of course Kit decided she couldn't look weak so *she* had to fight back, and the ensuing melee knocked over a display of Chardonnay, among other detritus. The cops were called. And here Kit sits, waiting for Pop to come bail her out. It's not the first time—there have been principals' office visits, a memorable harangue with a Girl Scout leader—but this is the first time Kit has landed in a police station.

Only it is not Pop who walks through the door. It's Nan, solo, looking positively bloodless as she calmly places her handbag on the table, removes her leather gloves, unbuttons her coat. She says nothing, and the combination of her silence and her methodical movements is unnerving. Kit feels she should stand up, begin talking, apologizing, but she can't seem to find her feet. Her heart is pounding. Why did Pop not come?

Nan sits down, folds her hands together on the table, looks at her with a face of stone. The words are all wrong, but Kit says them anyway. She's panicked, disoriented. Scared. She needs to play offense.

"This is all so stupid," she says, looking Nan right in the eye and feigning indifference. "They got this all wrong. We were just—"

"You were just browsing in a liquor store at night at the age of sixteen." A whisper that lands with the force of a scream.

There is dead silence for a minute or two. Kit knows whatever she says will be easily refuted. Her body begins to fill with panic, as if a spigot has been turned on.

"You can probably escape formal charges," Nan is now saying, "if you agree to pay for the damages, formally apologize to the security guard and the manager, and make a charitable donation somewhere in their names. My rough guess is you're looking at somewhere around fifteen hundred dollars total. Not counting an attorney, of course, if you need one. Which you probably do."

Kit coughs. "I know that's a lot. I . . . I'll pay you back."

"No," Nan says, leaning back in the chair. She folds her arms. "I am not paying a dime. You'll have to pay it now."

Kit thinks of her meager savings account, set up for her a few years ago to try and teach her the mechanics of banking. She has no idea how much is in it. If it's two hundred dollars it's a lot. "Nan, I don't have it. I . . . I can't pay that. But I promise, I will pay you back. Every penny." The spigot continues to flow, anxiety now oozing out of her pores.

Nan shrugs, stands, begins putting on her coat. "Well, I suppose that's your misfortune. Good luck to you." She retrieves her bag and gloves.

Kit bolts up from her chair, grabs Nan by the arm. "You can't . . . you can't just leave me here!" she cries. "OK, OK, I got it! I screwed up! I'm sorry! OK? Does that make you happy?"

Nan's stare is pure contempt. "Alas, very little you do makes me happy."

Kit feels like she's been gut punched. Nan has often expressed frustration and disappointment in Kit's behavior these last two years. But this, this is different. She's never seen Nan like this: remote, icy. Like she has finally been pushed too far. Kit needs to beg for forgiveness, promise to get her act together, but her pride is a boulder blocking the path. And so instead she lifts her chin up, exuding defiance. "You won't just leave me here," she says. "You're not capable of that."

The slap comes out of nowhere, swift and brutal, right across Kit's face. The force of it almost knocks her over. She puts a hand against the wall to steady herself, instinctively lifts the other to her cheek, registering the sting. Never, in Kit's entire life, has Nan ever lifted a hand to her. Her grandmother approaches, grabs her by the collar, eyes ablaze with fury.

"Let me tell you something," Nan whispers in quiet rage. "You have no idea what I am capable of."

She tugs Kit a little closer. Their faces are almost touching. Nan is in her early seventies but shockingly strong, the result of a midlife discovery of Zumba and Pilates. "Now let me explain what is going to happen. You are going to straighten out. You are going to do what you are told, and you are going to do it pleasantly and agreeably. Because if anything like this happens ever again, I will let you rot in here. Do you understand me?"

Kit nods weakly. And she does it. All of it. She cuts Jill off. Develops study habits. Slowly turns herself around. But she will never forget the look in Nan's eyes that night.

Josh knocks briefly on the bathroom door, shoving her back into the present. He enters without waiting for a response, yet another tic she finds annoying. He's dressed, a messenger bag flung across his chest. "Babe, I'm heading out." He looks at her more closely. "You OK?"

"Yeah, yeah, fine," she answers, mustering a weak smile. "Just a little queasy. I think I had some bad Chinese noodles or something."

"I keep telling you the food in that bodega is going to kill you," he says, bending down to give her a peck on the lips, but she turns her head slightly, causing him to awkwardly kiss her ratty hair instead. He stumbles back a step. "OK, well, later then." And he's off.

It takes another forty-five minutes to pull herself together, her face washed, hair in a clip, outfitted in a fitted blazer, slacks, and the sapphire necklace. She hustles up Canal Street toward the E train. She has no idea why she's coming unglued, why she's clearly freaking out, dropping balls, avoiding . . . what, exactly? She considers whether to call the shrink she was seeing a few years back, the doughy woman with the stuffy office who tried to take her down the road of tying her parents' death to her fear of commitment. Kit had drifted away after a month's worth of sessions. But maybe it would be different now. Maybe she needs it more now.

Or maybe Kit just needs to talk to the one person she's been avoiding. As she hurries down the subway stairs, her grandmother's words echo in her ears.

You have no idea what I am capable of.

*

Havre de Grace is a cute little burg near the mouth of the Chesapeake River, its slightly pretentious name (French for "Harbor of Grace") aside. Her brother-in-law, Russell, has picked her up at the train station and then, in an act of charity that reaffirms Kit's belief that Claire married extremely well, taken her nephews to soccer and given her a pass from being the cheering aunt on the sidelines. ("If it was the playoffs, it would be out of my hands," he'd joked.) Kit adores the boys, who at seven and five are warm and funny and still open to cuddling on the couch with her. She wonders if they will turn out to be teenage hellions like she was. She hopes not.

Now armed with an iced coffee, Kit strolls with Claire along the leafy Havre de Grace Promenade, at a bit under two miles round-trip the perfect walk for a sisterly catch-up. She's struggling to find an entry point, an almost impossible task during Claire's recitations of the tedious minutiae that comprises her suburban mom existence. If Kit never hears another story about the parking lot wars at Weis Markets, it will be too soon.

"Let's sit," Kit says, pointing to an unoccupied bench facing the water.

After they settle Claire looks at her. "What's on your mind, kiddo?"

Kit smiles. "What makes you think I have something on my mind?"

"I know my baby sister. You wouldn't impulsively visit unless there was something you wanted to talk about."

"Am I that transparent?"

"Evidently." Claire takes a sip of her coffee, looks out at the water. "Whenever you're ready."

Kit swivels to face her, flips her right knee onto the bench. "There *is* something I need to talk to you about. About Nan."

"What about her?"

There's no going back now, Kit thinks. So out it all flows. About finding the box in Nan's attic, the revelation of Nan's secret identity as Mercy Welles, her vanishing act in 1959. Claire takes it all in with surprising calm, interrupting only once or twice for clarifications, occasionally nodding seriously, the way you might if a doctor had just told you you needed surgery. Kit can almost feel her trying to process it all.

Kit pulls the old gossip blog up on her phone, shows Claire the pictures of their grandmother, young and gorgeous and flirting with matinee idols. Claire's face turns increasingly stoic. She wordlessly hands the phone back to Kit.

"I know it's a lot," Kit says.

Claire is quiet for a minute. Finally, she says, "You should have told me. Right away. You should have told me right away, Kit."

"I know, I know. I'm sorry."

Claire looks at her more intently. "So this is why you went on that work trip to Los Angeles?"

"Yes," Kit says. She talks about meeting Cass, the lost letters from Martha's Vineyard. "I was just trying to get my head around all of it. And I wanted to find more information, figure out what happened, before I told you."

Claire stares back at the water. "You should have told me right away," she repeats. "It might have saved us both a lot of trouble."

Kit studies her sister's impassive profile, trying to figure out what's going on inside her head. She hadn't been sure what to expect. But it wasn't this. "What do you mean?"

Claire turns back to her. "I mean," she says, in a voice now brimming with emotion, "that I want you to drop this. All of it. Now."

Kit searches Claire's face. "I don't understand."

"You're digging into Nan's private life, Kit. *Her* life. Not yours. You don't have any right to do that. If Nan had wanted us to know about this, about her life before us, she would have told us. She obviously had her reasons for not doing so."

Kit sits with this a second. "I have to admit this response is sort of coming out of left field for me. I mean, this is really upsetting me. Don't you see? Nan wasn't at all who we thought she was."

Claire's voice is taut. "She was *exactly* who we thought she was. She was the grandmother who sacrificed everything to raise two little girls who had just lost their parents. She was entitled to carry whatever secrets she wanted to the grave. And keep them buried there."

"Then why keep the box at all? She had to know we'd find it when she died."

"Do you know what's in every box tucked away in *your* place? I don't."

Kit leans back a bit, reading Claire's body language. "Did you know?"

"Don't be ridiculous. Of course not."

"And you're not even a little bit curious about the fact Nan had a whole other life we knew nothing about? That she changed her identity?"

Claire exhales wearily. "You've been in television too long. Not everything is a story, Kit."

"This is."

Claire jolts, as if she's just been hit with a prod, her eyes flashing with anger. "Don't you dare tell me you are thinking about airing all of this in public." The look quickly dissolves into worry. "Did you tell Lucinda?"

Somehow this has all gone terribly wrong. Kit had played through half a dozen possible reactions. Except this one.

"I had to," Kit says slowly. "There was no other way to get the L.A. trip done. I had just come back from bereavement and couldn't take any more time off."

"Oh my God," Claire whispers, leaning forward. Kit wonders if she's going to be sick, right there on the Promenade. She leans over, starts rubbing Claire's back.

"You have to promise me you won't let this on the air, Kit. I mean it."

Kit keeps lightly rubbing, slow, steady circles, trying to get her bearings. Time for some hard truths. "Claire, talk to me. Because honestly, I don't understand. I want to know about Nan's life. I *need* to know. And yet I don't. And so it's like this war going on inside my head. I want to keep the memory of the Nan we knew, but I also want to know who she really was. It's playing with me, making me act stupid."

"What else is new."

Kit stops rubbing, retracts her hand. "What's that supposed to mean?"

"It means," Claire says, turning to stare right into her eyes, "that Nan let you get away with murder. Admit it. And who knows why she did? But she did. And you put her through hell more than once, Kit, you know you did."

Kit flashes back again to the police station. "I accept that. But I made it up to her. Or I tried to. And a lot of teenage girls act out."

"*Teenage* girls, yes. You're pushing thirty, Kit. It's time to grow the fuck up."

It's like a brick to the face. Claire never curses. Ever. Kit feels the heat of anger snaking up her spine, spreading through her shoulders, up the back of her neck. "What the hell is this all about? Stop talking in riddles, Claire. If you have something to say to me, just say it."

And with that, a fuse is lit. Claire jumps off the bench, stands in front of her. "Fine. You want honesty? I'll give you honesty. You are a beautiful, smart girl. And yet you're wasting your life producing garbage cable television segments to appease the vanity of some egomaniac who hasn't been relevant in two decades and judges everyone by their clothes and where they vacation. You discard boyfriends like they're moldy blocks of cheese, though God knows none of them even last long enough to go bad. And I know you're abusing something—your face is puffy and waxy. I just have to hope it's only wine and nothing worse."

Kit stands up, now inches away from her sister. It's her turn to unload. "I have *no* idea why you're acting this way, or what it is that is triggering you to be so absolutely awful to me in this moment," she says. "I am trying very hard to understand. But you had better back the hell up. You're being vicious."

Claire appears unmoved, eyes cold in defiance. Fear? Pride? "I'm sorry if that was harsh," Claire says evenly. "But my point, which appears to have gotten lost, is that we all carry secrets we wouldn't want the larger world to know."

Kit scoffs. "Right. And tell me, dear sister," she says, "what deep, dark secrets are *you* hiding?"

Claire takes a step back, and for a minute they're just standing there, looking at one another. Kit searches her sister's face, looking for clues, for an explanation, *anything*, but only sees a stranger staring back.

And then Claire slowly starts to back away, one step, then two more, then three, then five. Finally she turns and begins running, down the Promenade, until she disappears around the curve.

Thirteen

S he does this," Russell is saying, calmly putting dishes in the dishwasher. "Though I have to say it's been a while."

Kit sits at the kitchen table, idly stirring a cup of tea slowly turning
cold. She finds it impossible to believe Claire does this at all. Ever. "It
just doesn't seem like her," she says.

Russell lifts the dishwasher door closed, takes a seat across from
her. "No offense, Kit," he says, "but you don't really know what seems
like her these days."

It pricks her, like a bee sting, sudden and sharp. He's right, of
course. For the past decade they've drifted, each wandering into very
different lives, casually waving from each other's shores. It's only
been in the last year, when Nan started to fail, that they saw each
other more regularly. God knows they weren't close in the adolescent
era—Claire the mousy girl going to church, reading moony poetry,
and earning straight A's; Kit hunting and pecking for trouble around
every corner. But somehow, when Nan was really fading, and then
after, Kit felt they'd found one another again, rebuilt some of that
bond they'd forged in those first few years after their parents died.
What would Nan think now?

Kit thinks of her grandmother and feels resentment bubble inside.
I don't really care what you'd think. This is all your mess. You and your secrets.

It's another half hour before the front door opens and Claire steps
inside, quietly tossing her keys into the dish on the foyer table. Kit
begins to stand—it feels like the thing to do—but something in Russell's eyes tells her to stay where she is. Claire ambles into the kitchen,
leans her backside against the counter.

"Boys upstairs?" she says quietly.

"Still chained to the iPad, I'm sure," Russell says.

Claire looks over to Kit, making eye contact for the first time. "Hey."

"Hey."

Russell takes the cue, awkwardly scrapes back his kitchen chair. "Well, now the nightly tug-of-war to get teeth brushed. Wish me luck."

Kit has spared Russell details of the fight, mainly because even now, hours later, she isn't quite sure what it was about. What exactly it was that caused her sister to make such a dramatic exit. "Want some tea?" she asks.

Claire nods, almost imperceptibly. "That would be nice. Bring it into the den. I'm going to make a fire."

Ten minutes later they sit, both staring into the fireplace—wood-burning, a preference Claire got from their grandmother. Nan was an adamant *no* when Pop wanted to convert the Rye fireplace to gas. *You need the smell, the snap and pop, the experience,* she'd said.

Kit finally breaks the quiet. "I'm sorry."

"I know," Claire replies. "But I suppose it might help if you knew what you were supposed to be sorry for."

Claire takes a sip of her tea, begins talking to the fire. "Do you remember when I called to first tell you about Russell?"

Remember? How could Kit forget? She had rarely heard Claire so . . . giddy. She'd met Russell at a Christian mixer at Tulane freshman year, and had fallen instantly and hard. Nan had been worried—Claire had so little experience with boys—but Kit had such fond memories of those calls, of Claire sharing the details of their dates, their first kiss. It was a time when they'd circled, if only for a little while, back into deep sisterhood. "Of course. You were positively gaga."

Claire smiles. "I was. I knew I was going to marry him within eight minutes of meeting him."

"A storybook romance."

Claire stiffens, eyes still fixed on the fire. "Not quite. There's a chapter missing."

For the first time her eyes leave the fire and look past Kit, back into the kitchen. Like she's checking to make sure the coast is clear. They can still hear movement upstairs, the clatter of the boys' bedtime ritual, Russell managing the show.

"I don't know if you recall, but the summer between sophomore and junior year I got an internship doing clinical research for a massive study in the psych department," Claire says. "It was incredibly prestigious. Unheard-of for an undergrad to get it, never mind a rising junior."

"I remember. Nan was proud, but upset you weren't coming home."

"Right. So Russell went back home to *his* family that summer, and I stayed on campus. Nobody's on campus at Tulane in summer—it's too beastly hot. But I didn't mind. At least not at first."

Kit feels foreboding drop into her stomach.

"One of the professors in charge of the study was very charming. And handsome. He made me feel special. Sophisticated. We'd occasionally go out after a long day. He taught me what made a wine good or not good, how to pick a truffle. Even suggested how to wear my hair. I talked to Russell every night. But . . . well, you can imagine. A young, impressionable girl with almost no experience with men gets her head turned by the worldly, older professor. It's hardly a new story.

"So one night, we're working late, and he makes his move. Right there in the office. I was . . . paralyzed. Because I *wanted* it to happen. For once I wanted to be the bad girl, to be the siren. And of course I also didn't want it to happen. I mean, I *loved* Russell. We had certainly fooled around a little, but our faith was important to both of us. I was going to convert to Catholicism. We'd agreed to wait. But in that one moment, in my waffling, I lost the battle. This man saw my indecision as weakness and he pounced on it."

Kit tries to jump a few moves ahead, figure out how all of this connects to Claire's reaction in the park. She leans over her knees, studying her sister's profile. "I understand," she says. "But Claire, you're not the first girl to ever be seduced by her professor."

"It's so much worse than that." And that's when Claire shuts her eyes tightly, but they are no defense for the tears that begin streaming in rivulets down her cheeks.

Oh my God. Now it makes sense.

Instinctively Kit turns back to the kitchen, checking to ensure Russell isn't there. She flings out her arm, grabs Claire's hand, feels the raw pain in Claire's squeezing back.

"I didn't know what to do," Claire whispers. "I didn't even realize it at first. I mean, I'd been late before. But then, when it dawned on me . . . all I could think about was Russell coming back to campus, having to tell him. My super-Catholic boyfriend, whom I had met at a church party, whom I was saving myself for. I couldn't. There was no way he would have gotten past that. Especially if he knew . . ." She stops.

That you didn't keep it, Kit thinks.

"No matter what, I'd lose him. If I went through with it, I'd have to drop out, go back to Rye, face Nan. And then what? Raise a baby from my childhood bedroom, at barely twenty years old? But the thought of terminating went against everything I believed in. My faith, my God, my moral compass."

Kit is quiet for a moment, absorbing all of it. Her heart aches, thinking of her sister, her steady, quiet, dutiful good-girl sister, facing such a horrible choice miles from home, completely alone. Finally, Kit asks the question, though she already knows the answer. "So, what happened?"

For the first time Claire stares at her directly. Only once in her life has Kit seen this look in her sister's eyes, this raw, devastating gloss of pain. At the age of nine, at the funeral of their parents. "Exactly what you think happened," Claire whispers.

Kit knows how incredibly difficult that must have been—like most women, she had her own pregnancy scare a few years ago, though mercifully her period showed up—but cannot imagine how hard that was for Claire, who in one procedure betrayed everything she believed, then hid it from everyone. And it is now, in this moment, that everything that happened today makes sense. Why Claire doesn't want Kit poking around in Nan's life. Why you should just let the past stay in the past. If not, old wounds get exposed. People get hurt.

Kit does the only thing she can think to do, which is to kneel in front of her sister, slowly folding her into her arms. And for a few minutes it's just the two of them, and Claire's tears, and the snapping and crackling in the fireplace, until finally Claire releases. Kit says, "I can't believe you've carried this all of these years. You could have told me."

"You were barely in high school."

"And later?"

"I didn't want to later. I just wanted to forget. But the truth is, you never forget. Even if you believe you did the right thing, you wonder: How old would he be now? What would he have looked like?" More closed-eye tears.

Kit sits back on her haunches, offers the only consolation she can offer. She takes both of Claire's hands in hers. "I'll stop digging into Nan's life. I'll let it go."

Claire smiles faintly. "That's very sweet," she says. "But no. You can't stop now. We all have baggage, Kit. It would be unfair of me to let mine interfere with something that may end up relieving you of some of yours."

"What do you mean?"

Claire pats her on the hands. "Go solve the case of our secretive grandmother. I have smaller tasks to perform. Namely," she says, standing up and wiping her eyes, "checking that my sons are, in fact, asleep."

And with that she walks out of the den, leaving Kit alone, ruminating on her words. Until Kit hears a faint buzzing coming from her bag in the kitchen. She pops up and dashes in, rummaging through a pile of receipts and lipstick tubes to find her phone. "Hello?"

"Kit, it's Jennifer Kauffman, at the Academy Library in Los Angeles," the voice on the other end says. "I think I may have caught another break in the mysterious case of Mercy Welles."

*

Kit steps out of 30th Street Station in Philadelphia and gathers her raincoat tighter around her. It's damp and wet, *the kind of cold that cuts right through you,* as her grandmother used to say. She wonders how long this will last, relating everything she does over a soundtrack by Nan. Although she doesn't want to think about what Nan would be saying right now if she knew what Kit was up to.

Bless Jennifer Kauffman and her doggedness. Kit wonders if she should recruit her for *Signature with Lucinda Cross*. The crackerjack librarian has tracked down Sy Sigmund's youngest son, an energetic seventy-four-year-old retired real estate developer named Aaron living in a condo in downtown Philly. When she'd reached him on the phone he'd said yes, he still had some of his dad's old files, but it was a scattershot collection no one had looked at in years. He made no promises. Kit didn't need any—she knew her way around a grimy box of forgotten records. And at least this time she didn't have to wing her way to L.A.

Fifteen minutes later the taxi has dropped her off at a building on Chestnut Street that smells of gefilte fish and talcum powder, and she now sits in Aaron Sigmund's living room as his wife alternates between handing around a plate of rugalach and peppering her with questions about Lucinda—what she's really like, who does her hair, how tall she is "in real life." Finally, Aaron cuts her off. "Elaine, enough! Leave the poor girl alone! She's here about Dad."

Elaine mutters something akin to "I was just asking" and harrumphs away, but not before pointing to Kit and then back to the rugalach.

Kit smiles at Aaron, who delivers the under-the-breath scoff all husbands deliver about their longtime wives. Kit has seen several photographs of Sy, and can easily see the resemblance, though Sy looked Aaron's age when he was in his early fifties. By contrast, with his full head of silver hair and fading tan, Aaron looks hale, hearty, the kind of man who lives for an early bedtime and early tee time.

"Did he ever talk about his clients? Maybe at the dinner table?" Kit asks him.

"Oh, I'm sure he did. But you know how it is. You're a teenage boy, you don't give a rat's ass about anything but the Dodgers and the girl in chemistry class who won't give you the time of day. I never paid much attention, to tell you the truth. I should have."

"So you don't recall the name Mercy Welles?"

He shakes his head. "No, sorry." He slides over a large oblong document box on the floor. "I have no idea what's in here," he says. "To tell you the truth, I have no idea why I even kept it. I guess because Mom and Dad had me late. I was only in my twenties when he died, so I kept thinking I would go through all of this one day, maybe write his biography or something, understand him better. Naturally, I did none of it."

Kit lifts the lid of the box, smells the dust of half a century as it wafts up to tickle her nose. She scans the mishmash of papers, files, clippings, books. *Let the treasure hunt begin.*

Aaron narrates as she riffles through the material, putting assorted items into piles she mentally labels as Possibly Useful, Useless, and I Have No Idea What This Is. She tackles the yellowed newspaper clippings first, a tricky task as many are on the brink of complete disintegration. Just as Aaron's constant dialogue—a stream of consciousness that pinballs from Sy's upbringing in Brooklyn to his hatred of travel to the mess of his estate, all the way up to whether Aaron's grandson is going to get into law school—is beginning to give Kit a headache, Elaine reappears, magically waving a phone and telling him said grandson is on the line. With a few minutes blissfully alone, Kit refocuses. But how do you find something when you don't know what you're looking for?

She's fifteen minutes through the piles, and beginning to feel the dull pulse of defeat, when she reaches back into the box, her fingers locating a neat stack of slim leather volumes. Kit extracts the top one, sees 1962 stamped in gold leaf on the cover. She sits back on her haunches, flips through it.

Appointment book.

In a second she's back on her knees, digging to the bottom and extracting the rest of the books. One by one she slides them off the pile: *1955 . . . 1961 . . . 1947 . . .* There are only seven total here; Sy had been an agent for at least twenty years. Two-thirds of the books are missing.

And then, second to last, her luck shows up. She holds up the book, wipes the dust off the spine.

1959.

Frantically Kit flips to May, uses her index finger to scan each page, flipping, scanning, flipping, scanning, flipping, scanning. Finally, Monday, May 18, noon: *Lunch with M. Welles, Sunset Tower.* That would have been just before Nan left L.A.

Kit keeps perusing through the summer, locating nothing but a mix of meetings, production notes scribbled in the margins, screen tests, assorted breakfasts, lunches, and dinners with people she's never heard of, no doubt back-of-the-house executives from the studios. Until mid-July. Travel plans. Scrawled over Wednesday, July 15:

Untd 3483 LA/NY, cr to WH, ferry MV 8 a.m. 16th.

United Flight 3483 from Los Angeles to New York. A car to Woods Hole, then the ferry the next morning to Martha's Vineyard.

Sy went all the way to Martha's Vineyard to see her.

Just half an hour ago Aaron had been telling her how Sy had hated to travel. And yet he picked up, in the middle of the week, and schlepped by plane, car, and boat to find Nan. It must have been terribly important. *Had she told him she was thinking of abandoning her career? And if so, why? Or was it worse? Was she in trouble?*

The letters to Cass. Certainly Mercy would have written Cass to tell her Sy had visited, and why. Did Cass really have them, or was that just Kit's wishful thinking?

Kit knows what she has to do. What she should have done right away.

She looks up, startled out of her thoughts by Aaron, now standing above her.

"Sorry, I didn't mean to frighten you. Finding any answers?" he asks.

She scrambles to her feet, wiping the dust off her pants. "I'm not sure," she says. "Odd question: Do you recall your father ever taking a trip to Martha's Vineyard?"

He looks puzzled. "Martha's Vineyard? No, I don't think so. Dad thought driving to Anaheim was torture. I couldn't imagine him going all the way to New England, especially in those days. Why?"

"Because," Kit says, picking up the appointment book, "that's where the answers are."

July 10, 1959

My dear Cass—

Greetings from the Atlantic! I read an item in one of the gossip columns in the Boston Globe that Constance Baxter picked another director for "She's Nothing but Trouble." Ha! Justice served. I suppose she found Louis wanting in the qualifications that truly mattered.

I suppose my big news is that it's official: I am doing a play here. I know, I know! I came here to do anything but act. But I met the most lovely piano player in a jazz trio, and he's also an aspiring playwright. He also happens to be Negro, and I can just imagine what Sy would say about that. But I've read his play and it's utterly charming. And I also feel that perhaps one of the reasons fate (via you) sent me here was to help someone like him get a start. It's going to blow my "cover" wide open, but that's the funny thing about these chilly New Englanders—those few who do seem to recognize me also seem wildly unimpressed to have a Hollywood actress in their midst. Thank God.

The exception, of course, is Vera, the waitress I mentioned in my last letter, who has affixed herself to me like glue, evidently basking in the joy of feeling like my best girlfriend for the summer. Though we both know only you could ever carry that title!

As for Ren, the mysterious oysterman, the jury is still out. I cannot deny that I find him attractive, but he is so remote in some ways. And what would be the point of a romance, anyway? I'm leaving in less than two months.

I will keep you posted, darling. Hope all is well on the lot and you are not biting off too many heads.

Love,
Mercy

Fourteen

Mercy hustled past the stately white colonials with their shiny shutters and hydrangea gardens lining Winter Street, on her way to meet Vera. She'd already put her off twice. And now with Bridie and Dennis at the White Whale, and Ren, and now Staxx's play coming up, the word was already out that she was here, anyway. The local paper had done an item on her starring role in the play—they'd photographed her riding one of the horses at the old carousel in Oak Bluffs. At least it wasn't a column in *Confidential*.

She glanced at the window of the California Shop—at their last meeting, Vera had breathlessly described the arrival of the new manager, Mrs. Ruth, from Nantucket—and as she passed she admired the Rose Marie Reid cotton satin Alhambra skirted swimsuit in the window. *That* is what she should be spending her time doing—mindlessly shopping, swimming, and sunning. Instead she was doing the exact opposite: fretting. Mainly about Ren.

Her diffident oysterman was like a jack-in-the-box, popping up suddenly, then retreating back into the shadows. He'd left another note under her door, asking if she was free for lunch tomorrow and stating that if she didn't leave word otherwise with Bridie and Dennis at the White Whale, he'd pick her up in the late morning. He told her to "dress casually." Should she tell him, she wondered, about her visit with Grace Chadwick, about what she'd learned about his identity, and his troubled family history? On one hand she relished the idea of smirking and asking him about his days as a teenage "hellion." On the other, all of that was no doubt the outgrowth of the tragedy of losing his father as a young teenager. And somehow she suspected that he wouldn't appreciate knowing she'd been gossiping—not her word, but, she suspected, it *would* be his—about him and his family.

"Yoo hoo!" came a shrill cry. Mercy walked toward the entrance to the Edgartown Drug Store, where Vera waited patiently, dressed in a drab salmon blouse, baggy blue jeans, and penny loafers. Her skin was even more freckled by the summer sun, and her hair was pulled back into a braided ponytail she was too old to be sporting. "Do I have a day planned for us!" she said excitedly as she pulled Mercy into the store.

And what a day it was: shopping for Elizabeth Arden cosmetics there, shopping at the Country Store and then Hall's (new swimsuits by Gabar and Catalina were now in stock), then a pop-in at the movie theater to see what was showing (rumor had it *Gidget* was opening later this week "and we *must* go"). There was the promise of a fountain ice-cream soda in there somewhere. It didn't really matter at this point if Vera kept her secret. And yet there was something about the girl—her neediness, her hero worship—that Mercy couldn't quite shake so easily.

Two and a half hours later, during which Vera had managed to stay silent for perhaps eleven minutes total, they were sitting in two metallic folding chairs under a green-and-white striped umbrella by the pool at the Harborside. Vera had objected to this unplanned stop, but quickly relented when Mercy had blithely declared the excursion was her treat. The money was well spent. She needed a drink. Badly.

It was a gorgeous midsummer day, the pool ringed with vacationers soaking up the sunshine, a brisk breeze wafting off the water. A monstrous white flagpole bordered the pool area, the stars and stripes billowing in the wind at the top. Mercy watched as a pair of sinewy boys took turns caroming off the diving board, ignoring the warnings of their exasperated mothers. Vera was droning on—again—with Mercy issuing the occasional polite "mmm hmm," until one of Vera's passing comments whipped her back to attention.

". . . I mean, the Sewards are just that kind of family."

"I see," Mercy replied, taking a casual sip of her chilled Sauvignon Blanc. *Damn. What did she just say?* "Though I'm not sure exactly what you mean."

"Just that Ren has never really fit in with them. I think that's one of the reasons we got close."

Mercy felt a shiver. Surely she couldn't be hearing this correctly. Ren . . . *and Vera?* She took a healthy gulp of the wine. "So, you two," she said, fighting to keep her tone casual, "you and Ren. You're . . . an item?"

Vera smiled demurely, attempting to play the coquette. She grabbed her straw and slurped up some of her banana daiquiri, which she'd ordered "to feel fancy." "Well, we've known each other a long time," she said. "I mean, we both grew up on this island, and that bonds you in a way. And we've both been sweet on each other at different points. It's just a matter of getting the timing right, I guess. But we'll get there. That is, if Mint isn't a big snob about it." A look of slight panic suddenly filled her face. "Oh, gosh, please forget I said that."

Mercy smiled. "Do you know Mint well?"

Vera took another long sip of the daiquiri. "Nobody knows Mint well."

Time to show some cards, Mercy decided. "You know, I gave Mrs. Chadwick a ride home from the market the other day. She told me about Mint's husband and his accident. How very tragic for all of them."

Bingo. Vera leaned closer. "Oh, yeah," she said, taking a glance around. "It really ripped them apart. Ellenanne, the daughter? Gone. And Ren, well, it's like that old saying about still waters running deep. But Patrick, Ren's younger brother, he seems OK. Maybe 'cause he was so young when it happened. And he was always Mint's baby. As for her, who knows? It's like I told you that day we met. She's always been a bit mysterious."

"Do you worry she won't approve of you and Ren as a match?"

Vera shrugged. "I don't think she approves of much of anything. Not that she should be so high and mighty. It's not exactly like she's from the highfalutins, either."

Mercy squinted. "What do you mean?"

"I mean, Mint came to this island to work for the summer. I don't know the whole story. But she was nobody until she got Jasper Sewards to the altar. She's been playing lady of the manor ever since."

Well, this is getting interesting. Had Mint been a gold digger? "Well, given that, she surely wouldn't prevent Ren from expressing his affection." Mercy had no idea why she was suddenly talking like a character written by Louisa May Alcott. Hazard of her profession, perhaps. She was always inhabiting someone else's character.

"I don't know," Vera said. She laughed resignedly. "But I guess I'll find out." She drained the last of the creamy drink, then held the glass slightly aloft. "Mind if I order another?"

*

The Martha's Vineyard Playhouse was an old saltbox building on Franklin Street, just off the main shopping district in Vineyard Haven and next to the First Baptist Church. Mercy had just pulled up out front and hopped out of the jeep, her eyebrows rising in surprise as she spied him walking out the front door.

"Well, well," Ren said, carrying his toolbox. "The leading lady has arrived."

She smiled, a bit too broadly. Pure reflex at this point. *Damn him.* "I am merely here to see the space," she replied.

"Staxx can be mighty convincing. And I've read his play. It's great."

He was right. It was. "And what, may I ask, is your role here?" she asked, nodding toward the playhouse. "Don't tell me you're auditioning."

"Hardly. Just the same as everywhere," he said. "Fixing what needs fixing." He plopped the toolbox down. She wanted to look away—his stares could do that—but was determined to hold his gaze. "So, did you get my invitation?" he asked.

"Yes. Rather cryptic, I have to say. And from your message about the dress code I assume we won't be going to the Charlotte Inn?" A subtle hint. She'd heard somewhere that the terrace was heavenly.

"Well, look who's already a local," he said. "No, sorry, this will be a bit more . . . rustic."

She flashed back to the walk on the beach at Gay Head, tried not to think about the kiss that came with it. "Wasn't our last outing a bit 'rustic'?"

"As I recall that was your choice." She smiled. He added, "And there are charms to be had other than at an elegant restaurant."

"I highly doubt that."

He laughed, lifting the box. "I'll take that as a yes. I'll see you tomorrow late morning. And remember—"

"I know, I know, 'dress casual,'" she said. "Be on time!"

He laughed even harder as he walked away. "Island time!" he said over his shoulder.

She climbed the steps and walked into the theater. The cast had had some table reads in a room at a local church, but this was the first time she'd been in the theater itself. It was hard to believe it was a little more than five weeks until opening night.

She inhaled the building's dank, earthy musk, like that of a cedar closet that hadn't been opened in years. The wood was all a dark-chocolate color, and there was slightly spooky sea-rope netting that hung from the rafters that almost gave the impression of moss, making the whole space feel like a Brothers Grimm forest. There was a small stage at the front, and a few rows of auditorium seating. The entire theater couldn't have seated more than 150 audience members.

She was ambling down the center aisle, still taking in the surroundings, when she heard her name. "Miss Mercy!" Staxx came bolting from the wings, leaping down from the stage to greet her. "Right on time." His smile—bright, wide, warm, beautiful—told her he was truly honored she was there.

"This is a really lovely building," she said. She meant it, too. It was hardly the Egyptian, but there was something about its relaxed, homey atmosphere that spoke to her. "Give me a quick tour?"

"I can do that," came a voice behind them.

Mercy turned to see a tall, broad-shouldered young man walking slowly toward them. He had the body of a linebacker but the carriage of a sophisticate. He wore a dark blue blazer over a sky-blue linen shirt, with cream slacks and polished brown loafers. His head was big and square, with a crooked grin that worked well with his wavy black hair.

He extended his hand to her. "Sorry, I didn't mean to interrupt. I'm Patrick Sewards."

Ren's younger brother. Of course. Same eyes.

"Mercy Welles," she said, taking his hand. "It's nice to meet you."

"We're all thrilled you're going to star in Staxx's play," he said. "We know you'll help put him on the map as the exciting young playwright he is." Patrick turned to Staxx. "I left the updated cost estimates on the table in the office," he said. "Why don't you read them over and we can talk about them after I give Miss Welles a tour."

Staxx's face dimmed. It was clear he had been intent on giving the tour, getting her excited about doing the play. After all, hadn't this all been his idea? But there was an unspoken arrangement between the men Mercy recognized all too well. She recalled Ren mentioning his brother was involved with the production. If Patrick had cost estimates, it meant he was the play's primary producer, or at minimum its major benefactor's representative, if Mint had coughed up the money. Mercy had been around enough movie sets to know that the people who bankrolled productions were the ones whose orders got obeyed.

"Of course," Staxx said, his stare now steely. He nodded briefly to Mercy before heading toward the office.

Patrick took her through the small space, relaying its history and some of the other plays that had been staged in it, including a production of *Hamlet*. They were soon back where they'd started. Patrick waved her into a seat in the last row, took one a seat away. "We are all so excited you are doing the play."

"I was hesitant," she admitted. "But Staxx can be very convincing."

He gave her a sly smile. "You still seem to have reservations."

She sighed. "Well, as you can imagine I came here *not* to work: to get away from acting. And it's been quite lovely, actually. This is a very soothing place."

"With many charms," he said. Sarcasm danced in his eyes.

She let it pass. "Yes. But very few people are aware I'm here. And part of me wants to keep it that way."

He nodded. "I understand. But this is a small seasonal theater, and one that hopefully will be very important to the community. An Oscar-nominated actress performing here will do wonders. The triumph of your altruism over your need for privacy is a credit to you. It's still very difficult for a Negro writer to have his work produced at all. This could be life-changing for Staxx."

"I know. Believe me, I'm happy to be here."

"Good." He stood, and she followed his lead. "I'm afraid I must be going. But it was lovely to meet you, Miss Welles. I look forward to seeing you up on the stage."

She thanked him for the tour, watched him walk up the aisle and out the door. His directness and self-assuredness were qualities very similar to Ren's, yet his stiff formality and courtly demeanor were nothing like Ren at all. And yet both of them had been raised by a clearly formidable woman whom half the island feared and the other half revered.

Mercy thought of one of her recent letters to Cass, her friend's constant criticism that she was always looking for a story. Perhaps that was true. But something told her the untold story of the Sewards family was one worth knowing.

*

He found her in the drawing room, a mix of burnished wood, heavy drapes, and polished accent tables littered with porcelain figurines, sipping her evening cup of tea. Two sugars, extra cream. More than one person had joked—behind her back, naturally—that no amount of sugar and cream could make her sweeter.

"Good evening, Mother," Patrick said, heading to the bar cart and uncorking the decanter of brandy. He poured a double into one of the cut crystal glasses, took a healthy swig. "And how are we this evening?"

Mint Sewards lowered the delicate Wedgwood teacup gingerly

back onto its saucer, sliding it onto the coffee table in front of the dormant fireplace. She was in her trademark knit cardigan and pearls, with a summer tartan skirt she wore long to hide the veins slowly advancing into view on her legs. She still considered herself relatively young—she was not yet sixty—but her body felt older, a result of the hardships of the younger years she'd endured before she'd met Jasper. Before she had reinvented herself as a completely different person.

She leveled a look of impatience. "I am not in the mood for pleasantries tonight," she said. "Tell me what you've discovered."

He refilled the glass, took a seat on the plush brocaded sofa across from her. "Well, your reports from the field seem to be correct. They're clearly involved. I'm just not sure yet to what degree."

"And you came to this discernment how?"

"I watched them from inside the theater. He was leaving as she was arriving. They talked for a bit."

"Did he see you?"

"We spoke our customary ten words as we passed each other inside. I'm sure he didn't notice me watching them. He was too busy watching *her*."

"Did you hear what they said?"

"No. But I didn't really have to. As Professor Birdwhistell might say, their 'body language' spoke volumes."

"There's no need to be vulgar, Patrick."

He sighed wearily, sipping the brandy. "You really do worry too much, Mother."

"You don't worry enough," she snapped. "It is precisely my worrying that has protected this family for a generation. I am not going to allow some random outsider to alight onto this island and threaten that."

He stood. "Perhaps it would be good to remind yourself that if it wasn't for you there wouldn't be threats to deal with."

He instantly regretted the words. *Over the line.* It didn't happen often. There was a reason for that.

She simply stared at him, her flat, bony face pale and impassive.

The stately grandfather clock in the hall chimed the hour, followed by eight laborious bongs that landed like punches.

Finally, she spoke, her voice low and firm. "I will remind *you*," she said slowly, "that if it were not for me, right now we would all be on the street somewhere in South Boston."

Their eyes met. *That's not exactly true,* he thought. *The correct statement would be, If it weren't for Ren.*

"We must find out what she's after."

Patrick looked away. "She seems to be 'after' nothing more than a vacation. And the play will keep her busy."

"If that's so, then we have nothing to be concerned about. But first she's asking my friends questions about me, about our family. Now I find out she's spending time with my son, with whom she may be developing a, shall we say, more personal interest. Surely you can understand my concern."

He shook his head. "I thought he was dating the waitress from North Tisbury. The Harding girl."

Mint scoffed. "Don't be daft. Vera's a flibbertigibbet. This . . . this is different."

He turned to her. "How can you be so sure?"

"Because," she said. "A mother knows her son."

Fifteen

She had done as she'd been asked and had dressed appropriately, in a light pink summer blouse (purchased on impulse at David's in Vineyard Haven), beige capri pants, and slip-on sandals, a colorful bandanna tied around her head as a makeshift hair band. She'd even thoughtfully packed a picnic lunch. Well, OK, so Bridie had packed the lunch: cold fried chicken, potato salad, and a bottle of sparkling wine. And provided the basket. But Mercy had paid for it. Surely that counted, didn't it?

She glanced over at Ren behind the wheel of the truck, where he looked extraordinarily relaxed and . . . happy. He wore a few days' worth of stubble; his face, arms, and legs boasted a golden tan that signaled his identity as an island outdoorsman. He wore a loose-fitting blue T-shirt and cotton shorts. His feet were bare.

"Isn't it dangerous," she remarked, "to drive with no shoes?"

He smiled, keeping his eyes on the road. "Not if you know how." Once they hit Chilmark he pulled the truck onto Brickyard Road. They drove through a heavily wooded area that suddenly cleared, leading to a small dirt lot and a sandy path with wooden stairs that descended to the beach. "Anyway, we're here."

Great Rock Bight was another of the many hidden gems that only the year-rounders seemed to know about. The trek down was long, hot, and dusty, the beach a mix of rocky stretches with pockets of soft, milk chocolate–colored sand. There was a huge boulder plopped in the shallow water, which gave the beach the aura of an old pirate's cove. At the top of the path the vista extended for miles, an endless view of navy-blue water stretching to the horizon. Down below on the right, at the edge of the water, Mercy could make out a nimble white and blue catboat, rolling gently with the waves, its triangular white sail fluttering in the warm late-morning breeze. On the side of the boat, in neat blue block letters, was painted the word PUDGE.

By the time they made it down to the beach she was exhausted. "Well, at least now I know why no one's here," she said, bending over to catch her breath. She looked around again. "But it is so incredibly beautiful."

Ren placed the food hamper and a large quilted blanket on the sand. "That it is. I love this spot because it's both so open and yet so private. The island is filled with these little pockets, if you know where to find them."

Mercy pointed over toward the skiff. "This is the boat you catch oysters on?" she asked.

"First off, you don't 'catch' oysters, you cultivate and farm them," he said. He put an arm around her, leading her toward the surf. "I'll teach you all the lingo."

"Can't wait."

"And no, you need a proper oyster boat for harvesting. They're better on the Pond. This is a Beetle Cat. And not one of those cheap imitations, either. Brought her all the way from Barnstable. The originals had engines, and they were intended for scalloping. They didn't even start making models with sails till the late thirties. But she handles so smooth. You'll see. It's just something I keep to zip around on. Something just for me." He looked over at her. "And now you."

Ten minutes later they were out on the water, the catboat nimbly skimming the tops of whitecaps as Ren deftly worked the keel to manage the centerboard, steering the boat farther out onto the water. At the other end Mercy leaned back, elbows resting on the side, and turned her face up to the sun. It was heavenly, being out on a sparkling summer day.

Being with him.

A few minutes later they were sitting together, the boat gently bob-

bing in the water, drinking wine. He picked up her right leg, propping her foot on his lap and gently rubbing. A rush of desire flowed
through her body. "We need to get you some lotion," he said, expertly
running his hands up and down the length of her calf. "You're going
to burn."

She shrugged. Between the wine, the water, and the company, at
that moment she didn't care if she ended up looking like a piece of
blackened toast. "That's what you get when you take a girl from the
Midwest out onto the high seas." She sighed. "Did your father teach
you to sail?"

His expression visibly darkened. "No," he said quietly. "Dad wasn't
much for the outdoors."

Her brain instructed: *Climb to safer ground.* "And *Pudge*? There has to
be a story behind that."

He laughed, and she slowly exhaled in relief. "Actually," he said,
"the boat is named for my sister."

Mercy recalled her conversation with Grace Chadwick, how she'd
told her Ellenanne Sewards had left the island at eighteen. *No one talks
about her anymore.* "Please tell me your sister's name is not Pudge."

"No, it is not. But you might say she was, well, a bit *round* during
her adolescent years. So my brother and I used to call her Pudge."

Mercy shook her head. "Boys! That's so cruel."

"Just brothers being juvenile and stupid."

She smiled. "Where is your sister now?"

The clouds descended over his face again, like a swift summer
storm. Ren removed her leg from his lap. "I should double-check the
anchor," he said, bounding toward the other end of the boat.

The more she got to know him, feel closer to him, the more she
realized that underneath his cavalier swagger lay a series of land
mines. Seemingly all surrounding his legendary but cryptic family.
How many had she stepped on already? How many were still there,
waiting to explode? And was it worth risking blowing herself up to
find out?

She watched him fiddling with the sail, moving levers, whirling
around the deck in a slight frenzy. Just then, a large gust of wind hit

the sail, knocking Ren off-balance and crashing back onto the starboard side. Intuitively she bolted up, about to run to his aid, but the crash had tilted the boat. He looked at her in alarm.

"No, don't—!"

The boat suddenly listed violently to the left. The two of them toppled into the water.

Mercy began thrashing, trying not to panic and failing miserably. "I can't swim!" she began yelling, taking in gulps of salt water. "Ren! Help! I can't swim!"

Within seconds she felt his strong arm around her waist, pulling her to him, his voice steady in her ear. "Stop moving. Just relax. Go limp. I've got you," he said.

She was still coughing when they reached the side of the boat. She flung her hands up to clutch the side, felt relief begin to take hold. He was now directly behind her, his own hands on either side of hers on the boat.

"I'm sorry," he said. "I lost focus there for a second. And I . . . I had no idea you couldn't swim." He squinted up toward the sun, shaking the salt water out of his eyes. "Don't they have lakes in Nebraska?"

She nodded. "Yes. You know what they also have? People who know how to steer sailboats." She heard him laugh behind her. "Now, help me up."

His arm was around her waist again. She felt her grip loosening as he began tugging her *away* from the boat. "Wh-What are you doing?"

Her grip gave way as he propelled them farther out onto the water. "Giving you a clearly overdue swimming lesson."

She began thrashing. "No! I did not sign up for a swimming lesson. I'm not even wearing a bathing suit!"

"Just the basics, I promise," he said. "Just to make sure if you tumble into the water again and I'm not there, you'll survive." He held her a smidge tighter. "Don't be scared," he said quietly in her ear, pulling her just a little closer to his chest. "Always be brave."

Was it worth arguing? And did she really want to? It felt good to be in a man's arms, in *his* arms, good to be out in the beautiful water, good to just . . . be. And so for the next thirty minutes she let him patiently show her the finer points of the doggie paddle, heard his voice saying, "Reach . . . and pull!" over and over and over, until she picked it up, slowly found the matching rhythm of her arms and legs, began floating around the edges of the boat.

They eventually moved to shallow water. He showed her how to freestyle, one arm in, then the other, kicking all the while, tilting the head for air, repeat. He was pleased at her quick study. She was pleased at pleasing him. She even managed to get in a playful splash with a deft kick of her left foot that left him pealing with laughter.

*

They were side by side on the beach, tired from all the swimming and drowsy from the food after, their bodies drying in the afternoon sun on the quilt. He wore only his shorts—men had an unfair advantage, being able to dry out shirtless—as she waited for her clothes to rid themselves of their seaweedy dampness. But it was so very peaceful, the only sounds the lapping waves rolling onto the beach, the caw of the seagulls, the gentle whoosh of the water against the giant rock.

"Boston," he said finally.

She looked over at him. His eyes were still closed, his face baking in the sun.

"Pardon?"

"Earlier. You asked me where my sister is. She's in Boston." He opened his eyes, sat up and propped back on his elbows, staring out at the sea. "I don't get to see her much." He cast her a quick side-eye. "I know Nancy Drew is curious."

She turned on her side, gazing at him. "Tell me about her."

"Ellenanne was—is—very different from me and Patrick."

She saw her opening and took it. "Patrick? The same Patrick who's producing the play?"

He nodded. "Yup. All part of the storied Sewards clan." He looked back out at the water. "But Ellenanne . . . she was always very nervous. Fragile. I have always thought of her as the heart of our family. I always wanted to protect her. I didn't do a great job."

"I'm sure you've been a wonderful brother to her."

"It's too late now. The heart of our family is broken." He shook his head and closed his eyes. "We all are."

Mercy had a million questions, and also knew now wasn't the proper time to ask any of them. So instead she simply reached over, gently brushing the side of his face with the back of her hand. "I don't think you're broken," she whispered. "I think you're beautiful."

He opened his eyes to look at her, and in that instant everything changed. Together, in unspoken mutual accord, they finally gave in to the feelings they'd been fighting ever since that first night of sparring at the bar of the White Whale.

He bent down as she reached for him. The kiss was gentle at first, longing, each of them tentative, still holding back a little. But it wasn't long until the connection gathered steam, energy, ferocity. They bit, gnashed, devoured, ravenous for one another, each finding something in the other that had been missing. Was anyone coming? Could anyone see? They didn't notice. They didn't care.

He trailed his lips down her neck, tracing her clavicle with his tongue, slowly, painstakingly working his way farther down, until he began to slowly open the wet blouse, one agonizing button at a time. More kissing, more nibbling, more gnawing of her flesh, her body writhing under his as she felt him thicken against her. She thought her head might explode.

He was fully on top of her now, covering her face with his as she clawed at his hair and, with her other hand, brazenly began sliding her fingers down the back of his shorts. He broke the kiss, his face now hovering above hers, his breath labored, his eyes dark pools of desire. "Are you sure?" he asked, heaving the words.

She grabbed the back of his neck hard and pulled his lips roughly onto hers, answering his query with a blistering kiss. "I'm going with my new motto," she whispered into his ear. "'Always be brave.'"

*

She was still attempting to shake the last of the salt water out of her hair when Ren pulled the truck up in front of her cottage. She was now wearing a wrinkled flannel shirt he'd had balled up in the backseat, her musty blouse on her lap. "I'll never get this smell out of my hair," she said, looking over at him slyly. "I'll be in the bath for days."

He smirked, then leaned over to nuzzle her neck. "Are you looking for company?"

She laughed, felt her face go hot. Edie Stoppelmoor, prim young lady of Beatrice, Nebraska, who had then furtively cohabitated with her fiancé in Hollywood, now wanton harlot being dropped off at home by her rakish new lover. Who was she turning into?

Whoever it was, she liked her.

"It's hard to believe you are the same man who was criticizing my wine pairing a month and a half ago," she said.

"I failed to see all of your hidden charms."

"And now?"

He was not much for out-and-out grinning. But he was grinning now. Big. "You continue to surprise me."

"And that's a good thing?"

"Very."

They sat, staring into one another's eyes. She could see a loving smile dawning on his face, like a room slowly filling with sun, and for reasons she didn't even understand, she fought, unsuccessfully, to keep her own joy contained. Impossible. And so they sat there, for a full minute, just grinning stupidly at one another, like two moony teenagers who'd just enjoyed a matinee and a malt.

She leaned over, kissed him gently. "Thank you for the impromptu swimming lesson. And the . . . unexpected adventure."

"They're always the best kind."

She clambered out of the truck and turned back to face him through the open passenger side window. "Don't forget," he said. "Reach . . . and pull."

She hopped up the few steps onto the porch, turned, watched him drive away. Thank God he'd finally gone—she could only imagine how wide the smile on her face was by this point. She stepped inside. And gasped.

There was Sy Sigmund, sitting in the living room, reading the *Martha's Vineyard Gazette* as if he were waiting for a doctor's appointment.

"Well, well," he said. "She finally returns." He scanned the paper. "Fascinating little place you've settled into here. Farmer Greene's in West Tisbury has a new shipment of fresh strawberries just in. Better get 'em while they last."

Mercy suddenly felt a bit light-headed, a combination, she was certain, of the unexpected tumult in the water, what had come after, and now, this. A head-on collision of her two worlds, happening right here in her cozy bungalow. She squared her shoulders. It was an effort to project a devil-may-care attitude that betrayed the limits of her acting ability. "Well, this is certainly a surprise."

He chuckled, stood, taking a minute to extract his blobby shape from the chair. He crinkled his nose as he assessed her damp, rumpled appearance, the man's flannel shirt. "You smell like you just got off a trawler for Santa Monica Seafood."

She felt the moment called for a hug, or at least some sort of physical contact, but couldn't bring herself to do it. Whether it was because of her waterlogged appearance or her head now doing swimming of its own, she wasn't sure. *Sy. Here.* "I took an unexpected swim. Seems like it's my day for the unexpected."

She spent the next twenty minutes scrambling—excusing herself to wash up and change into fresh clothes, pouring iced tea, arranging stale butter cookies on a plate—her mind whirling with questions and recriminations. Sy never left Los Angeles. Hadn't she heard a rumor that he once turned down a chance to represent Jane Wyman because she had insisted they meet in New York? And yet here he was, looking like an unmade bed, a bomb that just landed in the middle of her idyllic escape from the world.

Now caked in a fine film of talc (it was the best she could do in a pinch) and wearing a plain beige day dress, she laid out the refreshments and took a seat across from him. They spent a few moments making idle Hollywood chitchat—an unknown named Dolores Hart had landed the lead in *Where the Boys Are*—until Mercy decided it was way past the time to get to the point.

"So," she said. "Do I even need to ask how you found me?"

"Now, don't be too hard on old Cassie," he said. Cass hated being called Cassie (*It makes me sound like a dairy cow*), which is why, Mercy suspected, Sy always did. "When she found out why I needed to see you, she agreed that betraying Theodosia Burr was the thing to do."

"Who?"

"Another waif who was lost at sea. Look it up. Learn some history."

My God, he could be maddening. "Sy, what are you doing here? No one can get you to drive to Pasadena, never mind a cross-country journey to an island off the coast of Massachusetts. This has to be important."

"It is." He reached into the briefcase next to his chair, extracted what was clearly a script, and tossed it on the coffee table, where it landed with a small thud. She reached over to retrieve it.

"This is why you spent two days traveling across the country? To deliver a script?"

"Not just any script." He pointed to the document. "The script that is going to make you a star."

Mercy read the cover.

"WUTHERING"

BY BRENT BAKER

BASED UPON THE NOVEL "WUTHERING HEIGHTS,"

BY EMILY BRONTË

She looked up. "A new version of *Wuthering Heights*? The Olivier film is barely twenty years old. And flawless."

"This is a contemporary take, set in present day. Read the script. It's incredible."

She stared down again at the cover page. "Who's the writer?"

"New kid, army brat from Virginia. But he's got a way with words. I'm telling you: he's going to win Adapted Screenplay for this."

He was talking her language, and he knew it. She could feel the riptide of Hollywood creeping around her body, ready to suck her back out. "Producer?"

A sly smile crept across Sy's craggly face. "Kramer."

Mercy's heart skipped a beat. Stanley Kramer. The producer of

High Noon. The Caine Mutiny. The Defiant Ones. From the day he'd signed her, she had been begging Sy to get her an audition with Kramer. His films were meaty, deep works of cinematic art, with no resemblance to the glossy melodramas Sy was constantly sending her out for. His work since leaving Columbia and striking out on his own had been daring, original. Hollywood was already noisy with advance gossip about his new picture, *On the Beach,* a dystopian drama with Gregory Peck. Sy was right: with a script from Hollywood's new wunderkind and Kramer behind it, this picture would vault straight to the top. So would anyone in it.

"This doesn't feel like a Kramer project," she said, scanning the pages. "It seems far too feminine for him."

"Kramer lives to surprise people. He's signed Brando for Heathcliff."

Mercy's eyes flickered up from the pages. "Brando? For the brooding stable boy wandering the English moors?"

Sy exhaled wearily. "Try to follow the plot here, will you? I told you—this is a complete reimagining. It's set in current-day Brooklyn. Every A-list actress is vying for Cathy. Initial rumor was he was looking at Hope Lange. Debbie Reynolds pitched, which, let's face it, is a joke. Hayward wants it but is way too old. So is Constance Baxter. Liz Taylor sent Kramer a box of premium Cuban cigars. Every one of them knows this is pure Oscar bait."

The mention of Constance Baxter sent an unpleasant dart into her stomach. She ignored it, sank back into the sofa. "I don't understand. He'll never let me audition."

Sy leaned forward, put his elbows on his knees. "Why the fuck do you think I'm here? Kramer wants *you* for Cathy."

She felt the bottom fall out of her stomach. "Me."

"You."

She couldn't process. "Wh-Why?"

He cocked his head. "Honey, I know I'm a schmuck who's tough on you, but for Christ's sake, you do know you're talented, right? That you are actually *good* at this? They don't nominate people for Academy Awards who can't act. Or at least they normally don't. This is it. This is your shot. Stanley Kramer wants you to star opposite

Marlon Brando in a modern-day adaptation of one of the great classics in literature. This is everything we worked for. You should be over the moon in this moment."

Her head was spinning. "I . . . I am."

"Yeah. I can tell." He sat up straight, took a long sip of his iced tea.

"It's just a lot to take in, that's all. When does shooting start?"

"Next month. But you'll have to be in New York week after next for wardrobe fittings and makeup tests. Kramer's still meddling with some of the dialogue, but table read is set for the week after. All you have to do is get the writer to sign off."

Mercy's eyes constricted. It was almost unheard-of that a writer—especially a new writer—got the power to sign off on leads. "The writer negotiated cast approval?"

"Not for Brando, obviously," Sy said. "But he convinced Kramer he has a very specific idea for Cathy and he wants to meet the actress first. It's really a rubber stamp thing. But yeah, you'll have to meet him before we go to contract."

"When?"

"Day after tomorrow." He read Mercy's panicked expression. "Don't worry—turns out he's in Boston at the moment. So you'll just have to take one of those tiny flying death traps and have lunch with him. You'll be back in time for dinner."

"And then?"

"You'd have about a week to get your ass to New York."

She met the intensity of his gaze. She'd known it had to be big to get him to schlep all the way to Martha's Vineyard, and indeed, it was. She'd have to leave—soon. She'd also have to bow out of Staxx's play. He'd be devastated.

Would Ren?

He seemed to be reading her thoughts. "Do not tell me you are, for one instant, considering turning this down to stay on this godforsaken land of the Pilgrims. Please, tell me that is not possible."

Mercy could feel panic splashing inside her body. He was right. It would be sheer insanity to turn this down.

And yet.

"Who is he?"

Sy's question shook her out of her scrambled brain. "What? Who?"

"Tall, dark, and seaworthy," he said. "The guy in the truck. The one treating your neck like it was breakfast."

She looked at him archly. "You were spying on me?"

"I was *waiting* for you. It's a big window. I looked out. Sue me."

"He's just a friend."

He scoffed. "Right. Is he worth throwing away your career?"

She began shaking her head. "It's not like that. You don't understand—"

He put his hand up to cut her off. "I understand plenty. Look, I indulged this little fantasy when you decided to take off. I didn't argue. When I found out what had happened with Louis, who, by the way, I always knew was a complete asshole, I didn't bother you then, either. But this—this is your moment. Right here. Don't be a *meshuggeneh*. Do. This."

He was right. Every single word.

But.

The peace and healing she had found here. The sense of new purpose. Staxx, and the play that could make his career. Ren. This unexpected curve from Sy had arrived just as what she had been afraid to admit this afternoon was now coming into focus.

She was falling in love with Ren.

She needed to buy time, clear her head, look at the situation without the churn of emotion roiling her insides.

She spoke quietly. "I know you're right in everything you say. I do. I just need a day to think about it." He began protesting. This time it was her turn to cut *him* off. "A day isn't going to make any difference, Sy. Please, just one day. Twenty-four hours. I'm not asking a lot. There are things happening here . . . it's too much to explain. Just give me a day. One day." She managed a small smile. "You can spend the evening eating a nice lobster roll."

"*Traif!*" he said. "They'll kick me right out of Beth Israel."

"You haven't stepped foot in Beth Israel since Aaron's bar mitzvah." She stood up. "Where are you staying?"

"Smiths' Inn."

"Perfect. I'll meet you there tomorrow afternoon for lunch. Noon."

He stood. The mirth had left his eyes. Old Sy, back to business. "Breakfast. Ten o'clock. I'm leaving on the early afternoon ferry. And hopefully, the next day you'll be headed to Boston."

He donned his fedora, grabbed his briefcase. As he walked past her out the door, he leaned down, picked something up off the porch. An envelope. "For you," he said wryly. "No doubt more correspondence from out at sea."

He tipped his hat sarcastically and lumbered down the steps and onto the sidewalk. Mercy inspected the envelope. Expensive cream linen, with her name in carefully written script on the front.

She extracted a matching notecard trimmed in navy, the word SYCAMORE in raised letters at the top.

> My dear Miss Welles—
>
> It seems that some dear friends and both of my sons have been enjoying your company during your visit to Martha's Vineyard, but I have not yet had the pleasure.
>
> I do hope you will come for tea tomorrow at 4. I look forward to getting to know you.
>
> > Most sincerely,
> > Margaret Sewards

Sixteen

Mercy drifted into the White Whale and took a seat at the bar. The pub had just opened—it was barely past eleven in the morning—and there were only two tables occupied. It struck her that every time she'd been in here it had almost always been empty. She made a note to try and return during the dinner hour or after. She'd like to see the place full, humming with conviviality.

Dennis came over, slid a glass of white wine in front of her.

"Oh, Dennis! Thank you, but no," she said. "It's far too early in the day to be drinking."

He chuckled the hearty laugh of the Irish bartender. "It's never too early to be drinking," he said. "Besides, you look like you need it."

This much was true. She'd just left breakfast with Sy; by now he had checked out. Not that it was much of a breakfast, anyway. He had wolfed down a plate of eggs and bacon (so much for no *traif*) while she had sat picking at half a grapefruit, trying to find the words she knew she had to say. She'd been up half the night reading *Wuthering*, picturing its sullen leading man and star director and rising writer and all of the trappings that she'd yearned for since arriving in Hollywood from Beatrice. Sy had been right: the script was spectacular, a fresh, riveting, bold interpretation of the novel. This was a whole new take on Catherine Earnshaw. The role of a lifetime. In the end, she had given Sy the only answer she could give.

She had said yes.

She would fly to Boston tomorrow, meet Brent Baker, the screenwriter, then come back to pack and settle her affairs here before leaving. Well, one affair, anyway.

Hadn't she known all along she had to take it? Yes, she had made a commitment to Staxx to do his play—a play that could change his life—and would now be breaking that promise. But she justified it by telling herself that with leading lady stardom she would have new leverage to help him, to bring him to Hollywood, introduce him to the right people. Certainly that would prove far more valuable than appearing in a local production in Vineyard Haven. In the long run, Staxx would fare far better with her decision.

Ren would not.

He had been the wild card in all of this. Never, in escaping to Martha's Vineyard, had she expected to find love. She had no guarantee, she had told herself, that their fledgling romance would continue past today, never mind the following months or years. How was that going to work? He'd never leave. Was she just going to throw everything away and move to some tiny island plopped in the middle of the Atlantic? She was not.

But then, why was there part of her that wanted to?

She took a slug of the wine.

"That's supposed to be helpin', not making things worse," Dennis said from the other end of the bar. He ambled over. "Do you want to tell me what's botherin' you, love?"

Bless him. In the weeks she'd been here he had taken a genuine interest in her, asking questions about how long she was staying, what she was enjoying about the island. Bridie was clearly running the day-to-day at the pub. But it was Dennis, she felt, that was its heart. She smiled.

"Nothing that won't work out on its own," she said airily.

"Heard you were out at Great Rock Bight yesterday. Did you have fun?"

The question startled her a bit. How did he know that? "My, you do keep up with everything that happens here, don't you?"

"Ren was in here last night for a quick pint. He mentioned it. Beautiful part of the island there. Did you enjoy it?"

"I did. I could have done without the swim, though."

He cocked his head. "You don't fancy the water?"

"I'm afraid the water doesn't fancy me. I've never learned to swim." There was something in his eyes, a devilishness, that made her want to open up. That, and the fact that he had known Ren since childhood. She was dying for more recognizance. "Ren is . . ." She struggled to find the words.

"Ren is the salt of the earth," he said. "And now you're in an island romance with him. Don't worry. You're not the first." Catching her blanched expression, he quickly corrected course. "Now, now, I didn't mean it that way. I mean, lots of people come here from all over and have romantic adventures for the season. It's part of the place's charm."

She cocked a brow. "Was that part of its charm for you?"

He laughed. "You could say that. It's how I got here. I met a lovely lass in Boston turned my head right side out and back again. She came here, I followed her. I was desperately mad for her."

Mercy could picture it: young Dennis, the earnest, scrappy Irishman, holding his woolen cap and a bouquet of wilting wildflowers, courting the elusive girl he'd chased across the water. And yet here he was, years later, with no sign of her. "What happened?"

He shrugged. "She married someone else," he said quietly. "Went back to Boston. That also happens a lot. Island romances, they're tough to sustain. Especially for the locals who get smitten, only to have the objects of their desire leave them once the weather turns."

He eyed her evenly and she felt his judgment washing over her, seeping into her bones. He had no idea just *how* soon she was leaving. She hadn't planned on this romance, on feeling this way. Falling for Ren had only managed to show her how shallow her relationship with Louis had been, how much of a blessing discovering his indiscretion had proved to be. Now she had the real thing, could feel it, and she was going to discard it to go make a movie. But she would come back. She'd explain to Ren that once filming ended she'd come back, stay longer next time. He could visit California. Surely there were oysters off the coast of California? He'd want to do that.

Wouldn't he?

Dennis slapped an oversized ledger onto the bar. He opened it, retrieving a pen lodged behind his right ear. "Time to write a few checks." He pointed the pen to the heavens. "A good Irishman always pays his bills!"

Mercy watched as he scribbled out three checks. Her eyes focused in as she watched him sign. "Wait," she said, crooking her head to get a better look. "You're signing these 'Bridget deCoursey.' That's forgery!"

He grinned, setting the checks aside and closing the ledger. "Do it all the time. I could fake da Vinci's signature on the *Mona Lisa* and nobody'd be the wiser. Missed my calling. Here." He ripped a small piece of paper out of the ledger and slid it across the bar to her, pen on top. "Write something and sign it."

She tentatively picked up the pen and scribbled out a short greeting and her name, pushing the paper back toward him. He inspected the signature for a few seconds, then he picked up the pen and wrote his own version underneath. She gasped. The two sentences were practically identical.

"My, that's incredible," Mercy said. "And a bit alarming."

"If you ever get tired of signing those black-and-white photos, I can offer services at a reasonable rate." He winked at her, then scooped up the ledger and scurried down to the other end of the bar, where a couple who'd just entered was scanning about for a table.

Mercy glanced at her watch. Already half past. She was due at the theater for rehearsal at noon.

How would she tell Ren? She should tell him first. But she had a more immediate problem. How could she go through with a rehearsal for a play she knew she wasn't going to appear in? She grabbed her purse and slid off the barstool, mentally rehearsing her speech to Staxx.

*

It had all gone wrong.

Staxx had fallen ill—food poisoning, she'd been told—and in her flustered state Mercy couldn't find a reason quickly enough to explain why she couldn't rehearse without him. The director, a stern, brassy woman who had gotten the entire playhouse "off the ground, on my back," as she was fond of telling anyone within earshot, had gotten the cast together and run them through a fair amount of the blocking for the first act. Mercy had sleepwalked through the process, which had been duly noted not only by the director but the rest of the cast. It had certainly caught the attention of Patrick Sewards.

"I'm so glad you could come to tea," he said. She was now sitting in the passenger seat of his blue MGA 1500 Roadster, holding her straw platter sun hat to her head, as they curved around the back roads of Edgartown toward the looming cliff that housed the Sewards mansion. "I was afraid you wouldn't be up to it after that rehearsal."

A dig at her dismal performance today, gift-wrapped in faux cheeriness. She let it go. The truth was that among ruminating over the new movie, Ren, and Staxx, she'd completely forgotten about Mint's invitation to tea. It was only as she was walking out of the theater that he'd offered to follow her back to Edgartown and drive her himself, "because I assume you'll want to change first." How . . . gallant.

Her first instinct was to cancel, but it would have been far too rude to do it this late. She was also feeling guilty: Didn't Ren have a right to know his mother had asked her to tea? Too late now. And her curiosity about Mint, stoked at that first glimpse through the window of the Mansion House Inn with nosy waitress Vera, had only grown since. Mainly via some questions she couldn't reconcile: How did the grande dame of Martha's Vineyard raise rakish and charming Ren? Why were they so clearly estranged? And why did Ren feel the entire family was broken?

She smoothed the folds of her rayon dress—green, to bring out her eyes—and fidgeted with the wide white belt. It felt like she was going on an audition.

Wasn't she?

"I'm sure you've heard much about Mother already," Patrick said with a laugh. "It's possible some of it is even true."

"People really admire her" was all Mercy could offer in return. She looked to the right at the passing scenery, rolling her eyes at herself.

"Well, I'm sure Ren has had plenty of commentary to offer."

Her head snapped to the left. How did he know? Surely Ren hadn't mentioned anything to his brother. From what she could tell they barely spoke. She found herself at a loss for words.

Patrick shot her a glance. "Don't look so stricken," he said. "It's a small island. People talk." He laughed softly. "I have to say, you're probably the classiest girl he's ever dated."

"We're not dating." The words were rushed, defensive.

He nodded. "Whatever you say." They made the turn up the winding gravel drive and he threw the car into park. "Welcome to Sycamore."

Up close the house was even more impressive than from the view from Grace Chadwick's kitchen, an L-shaped monument to traditional New England architecture. The outside was painted a pristine toothpaste white, with glossy black shutters and four gabled slate roofs that housed two chimneys on either end. Huge lead-paned windows, each outfitted with a window box overflowing with tea roses and fit for a cottage in the English countryside, looked out over the bluff to the sea below. A wide porch, painted slate gray, wrapped around the house. To the left stood a wide, beautiful old sycamore tree of deep green, with endless twisted branches that led down to a battered, gnarled trunk. Patrick waved at it grandly. "Hence the name," he said.

Mercy shook her head at the tree's sheer beauty. "You don't mean to say . . . this tree dates back to the sixteen hundreds?"

"Highly doubtful," he said. "Sycamores usually top out at two hundred years. We think this one was probably planted somewhere around 1840. That's when the largest addition to the house went on."

Patrick led her through a deep-red door replete with an imposing brass knocker, past a curving mahogany staircase and into an expansive drawing room. The space was flooded with light from the windows on three sides, and accented with the tufted furniture and silver and crystal accessories that signaled old-money status and privilege. A maid in a crisp uniform was arranging madeleines on a tray next to a bone china tea service. She nodded demurely to Patrick, then left.

Mercy was standing by the massive white fireplace, admiring an oil painting of an old sea captain, when she heard a strong, feminine voice behind her. "That's Elias Sewards."

Mint wore a plain silk pink blouse and navy pencil skirt that accentuated her slim frame and set off her pale complexion. Unlike so many of the women on Martha's Vineyard, all ruddy and freckled, she seemed almost made of porcelain, which only added more drama to her enigmatic air. She had a long, angular face with prominent cheekbones, and a tiny mouth that held just the slightest smear of pale rose lipstick. She was thin, wiry, but carried herself with a steely, Barbara Stanwyck–like confidence.

"Everyone called him Quill," Mint was saying, now standing next to Mercy as they both glanced back up at the painting. "No one could explain why, because as far as I know he never wrote a word." She met Mercy's eyes and smiled. "New Englanders and their quirky monikers. Someday I must share with you the tortured tale of how I came to be nicknamed for an after-dinner candy."

Mint waved Mercy onto the sofa and they sat, exchanging introductory pleasantries and commentary about the weather as Mint poured the tea and Patrick circled in the back of the room. His casual pacing made Mercy uneasy, as if she were a prized steer being inspected to see if it was worth the purchase price. Sensing this, Mint spoke.

"Patrick, please either do sit down or take a stroll. You look like a father outside the delivery room."

He laughed, downed the rest of his drink, and walked out of the room.

"Boys," Mint said, shaking her head as she handed Mercy a delicate cup and saucer. "Well, I'm just so delighted you were able to come. I feel like I have been missing out getting to know our famous island guest."

"I wouldn't say 'famous.'"

"Oh, you're being modest, my dear. I've seen two of your pictures and you were marvelous in each. And Patrick tells me you're going to be positively brilliant in the play he's producing."

Coming here was a mistake, Mercy thought. *A huge, huge mistake.*

She smiled wanly at the compliment.

"Of course, I'm sure you're anxious to return to your glamorous life in California." Mint lifted her own teacup, taking a long, luxurious sip. It was suddenly quiet, the only sound the faint roar of the sea beyond the open windows.

Now they were getting somewhere. Clearly this was the raison d'être behind the invitation—to confirm Mercy would be leaving Martha's Vineyard after the play was over. How much did Mint know? Ren was approaching thirty. He was a bit old to have a mother meddling in his love life. But it was clear Mint Sewards was no ordinary mother.

"I haven't really finalized my plans yet," Mercy lied. She had no intention of telling anyone about *Wuthering* until she'd spoken to Ren. "But whenever I go, it will be hard to leave. I have quickly experienced, and appreciated, the charm of this island."

She caught a fleeting flicker of something whip across Mint's face.

"This is a glorious house," Mercy said. "Like something out of a book."

Mint nodded. "It's been in our family for three hundred years. Which makes it very charming, and also a very large and expensive pain to maintain."

Mercy smiled. "And it's just you and Patrick here while he's home from law school? I know Ren lives elsewhere on the island. And . . . your daughter?"

Mint's blue eyes flashed and Mercy basked in the bull's-eye. The elder woman took another languid sip of her tea, carefully calibrating her response. "Ellenanne was always a dreamer," she said casually. "She wanted a more cosmopolitan life than a sleepy island could afford. Of course, as a mother you always want your children close. But you must also allow them to find the paths that lead to their own happiness."

Mercy's mind whirled as she pieced together all of the details. The island rallies around a wealthy widow, but the family fractures: the eldest son turns his back on his mother, so much so that he doesn't even acknowledge they're related. The daughter flees at the first opportunity. The youngest takes on the role of devoted son. And now the matriarch spends her time meddling in all of their lives. Or trying to.

They drifted into less choppy waters: restaurants, diversions, the early history of the Sewards family. They talked about their mutual admiration for Grace Chadwick, and her charming assertion that she was a "washashore." "And you, Mrs. Sewards?" Mercy asked. "Does your own family lineage extend all the way back to the founding as well?"

Mint smiled. "Oh, hardly. No, no. I came here as a young woman. I was working as a governess for the summer when I first met Jasper one afternoon in Vineyard Haven. I had no idea who he was."

Mercy felt emboldened. "And was it love at first sight?"

Mint raised her eyebrows. "Hardly. I found him to be boorish and self-absorbed. But he was also very charming, and very persistent." She looked Mercy in the eye. "A bit like Warren."

They held one another's stare for a moment. Mercy had been careless, enjoying the dance only to realize, too late, that Mint had been slowly backing her into a corner. There was only one way out.

"Is there something you would like to ask me, Mrs. Sewards?"

Mint continued to watch her, inscrutable, when Patrick's voice intervened.

"We don't want to keep Mercy, Mother," he said, slowly sidling up next to the sofa. "She's had a long day of rehearsal. I should be getting her back."

Mint stood, extending her hand. "It was so lovely to finally meet you, Miss Welles. I do hope you'll visit again before you leave us."

A few additional perfunctory pleasantries were exchanged as Mercy was escorted out. Mint closed the door tightly, watched from the window as Patrick and Mercy got into the car and drove off.

She never panicked, prided herself on never, ever panicking. She had the history to prove it. But there was a twinge, a small pocket of disquiet, lodged inside her brain. A voice. She didn't know why the voice was so strong. Why it kept saying the same thing, over and over.

This girl could ruin everything.

*

Mercy walked through the lobby of the Sheraton-Plaza Hotel in Boston's leafy Copley Square, threading her way through the pockets of tourists, businesspeople, and servers bustling about. She caught her reflection in an oversized gilt mirror and immediately wished she'd picked another outfit, eyeing her two-piece pink peplum suit with cap sleeves with a newly critical eye. She stopped, futzing again with the button-back belt, then noticed a small smudge in the palm of her left glove. *Great.* She had wanted Brent Baker to see an actress with poise, confidence, but also the vulnerability needed to play Catherine. What she saw looking back in the mirror was a young woman swamped in self-doubt.

Sy had told her the writer would meet her in the lobby, but there were at least forty men here, some in couples or small groups, and at least a dozen alone. How could she know which one was him? She walked up to the concierge. "Hello. I have an appointment with a guest, Brent Baker. He had told me he would meet me here. Could you possibly direct me?"

A gaunt man with the bearing of an undertaker, the concierge raised his eyebrows slightly. "Ah, yes. Miss Welles. Mr. Baker is expecting you. He's just over there," he said, waving his arm toward the lounge. "The gentleman in the seersucker suit."

Brent Baker sat, coffee cup in hand, engrossed in a copy of the *Boston Globe.* He was undeniably handsome in a Midwestern way, with an angular, diamond-shaped face, a wide nose, and prominent ears, his dark brown hair carefully oiled and expertly parted on the side. He boasted a thin, rangy physique that projected a youthful vitality, like that of a college runner, augmented by well-placed lines around his eyes and mouth that added a touch of experiential gravitas to his appearance. His eyes flew up as she approached, and he quickly discarded the paper as he stood.

"Miss Welles," he said, extending his hand. "How nice to finally meet you."

"And I, you, Mr. Baker," she said, before blurting out, "I am incredibly nervous."

His smile was wide, warm, gracious, and he waved her into an ornately embroidered chair by his own. "Oh, please, don't be. You're the veteran here. I'm the one rather new to all of this fuss."

"Get used to it. Your screenplay is worth every ounce of the excitement it's generating."

He nodded slightly. "I'm very humbled."

He called over the waiter and she ordered a lemonade. They spent the next hour talking about everything: the script, how he had come up with the idea, how gobsmacked he had been by the reaction to it, Brando. He told her a hilarious story about meeting Sy in Los Angeles and the unfortunate tuna salad sandwich episode that followed.

"I have to say," she said, "it is very rare that a writer gets casting approval. You should feel very honored."

He nodded. "Well, obviously I didn't approve Brando, but he's Brando," he said. "But yes, I was forthright with the studio that I had a very definite idea of who Cathy was, and I wanted to know the right actress was going to be cast." He looked at her. "Which brings me to wanting to ask if you would mind running through some lines. Just so I can get a sense of what you would bring to the character."

"Of course." She had anticipated this, had rehearsed a particular scene midway through the story. As she reached into her bag for the script, however, he interrupted. "Oh no, not here in the lobby," he said, smiling. "My copy of the script is in my suite. We can go there and won't have any noise or prying eyes. And I'll be able to hear you without the din."

A pebble of foreboding dropped into her body, creating a slight ripple in her stomach. She wasn't naive. Tales of the casting couch abounded in Hollywood, though the story was almost always one of the director or leading man and the aspiring starlet looking for her big break. But Mercy knew directly that women were not immune from culpability. She thought back to a half-dressed Louis, opening the door holding the ice bucket as Constance Baxter lounged somewhere in the recesses of the hotel room at the Chateau Marmont.

Brent was looking at her expectantly. "Is everything all right?"

Kramer. Brando. Brontë. He seemed pleasant, affable, and hardly like a predator. She exhaled. "Of course. Lead the way."

Five minutes later he swung open the door on his top-floor suite, the centerpiece of which was a series of rounded floor-to-ceiling windows. She walked over to the middle one, which overlooked the lush green park below. "What a lovely view," she said.

He had walked up behind her. And then it came. His hands on her elbows, rubbing her arms. "I couldn't agree more," he whispered into her ear.

She froze. She expected to be overcome with fear, and there was a tinge of that. But whether due to his slight frame or her own deep-down sense of preparedness for this possibility, in that moment what she felt mainly was crushing disappointment. How many other actresses had Brent Baker "met with," then discarded? Giving in was not an option. But the impact of that decision hit her with a force that had her trying to catch her breath. This had been the role of a lifetime, the role that could have made her a star, defined her career. But she had no guarantee that even if she did succumb to his seduction that he wouldn't simply cast her aside, go back to Kramer and tell him the reading had been terrible, that they had to "keep looking" until all of his carnal appetites were sated.

Maybe she could still salvage this. She whirled around to face him. "We should get to the reading," she said, issuing a tight smile then deftly stepping around him into the room. In businesslike fashion she extracted the script from her bag, then took a seat on a Queen Anne chair.

His eyes narrowed as he walked over, hands in his pockets, stopping in front of her. "Look at me," he commanded.

She glanced up, feigning congenial indifference.

And then he was suddenly there, bent down, his hands gripping both arms of the chair, his face inches from hers, his breath hot. She fought to remain impassive, holding his fiery gaze. "You're very attractive," he was whispering. "You have the kind of presence all great actresses yearn to have, but so few do. I could make this role yours, right here, right now. I just need a little more. A little . . . " he scanned her body, "*taste* of what you'd bring to it." He smiled again, more broadly, exhibiting a perfect row of neatly capped teeth. No doubt installed while he was home one summer from boarding school, leering at the housemaid as he waited for the annual family trip to the Cape.

She remained rock still, looking right at him. "I think I need to clarify things," she said slowly. "Well, one thing. And that is if I get this part, it's going to be because I am the best actress for it."

"Of course." He bent down farther, began dropping a few soft kisses on the side of her neck. "I only want the best."

She didn't know what it was—the unctuous feeling of his coffee-scented breath on her neck, the feeling of claustrophobia now enveloping her, a momentary memory of Ren, trailing his mouth down her body on the deserted beach—but whatever it was, she knew she had to act. Now. Before he took control. And she lost control of everything.

She kicked him, hard, heel first, directly on his left shin, and the force and shock of it sent him staggering backward, until he collapsed onto a nearby settee. Mercy swiped her bag off the floor and stood. He was still sitting, rubbing his shin, his eyes shining with anger. "You're an idiot," he whispered.

Mercy flung the script at his feet. "Perhaps," she said. "But at least I'm one who kept her dignity."

She stalked out of the room, slamming the door behind her. What would Sy say? It didn't really matter. As she pressed the elevator button, the only thing she knew *did* matter in this moment was getting back to Martha's Vineyard. To Ren. She smiled as his words in the water echoed in her brain.

Always be brave.

July 21, 1959

Dear Cass—

I love you, so I am going to forgive you for telling Sy where I am. I also know you were only trying to do the right thing, which you always are. As I am sure he mentioned, I was up for the lead in the new Brando movie, a modern retelling of "Wuthering Heights." I have to tell you, the script was worth all of the hype. But Sy sent me to Boston to meet with the writer (I cannot recall an instance where a new writer got casting approval, but it's evidently a new day in Hollywood), and, well, let's just say it didn't go very well. Remember that story I told you about the Lux soap commercial audition I had, right after we moved in together? Picture that, only ten times worse.

I called Sy and told him what happened and not to bother me for the rest of the summer. But now, I am wondering if even that isn't long enough. Do not faint onto the couch, but I am starting to wonder if show business is for me at all. The relentless pursuit of the "next thing"—the next role, the next award, the next contract—is it truly all worth it? I suppose if you're Joanne Woodward and you're coming home to Paul Newman every night it is, but how many people get to be Joanne Woodward?

I have been thinking about Diane Varsi. I think we've been on similar tracks, she and I: young ingenues, next big star, nominated for Oscars, all of that. She had the world on a string after "Peyton Place." And then a few months ago she quit the business and moved to Vermont. Someone wrote that she had just wanted to live an authentic life. I'm beginning to see what that's about.

I remind you once again that all of this is your fault. You are the one who sent me here to gather myself, and put me on this journey of self-discovery. It's been eye-opening.

I am seeing Ren tonight. I have to admit it, Cass. I love him. I didn't expect to, and I don't want to, but I do. And I feel I owe it to myself to see it through, whatever happens. On the surface I know how impossible this all is: the actress and the oysterman. Ironically, it's something . . . out of a movie. But all I know is I want to be with him. And for now, that's enough.

Fondly,
Mercy

Seventeen

Kit sits in the small conference room, the long table littered with heavy textbooks, volumes, and folders spewing out photocopied articles, photos, sketches, and myriad other historical ephemera about the first ladies of the United States. Ratings for *Signature with Lucinda Cross* have been soft, and its host has decided some lighter feature fare is in order to goose viewership. What is going unsaid is that Lucinda's contract is up for renewal in a few months, and she needs to show some positive momentum. Which means eyeballs. To her credit, she refuses to plumb the depths of the culture for a cheap win—an intern who suggested a segment on supermodels battling climate change was quickly silenced—which has led to this multipart series on first ladies, "the women behind the men," from Martha Washington onward. Kit had meekly suggested broadening the scope, perhaps doing a series on female trailblazers and including women such as Elizabeth Cady Stanton or Margaret Sanger, but Lucinda had dismissed it. ("No one wants a tour of noted lesbians of the twentieth century," she remarked drolly.) Lucinda has assigned Priya to help. So they have divided the list of first ladies, calling historians and searching for story hooks to weave the narratives of these disparate women together. Which is how she now finds herself in this moment, frantically scribbling notes about dresses, teas, and the occasional assassination.

"Well, you look like you're having fun," Priya says, walking into the room carrying a midsized bulletin board. She's wearing a bright tangerine jumpsuit accented with a particularly busy Pucci scarf and way too many bracelets. She looks like a fashionable Creamsicle.

"A blast," Kit answers, leaning back in her chair and tossing her pen onto the yellow legal pad. "Did you know Caroline Harrison founded the Daughters of the American Revolution?"

"Alas, women who look like me are not eligible for membership in such institutions. We were just the ones colonized. But I can tell you that Nellie Taft planted the first cherry trees in Washington. Perhaps a more enduring gift than the old DAR."

Kit puts her face in her hands. "I so don't want to be doing this right now."

"I know," Priya says, propping up the bulletin board. "Which is why I brought you this."

"Which is?"

"Motivation. To get you back to what you really *should* be doing."

Kit knits her eyebrows in confusion as Priya flips the board around, revealing its contents. It's a crazy mix of Post-its, diagrams, timelines, photos, and notecards. There's a photocopy of the picture of Nan and the mystery man, a map of Martha's Vineyard, the flyer for the play. It looks like a mash-up of a serial killer's manifesto and a blog on Pinterest. Kit looks closer, sees a series of pictures of Nan as Mercy Welles, selected factoids from her own nascent investigation into that mysterious summer.

"Here is where we are so far," Priya is saying, and Kit notes the "we" in her statement. She has leaned on Priya for background help and off-the-books research far too much—she'd be fired instantly, and probably rightfully so, if Lucinda got wind of it. But now Kit's enthusiasm is waning. She has been doing poorly at work, distracted by all of this. After she left Sy Sigmund's son in Philadelphia, she knew her next logical step: if she wanted to get to the bottom of what had really happened to change the course of her grandmother's life, she would have to go to Martha's Vineyard herself. Except she couldn't. At least not now. She'd just been on bereavement, and then taken another gift week in Los Angeles. There was nothing left in the time-off bank.

She focuses back on Priya mid-sentence. ". . . and that's where the trail goes cold. It picks up again in the spring of 1960, which is when your grandmother was in New York, living at the women's hotel. She eventually meets your grandfather, and we know the rest of all of that. But it's this period"—she points to a gap on the board, marked by a blank notecard—"which is where the answers are. After Sy visits, but before she comes to Manhattan. Something happened in here that made Mercy Welles throw everything away."

Priya catches the hurt that flashes into Kit's eyes, begins a tactical retreat. "Or, rather, what made her make a radically different choice to reinvent her life as she knew it. Which turned out to be wonderful and included raising two lovely granddaughters she positively adored."

Kit manages a weak smile. "Nice save."

Priya winces. "Thanks?"

"I have to back-burner the whole riddle of my grandmother's missing life for a while," Kit says. "I've got too much going on right now."

Priya looks at her archly. "Like what: Florence Harding's lunch menus and random late-night visits with your emotionally unavailable guitarist?"

Kit shoots over a warning look. "Careful."

"OK, sorry, over the line, over the line. But c'mon, Kit. This is important."

"So is being able to pay my rent."

Priya pulls out a chair, plops down. "Ask Lucinda for a leave of absence."

Kit laughs derisively. "She'll never go for that."

"Kit, this revelation about your grandmother is affecting you more than you're admitting. And I get why you want to put a pin in it. But you'll always wonder, and I think that prospect is much worse than what you may find. This woman raised you, Kit. She loved you, sacrificed for you, she made you the woman you are today, all while holding back a part of herself that for some reason she didn't let you know about." Priya waves her hand around the table. "Nothing against the Caroline Harrisons, but it's the women like your grandmother whose stories we should be telling. Because they also tell us who we are."

Kit is slightly astonished that of all the many things she is feeling in this moment, the most prevalent one is pride. She's proud that Priya has started to come into her own, to develop not only story sensibility, but her own carefully considered and measured view on the world. Her own voice. One that also carries with it the distinct ring of truth.

"I can't just bolt my job, Priya."

"I think that if you went to Lucinda, explain, she'd at least give you a leave of absence for a month or two."

"Which leaves me with no income for a month or two."

"And half the proceeds from the sale of your grandmother's fat-ass house. C'mon, Kit, stop making excuses. You can do this, and you *should* do this. You should go to Martha's Vineyard. The question is: What's really holding you back?"

The room is quiet for a few seconds. Kit listens to the droning of the network feed in the distance, which sounds like Charlie Brown's teacher. Finally, she says, "Maybe I'm afraid of what I'll find."

Priya smiles gently. "OK, final dose of motivation." She reaches into her pocket, extracts an orange Post-it, slides it across the conference table. There's an address on it, in Jackson Heights. Kit looks at Priya. "What's this?"

"Another piece of your puzzle," she says proudly. "I found Stanton Williams."

*

Priya, for all her . . . well, "Priya-ness," can be shockingly good at tracking down sources. It's the element of surprise—people were always looking at the kooky, crazy-quilt packaging and underestimating the cunning girl hiding beneath it. In any event, Priya has tracked down Stanton Williams, alive but evidently not all that well, living in a nursing home in Jackson Heights, just off the BQE.

The facility itself is old and smells of too much pine cleaner, but it is clean and bright and reasonably well maintained. Kit approaches the woman behind the front desk in the lobby. "Hi," she says. "I have an appointment to see a resident named Stanton Williams. His daughter said she would meet me here."

Sarah Williams had been, understandably, a tad confused by Kit's call. But how did you succinctly explain the journey of trying to put together the jigsaw puzzle of the secret life of your grandmother? Kit had managed to outline enough of the tale to both intrigue Sarah and get her to agree to facilitate a meeting. This was Kit's big break—the chance to finally talk to someone who actually knew Nan during that fateful summer, who had been *on* Martha's Vineyard with her.

A few minutes later Sarah walks through the front doors holding a piping paper cup of coffee. She is a tall woman, in her early fifties, a nursing supervisor at Columbia Presbyterian with curly shoulder-length hair and a smooth mocha complexion that belies her age.

"I'm sorry I'm a few minutes late," she says, shaking Kit's hand and then taking a seat next to her on the worn leather sofa in the lobby. "But I am nothing without my morning caffeine."

Kit once again expresses her gratitude for doing this, what it is she's after. Sarah listens intently, sipping her coffee and taking it in.

"So you knew nothing about any of this until after your grandmother died?"

"Not a glimmer."

Sarah whistles lowly. "Wow. And you say Dad had written a play for her?"

Kit hands her a copy of the flyer. "I'm not sure he wrote it *for* her, but as you can see, she was definitely set to star in it. I mean, they had to have at least gotten to the rehearsal stage if they were marketing it. But as far as I can tell, there is no record of it ever having been performed publicly. Did your father ever talk about it?"

Sarah peruses the flyer. "'Stanton Williams.' That's funny. Everyone always called him Staxx. I knew he had written a few plays, screenplays, but to my knowledge he never had anything produced." She inspects the flyer more closely. "But I mean, this is him. He was definitely on Martha's Vineyard then. He played piano in a jazz trio at one of the hotels. But fifty-nine would have been right around the time he came to New York."

"Your family had a house there? On the island?"

"My great-grandparents owned a modest place," she says. "But we were not really the fancy Blacks. They were the ones with the grand houses. I don't know how much you know about the history, but Oak Bluffs was one of the centers of Black intellectual life in this country in the early and mid twentieth century. Sort of like the Harlem Renaissance at the beach. You have to remember, financially successful Blacks who were doctors and lawyers couldn't go to the white country clubs or hotels. So they had to make their own place, their own safe haven. They did it on Martha's Vineyard."

"That sounds fascinating."

"It was. Is. But anyway, you didn't come here to hear all of that. I'll take you to see Dad. But it's like I explained on the phone: I don't know how helpful he's going to be. His dementia runs in and out, like the tide. Some days he's pretty good, some days he's not. It's a fifty-fifty shot that he will even know me. So I just need you to be prepared."

Kit nods. "I understand. But if he can give me even a nugget of something, it will help."

On the walk to Staxx's room Sarah fills her in on the rest of her father's life. He moved to New York in late 1959 to try and break into playwrighting, but Broadway was then truly a Great White Way. He became discouraged and gave up the dream and returned to music. He played keyboards in a series of house bands, including briefly for Ed Sullivan, and taught music as well. He met Sarah's mother in the early sixties, and they had five children. "All in all, it was a pretty good life," Sarah is saying as they reach the door of his room. "But I don't think he ever really got over not realizing his dream."

*

It has not gone well.

From the moment they walked into the room Kit could tell Staxx was not mentally present. His eyes were gray and hollow, with the faraway look of the very old. Despite his cotton robe and pajamas he looked almost majestic, with a ring of coarse gray hair around his head and a matching close-cropped beard. Sarah has done her best, coaxing him, explaining who Kit is and why she is there, trying to prod his mind back into the room, to no avail. Staxx has continued to stare out the window, unmoved.

Sarah is sitting in front of him, his hand in hers, lovingly rubbing it with her thumb, when Kit finally walks up next to her, puts a gentle hand on her shoulder. "It's OK," she says. "I always knew it was a long shot. I don't want to upset him. I can go."

Sarah looks up at her briefly, then back at her father. "Time to bring out the heavy artillery," she says, and takes Staxx's hand more forcefully in both of hers. "Daddy," she says, "how 'bout we sing our song, OK? Can we do that? Just us. Let's sing it." She begins singing, mellifluously.

Kit recognizes the tune. "Nature Boy," by Nat King Cole. They used it for a Lucinda special a few years ago about the Lost Boys of Sudan. It's a haunting, melancholy tune, even more so via Sarah's lilting voice.

Staxx slowly turns his head, and Kit can see it, like a curtain slowly rising, as his eyes come into focus as the song goes on. He nods slightly, a seraphic smile forming on his lips, until, at the very end, he joins Sarah in the close.

The greatest thing is to love, and to be loved in return.

The sudden sound of his voice, deep and delicate, coalescing in harmony with Sarah's, has Kit's eyes welling. Sarah looks up at her, a tear now trailing down her own face. "He's ready now," she whispers. "But you better be quick."

She stands, moves behind the chair and lets Kit sit across from him. Kit explains again who she is, what she's doing there. Staxx's eyes constrict as he surveys her.

Finally, he utters, "Mercy."

Kit's heart leaps. "Yes, yes, that's right. Mercy was my grandmother."

He nods. "You have her eyes. She had the most beautiful green eyes."

"Yes, she did. Do you remember how you met her, on Martha's Vineyard?"

"I *recruited* her," he says muscularly, and the sudden brio in his voice surprises both of them. "She came to hear us. Mercy. She was going to do my play."

"Yes, she was. *The Rose of Aquinnah*." Kit unfolds the flyer, puts it in front of him. "See? Here's the advertisement for it." He glances down at it. "Staxx, do you remember? Did the play go on?"

He looks up at her and their eyes meet, and Kit can see the sadness. He shakes his head slowly. "No."

Then he tells her why.

Eighteen

Kit edges stealthily onto the set, slipping a few feet behind Camera One as Lucinda finishes up with her last guest, a Yale professor discussing the intersection of cryptocurrency and Mexican drug cartels. Her preshow prep session had been inadvertently hilarious, punctuated by Lucinda's blithe query about whether cryptocurrency had its own color, like silver or gold.

"Well, thank you so much, Dr. Elker, for this fascinating discussion," Lucinda says. She turns to face the camera. "And thank all of you, as always, for joining us. Until tomorrow, I'm Lucinda Cross, with my signature." Fade to black as Lucinda's fake handwriting unfurls slowly across the screen.

"And we're out!" the director shouts.

A flurry of moving bodies and equipment ensues, Lucinda hustling past the hub as Priya dive-bombs in with Lucinda's late afternoon mocha latte. The host swoops it up with the alacrity of a vulture, and as she passes instructs Priya over her shoulder to make sure her driver is downstairs in ten minutes.

Kit feels like her body is nothing but a tangle of live electric wires. Staxx's revelation about why his play was scrapped keeps rolling around in her brain. It's raised so many new questions. But also answered one: what she has to do now.

Priya sidles up and together they watch as Lucinda walks toward her office. "No time like the present," Priya says.

Kit keeps her eyes peeled on Lucinda's steadily receding frame. "I'm thinking maybe tomorrow would be better."

Priya nudges her. "Don't be a coward. It's not a good look on you.

But I have to say, those Alexander McQueen cigarette pants most definitely *are*."

Kit rolls her eyes, starts walking toward Lucinda's office. She may have the delivery of a 1980s mall girl, but Priya is right: it's time to talk to the boss.

Her visit with Staxx and his divulgence, delivered just before he retreated back into his mind's murky haze, had cemented her course of action.

Kit walks into Lucinda's office to find her shoving a leather Hermès Ulysse portfolio, stuffed with background research she won't read, into a monstrous tote. "Douglas is forcing me to go to this ridiculous gallery showing for his niece," Lucinda says with a harrumph. Douglas is Lucinda's husband, though no one is quite sure what number husband he is. "Midtown traffic is going to be heinous."

"I need to talk to you briefly about something."

"All right," Lucinda says, hoisting the bag onto her shoulder. "Walk with me."

As they head toward the elevator bank, Kit rolls out the speech she's rehearsed. "I want to reiterate how much I appreciated the trip to L.A. And I know I don't have any time left to take, given how much I've been out lately. But I feel I really need to go to Martha's Vineyard. It's already October and a lot of the resources I need to check out there may close up or even disappear starting really soon."

Lucinda pivots in the waiting area, a look of annoyance on her face. "Oh, good Lord. We're still on the trail of the grandmother's missing summer?"

Kit takes in a deep breath. "Yes."

"Look," she says, with more than a mildly patronizing tone, "when you first brought this to me, I thought this could make a cute little story, but now I can't even remember the details. Actress or something?"

"A cute little story." *Everything I've ever known is upended and that's what you call it.* Kit feels herself stiffen. "Yes."

"We have sweeps next month and some really ambitious packages to put together, including the first ladies, and with Andy out on paternity leave I'm already a producer down. I just can't afford to let you go gallivanting off right now."

Kit wants to tell her that last month the Nielsen Company announced they were doing away with sweeps, which Lucinda would know if she ever perused any of the material stuffed into her pricey tote. She decides to ignore the use of the word "gallivanting," even though it's completely infuriating. "I would take the time without pay. Just a week. Two, tops. I hear you about the staffing. I would arrange coverage."

Lucinda delivers a silent, icy stare, sighs as she pushes the down elevator button. "I have to say, I am disappointed in you, Kit. I did allow, and even underwrite, the Los Angeles excursion. And now, to have you trying to guilt me into giving you more time off . . . frankly, I am a bit appalled at your selfishness. Particularly for some silly goose chase. I'm sorry. The answer is no."

Kit isn't sure what tips her over the edge—Lucinda's cruel, dismissive tone, the reminder that she is incapable of any form of empathy, the harsh summation of this life-changing event as a "silly goose chase"—but whatever it is, Kit feels it like something snapping inside her. She actually registers . . . relief. If she has any regret in this moment, it's for having spent so much time trying to curry the favor of this monstrous person to further her career. Perhaps that's what Nan is really paving for her here: a way out.

Always be brave.

"I see. In that case, I'll be handing in my notice."

Lucinda eyes her appraisingly as the elevator doors whoosh open. She walks casually in, spins around to face forward. Her eyes drift upward, toward the floor numbers, but her expression is seething. "Leave your key card on your desk" is all she says before the doors slide silently shut.

*

The Martha's Vineyard Historical Society, part of the Martha's Vineyard Museum, is housed in an elegant Shaker-style structure in the heart of Edgartown. Kit has tossed her bags onto the bed at her cozy

Airbnb on Beach Road and hustled here, anxious to begin her ground investigation.

The librarian at the front desk, a warm, cherubic older gentleman named Bernard, has dug out a bound volume of paper editions of the *Vineyard Gazette* from 1959 that she now flips through, a page at a time. She's going in order from May on, looking for any mentions of Nan, any stories that might confirm what Staxx told her about the aborted play, when she feels a presence next to her.

"Can I help you find something specific?" a voice asks.

Kit looks up and meets the gaze of a young man, late twenties maybe—she's terrible with ages—with dark brown curly hair that grazes over the collar of his hunter-green cashmere sweater. He has mischievous eyes the color of caramel and a manicured five o'clock shadow on his face, and he wears artsy round tortoiseshell eyeglasses that deliver a "hot for teacher" vibe. Josh the vampiric bassist he is not.

He leans down, rests his arms on the back of the chair next to hers. "Sorry," he says, "didn't mean to intrude." He smiles, and she feels something flare inside her. She catches herself staring a beat too long, quickly turns her attention back to the newspapers.

"No, no," she says. She absently turns a page. "I . . . my grandmother stayed here for the summer a long time ago, and I'm sort of on a little adventure trying to retrace her steps." Broad strokes. She doesn't need the whole island knowing what she's up to.

"Ah," he says. "So, sort of like a trip in her memory, then?"

"You might say that." She glances back up at him, trying to appear nonchalant. "Do you work here?"

He nods. "I'm finishing up my doctorate, or shall I say, attempting to, and doing a bunch of research for it here. I help out so they don't kick me out."

"He's being modest!" Bernard yells over from the front desk. "Seth knows more about the history of Martha's Vineyard than anyone. Ask him anything."

Kit arches an eyebrow. "You're a local, then?"

"Born and raised," he says. "But I teach at Brown as a G.A. Or at least

I usually do. I took this term off so I could finish the research and finally get this dissertation written." He pulls the seat out. "May I?"

She waves him in, trying to ignore the fact that she's now far too focused on his full lips. He extends a hand. "I'm Seth Cabot."

"Kit O'Neill."

"From?"

"New York."

"Ah. We get a lot of New Yorkers. What do you do in New York?"

"I'm a television news producer. Or at least I was, until recently."

"And you're trying to piece together your grandmother's summer here. So, I take it she's . . ."

"Gone, yes. A few months ago."

"I'm sorry."

"Thank you. This island was a very important place to her."

He nods. "It is for a lot of people. It's funny, Nantucket gets all the hype, but the Vineyard . . . you either get it or you don't. It's not glamorous like Nantucket or P-Town. It's more chill, maybe a bit more . . . mysterious."

"That's an interesting choice of adjective."

He grins. "I don't mean it in the *American Horror Story* kind of way. I mean that it has little hidden pockets and coves and history buried everywhere, just waiting to be discovered. It doesn't show all its cards."

"So is that what your dissertation's about? 'The Martha's Vineyard You Don't Know'?" *Ugh.* "Sorry. I was trying to be clever and that just came out condescending."

He laughs softly. "I certainly *hope* it has more depth than that, or my committee is going to toss me right out of the room during the defense. It's actually about the Wampanoag, the original Native American inhabitants of Noepe. That's what this island was originally called before those pesky Puritans showed up."

"And ruined everything."

He laughs. "Isn't that so like them?"

"And Martha, of Martha's Vineyard fame? How does she fit into this picture?"

"Oh, for that you have to go back to a British explorer named Bartholomew Gosnold. But that's a much longer story." He trains those caramel eyes on her. "Maybe I can tell it to you sometime over a glass of wine."

She did not come here for wine with a cute historian with good teeth and prep-school looks whom she began fantasizing about kissing maybe ten seconds after she laid eyes on him.

She smiles and says, "That would be nice."

August 11, 1959

Dear Cass—

Greetings from glorious Edgartown. The weather has been spectacular of late here in the height of summer, and I have been out and about enjoying it, drinking lime rickeys and dancing at the Chilmark Tavern. Ren took me to this place called the Lamppost in Oak Bluffs, and the owner told me Burl Ives used to sing there. "I have never seen a man eat so much popcorn in my life," he said. Ren and I roared.

Did I tell you Ren taught me how to swim? Me, who wouldn't even go into the pool at the Beverly Hills Hotel during that ridiculous photo shoot I did with the Marines from Camp Pendleton for that magazine feature on "the emerging young stars of Hollywood." Remember how the photographer wanted the boys to throw me into the pool for the photo? Thank God Sy was there to prevent it.

Play rehearsals are going well. I never imagined myself as much of a stage actress, but I am enjoying it. There is so much riding on this for Staxx, though—he's a nervous wreck, which is making me nervous, too. Ren's brother has been lurking around, ostensibly to check on his investment, but I suspect it has more to do with his mother than anything.

I don't think I told you that I had tea with her a few weeks ago. It was clear to me that she was on a fishing expedition to see how serious things were between Ren and me. Why is she meddling in his love life when he's a grown man? It makes no sense to me. But I can see why half the island worships her and the other half is scared to death. She's the type Gladys Cooper has been playing for decades.

Anyway, the tea went fine and I felt I held my own, but now the trouble is I never told Ren. It's clear they are deeply estranged, and I don't know why, but I do know he would not take kindly to the fact that I had spent time with her. It's all so silly, because it was nothing, but now it's been a few weeks and it feels like a secret. I keep trying to find the right time to bring it up, but then

I always talk myself out of it because selfishly, I don't want to ruin the moment. Now I wonder if maybe I don't need to at all? What do you think?

I'll let you know how things turn out with the play. Wish me luck.

Love,
Mercy

Nineteen

Mercy was resting her head on his chest, her right leg thrown over his right, casually circling his right nipple with her finger. She loved being able to do this, to take what she wanted, to be carnal, to be selfish, to want to give everything and to take everything, to be . . . in love. Ren lay back, relaxed, smoking a cigarette, looking out the bedroom window of the cottage as the cloudy sky slowly brightened.

"I've got to get up," he said. "I have a couple of jobs to get to."

She snuggled in closer. "No, no," she protested. "You promised you'd teach me how to make your famous vanilla apple pie."

"That was supposed to happen last night. But someone had other plans."

"Don't blame me for turning into a shameless hussy. That's all your fault."

He kissed her temple. "So it is."

It had been three weeks since the meeting with Brent Baker in Boston. Three weeks of unexpected bliss. Mercy had returned to the island with a new determination not to let other people dictate her future. She had made a collect call to Sy—he was still fuming about the cost—and explained the entire episode. He had offered to call the studio, even to call Kramer. But they both knew how Hollywood worked. Either the studio would overlook their new star writer's bad behavior in order to make a blockbuster, or Baker would go a step too far with the wrong actress attached to the wrong husband or executive and blow himself—and the project—up. That's how it always went. For all of her initial, and significant, disappointment, Mercy had quickly come to see it all as a sign from God that she was meant to come back here. Back to Ren.

He managed to extricate himself from her entanglement and clambered out of bed, slipping into his underwear and pants. "Maybe you should keep an outfit here," she said casually, propped on an elbow, "instead of always leaving looking like a dirty hamper." He cocked an eye at her, and she laughed. "Oh, my," she said, "was that too much of a commitment to suggest for the rogue oysterman?"

He grinned wickedly, picked up his pillow, and tossed it at her head. She deftly avoided it, and in one super-swift motion picked up her own pillow behind her and launched it over her head, straight at him. It hit him right in the midsection before dropping to the floor.

Ren's eyes danced with mischief. "Oh, lady, now you're in for it," he said, taking a few stalking steps toward the bed. Mercy began slowly retreating behind the covers. She dissolved into hysterical giggling as she prepared to fight him off—and happily lose. "No, no, Ren! Don't! I swear—"

He pounced back onto the bed, covering her body with his, kissing her neck, nibbling her ear, caressing her hair. She had unlocked something in him these past few weeks, a lightness she had been thrilled to discover. She had not verbally confessed her deepest feelings. Nor had he. But somehow, words didn't need to be spoken. They knew.

They made love again. Once more, they found themselves where they had begun that morning, wrapped around the sheets and one another. "Tell me more about you," Mercy said, delivering a soft kiss to his clavicle.

He exhaled deeply. "You seem to want to know everything about me."

"Don't you want to know everything about me?"

"No."

"Why not?"

"Because who we *were* doesn't matter," he said. "It's who we are now that does."

She was quiet for a moment. "I just want you to let me in."

"You are in."

"It doesn't always feel like it." She was circling back into sketchy territory, risking ruining a perfect morning. But even now, after three more weeks of beach walks and fudge from Averill's Bakery and window shopping (she was still paying winsome visits to the sapphire necklace), and one fun and raucous clambake sponsored by the volunteer firemen's association that had ended with banjo playing in the wee hours, her mind kept coming back to his family, to his estrangement from them.

Why did she need to know? She thought perhaps it had to do with Louis, with being blithely unaware that the man she had been planning to marry was someone else entirely, keeping secrets. She needed to be sure that in risking her heart this time around, all the cards were showing.

"I'm sorry," he said. "I'm doing the best I can."

She nodded into his furry chest. "I know. I'm sorry, too. I'll try to be more understanding."

He sat up on his elbows. "Would teaching you how to make the best vanilla apple pie in the world help?"

She grinned. "Definitely."

*

He slid the pie into the oven. Already the tiny kitchen smelled heavenly. He had been methodical and patient, showing her how to roll out the pie crust, boil the sugar, pinch the dough, assemble the gooey mix of sliced apples, caramel sauce, vanilla, and lemon zest, then delicately lattice the top. Ren now stood at the sink, washing crusty residue off his hands.

"Who taught you how to do this?" Mercy asked, sitting on the kitchen counter, sipping a cup of tea.

"My grandmother. She was a terrific baker."

"Which is tougher: baking or oystering?"

"Oystering, for sure. You plant bushels of scallop shells on the bottom of the Pond and hope you get a heavy set, but there are times when blight wipes out the whole crop. There's a lot of luck involved. Baking, on the other hand, if you follow the instructions and have the right ingredients—a hit every time." He opened the oven door slightly, eyeballing the pie. "I always threaten to enter this at the ag fair, but I never do."

"What's the ag fair?"

"The Martha's Vineyard Agricultural Society's Annual Cattle Show and Fair," he said. "It sounds a lot more formal than it is. It's out in West Tisbury. Been held almost a hundred years now. We'll go. But I guess it won't be so novel for you. I'm sure you went to your share of county fairs growing up."

"We were more church potluck kind of folks," she said. "Daddy wasn't one for crowds."

He eyed her sitting on the counter, clad only in his fisherman's sweater—they'd had an unexpected cold front a bit ago, and now on cooler nights she practically lived in the thing. He smiled at her devilishly. "If only the church ladies could get a look at you now."

She hopped off the counter, wrapped her arms around his waist. "I'm sure they'd say I look swell," she said. She reached up, began playing with his scruffy beard. "And look who's talking, mister—is that a gray hair or two I see? You're beginning to look like old Quill Sewards."

His eyes constricted, and she knew instantly the grave mistake she'd just made.

He pushed her away with enough muscle to send a message as his eyes flashed with accusation. "How do you know what Quill Sewards looks like?" His voice was low, the words deliberate. "How do you even know who he is?"

They both knew there was only one way she could have known who he was. And that was if she'd been in the drawing room at Sycamore.

"I . . . OK, Ren, you have to let me explain."

"Explain what?"

She grabbed his arm in panic. "Yes, I was at Sycamore. Your mother invited me to tea."

His voice was even lower now, a whisper laced with quiet wrath. "When?"

She paused. "A while ago. Your brother took me."

His eyes were a carousel of anger, disbelief, betrayal. A bullet might have had less impact.

"Ren, I was going to tell you, I swear, you have to believe me," she said, rambling, trying to get it all out as quickly as possible so she could move on to the apologizing, the making up. She told him about how Mint had written her, how she had actually forgotten about it until Patrick had reminded her after rehearsal at the theater, how it had just been a nice, short tea and that they had not even discussed him and it was all nothing and then she'd had to go to Boston and she meant to tell him when she got back and he had to know she would never—

He shook his arm free. "You got back from Boston weeks ago," he said. "*Weeks*. And you never thought to mention this. After you knew about my relationship with my family. How hard it was for me to even speak about it. You knew, and you kept it from me. All this time."

Tears sprang to her eyes. Far worse was seeing them beginning to form in his.

He stalked out of the kitchen and she scurried after him like a mother chasing an escaping toddler, desperate to keep him there, to explain, to let him scream and yell if he wanted, to get it all out, but then to begin retracing the steps back to a few hours ago, to waking up in each other's arms.

Ren scooped up the rest of his things, shoved his feet into shoes. Mercy kept babbling, explaining, pleading, hating herself for her own debasement in this moment but feeling she deserved it. She was frantic to calm the storm. The storm had other ideas.

He stalked out of the bedroom toward the front door.

"Ren, please!" Mercy screamed through her tears. "I'm sorry! You have to believe me!"

He spun around. The wounded look on his face was worse than anything she had ever witnessed. "I trusted you."

"Don't you see, I was just trying to find out who you are. The only thing I have ever wanted is for you to let me in. People who love one another have to let each other in."

His eyes were pure ice. "I don't love you."

He turned and walked out, slamming the door behind him.

She collapsed onto her knees. In the recesses of the kitchen, a bell tinged. The pie was done.

Twenty

Ren found his mother in the study, sipping coffee and flipping through an issue of *Town & Country*. She prided herself on her ability to remain implacable in any situation, a trait she had certainly not exhibited as a young wife, but which she'd honed in widowhood. But his stormy entrance into the foyer and stomping into the room had caught her off guard, reflected in the momentary look of panic that briefly drifted over her face.

"What are you up to, Mother?" he thundered.

"Why, it's lovely to see you, too, Warren," Mint said, gently closing the magazine. "It's been some time since you've graced us with your presence here."

"Not long enough." Ren took a step closer. He could see her twitch momentarily. Controlling Ellenanne and Patrick was one thing. Their history, his and hers, was far more complicated. As she might say, "untidy." "I will ask you again: What are you up to?"

She shook her head slightly. "You're speaking in riddles. I don't know what you're referring to."

"Don't play coy. It doesn't suit you. Why did you invite Mercy Welles here?"

Mint casually picked up the coffeepot, began refilling her own cup and then pouring another. "Have some coffee, Warren. It'll calm your nerves."

"In five seconds I am going to take that pot and I am going to smash it against the wall if you do not answer me. And that will be just the start. I am not playing games here."

Mint looked at him appraisingly. She had seen him out in public, of course—it was a small island—but she was trying to remember the last time he'd actually been *in* the house. A few years now. The day Ellenanne had left. He'd taken her to the ferry.

"A son begins spending time with a young Hollywood actress, his mother is curious to know her," she said. "It's that simple."

"Nothing with you is ever simple."

"Oh, do stop being so dramatic, Warren."

Another voice, behind him. "What's going on here?"

Ren turned to see Patrick walking cautiously into the room. "I could hear you two all the way upstairs," he said. "Ren, what are you doing here?"

Poor Patrick. He had been so young when their father died, so confused about everything that happened after. He'd only been a small child, robbed of any semblance of normalcy. Not that what had come before all that had been so normal, either. But as Ren and Ellenanne had retreated to their respective corners, plotting their escapes, Patrick had clung to Mint, unsure and afraid, perfecting the role of the good son and confidante that he'd played ever since. Ren had tried to maintain some semblance of a relationship with him—they'd gone to a Red Sox game last year—but their mother was somehow always there between them, an enveloping fog obscuring each brother from the other.

"Stay out of this, Patrick," Ren said, turning back to Mint. "This is between Mother and me."

"It seems Warren is upset that I had the gall to invite Miss Welles to tea."

Patrick scoffed. "It's not a big deal, Ren," he said. "It was barely an hour."

"Nice of you to tell me," Ren replied. "Mercy said *you* drove her here."

Patrick shrugged. He picked up the extra cup of coffee, began adding cream and sugar. "I have to say, though," he said casually, "she's a kicky little palomino. Well done."

"Shut your mouth," Ren said.

Patrick smirked. "Ooooo, Mother, I think we've hit a nerve," he said, taking a sip of the coffee. "Has our stoic, stony Ren finally found . . . love?"

Ren's punch was swift and brutal, landing squarely on the corner of Patrick's jaw and sending the coffee cup and saucer flying across the room, where they hit the parquet floor and shattered into pieces. Patrick bolted backward, landing awkwardly on the side of an over-stuffed wingback chair. Mint leapt to her feet.

"Warren! You will leave this house immediately!"

"Yeah, brother," Patrick said, massaging his jaw, "wouldn't want to keep that little piece waiting," causing Mint to declare, "Oh, Patrick, shut up!"

Ren lunged for him, grabbing him by the collar with both hands and shoving him up against the fireplace mantel. "One more word, little brother," Ren whispered. "Go ahead. One. More. Word. I dare you."

"Warren! Stop!" Mint flew over to the mantel, swatting at Ren's arm, trying in vain to get him to release his grip. "I said stop!"

They stood, the three of them, no one moving, no one speaking, for seconds that felt like hours, the only sound in the room the heaving breaths of the brothers. Finally, Ren let go with a final push. The two men kept their eyes locked, unblinking, as Ren slowly backed away.

Mint spoke quietly. "It's time for you to go, Warren."

"I'll go when I'm damn well ready to go."

"You will not speak to me that way."

He turned to her, his eyes ablaze. "You don't get to tell me how to speak. You don't get to tell me to do anything."

She returned his angry stare. "I will remind you that this is still my house. I am still the head of this family."

"You *destroyed* this family!"

Mint's eyes glittered with defiance. "As usual, you have no idea what you're talking about. Did you know your Hollywood concubine has been asking questions all over this island about me, about us? She spent an afternoon grilling poor Grace Chadwick in her kitchen! And that's just the tip of the iceberg. I have a duty to protect this family's good name."

Ren glowered back. "This family's name hasn't been good in fifteen years," he said. "You made sure of that."

It was Patrick's turn to speak. His voice was low, measured. "OK, Ren. You've made your point. Enough."

Ren pointed a warning finger at Mint. "Stay out of my life. I will not repeat that. But let me assure you, if I have to come back here," he said, spitting out the words, "next time it will not end this well."

He stalked out of the room, slamming the front door so hard it wobbled the vase on the foyer table.

*

Mercy sat at a table for two near the window at the White Whale, staring out onto the street. The place was crowded and fairly noisy, reflecting the height of the tourist season. She had wanted to come back and see the pub at its honky-tonk best and had now gotten her wish, only to regret it. At this moment she wasn't in the mood for crowds, for conviviality. She was in the mood for Ren to walk through the door, come up to her, and tell her that he forgave her and that everything was going to be all right.

She thought back to earlier today, to what she had decided to do and whether, in hindsight, it had been a huge mistake. Why had she even done it? Maybe because Labor Day was quickly approaching, and with it an official end to her island adventure. Maybe because it had been a week since Ren had shut her out, and she had nothing left to lose. Nothing left to find but the truth.

Mercy had gone to the public library, flipped through the Boston city phone directory, and found Ellenanne Sewards's address. What would Ren say when he found out she'd written his sister? It would only make everything worse. But even if he was angry all over again, perhaps it would force him to confront her, to see her, to *talk* to her again.

Opening night of *The Rose of Aquinnah* was just four days away. There were pockets of excitement about it around the island, people occasionally stopping to gawk at her on the street or asking for an autograph. She fought the distraction of the loss of Ren by continuing to remind herself of what this could do for Staxx's future. And also, perhaps, for herself. She'd taken a bus from Nebraska armed with nothing but guile and a dream, and a few years later had been nominated for an Academy Award. It was time to remember she was an actress, and a good one at that.

Now she sat waiting for Vera, a long-promised lunch she had already begged out of once but could not again. Not that it really mattered anymore. Their initial bargain was long moot. But Mercy was nothing if not a polite Midwestern girl, even if while here she had also become quite a prurient one. A deal was a deal. It was only for another two weeks, when the lease on the cottage expired.

And then . . . what? It was the question she had been putting off, too busy relishing the gloriousness of the romantic days and nights that had followed her return from Boston and l'affaire Brent Baker. Her Hollywood life seemed so distant now, so . . . unimportant. What was waiting for her back there? And was it more meaningful than what she had found here?

Bridie passed by, holding an empty tray, and plopped down in the chair opposite her. "Ginger ale," she said, nodding at Mercy's half-full glass. "If you don't mind my sayin' so, you look like you could use something a wee bit stronger."

Mercy smiled weakly. "Perceptive."

"Want to talk about it?"

"Not really."

"Do it anyway. You'll feel better."

Maybe it was the timing. Or maybe it was just Bridie's lilting Irish accent. Mercy was reticent about sharing the whole, sordid tale, but she knew Bridie was right—keeping it to herself and continuing to ruminate, replaying everything over and over in her head, wasn't going to help, either. So out it came, in all its complicated glory, ending with Ren's unceremonious departure from the cottage. "I just wish I could understand why it was such a big deal that I had tea with his mother," she said. "We never really discussed him."

Bridie nodded in sympathy. "You have to understand something, love. Ren has been through a lot with Mint. They all have. She hasn't always been the duchess of the manor. In her younger days she was a very different woman."

"How so?"

"Remember, she wasn't born into the fancy world she married into. Being Jasper Sewards's wife was hard, and she didn't bear it well. She felt everyone was looking at her, looking *down* at her, almost like she was the mistress instead of the wife. And you have to remember the year-round community here is small, and was even smaller then. There wasn't any place to hide. There was constant chatter that she'd trapped him into marriage."

"So Ren was . . . ?"

"No. Born ten months after the wedding, almost to the day. But that didn't stop the talk. And Mint was very sensitive to that. She started drinking, taking pills to calm herself, that kind of thing." Bridie looked around the room, leaned in a bit. "God strike me for gossiping, but she was a bad mother to those children. I'm not sayin' it was all her fault, mind you—Jasper could be a terrible man, and I don't like to speak ill of the dead but it is what it is. It was very hard on them. Especially Ren. He took on the role of protector of the other two. And her."

"So Ren's father? He was . . . hurting them?"

Bridie stiffened. "He was not a good man. I'll leave it at that."

A shrill voice from slightly above them interrupted. "Hi! Sorry I'm late!"

Vera was wearing a loud blue gingham dress that was a bit too snug, making her look like a slightly chubby Dorothy on her way to Oz. Bridie stood to relinquish the seat, when Vera spied people she knew at a back table and began waving. "Oh, I just have to pop over and say hello," she said, tapping the table. "Be right back!"

With Vera safely out of earshot, Bridie leaned back down to Mercy with some final words. "Watch what you say to that one."

Mercy looked over at Vera, now talking animatedly to a couple. "Why do you say that?"

Bridie stood erect. "It's always the ones who look like the simple-tons," she said, "who have the most devious minds."

Twenty-one

Mercy pulled up outside the house in Oak Bluffs to find Staxx waiting. Today had been the final dress rehearsal before Saturday's opening, and it had all gone beautifully. The cast had been in a great mood, one elevated even further when Bridie and Dennis had thoughtfully showed up with sandwiches and beer at lunch break.

Staxx had changed into a beige linen suit with a sky-blue shirt and bow tie, a matching pocket square folded perfectly into his front breast pocket. The contrast of the light suit against his luminescent dark skin was arresting. He almost skipped down the front steps to open her door, like a jumpy suitor trying to impress his date before escorting her into the formal.

His family was throwing a dinner in his honor to celebrate the play opening this weekend. Evidently there had been a spirited discussion about throwing it *after* the opening, but Staxx's aunts had said they were old and not going to eat dinner at eleven o'clock at night, no matter what the occasion.

The gabled gingerbread house was one of several all in a row, painted in hues of hunter green, orange, and maroon, with a thin trail of white trim along the porch railing. It made Mercy's cottage look like slum housing.

"I really wish you had let me drive you," he said as she alighted from the jeep. "I am feeling very ungallant."

"It didn't make any sense for me to come with you from the theater and then make you drive me all the way back there to get the jeep."

"Right. Because it's *so* far."

"I can make my own way around. I am a modern young lady."

He grinned. "Yes, you are."

She looked over his shoulder. "This house is adorable. Shall we go in?"

He pulled her gently aside. "I think you may need a little lay of the land first. Sort of like a . . . passport to Oak Bluffs."

She pushed her brows together in confusion. "I need a passport to go from Edgartown to Oak Bluffs? How did nobody inform me of this?"

"Two similar towns, two completely different worlds," he said. "You're used to being only with white people, listening to white people, looking at the world the way white people do. This is the very opposite of that."

"What are you trying to say?"

"Only that we're used to this experience. Everyone here, we're used to being the only people who look like us in a room. You're not. And it can be . . . jarring for white people when they realize that, for the first time, *they're* the ones who are different."

She hadn't really thought about it. But what did it matter? She had never considered herself prejudiced. "You forget I live in Hollywood. I know lots of Negroes."

He scoffed gently. "Smiling at the people picking up your plates after lunch doesn't count." She began a retort and he put up a hand. "And if you mention saying hello to Sammy Davis Junior I am going to slap you upside the head."

She folded her arms, smirking. "OK then, professor, educate me."

"This won't be different than any other party you go to. Except some of the lingo you won't understand, some of the food you will never have eaten, everyone will talk and laugh a lot louder than you're used to, and Uncle Lester will look at you like you're an exotic museum exhibit."

She burst into laughter. Then he did.

"And Miz West is here," he said.

"Miss West?"

"Dorothy West. She's the founder of the Cottagers Club. They're basically a bunch of fancy Black ladies who make sure that the white people know we're here and just as good as anyone else. They raise money for charity. But mainly, they exist because it gives Miz West an excuse to write about them in a column in the *Gazette*."

Mercy smiled wryly. "This is more like Hollywood than I thought."

He crooked his elbow to her. "Lesson over. Shall we venture in?"

She threaded her arm into his. "Ready if you are."

For all of Staxx's preamble, nothing could have prepared Mercy for the world that unfolded inside the house. Men in beautiful, fitted suits held court, drank brandy, and elegantly smoked cigarettes in small pockets peppered throughout, some holding quiet but urgent conversations, others engaging in raucous, animated storytelling that had their respective circles in stitches. The women were a varied lot in both age and size, though each seemed to boast the same silky skin and pleasant smile, none more so than Dorothy West herself, who with her heart-shaped face and elegant manners looked like a sister of Lena Horne. Each room was a hive buzzing with everything from idle island conversation and political arguments to family updates and discussions of literature. Mercy was astonished to discover a world she never knew existed: here were the Black doctors, lawyers, professors, and artists who had found a place of their own to build a community, in a country where none of them could join a country club.

To a person, the guests greeted her with impeccable manners and genteel civility, even if several couldn't quite hide their astonishment at the waifish white girl suddenly in their midst. Navigating the food proved thorny. Fried fish, cornbread, salt pork, mustard greens, hush puppies, sweet potato pie—how did so many of them stay so slender? Mercy nibbled just enough to be polite.

After everyone had eaten, a wizened older gentleman stood in the middle of the living room with a raised glass, gently tapping on it with a spoon to get everyone's attention. He was Benjamin Coleman, one of Staxx's seemingly endless supply of uncles. "My dear friends and family, I'd like to say a few words in praise of my talented nephew," he said. "He has made us all so very proud. His first play is being produced, and now the world will see his genius. Now, some of you may recall that I have done some writing—"

"I *knew* he'd find a way to bring it back to hisself!" a gregarious woman holding a large piece of cake screamed from the back of the dining room, and the house erupted into roars. Soon others were shouting, talking over one another, until Benjamin once more took up the clanging spoon more forcefully in a clumsy effort to restore order.

"All right, all right now!" he shouted. "As I was saying, I want to offer a toast to my talented nephew. And to the young lady from Hollywood who graciously agreed to star in his play." He scanned the crowd. "How *will* I find her in this gathering?"

More laughter as all eyes turned to Mercy, standing near a mantel clock in the living room. Staxx was called front and center to deliver a few words. He talked movingly about his dream of being produced, the encouragement he had received from the people here. He asked Mercy to speak, but she demurred—emotion got caught in her throat as she understood, perhaps for the first time, what this moment truly meant for him.

It was after nine when he walked her out to her car. "Thank you for a lovely evening," Mercy said. She turned around and gave him a delicate kiss on the cheek, which did not go unnoticed by two men standing on the porch, smoking. Both delivered hard glares; one gave a slight harrumph. They walked slowly back into the house.

"Ignore them," Staxx said. "And no, it's not because of that."

"Because of what?"

"You're thinking they did that because you're a white lady giving a colored man a kiss. But that isn't why they're mad."

"Why are they mad?"

"Because you remind them that I am not doing this at the Shearer."

Mercy knew about the Shearer. Technically called Shearer Cottage, it had been built in 1912 as a hotel catering to Black visitors and now also operated as an open-air theater staging Negro productions. "So, why didn't you?" she asked.

"Look, the Shearer is real important to Black folks on this island. It's important to *me*," he said. "But there was gonna be a whole lotta politics having a 'white play' put on at one of the only Black stages in the country. And it wasn't worth it. What they're really mad about is that I wrote a 'white play' at all."

"You could have written a play with Negro characters."

He shook his head. "That's just the point. Why do I gotta get stuck only writing what I already know? There's no future in that. No offense, but I don't want to write *A Raisin in the Sun*. It's brilliant. But I've lived that, I don't need to write it. I want to write *The Teahouse of the August Moon*. I don't care if they think I'm being all high and mighty, or forgetting where I came from. That's their damn business. I have bigger dreams. And I am done apologizing for them." He smiled weakly. "And I'm sorry for cussin' in front of you."

"I'm not quite as delicate as you think." She touched his arm gently. "And I think you have a really bright future ahead of you. Talent always wins."

He laughed. "Oh, Miss Mercy, you have a lot to learn."

She eyed him quizzically. "I thought I *was* learning. What's left?"

"A lot. Like what it's really like to be a Negro in the United States. You have no idea what it feels like to walk into a restaurant and see a bunch of empty tables and have the maître d' say, 'Sorry, we're all full.' Or to stand on a street corner in New York trying to hail a taxi and seeing empty cab after empty cab fly by, like you're invisible. In our world, talent doesn't win at all." He took in her wounded expression. "Don't feel so bad. We're used to it. We just have to work harder for our breaks, is all. Just a fact of life."

"It shouldn't be."

He shrugged. "Lots of things that shouldn't be." He opened the door of the jeep. "Now, you drive safe and go right home. I need you fresh and rested for opening night."

"Aye, aye, captain," she said.

He backed away and she opened her purse to take out her car key. *Hold it*—she began rummaging through the bag. *Oh, no*. The car key was there, but not her key to the cottage. She recalled locking the front door when she'd left for dress rehearsal. But then later, afterward . . . she'd taken out her comb and lipstick at her dressing table to freshen up for the party. The house key must have slipped out of her bag. That meant it had to still be at the theater. *Damn it!* She had been meaning to put all the keys on one ring.

Mercy gave the horn a slight tap and Staxx came ambling back over. She explained the dilemma. "Do you have a key to the theater?"

He did. Ignoring her protests, he insisted on accompanying her, saying it wasn't right for a young lady to be roaming around a dark theater by herself at night, even if it was on Martha's Vineyard. He would borrow his cousin's car, follow her there.

*

There was an ethereal beauty to the theater cloaked in darkness, the only light the moonlight streaming in through the skylight above the stage, where the set of the diner stood ready, waiting for Saturday night's opening curtain. Mercy and Staxx stood quietly, looking out at the rows of empty seats.

He grabbed her hand. "Thank you," he whispered, "for giving me this."

She looked at him. "No," she replied. "Thank *you* for giving me this." She squeezed his hand before letting go. "I'm just going to dash to the dressing room and hopefully find the key. Be right back."

Her hopes for a quick retrieval—that the key would be right on the table, or right by the chair—were immediately dashed. For several minutes she poked around the small dressing room, until her luck turned: she found the key under the wastepaper basket.

Mercy rushed back out onto the stage. "Good news! I found—"

She spied his body immediately.

He was sprawled on his stomach on the left side of the stage. She ran toward him, dropping to her knees. She began frantically shaking him. "Staxx! Staxx! Can you hear me?!"

She cupped the back of his head. Something wet. She held up her fingers.

Blood.

She jumped to her feet, frantically surveying the dimness.

Someone was here.

Her heart pounded. There was ringing in her ears. A phone. Where was the phone? Somewhere in the back office, no doubt. No. Better to just run out the back door where they'd come in, flag someone down to call the police, get an ambulance.

She fled to the back door, but it wouldn't open. Why wouldn't it open? She looked at the door, frantically twisted the knob again. Nothing.

New plan. She tore back toward the stage, down the side stairs, up the aisle and through the small lobby, pushing the exit bar of the front door. But it, too, wouldn't budge. She tried again, and again, but while the bar kept moving the door did not. Locked.

She fought the growing wave of panic now roiling her body. Someone else was here. They had attacked Staxx.

Her mind whirled, trying to calculate her options. She could make a run for backstage, try to find the phone. But who was here? Where were they hiding?

And then, a singular, acrid smell.

Smoke.

She lurched back toward the inside of the theater. A line of bright orange flames was racing its way up the left side of the stage curtain, steadily advancing toward the top.

August 16, 1959

Dear Miss Sewards,

I apologize for just randomly writing you, but desperate times and desperate measures and all of that, I suppose.

I am currently staying for the summer on Martha's Vineyard, and in that time I have become acquainted with your family, most specifically your brother Ren. He and I have gotten very close these past few months, but I seem to have ruined it all by inquiring too much about your family and its history here, including accepting an invitation to tea with your mother at Sycamore.

I honestly don't mean to draw you into all of this, but I am left bereft and confused by this turn of events. Any light you might be able to shed here, and more specifically on how I might repair my relationship with Ren, would be greatly appreciated. I have no doubt if he finds out I have written you he will be even more cross with me, but I feel at this point I have little left to lose. I care about him deeply. If I didn't, I wouldn't be going to these lengths to try and repair this rift.

I am not trying to rip open old wounds from your family, but merely understand what is happening and how I can be there for him. He has talked so affectionately of you that I felt it was worth the chance to inquire if you might be able to offer any insight or assistance that might be useful.

If you do not wish to respond, I will of course completely understand. Just please know my motives are pure and only grounded in my deep affection for your brother.

Most sincerely,
Mercy Welles

Twenty-two

Following her initial visit to the historical society, Kit has spent two days exploring Martha's Vineyard. She wants to get a better sense of the place, its history, its people. Wants to capture a feeling, a sense of what her grandmother found here that fateful summer. She's had amazing fish and chips with tangy tartar sauce and malt vinegar at the Newes from America pub, sat in the serene quiet of the Old Whaling Church, bought a sweatshirt for Priya at the Black Dog General Store. She's beginning to get it. There is a peace and calm here that is uniquely renewing.

On her third morning she walks back through the front door of the society and finds Seth Cabot behind the desk, rummaging through some old maps. The only other person here is an elderly gentleman sitting at one of the wooden tables, who appears to be perusing a collection of vintage postcards. Seth glances up as she approaches, and his face breaks out into a big smile. Kit again tries to ignore how good-looking he is, and that she spent just a little extra time this morning picking out a flattering outfit—light pink crewneck sweater, hip-hugging jeans, canvas jacket that brings out her eyes—just in case he was here.

"Flying solo today?" she asks him.

"Bernard's at a doctor's appointment," he says, pushing the maps over to one side. "Can I help with something?"

"Oh, that's OK. He told me he'd call some of the old-timers to see if anyone remembered my grandmother from back in 1959. I wanted to see if he'd had any luck."

"Ah, right. How goes the great memory lane tour?"

"I'm sort of working from the outside in," she says, even though she has no idea what that even means. "I want to keep looking through those old *Gazettes* from 1959."

"Coming right up," he says.

She spends the next hour combing through the rest of the old newspapers. She finds a front-page story announcing that film star Mercy Welles is going to star in *The Rose of Aquinnah,* which features a wonderful photo of Nan laughing atop one of the horses on the Flying Horses Carousel. And then, in the August 27, 1959, edition, the story she's been looking for, right on the front page. The story that confirms what Staxx had told her.

HAVEN PLAYHOUSE DAMAGED IN FIRE
PLAY WITH FILM STAR MERCY WELLES IS CANCELED
Damage will take "months" to repair

VINEYARD HAVEN—A fast-moving fire swept through the rear of the Martha's Vineyard Playhouse on Spring Street last Wednesday night, just days before the theater was set to open a week-long run of a new play headlined by Academy Award–nominated film star Mercy Welles.

Officials said the cause of the fire, which was contained to the stage and rear of the theater, was still under investigation, but that it was possible faulty electrical wiring was the culprit. Firemen from the Tisbury, Edgartown, and Oak Bluffs companies responded quickly to the scene and had the fire under control within an hour, according to Fire Chief Stanley C. Morgan. No one was in the theater at the time, and there were no reported injuries.

"We're lucky this happened during the off-hours, when no one was present," Chief Morgan said.

Miss Welles, who was nominated for a Best Supporting Actress Oscar earlier this year for her role in the drama "The Lovely

Dream," has been summering on Martha's Vineyard and was set to make her local stage debut in the new play "The Rose of Aquinnah," written by local playwright Stanton Williams, a resident of Oak Bluffs. Theater officials did not have a timetable on when the play might be rescheduled.

The theater opened in 1930 . . .

Seth makes copies of both stories and hands them to her. Kit digs into her bag, extracts the notecard, along with the photograph of the mystery man and Nan. "Thanks. Now maybe you might be able to help me with these. Do you have any idea what 'Sycamore' is? Or who the man in this photo might be?"

Something registers in Seth's eyes—a flicker of recognition—and then vanishes just as quickly. He examines the handwritten message on the card closely: *Nancy—Something to remember me by, or to stow away in the attic. R.* He turns his attention to the photo, his eyes focusing intently. Finally, he looks up.

"The woman in the photo? That's your grandmother?"

"Yes. As you can see from the story you just photocopied, she was scheduled to perform in a play here"—Kit pulls out the playbill for *The Rose of Aquinnah*—"but because of the fire it never opened."

"It seems like your grandmother had herself quite a little adventure," Seth says. "No wonder you're retracing her steps."

"You don't know the half of it. Actually, I drove past the site of the theater, but it's not there anymore."

"No, that particular theater was torn down sometime in the 1970s. The one on Church Street was a Masonic lodge until 1982, when it was bought and turned into what's now the Vineyard Playhouse. It was completely renovated a few years ago. Though today the flashier stuff is staged at the Performing Arts Center."

All very interesting—if she'd been a tourist on holiday. She tapped on the notecard. "Do you know what 'Sycamore' is, or where it is?"

He picked it up, nodding. "Yes. Sycamore is the name of the old Sewards estate here in Edgartown. Situated on a cliff overlooking the harbor."

Kit felt the hairs standing up on her arms. Finally, a strong lead. "The Sewards? They're a family here?"

"More than that. One of the founding families of Martha's Vineyard. Been here since the sixteen hundreds."

"Are they still here?"

"Yes. Or at least a branch is."

"Can you make an introduction for me? It's likely that the man in this picture is the same man who wrote the note. Maybe he was part of the family. He might even still be alive."

Seth winces. "That's going to be a little tricky. The Sewardses are *notoriously* private people. I can't imagine they're going to want to talk to a television producer who wants to poke around in their family history, however innocently."

"But I'm not a television producer. At least not at the moment," Kit says. She tries to keep the pleading, the desperation, out of her voice. "We don't have to tell them that part of my bio, do we? Honestly, this is not a 'story' for me. I just want to know what happened to my grandmother that summer."

He eyes her quizzically. "There seems to be more to this than you're telling."

She has a decision to make. Can she trust him? She holds his gaze, her mind whirring. At this point, does she have a choice? He is a lifelong islander and a historian whose help will be invaluable if she wants to get to the bottom of this once and for all. Her unexpected, visceral attraction to him—he is so unlike anyone she's ever been interested in—aside, Seth Cabot is, she knows, her best bet to solve the long-buried riddle of Mercy Welles.

"Perhaps we should sit down," she says.

And so Kit tells him the story. How Nan raised her and Claire, Nan's death, the cleaning out of the house, finding the box with the souvenirs inside, learning about her grandmother's secret past, the trip to see Cass Goldman in L.A. She leaves out certain elements, like Claire's reason for wanting to leave it all alone. She ends with her visits to Aaron Sigmund in Philadelphia and to Staxx in New York before arriving here.

Seth issues a low whistle. "Wow. That is some tale."

"Yeah, I know. But that's just it: I don't have the ending. But if I can discover who 'R.' is—I assume the mystery man in the photo—perhaps I can learn what happened. What made Nan turn her back on her career in Hollywood and reinvent herself as someone else in New York."

He cocks his head. "Maybe it was less a reinvention of who she *was* than a rediscovering of who she'd *been*. Lots of people walk away from fame because they determine it's not worth it."

Kit shrugs. "Maybe."

Seth picks up the photo, inspects it again. "Well, I can contact the family, see if they'll talk to you. But I can't promise anything." He smiles. "But if they do agree, I will be collecting a finder's fee."

Kit experiences a shiver of delight. How long has it been since she's been truly flirted with? "Oh, really. And what might that be?"

"Dinner. You're buying."

She crosses her arms. "And if they don't agree?"

"Still dinner. I'm buying."

She fights to contain the beam now breaking out on her face. She extends her hand. "Deal."

*

"So, how are you feeling?"

Priya's voice, on Bluetooth, fills the rental car as Kit pulls over on South Water Street, waiting to make the turn onto the access road to the Sewards estate. She's early.

"Nervous," Kit says. "I have to say, given what Seth told me, I'm kind of surprised that they agreed to this at all. But I think he vouched for me. It'll be worth the dinner I now owe him."

"Mmmm . . . Seth," Priya purrs. "I googled his photo. That jawline! It's like if Ryan Reynolds had been an egghead instead of just pretty. Delish."

"Down, girl. We're not here for that."

"Mmm hmm. Keep telling yourself that."

"I feel like I'm getting close, Priya. That the answers are just within my grasp."

"Then go get them. And then please come home so we can drink pink champagne at Gotham and I can spill all of the ridiculous Lucinda stories you've been missing."

Kit glances into the rearview, checking her makeup for the eleventh time. "OK, it's showtime. Wish me luck."

Ten minutes later Kit is shown through the front door of the grand house that is Sycamore by Laura Milleneux, the current descendant living within its storied walls. Laura is a slim, attractive mid-fiftysomething woman in a cream sweater and black slacks with dark, wavy hair and a perfect manicure. She waves Kit into the sitting room, where a wooden tray with a coffee service sits on a burnished mahogany table. "Thank you so much for seeing me," Kit says, taking a seat on one of the sumptuous club chairs by the fireplace.

"My pleasure," Laura says, beginning to pour. "Seth tells me you have a bit of a mystery on your hands."

"You might say that. My grandmother was an actress in the 1950s who was on her way to what appeared to be a rather successful career. But then she came here in the summer of 1959 and never went back to it."

"Well, that doesn't seem so mysterious. I'm sure a lot of actors reconsider their career paths, do they not?"

"I'm sure they do. But the fact is she kept that whole part of her life a secret. I only found out about her . . . 'other identity' after she died. So here I am, trying to fill in the gaps. Which brings me to this card and this photo." As Kit hands them over, a man with salt-and-pepper hair, dressed in a Burberry golf sweater and chinos, walks into the room. He introduces himself as Mark, Laura's husband. He sits down on the arm of the sofa, looking over Laura's shoulder at the photo. "Wow" is all he says.

"Yes," Laura adds, nodding. "That's definitely my uncle Ren."

"Is he still . . ." Kit inquires delicately, "with us?"

Laura sighs. "I'm sorry, no. Actually, there's no one left from that generation, I'm afraid. My father, Patrick, died more than five years ago. And my aunt, Ellenanne, died relatively young, about twenty years ago now. Breast cancer."

Kit's heart sinks. "And the card? Does that handwriting look like Ren's?"

Mark nods. "Yes. I handled all of his legal affairs later in life. He always signed his notes with his initial. It was sort of his trademark."

"Do you happen to recall him ever mentioning the name Mercy Welles?"

They look at one another. "No," Laura says. "Uncle Ren was not exactly a big talker, if you know what I mean. I think he probably talked to his oysters more than people. He was more the strong, quiet type. A Clint Eastwood kind of guy."

"Did he marry? Have children?" Kit asks.

"No, he never did," Laura says. "He kept to himself most of the time." She leans forward, clasping her hands together. "I'm sorry. We're not being very helpful."

Kit studies Laura's expression of sympathy, then smiles weakly. "No, it's fine. It was a long time ago. It's only natural the trail would be pretty cold."

They make additional small talk. Finally, Kit gathers her things, and Laura and Mark walk her to the door. They tell her to call if she has additional questions, wish her luck with her search.

As she climbs into the car a nagging feeling, one that began almost from the time she entered Sycamore, blooms more fully. Kit has been a cable news producer for a few years now, is used to talking to people, reading their mannerisms and body language and inflections during preinterviews for Lucinda. She has developed a skill for knowing when someone is holding back, when they know something and aren't disclosing it.

When they're lying.

She can't shake the feeling that Laura Milleneux is doing just that.

Twenty-three

They've had dinner at the Port Hunter, a redbrick, Brooklyn-looking restaurant, part sleek, part old-school cool, with lots of polished wood and exposed ceiling beams, located on Main Street in the heart of downtown Edgartown. Seth had ordered the fish tacos, in part, Kit suspected, because they were among the cheapest items on the menu and he wanted to be respectful of her paying the tab. She'd had the catch of the day, perhaps the most delicious striped bass she'd ever tasted.

The dinner conversation had been light and easy, no awkward pauses or weird revelations, a rarity for Kit on a date, even though she wasn't sure this counted as a date. Seth had asked how it went with Laura Milleneux, and Kit had shared the highlights, as well as her gut feeling that there was more of the story still missing.

The night is unusually warm for October, in the high fifties, as they walk down the brick sidewalk of Main Street toward the beckoning light-dappled water of Katama Bay.

Kit inhales deeply, draws in the woodsy smell of the crunchy leaves mixed with the salt air. They amble down toward the yacht club, make a left onto Dock Street, strolling alongside the harbor on the right until they reach Memorial Wharf and the Chappaquiddick Ferry. Kit took the Woods Hole ferry over to the island after driving up from New York. This looks like a baby ferry by comparison. She nods over in its direction. "How often does this run?"

"Continuously, till midnight. At least until the derby ends. Then till ten."

"The derby?"

"The Striped Bass and Bluefish Derby," he says. He takes in her puzzled expression. "It's a thing, OK? This is a small island with quixotic people and traditions. It has 'things.'"

She folds her arms. The air has turned chillier. "You want to head back?" he asks.

"In a minute." She looks again to the ferry port on the left. "What happens if you lose track of time and miss the last ferry? You swim for it?"

"Oh, I wouldn't recommend that," Seth says. "It's only a tenth of a mile, but swimming in pitch darkness at night in really cold water, it will feel *a lot* longer."

They stand at the wharf rail for a few moments, saying nothing. Inside, Kit's brain is blaring one message, over and over: *Stay focused.* She cannot remember the last time she has been with a man with whom it feels this comfortable saying nothing. Just . . . being. Yes, he is easy on the eyes, and that's part of it. She admits that. But there is something else going on here. Does she have the courage to admit *that*?

She thinks back for a moment, to her college boyfriend at NYU. By then she'd straightened herself out—the hell-raising teenager had long been retired. He'd hung in with her for the better part of two years, until one day he finally turned to her and said, "We've gone as far as we can go."

"What do you mean?" she'd asked.

"I mean," he'd said, "that you won't let down your guard. Or whatever you want to call it. But I can't continue to be with someone who won't let me in."

Have I ever really let anyone in?

"Where have you gone?"

Seth is looking at her, studying her face, tugging her back into the present. She stares into his eyes, and they are beautiful. But most of all, they are kind. Finally, she says quietly, "I didn't know them."

He looks at her wordlessly.

"I think that's why this is so important to me, to find out what happened to her here. I think it's because of my parents."

He says nothing, just maintains eye contact.

"You see, I know *of* them," Kit continues, "but I never got the chance to know them as people. It's funny, growing up I used to hear my friends bitch and bitch and bitch about their parents, and I thought, *You don't know how lucky you are to have parents to bitch about.* But I had Nan and Pop, and they did a great job, especially when I turned into—" She stops. "Well, let's just say I was a 'challenging' teenager. Pop was laid-back and warm, a nurturer. But he was a grandfather in the true sense of the word, you know? And there was also this sadness about him he couldn't really shake. I don't think he ever really recovered from losing my dad so young, so suddenly. Nan was different. She was also warm, and hilariously funny. But she was also the disciplinarian and the caretaker and the cook and all the rest of it. She was the *glue.* And she never complained, never once showed an ounce of impatience or resentment that she had to raise two additional children at a time she should have been condo shopping in Florida." Kit pauses, glances back out onto the water. "I guess what I mean is that Pop, I couldn't see what made him tick. But Nan . . . before all of this I would have sworn that I knew her better than anybody. And now it turns out I didn't know her at all."

"Of course you did."

Kit shakes her head. "Not the most important part, the part that seems to have changed her life, who she literally *was,* forever. She was one person when she came here, and someone else entirely when she left. Right down to the name."

"Or," he says, "you could flip it. It's like I told you before. You might say she found herself here. That she went back to her most authentic self. Who she'd been *before* all of the Hollywood stuff."

"I suppose. But when I really ask myself why this has rattled me so much, why this is so important, I think that's it. Because she was the one person I thought I really knew, inside and out. And now I find out she had this secret life. That my sister was carrying her own secrets. It makes me wonder if you can ever really know anybody."

Seth looks at her with an intensity that is both tempting and unnerving. "Does anybody really know *you?*"

She barks out a small, melancholy laugh. "I doubt if anyone wants to know the real me."

He reaches over and caresses her chin with his thumb, and she feels something stir. An ache, a yearning long suppressed. His voice is a whisper. "I do."

He leans over, and it is seconds that feel like hours before his lips are full and soft on hers. His fingers gently caress the back of her neck as he softly nibbles, explores, tastes. As she slowly reaches up and cups his face, everything else—Nan, the island, her own brokenness—slowly fades away.

Kit doesn't know how long the kiss lasts. She only knows that it is perfect. The best kiss she's had in a long time. Maybe the best she's had, ever.

They break apart, faces now mere inches from each other, and they hold each other's smile wordlessly until Seth says, "That was nice."

"It was," she agrees. And then, a low hum of buzzing, coming from her bag. He chuckles. "And here I thought we were having this perfect Hallmark movie moment."

She scrunches her face in apology as she steps back to fish out the vibrating phone. "I know, I know, I'm sorry." She looks at the caller ID, flashes it to him. "It's Bernard. So technically this interruption is partly your fault."

He throws his hands wide in protest as she clicks to answer. "Hi, Bernard," she says cheerily, still looking at Seth. "How are you?"

"I'm so sorry to call so late," he says. "Are you out and about?"

"Just out for a brisk walk on the wharf. What's going on?"

"Good news. I found someone who remembers Mercy Welles."

Kit's heart leaps with excitement. "Who?"

"She says she was your grandmother's best friend that summer," Bernard says. "Her name is Vera Kolchak. But back in 1959, she was known as Vera Harding."

*

Vera Kolchak lives in a modest one-story saltbox in Chilmark on the west side of the island, just off Middle Road. The place has seen better days—the roof sags in spots, some of the shingles are cracked and broken, the railing needs a good stripping and repainting. Vera herself is much like the house: old, sturdy, and in desperate need of a refresh.

She sits in a wide rocker accentuated by knitted doilies on the arms and a patchwork afghan thrown over the back. Behind her on the wall hangs a framed embroidered cross-stitch that says *Live. Laugh. Poop.* She's got a wide, flat face and a body to match, and is dressed in a roomy navy sweatshirt and burgundy slacks, her shoes big, ugly black bricks that are the elderly's respite from bunions, arthritis, and other such maladies. She lives here, she says, with her divorced daughter and her teenage grandson, "both ingrates," though she is quick to add that the daughter works at the alpaca farm in Vineyard Haven, and if Kit wants a deal on a blanket or sweater, she can probably get her a discount.

"But you're here to talk about Mercy," she says, eyeing Kit cautiously across the small living room coffee table. "My, I haven't thought about her in many years. She was your grandmother, you say?"

"Yes," Kit replies. "She died a few months ago."

"I'm sorry. She was a nice girl."

"Bernard tells me you and she were close, that summer of 1959."

"Oh, yes. Almost inseparable. We were both in our twenties, but I swear we were more like two teenagers at a slumber party! We just clicked right away." Vera tells her about their initial meeting while she was waitressing at the Mansion House Inn, their shopping trips and movies, a memorable day where they sat "and were fancy" at the Harborside, drinking fruity cocktails.

Kit takes it all in, nodding where appropriate, as her brain tries to process what she's hearing. Vera does not, in any way, seem like someone Nan would have befriended. In fact, Kit has quickly determined that Nan would likely have found Vera vapid and insufferable, "a silly goose." It doesn't add up. But as Vera provides further detail of their adventures, it seems clear that they did, in fact, spend a decent amount of time together. Suddenly, Vera's eyes focus on Kit's neck. With a bony finger she beckons Kit to lean over the table.

"This," she says, taking the blue sapphire at the end of Kit's necklace into her hand. "This was your grandmother's."

"Yes, it was."

Vera nods. "She got it here. I don't know how many visits she made to Ethel Roberts, staring at it in the window."

There is something off in Vera's eyes, almost a hint of . . . jealousy? in how she is talking about the necklace. "You were with her when she bought it?"

"No, no," Vera says casually. "Your grandmother and I, we had sort of, well, drifted a bit by the end of that summer."

"So she never spoke to you about quitting acting?"

Vera shakes her head. "No."

Kit leans back, surveying Vera a bit more carefully. There is something in her body language that is stiff, almost defensive. "Were you around when the theater caught fire?"

"Oh, yes. That was big news. Mercy was lucky to make it out of there."

Kit's blood freezes. "Wait. She was *in* the theater when it caught fire?"

"Yes," Vera says casually. "She sure was."

"But I read the newspaper account. There was no mention of anyone being in the theater at the time."

"I know. The Sewardses have always been able to control what is and isn't in the paper."

Kit feels her head beginning to spin. "The Sewards? What did they have to do with it?"

Vera's expression changes, devolves into the slightly chagrined look of someone who knows they've said too much. "I just mean, they were the people who owned a lot of the businesses back then, a lot of real estate. They didn't like any bad news about the island in the paper." She begins glancing casually around, as if physically searching for new talking points. "It was such a shame for the colored boy who wrote that play. He thought that was going to be his big ticket out of here. But I don't think he ever came to much."

Kit blanches at the language, the cruel summation of Staxx's career, but remembers she is not here to like Vera. She's here to gather information.

"How did you know Mercy had been inside the theater?"

"I can't quite remember," Vera says. "I guess she told me."

Kit conjures the details of the fire. It happened the Wednesday before opening night. "Did she say why she was there at that hour?"

Vera shakes her head. "Not that I recall. You'll have to excuse me. I'm an old woman and my memory isn't quite what it was."

Kit asks a few more questions about the fire, but gets shut down each time. She can't risk Vera clamming up for good. She zooms back to safer subjects—more about what she and Nan did, where they went—and gets more details about shopping, lunches. It all seems perfectly banal. Kit tries inching back to meatier territory. "Did Mercy date while she was here?"

"Well, she was a movie star and very pretty, so of course she had some attention from potential suitors," Vera says. "But I don't think there was anyone special."

Kit slides the photo across the table. "Not even him? This is Ren Sewards. Did you know him?"

Vera pulls her reading glasses up from the silver chain around her neck to inspect the picture. She looks at it in silence for a full twenty seconds, her lips pursing. Finally, she says, "Yup, that's Ren all right. He was sort of the black sheep of that family, to tell you the truth. Difficult man. Troubled, even, you might say. I think they may have spent some time together that summer." She taps the photo. "Well, I mean, clearly they did. But I don't think it was anything serious."

Vera hands the photo back to Kit. That feeling she had at Sycamore—of something not being said—returns even stronger this time. Vera delivers a wan smile and Kit returns it in kind, as if both women are engaged in a poker game. Each intent on not showing her cards.

*

Vera closes the door, watches from the window as Mercy Welles's granddaughter climbs into her car and slowly pulls away. She should feel bad about all the lying. But the thought of the generous check now sitting in the top drawer of her bedroom dresser quickly assuages the guilt. She'll get her next-door neighbor to drive her to the bank tomorrow. Her greedy daughter doesn't need to know about this. She'd have her hand out quick as a flash.

It's too bad, Vera thinks. *I was prepared to tell her all of it. The whole, ugly story. Editing out my part a bit, but still, I was going to tell her. Even if she did act all high and mighty, like she was better than me. Although I shouldn't be surprised about that. Wasn't her grandmother the exact same way?*

An hour later the yellow wall phone rings. Vera picks up.

"How did it go?" asks the voice on the other end.

"Fine," Vera says. "She doesn't suspect a thing."

August 18, 1959

Dear Ren,

Hi. I never write letters, so you should feel special! But we haven't had much chance to talk this summer, and I wanted to approach you about something important, so I am writing to you.

I know you have been spending a lot of time with Mercy this summer, and I want you to know I understand. She is very pretty and a movie star and any man on the island would want to be around her. But she is also leaving right after Labor Day to go back to California. I just want you to know that you can count on me after she's gone. We have always been there for each other, and I will always be there for you. We have a unique bond nobody can break. We island folks have to stick together!

I hope we can have a nice dinner in September and catch up. We both know how lonely it can get here after the season. I just want you to know I am always here for you. Hope to see you at the Ag Fair!

Fondly, Vera

Twenty-four

Mercy bolted awake, drenched in sweat. Sitting up, she looked around the dark quiet of the bedroom. The fire was over. She was home. She was safe.

For now.

She found herself shivering, replaying the terrible night in her head.

Staxx had been lying at the end of the stage, unconscious. The front door to the theater had been locked. She'd watched the flames galloping up the stage curtain.

She'd made a decision: she would find a chair, break one of the front windows, climb out, and start screaming for help. It was her only way out. She had to get aid, find someone who could come in and carry Staxx out before the whole place went up in smoke.

She had begun running down the aisle when she'd felt a sharp hand on her arm. She screamed, only to find . . . him.

Ren.

"You can't go back that way!" he'd thundered. "It's too dangerous!"

Where had he come from? No time for that. Mercy had looked again at the spreading fire, then back to the lobby. She pointed to the stage. "Staxx has been attacked! He's bleeding and unconscious! And the front door won't open!"

He'd shaken his head, released her arm. "Follow me!" he ordered. He'd run back toward the lobby, her trailing right behind. "Stand back," he said. He stood against the lobby wall, then rushed at the door, lifting his right leg at the last moment and, with all the force he could muster, smashing it open. He turned back to her. "Get in the jeep and go back to the cottage. Now."

"But Staxx—"

"I've got him! Mercy, now! I'll meet you there."

The forcefulness of his command was not to be ignored. She had done what she'd been told, leapt inside the jeep and peeled out of the lot. Halfway down Edgartown–Vineyard Haven Road she'd heard the faint blare of sirens.

She'd drifted into a light sleep waiting for him, but had awakened when he'd come in well after one. After assuring her Staxx was safe and would be fine, he'd insisted she go back to bed, told her he'd crash in the living room, that he knew she had many questions and that they'd talk it all out in the morning.

Now she stood up and slipped on her silk bathrobe before opening the bedroom door and padding into the living room. Moonlight poured through the front window, framing Ren's sleeping body on the small sofa. He was in a button-down shirt and light gray pants, his feet dangling over the side of the armrest. She could still smell the smoke on his clothing.

She'd just sunk into the armchair opposite him, studying his face, when his eyes fluttered open. "I'm sorry," she whispered, curling her feet underneath her. "I didn't mean to wake you."

He cleared his throat. "It's fine. Just dozed off for a bit. I thought you'd be out from exhaustion."

"Just the opposite. I can't sleep. My mind won't shut off."

He rubbed his face. "I know the feeling."

"Ren, I know it's the middle of the night and I know you're tired and we can still wait until the morning, but I just have to ask: Why were you at the theater?"

He looked at her stonily. "You think I snuck in, knocked Staxx out cold, and set a fire?"

She sighed, exasperated. "Of course not." She played with the belt on her robe. For some reason she didn't want to look at his face. "I didn't say I wasn't *grateful* you were at the theater. I don't even want to think about how it might have turned out otherwise." She leaned back, ran her fingers through her tangled hair. "Poor Staxx."

"He'll be OK. Physically, anyway." He pulled himself up, sitting upright on the couch. "But you're right. He'll be devastated about the play."

"Did you take him to the hospital?"

"We had to get him out of his smoky clothes first. But yes. He needed some stitches, probably has a concussion. They're keeping him for observation."

"Was he conscious? Did he say anything about who hit him?"

"He was too out of it."

"Did you speak to the police?"

"No. As far as they know, the theater was empty."

"Why?"

"Because it's better that way."

"I don't understand," she said. "We have to tell them what happened. He was brutally attacked. Someone committed arson! They have to investigate."

"They will. Look, it's unpleasant to consider, but even for a liberal island like Martha's Vineyard there are bound to be people who don't like the idea of a white woman starring in a Black man's play. There might have been one or two who were out to stop the play from happening, and then you guys happened to come into the theater while they were doing it."

A reasonable explanation. But something about it didn't ring true. "You never answered my question," she said. "Why were you at the theater?"

"I followed you from Staxx's party. He'd invited me to join him for a drink after the dinner, and I had gone back and forth about going," he said, looking back at her, "for obvious reasons."

"I wasn't aware you knew him that well."

"I've done work at the theater, and he's done some odd jobs with me in between gigs at the Harborside. It's—"

"A small island. I know. Go on."

"By the time I decided to go, it was late, and as I pulled up you were pulling out, and he was following you. I assumed that he was following you back here to make sure you got home OK. So I followed both of you. I figured once he left, maybe we could talk. But then you guys ended up pulling into the theater lot. I decided to go home. But then, about a mile down the road, I changed my mind and came back. That's when I saw the smoke."

"How did you get inside?"

"Stage door."

"But I tried to leave through that door to go get help. I couldn't open it."

"That's because someone had wedged a two-by-four across the handle outside." He looked at her soberly. "This was no accident, Mercy. I mean, maybe getting violent with Staxx was. But someone was trying to trap you guys inside the theater."

"Ren, that's way beyond a couple of racists trying to cancel a play."

He exhaled wearily. "I have to agree."

"So all of this," she said slowly, "was planned? Why? Who would do such a thing? And how could they have possibly known we were going to be there?"

"Why *were* you there?"

She told him about her missing house key, about losing it during the rehearsal, oddly finding it underneath the wastepaper basket in the dressing room. "But nobody knew that I had to go back to get the key except Staxx."

"Unless."

"Unless what?"

He looked toward the ceiling, as if trying to pull it all together in his head. "Unless someone took the key out of your bag deliberately. And knew you would have to return at some point to get it." He met her eyes again. "Who else was at the theater today?"

Mercy began reciting the list: Staxx, the half dozen members of the cast, the director, the stage manager, the lighting man. Then she added, "And your brother."

"Patrick was there today?"

"He's the producer, Ren," she said quietly. "Of course he was there."

The revelation hung in the silence for a minute. Finally, she broke the stillness. "Why?"

He sighed again. "Why what?"

"Why would Patrick do something like that? Because I know that's what you're thinking."

He said nothing. She got off the chair, walked to the sofa, sat down next to him. She took his reluctant hand in hers.

"I'm sorry," she said. "I should have told you about the visit to your mother."

"Mercy, it's not the time—"

"It's the perfect time. You were right. You have opened up to me and you have trusted me and I should have told you right away, the minute I got the invitation. But Ren: Staxx, me, you—we all could have been seriously hurt, or worse, tonight. You have to tell me if you think your brother might be capable of this. And why he would do it. It's my life, too. I have a right to know."

He looked at her in the shadows of the room for a long moment. "I lied, you know," he whispered.

"About what?"

He reached up, cupped her face. "About not loving you."

She tilted her cheek into the coarseness of his palm. "I know."

He leaned in and kissed her, softly at first, then a bit more urgently, taking both hands now and holding either side of her head, his thumbs gently caressing her temples, his mouth full and intense on hers. He took her hands in his, staring at them. "I do want to tell you. Everything. But I just need a bit more time, Mercy. I . . . I've never . . ." He looked back at her. "It's hard for me to . . . open up. With anyone. I keep thinking about what you said, about wanting me to let you in."

There was so much she wanted to say. But somehow she knew it was the time to listen, not to talk.

"I wanted to talk to you after the play was over. So you wouldn't have any distractions. But now, well . . ." He looked up. "Tomorrow night, after the ag fair. We can talk then. I just need . . ." He trailed off.

She caressed his hands. "What, Ren? What is it that you need?"

He looked at her. "I just need one more day of us the way it was.

Before all of this. When it was just us, sitting together at dinner, or walking on the beach, or . . ." He smiled, a hint of devilment in his expression.

She couldn't help but smile back. "You're a rascal, you know that?"

"I do. So . . . Can you wait till then?"

"That depends."

He cocked an eyebrow. "On?"

"On whether you can throw in a little incentive to the deal."

He leaned over, kissed her softly again. "I think I can do that."

He stood, and in one swift motion lifted her off the sofa and into his arms, and carried her into the bedroom.

*

He tried to answer her, to converse—Staxx was nothing if not always polite—but there was no hiding the raw bitterness in his eyes. He lay in his hospital bed, glancing absently out the window. He seemed to be intently focused on a pigeon perched on the outside sill. Finally, he spoke. "I should be home right now, rummaging through my closet, figuring out what suit I am going to wear to the premiere Saturday," he said. His voice was monotone, devoid of any emotion. "Instead, I'm wearing this." He pulled at the hospital gown, his eyes still fixed on the bird.

Mercy shifted uncomfortably in the visitor's chair by the bed. Out in the hallway she could hear some of his relatives engaged in animated conversation, seemingly oblivious to his depression.

"I understand how devastating this is. I really do," she said softly. "This meant a lot to me, too."

"You didn't have everything riding on it."

"No, you're right. I didn't. But it won't be in vain. I'll introduce you to my agent."

"Old white man who represents young white girls ain't gonna be interested in anything to do with some random Black guy his client met on vacation. Let's be serious, Miss Mercy."

She started to offer a counterview but stopped. Mainly because he was correct. Even if all of that weren't already true, Sy had no interest or any real connections to the world of theater. He was a Hollywood agent: film and television. And there was not going to be any easy path for Staxx to break into either of those. Finally, she said, "We have to be thankful we both got out of the theater alive. It could have been far worse."

He shrugged slightly.

"What do the doctors say?"

"I should be getting out later today. They were worried about bleeding on the brain or something, but looks like it's just a good ole concussion. I still wish I knew who did this. I'd love five minutes back in that theater with them. Only this time it'd be a fair fight."

Staxx had no recollection of who'd hit him. One minute he was standing there, waiting for her to come back from the dressing room; the next he was out cold. Whoever had attacked him had come stealthily, from behind.

"I just don't understand who would do this," she said.

"Somebody who didn't want a white woman in a Black man's play."

It still remained the obvious explanation, and the one that had gripped most of the island as news of the fire had spread. But it still felt off. It was too pat, too . . . easy. Then there was the question of Ren. He had made sure that no one knew the three of them had even been in the theater, explaining Staxx's journey to the emergency room as an accident. Why all the secrecy? Why not tell the police the truth?

What was he hiding?

She'd finally get her questions answered tomorrow night. After the ag fair.

Two large women in sensible shoes and dresses that made loud rustling noises when they walked entered the room, one holding a covered pie dish. Mercy took the cue and, stopping to lean over and plant a gentle kiss on Staxx's forehead, left, promising to check back on him soon.

She was heading toward the exit when out of the corner of her eye she spied a vaguely familiar face at the end of the hall. As she walked closer, she placed him: Jimmy Chadwick, Grace's son. She hadn't seen him since the day they'd met two months ago, when she'd driven Grace home from the market. He was standing outside a room, fishing for something in his pocket. As she drew closer, he looked up.

"Miss Welles," he said in a bit of wonder. "Well, this is certainly a surprise. I mean, a nice surprise, of course. Are you here to see Mom?"

Mercy glanced at the nameplate by the hospital room door.

CHADWICK, GRACE.

Oh, no.

"Actually, I was just down the hall, visiting a friend," Mercy said. "I didn't know Grace was in here. Is she OK?"

He shook his head gravely. "I'm afraid she's suffered a stroke. They're taking good care of her, but . . ." His eyes went misty. "We're not sure what's going to happen."

She reached out for his forearm. "Oh, Jimmy, I'm so sorry. I wish I'd known. I would have brought flowers."

"Would you like to see her?"

Mercy glanced back at the doorway, unsure. "Is she well enough for visitors?"

"I think it would do her a world of good. You know, she told everybody you had driven her home that day, and how generous you were to give her the last pound cake at First National! She really enjoyed your visit. We don't get a lot of movie stars here. It made her feel special."

Mercy smiled. "I'm so glad. Well, if you think she'd be all right, I'd love to pop in and see her for a few moments. Can she speak?"

He nodded. "She's pretty weak, but yes. C'mon, I'll take you in."

*

Grace's appearance had been a shock—her graying hair was tousled and unkempt, her skin ghostly white—but her eyes opened wide as Mercy entered. Jimmy explained Mercy's visit to the hospital, and the three of them had chatted briefly about how Grace was feeling, what the doctors said, who had visited earlier, Mercy chiming in with appropriate encouragement and assurances of her full recovery. There were a few modest bouquets of flowers positioned around the room, and one large crystal vase overflowing with two dozen long-stemmed white roses. Mercy didn't even have to ask who those were from. They had "chilly grand gesture" from Mint written all over them.

Finally, in a feeble voice, Grace said, "Jimmy, can you give us a moment, please? I'd like to speak to Miss Welles alone."

Jimmy nodded, then headed to the cafeteria. He reminded Grace that her other son and his wife would be coming in from Wareham in the afternoon, then left the room.

Grace beckoned Mercy closer, taking her hand in hers, guiding Mercy to sit on the bed next to her.

"What is it, Mrs. Chadwick? Are you all right?"

Grace shook her head. "It's a sign, you coming here today."

"A sign?"

"From God. He's taking me soon. He wants me to confess."

Mercy tried to mask her look of astonishment. What was she talking about? She began to wonder if the stroke had affected the older woman's brain function. "I . . . I'm not sure what you mean, Mrs. Chadwick. Do you need a clergyman?"

Grace shook her head adamantly. "No, no, no. I need *you*. I need you to hear what I'm saying. That day you took me home. You were asking questions. About the Sewards. About Mint."

Mercy flashed back, recalled staring at the view of Sycamore from Grace's kitchen window. "Yes, I remember."

Grace's watery gray eyes gazed at her intently. "You asked me about Jasper. About how he died."

Mercy felt her heart begin to beat faster. "Yes," she said quietly. "I did."

"Have you ever been married, Miss Welles?"

"No. I have not."

"You have to understand something," she said, squeezing Mercy's hand. "It's very, very hard for women, especially for those who make bad choices. It was even worse fifteen years ago. Jasper was not a good man. He hurt her, beat her, constantly. The children, too. She was able to protect Patrick, but for Ren and Ellenanne . . . It was horrible for her."

Mercy didn't want to hear another word. And wanted to hear it all.

"It's all right, Mrs. Chadwick," she said soothingly. "You can trust me. Go on."

Grace looked down at their joined hands. "I made a terrible bargain," she said, her voice now barely audible. "You have to remember, that was during the war, and it still felt very much like the Depression. You're too young to remember, but it was a terrible, scary time. We'd lost almost all of our money when the bog flooded, and there were some pretty lean years afterward. We didn't know what we were going to do, what would happen to us, the kids. Mint swooped in to help, made sure John got a new job with the WPA, that we didn't lose the house. She began inviting me to things, introducing me to the great ladies who ran the charities here. It was nice, I have to tell you. To feel important, to be part of 'society,' even if it was as someone's ward. Mint told me it was a new lease on life for her, for both of us. Just as long as I didn't tell anyone."

"Tell anyone what, Mrs. Chadwick?"

A sob caught in Grace's throat. "What I saw that night, standing in my kitchen. That Jasper didn't fall over the cliff in a drunken stupor." Her eyes flicked back up to meet Mercy's. "That she pushed him."

Twenty-five

She had wanted to know more. She had wanted to know what Ren had been hiding.

Be careful what you wish for.

By the time she put the jeep in park in front of the cottage she was reeling. It was all making sense now.

Mint Sewards had killed her husband.

It explained everything. Why Ren had withdrawn, why his sister had fled. Had they watched her do it? It explained why Patrick had taken on the role of the devoted son. Jasper Sewards had died in 1944. How old would Patrick have been then? Seven? It was possible he didn't even know the truth.

Then there was Mint's game of chess with Mercy over tea, trying to determine how much Ren had told her, how vulnerable her secret was to being exposed. Mint couldn't risk Ren getting too close to anyone. Couldn't risk him revealing the secret she'd spent fifteen years protecting.

Mercy slid her bag off the seat and alighted from the jeep, wearily trudging up the steps of the cottage. She suddenly felt very tired. She'd gotten almost no sleep last night. She needed to lie down, escape her cluttered head. Then—

Footsteps, on the stairs behind her.

She whirled around, only to find a slender, freckled young woman around her own age looking up at her. The girl had alabaster skin, wavy, flaming red hair, and kind but melancholy eyes. She was dressed simply, in a pale green blouse, plain ivory slacks, and a pair of burgundy penny loafers. "Miss Welles?" she asked.

Mercy let out a breath. Another autograph-seeker. One whose timing could not have been worse.

"Yes, yes I am," Mercy said. She waited for her visitor to produce paper and pen. "Is there something particular you would like me to sign?"

A slight look of chagrin draped over the young woman's face. "Oh, no, I'm not here for an autograph," she said. "I'm Ellenanne Sewards."

*

They sat in the living room, the silence awkward and engulfing, each of them gingerly sipping the pink lemonade Mercy had poured. Mercy was trying to reconcile everything that Grace Chadwick had confessed in the hospital with this surprise guest. By writing her, Mercy had hoped that Ren's sister might respond in kind. She had never considered the possibility that Ellenanne, who had fled the island to escape her family, might actually appear.

"I'm sorry for the sneak attack, Miss Welles," Ellenanne said finally. "It's just that I didn't want anyone to know I was coming."

"I understand," Mercy said. "And please, call me Mercy. I'm so very grateful to you for making the trip. I know this can't be easy, being back here."

"It's certainly brought a mix of emotions, that's for certain. But you know, when I finally stepped off the ferry I realized how much I've missed it. Despite everything that's happened, I have a lot of happy memories here." She took a sip of the lemonade, then looked Mercy squarely in the eye. "So, I don't have a lot of time. My boyfriend is waiting for me. But I know you have questions. And I wanted to come and answer those that I could."

"I want to say how thankful I am for your willingness to do that. But first, I must ask: What made you decide to come?"

Ellenanne let out a long sigh. "You know, we've all paid such a terrible price for Mother," she said. "Ren more than anyone. I mean, Patrick became Mother's confidante, and it's worked out for him. At least I think it has. And I . . . I'm better now. I'm a teacher, and my boyfriend had never even been to the Vineyard before today and doesn't seem to have any interest in returning. But Ren . . . he's always been such a loner. And then you wrote, and I read up about you, and it just seemed so right to me: of course only someone from the outside, someone who had lived a far bigger life, could have managed to pull Ren out of himself, back into living again. And I so want that for him. I really do. He's been such a tremendous big brother to me. If I can help him, I want to do it."

A million images raced through Mercy's brain. Had the children *witnessed* Mint push Jasper off the cliff? She couldn't imagine how deep a scar that would leave. Clearly Patrick had not—or if he had, he didn't recall it. But it was the likely explanation for why Ren and Ellenanne had turned on Mint, fleeing her orbit as soon as humanly possible.

A question interrupted her thoughts. "Now, I have to ask," Ellenanne said, "how much has Ren told you? About . . . our past?"

Mercy knew she had to tread carefully here. Hadn't she repaired her relationship with Ren just hours earlier? She fully intended to tell him everything—about her unplanned visits with both Grace and Ellenanne, and everything she'd learned—but now, in the moment, she needed to be cautious about what she said and how she said it. "Truthfully, very little," Mercy said. "But it's a small island, and as I have gotten to know Ren better, others have chimed in with . . . observations."

Ellenanne smiled wryly. "You mean 'rumors.'"

Mercy shrugged. "Honestly, Ellenanne, like you, I just want to help him. To know him. Because . . ." She trailed off.

"Because you love him."

"Yes. Because I love him."

"And these 'rumors.' They concern how my father died?"

Mercy admired the young woman's directness. "Among other things."

Ellenanne nodded. "I can't say I'm surprised. I mean, when your father literally falls off a cliff, there are bound to be questions. Especially since it was something of an open secret that my parents' marriage was hardly idyllic. But as I am sure you've heard by now, my father was a hard, mean man. At times, a vicious one. And an alcoholic, which was also well known by the year-rounders. I think our name, our legacy here, was hard to live up to for him. That's why he and Mother moved back to Boston for the first few years after they were married. But our family business—the real estate, the retail spaces, the dairy farm—they're all here. It was only a matter of time before he had to move us back."

"How old were you then?"

She looked to the ceiling. "Oh, I guess about five. Ren was nine. Patrick was just a toddler."

"Go on."

Ellenanne leaned back in the armchair, crossing her legs. "My mother was not equipped to deal with him. She was a parlormaid who suddenly found herself married to the scion of the first family of Martha's Vineyard."

Mercy's eyes tapered in curiosity. "I was told your mother had come here as a governess."

Ellenanne laughed. "Oh, well, that's certainly the story she's crafted, but no. The truth is she was working as a maid for a wealthy family in Beacon Hill that had a vacation home here. One summer, at the last minute, their governess eloped, and they needed someone to watch their children, so they brought Mother. That was sometime in the mid-1920s. She met Dad and they married, which raised more than a few eyebrows. I think it's painfully obvious that each married the other for the wrong reasons. She had evidently secretly been engaged to a working boy in Boston, but she wanted position and financial security. My father was under pressure from my grandfather to settle down and start a family, and he wanted a woman who would be obedient, someone he could completely control."

"Not exactly Romeo and Juliet."

"No. They made a terrible bargain. I don't know how he was those first few years. My memories of him are all coated in his meanness. Between that and the eyes of the island old guard on her, Mother began taking pills and drinking to cope. She'd pass out in the middle of the day. Then Dad would come home and the house would be in disarray and he'd be even worse, striking her. Eventually striking us." She looked away a bit, gathering herself. "It was rather brutal, to be honest."

"I'm so very sorry," Mercy said. "It sounds horrible."

"I think a lot of it had to do with my father not being able to escape his own father's shadow. My grandfather wasn't exactly a peach, either. But our grandmother was just lovely. She was the bright spot of the family."

Mercy smiled. "Ren told me she taught him to bake."

Ellenanne laughed. "Yes! She did. Her famous pie." She smiled. "That makes me happy, to know he's shared that with you."

She talked a bit more about growing up, a few rare fun times they'd had together as a family. It appeared that much of the Sewards fortune had been lodged in durable goods that had proved to be a sturdy barrier against the harsh winds of the Depression, only burnishing the family's luster further. "But by the early 1940s, everything truly changed," Ellenanne said. "My grandfather died. My father was the only boy of three, so naturally control of the businesses was passed to him. Dad began going to Boston for these mysterious business trips, sometimes for weeks at a time. It was bad when he was here, but worse with him gone. Mother became even more unhinged."

Mercy sat quietly, taking it all in. It was almost impossible to reconcile the image of the steely Mint Sewards she'd met with the lost, self-medicating harridan her daughter now described. "Can you tell me," Mercy asked, "about the night your father died?"

Ellenanne's gaze was intense. "How much has Ren shared with you?"

She couldn't lie. "Honestly? Nothing. But Mrs. Chadwick told me a version that was quite shocking."

Ellenanne seemed surprised. "She did?"

"She's in the hospital and very ill," Mercy said. "I went to see her. I think she needed to clear her conscience about what she saw that night."

"I see," Ellenanne replied. She was quiet for a second, as if deciding how much to reveal.

Finally she said, "That night, Dad was drunk. More so than usual. Mother was jumpy, also more than usual. We ate dinner almost in silence. I remember it so clearly because Mother kept generously refilling his bourbon, which wasn't like her.

"Every night, like clockwork, my father went out front onto the bluff to smoke a cigar. It was his ritual while Mother got us ready for bed. Only that night . . . " She paused. "That night, she stayed downstairs." She was quiet for a moment, staring out the front window. She turned back and said, "And then suddenly . . . he was gone. Over the cliff. A fishing trawler discovered his body near Gay Head a few weeks later."

Mercy leaned forward. "Did you see . . . ?"

Ellenanne nodded slightly. "I was in my bedroom upstairs. It overlooks the bluff. Some things you know you'll never forget."

An eerie stillness filled the room. Mercy was at a loss for words. How do you survive watching your mother kill your father? "I'm so very sorry," she said finally. "For all of you. No child should have to endure what you and your brothers did."

"Thank you," Ellenanne said quietly. "I won't lie, it's been hard. Our lives were never the same. Although Mother's certainly improved. She quit the pills, pulled way back on the booze. She started over, joined boards and committees, gave big donations. She turned being the Widow Sewards into a successful career." She looked back at Mercy. "Your letter mentioned you met her?"

"Yes. It was interesting."

"I bet. She needed to size up the competition."

"For Ren? But they don't even speak, as far as I can tell."

"That's not what I mean. For the past fifteen years she's been living in this state of fear, carrying this slight hum of anxiety that at any moment her secret would be revealed and she'd lose it all. She bought off Grace Chadwick. That leaves me and Ren. I'm gone now, so she's not as worried. But Ren . . . Ren will never leave here. The sea is in his blood."

"I still don't see what that has to do with me."

"As you are well aware, it is not easy to break down Ren's defenses.

But somehow, you have. And that must scare Mother to death. Because if Ren tells you the truth, then her secret is out. And out to a fancy actress who, if she stays here, or God forbid marries her son, might attract national reporters. 'The movie star and the oysterman.' It almost writes itself. And—"

Mercy began to see. "If reporters begin to look into the family background of the actress's seaman . . ."

Ellenanne nodded emphatically. "Exactly."

More pieces locking into place. The fire at the theater. No play meant no reviews drifting back to Boston or New York, no record of her being here. It had been unthinkable that Mint could be capable of such a thing. But a wealthy woman who had murdered her own husband and then reinvented herself with his wealth and standing could be capable of just about anything to keep that a secret.

Ellenanne looked at her watch. "I should be going," she said.

As they stood, Mercy studied the girl's face. How had she not noticed immediately on the porch? She and Ren had the same eyes, the same slightly crooked mouth. Mercy felt a sly smile escaping.

"Is something . . . amusing?" Ellenanne asked, curious.

Mercy shook her head. "I'm so sorry. This is one of those moments where your mind just plays tricks. Have you ever been in a very serious moment and then, for no apparent reason, your brain just drifts over into the most absurd, inappropriate thought?"

"I have," Ellenanne said. "So tell me: What absurd, inappropriate thought are you having in this moment?"

"I have to ask," Mercy said. "Did your brothers really call you Pudge?"

Twenty-six

Mercy carried the small wicker basket with the care of a new mother bringing her infant home from the hospital. It had taken her all night and three tries, but in the end she felt she'd finally mastered the task. She'd told herself that she had done it to feel like a local.

But the truth was, she'd done it for him.

"And what have we here?" an older gentleman in a linen blazer had inquired as she'd walked up to the long table, draped in a pink checkered tablecloth.

She gently laid the basket down. "Vanilla apple pie," she said proudly. "My official entry in the pie contest." He smiled and jotted down her name and entry number on his notepad, then slapped a ticket with the number 14 on the basket and gave her the other half. "Good luck to you, miss."

Ren had wanted to escort her onto the West Tisbury fairgrounds. But she had wanted to surprise him by entering her pie secretly, so she'd told him she would meet him here. It was Friday, the second day of the fair and the most crowded, because all the best events and contests happened on Friday. It was sheep day, a hundred different breeds baa-baa-baa'ing their way around their various pens, as well as the day of the dog show. The poultry show boasted more than seventy pens of hens, roosters, turkeys, ducks, guinea fowl, and pigeons, along with the random rabbit thrown in.

The morning had dawned cloudy, but now, at barely noon, the air around the fairgrounds was thick with heat and the pungent smell of horses and livestock. Mercy had selected a flowing white sundress for the day, and as she walked the grounds and passed the cattle show and the setup for the oxen pull, her spirits lifted. Tables were stocked with flower arrangements bursting with dahlias, marigolds, zinnias, and roses, and bushels of just-picked fresh vegetables for sale. Booths sold crafts and quilts. Bonnar Atwood Interiors had erected a small house, right in the middle of the grounds, complete with its own garden. In the distance, a Ferris wheel turned lazily into the sky.

Today was her chance to pause all the terribleness that had bubbled to the surface these last forty-eight hours. To not think about the fire, or Grace Chadwick's confession, or Ellenanne's revelations. All of that would be dealt with later tonight. But for today, reprieve. A chance to fulfill Ren's fervent wish. To just be happy.

People hustled toward and past her, greeting one another and laughing, exchanging hugs and gossip and inquiries about relatives' health. They discussed the odds on everything, from who would win the top prize for champion horse to the Sunnyside Award, given to the family that contributed the most to this year's fair.

Mercy passed around a corner to find a small stand proffering hot soup and instantly recognized the figure of Bridie deCoursey carefully spooning thick, buttery bisque into small bowls. "Oh my goodness, that smells delicious!" Mercy said, leaning over to give her a hug. Dennis sidled up next to Bridie, delivering a brief hello that seemed to belie some stress he was experiencing. He proceeded to argue to Bridie that they'd evidently been shortchanged on the propane. Mercy stood silently, smiling at Dennis's cranky complaining and spooning the yummy soup Bridie had poured for her, when she felt a strong arm encircling her waist. She looked up, saw Ren's smiling face.

"Good morning," he said. "Early lunch?"

"I had to," she said, spooning some bisque and feeding it to him. "Clearly you understand why."

He swallowed the soup and laughed. "I do. Bridie, that's incredible."

"Chunky lobster, fresh tarragon, and the right white wine," she replied matter-of-factly. "Those are the keys. All you have to do is get out of the way."

"Well, hello!" came a voice from the left. Mercy, Ren, and Bridie turned to see Vera, wearing a straw hat the size of a Thanksgiving turkey platter, now standing in front of them. She spied Ren's arm around Mercy and delivered a tight smile. "Well, don't you all look ... cozy."

Dennis interjected, "Ren, could you do an old man a favor and help me with these other tanks? They're just over in the truck."

As the men departed and Bridie ladled out soup for a few new customers, Vera gently pulled Mercy aside. "So . . . ." she said, "you and Ren, you're ... together now?"

"We've spent some time together this summer, Vera," Mercy replied. "You knew that."

"Well, sure I did. I just ... I guess I thought it was more like a summer fling thing. But you two look . . ." She tried to feign indifference and failed miserably. "Are you considering keeping on past the summer? Not that that wouldn't be wonderful, of course. But I thought you were due to go back to Hollywood in a week or two. I'm sure you must miss your glamorous life there."

Mercy weighed her response. A memory floated to the top of her brain. Vera, sipping a fruity cocktail at the Harborside Inn after their day of shopping, talking about herself and Ren. *We've both been sweet on each other at different points. It's just a matter of getting the timing right.*

Clearly Vera had no idea how deep the feelings had grown between her and Ren. But of course, that was a fairly recent development. There was no way Mercy could have known that the brusque, cranky oysterman who had insulted her wine and sarcastically fixed her faucet would turn out to be ... love.

And the truth was Mercy still didn't know how to answer. How was this all going to work? A question for another day, but she didn't want to lie to Vera, either. Lying by omission had caused her nothing but trouble the entire summer.

"Well," Mercy said slowly, "I'm not at all sure what I am going to do, Vera. I will say that my summer here has proven to be truly magical, and I am sure I am not alone when it comes to people who come here for the first time and fall in love with the place. I guess we'll just have to see."

"Yes," Vera said with artificial cheeriness. "I suppose we will."

The men had returned with the propane tanks, and Ren sauntered up next to Mercy. "So, ready for a tour of America's greatest county fair?"

She smiled, and—whether out of devilment, affection, or both—threaded her arm into his. "Yes. I'd love that."

As they walked away, Mercy could feel Vera's emanating scowl boring into her back as she remained planted by Bridie and Dennis's booth, stewing in her own kind of soup.

*

Mercy sat at the small kitchen table, licking the stamp and affixing it firmly to the right corner of her latest letter to Cass. What a tonic it had been this summer, being able to share all of her feelings, up and down and all around, with her treasured friend all those miles away. Cass had been terrible about writing back, but picturing her unfolding Mercy's letters and taking in everything that was happening had given her a very singular kind of comfort.

She went back into the bedroom, fiddled with a hair band. On the dresser she spied the bright yellow ribbon that blared SECOND PRIZE, her shocking runner-up finish for the vanilla apple pie. It had been worth it for the look of pride and love that had overtaken Ren's face, and was still on it when the fair photographer snapped the picture she insisted he be in.

He'd had an emergency somewhere—something about a broken boiler at a restaurant in Vineyard Haven—but said he'd meet her at the cottage as soon as the job was done. She started to feel the slow creep of adrenaline. How would he react when she told him what she'd learned? That she had written his sister, and that Ellenanne had then shown up on her doorstep? She shook her head. She would tell him everything, just as they'd promised, and it would all be fine. It would all be out in the open, and they could move on. To whatever it was that lay ahead.

She jumped at the knock at the door. "Coming!" she yelled. She threw her hair into the hair band, applied a few final droplets of perfume, and hustled toward the door.

Only to open it and find . . . Vera, now holding her ridiculous cartwheel hat.

"Vera . . . hello," Mercy said. "I . . . I wasn't expecting you."

Vera blew past her into the cottage, wheeling around and thrusting out a piece of paper she held in her right hand. "I know. I'm just here as a favor to Ren. He caught me as I was walking out of the fair. He asked me to make sure you got this."

Mercy took the note and opened it. She immediately recognized Ren's handwriting.

> So sorry. Got called to another emergency on Chappy. Can you meet me? Ferry isn't running this late but I've arranged for Dennis to take you the short trip by boat. He'll meet you at the wharf. Don't worry. Everything is fine. Will explain everything when you get here. R.

Mercy narrowed her eyes, rereading the note. She was confused. Chappaquiddick, the tiny island off the coast. Why did he want to meet there? She suddenly felt unsettled. They were going to have a nice, long talk, quietly, together, at the cottage, and now she had to get into a small boat in darkness. Did it have something to do with Ellenanne? Had he found out she'd been here? A hundred different theories ricocheted in her mind, all colliding into one another.

"Is everything OK?" Vera asked.

Mercy glanced back down at the note. *Everything is fine.* Why didn't it feel like it?

"Yes, of course," she replied, folding the note and shoving it into her dress pocket. "I need to get down to the wharf and meet Dennis."

"Oh, I'll walk you down."

The last thing she needed was more of Vera's snooping questions.

"No, no," she said, a bit more forcefully than she'd intended. "I mean, I still have to do some quick things here. But if you're walking that way, would you mind telling him I'll be there soon?"

She couldn't read the mixed emotions on Vera's face, and in that moment had neither the time nor patience to decipher them.

"Of course," Vera said. "I'll tell him."

Twenty-seven

Ren was late, a fact of which he was all too aware, but he'd had to stop by his cabin to shower and put on fresh clothes. There was no way he was going to do this, tell her everything, tell her how he truly felt about her—about them—and do it smelling like sweat and putty. He'd rehearsed the speech a dozen times. As he made a right and drove toward the cottage, his heart began beating faster.

Would she understand? He believed, deep down, that she would.

Would she still love him? God, he hoped so. He didn't know much, but one thing he knew for sure: he had never loved anyone the way he loved her.

He pulled the truck over in front of the cottage and found her sitting on the front step of the porch, waiting for him.

Only, it wasn't her.

His eyes focused more intently as the young woman rose, her expression expectant.

He got out of the truck to see Vera Harding, nervously fidgeting with her ridiculous hat, walking to meet him on the sidewalk.

"Hi," she said.

Ren looked past her, through the cottage window into the empty living room. The night was still, quiet. There was no sound on the street other than the gentle clicking of the crickets and the soft rustling of the bushes in the night breeze. He looked around, confused.

"Vera, what are you doing here?" he asked. "Where's Mercy?"

Looks of defiance, quickly replaced by faux concern, passed over Vera's face in quick succession. She dug into her pocket, extracted a piece of paper. "She asked me to give you this."

Ren kept his scowl trained on her as he carefully took the paper. He unfolded it, struggling to read it in the dim glow of the nearby streetlight.

> Dearest Ren—
>
> I'm so sorry. I know we were supposed to talk tonight, but I just couldn't face it.
>
> I have decided to leave Martha's Vineyard tonight. I know this is difficult and cowardly, but it's what I need to do, since staying would only make it harder for both of us. We both knew this day was coming. We live very different lives, and it's time we admit it. I will always be grateful for this summer, and for having met you.
>
> I wish you every happiness. Please forgive me.
>
> Love, Mercy

His eyes flicked back up to meet hers. "Is everything OK?" she asked.

He slowly folded the note, nodding. "It appears Mercy has left."

Vera nodded, jutted her lower lip out just a bit. "Yes, I know. She had a suitcase with her, and I think she's arranged for the rest of her things to be sent. I'm so sorry. I know you two were . . . close."

He said nothing, just continued to stare at her.

"I told her she should stay to say a proper goodbye. But it must have been something very important that took her away so suddenly. Maybe a new movie." She moved closer, put her hand on his arm. "Did you get *my* note?"

He ignored the question. "How long ago did she give you this?"

"I don't know, maybe an hour ago?" She began stroking his arm. "Do you want to go somewhere, have a beer, talk a bit?"

"That's very kind of you, Vera."

Her look of pity intensified. "Ren, it's like I wrote. I just want to help—"

In one, lightning-fast motion he flipped her hand up and grabbed her by the forearm, pulling her roughly to him. His eyes bored into hers, which were now brimming with fear. "Ren, stop! You're hurting me!"

He tightened his grip, jerked her arm even harder. "You have exactly five seconds to tell me where she is, Vera."

"I . . . She told me to give you the note. I don't know what you're talking—"

He grabbed her other arm. Their faces were now inches apart. "Do I look like a chump to you, Vera? Is that what you think, after all these years? That some ridiculous forged note would work? *Where is she?!* Tell me, now!"

For a few seconds the only sound was the two of them breathing—Ren's heaving rage, Vera's gulping terror—as each looked into the other's eyes and saw an enemy staring back. "It wasn't my idea. You have to believe me," Vera whispered.

"Vera, I have never hit a woman in my life, but I swear to God . . ."

She looked into his eyes—wild, feral.

There was only one way out, and she took it.

*

The wharf was relatively tranquil at this time of night, the normal gaggle of late-evening strollers no doubt too pooped out after a long, hot day at the ag fair to be up for another wander by the moon-dappled water of the harbor. It didn't take long for Mercy to find him standing by the boat slip, smoking a pipe.

"Dennis!" she exclaimed. "Thank God. So you can run me over to Chappaquiddick? Ren made it sound rather urgent."

He looked at her intently. "Don't worry, I'll get you where you need to go, no problem," he said. "Come, let's go down to the boat."

"Oh, hold on," she said. "I just have to mail a letter." She scurried over to the mailbox and dropped in her latest update to Cass, then hurried back. "OK, I'm ready."

Dennis helped her climb into the small vessel, and she took a seat at the rear, next to an old blanket and a rusty metal thermos. The boat was a sporty red and white Chris-Craft runabout made mainly of wood, with an outboard motor that slowly gurgled to life. In a few moments the boat was skimming out onto the water, Dennis at the till, Mercy nestled in the aft, in the direction of the small patch of sand that comprised Chappaquiddick.

"I don't understand why Ren would ask me to meet him here," Mercy yelled above the humming din of the motor. "I've never even been to—"

Dennis had his back to her, his figure ramrod straight as he intently steered the boat out onto the open water. Mercy looked to her left, saw Chappaquiddick slowly growing more distant. "Dennis?" she yelled again, pointing to the island. "I know I'm hardly an expert on local geography, but shouldn't we be heading over there?"

He didn't answer. The boat continued to chug farther out to sea.

Mercy whipped her head around, watched Chappaquiddick growing smaller under the moonlit sky. She peered harder, made out the shape of something slowly lumbering toward it. The ferry. The ferry was still running. *Wait*—

Something was wrong.

She got her bearings and stood, holding the gunwale with her right hand as she slowly inched her way toward him. Finally, she grabbed his shoulder with her left arm, spinning him partially toward her.

She didn't recognize the face of the man now looking at her. Gone was the impish, genial Irishman she had laughed with at the White Whale. His eyes were hard, almost dead. His mouth ran in a grim, straight line across his face. Mercy felt the bottom drop out of her stomach.

"Dennis, what's happening? Why are we moving away from the island? I don't understand!"

He sloughed off her grip, sending her careening to the back of the boat, where she landed with a hard thud. "Quiet!" he thundered. "Just stay there and this won't be any worse than it has to be."

She fought to stay focused, to keep the terror now swamping every one of her senses under control. This didn't make any sense. Why would Dennis have lured her out under false pretenses? Where was Ren? Why—

And then, eyeing the back of him, standing straight as a statue, legs slightly apart, steering the boat farther out, the clouds inside her brain slowly parted.

She recalled that day at the bar, watching him scribble Bridie's name on all of those checks, then duplicating her own handwriting. *I could fake da Vinci's signature on the* Mona Lisa *and nobody'd be the wiser.*

His ardent defense of Mint, that first time she'd asked about her. *One of the finest women to ever step foot on this island.*

Dennis. All this time, it had been there, right under her nose. Dennis had been the boy Mint was supposed to marry. He'd followed her to Martha's Vineyard to win her back. But it hadn't worked. *She married someone else. Went back to Boston. That happens a lot.*

Only Mint didn't stay in Boston. She'd returned. Had they carried on a secret affair? Dennis must have known that Jasper was an alcoholic who had been beating Mint and the children. Mercy could picture a young Margaret Sewards, overwhelmed and coping with life through pills and booze, terrified for her children, pleading with her jilted suitor. *I should have married you. I only loved you. I can't live like this. You have to help me.*

And he had. He'd been a young policeman, right in Edgartown. He could have easily made sure her crime never saw the light of day. Perhaps Mint had then staked his purchase of the pub. It was all so neat. Until Mercy had shown up, poking into the past.

Suddenly, the motor went quiet. Mercy could still make out Chappaquiddick in the distance. Dennis remained standing, immobile, now looking up toward the brightness of the moon. He slowly turned to face her.

"You, and Mint," Mercy said. "You never stopped loving her. Even now. Even after helping her kill her own husband."

His face darkened. "You will shut your mouth. Do not speak of her."

She shook her head in utter disbelief. "You set the fire at the theater. You attacked Staxx."

He sneered back at her. "You were so thrilled when we showed up with the sandwiches and beer for your silly play rehearsal," he said.

"It didn't take much to find your key and hide it. I knew you'd have to come back to get it. I just didn't count on you having company. I never meant to hurt the boy. He was just in the wrong place at the wrong time."

"You tried to kill us."

"Bah! Just a little scare. I was going to open the door once you'd gotten enough smoke to send a message. But then your hero had to show up. I don't know what's gotten into him since you arrived."

"Love," Mercy replied defiantly. "He loves me."

Dennis scoffed. "He'll forget you were ever here."

"Why? Why are you doing this?"

He was quiet for a moment, staring at her impassively. Finally, he said, "I know you'll find this hard to believe, but this was not at all what I wanted. You brought this on yourself. All you had to do was have a nice little holiday, go back to where you came from." He shook his head. "I thought after the play was canceled, you'd go, especially since Ren told me he had broken things off. But that was my own error. Turned out in stopping the play I only restarted the two of you."

"I still don't understand. I am no threat to you. To anybody. I don't understand why any of this is happening."

He retrieved a note from his jacket pocket, tossed it over to her. "*This* is why this is happening."

A letter, addressed to her by first name only. No postmark. Mercy took it out of the small beige envelope, unfolded it. It was almost impossible to read by the pale light of the moon, but scanning it Mercy could make out the signature at the bottom: *Ellenanne Sewards*. A thank-you for allowing her to come, to unburden herself, to finally speak the truth. Someone had intercepted the letter. Mercy closed her eyes for a moment. Of course. "Vera," she said out loud.

Dennis nodded. "As foolish a girl as you'll ever meet, no doubt. But useful. Took me a while to convince her that you and Ren were truly an item—denial is a powerful thing in silly girls, but jealousy is an even stronger one. Eventually she came around, began doing some snooping for me. She saw Ellenanne going into your place, and later she intercepted the letter. That's when I knew I had to act. Tonight."

"But I . . . I don't know anything," she said. It sounded feeble.

"Don't lie to me. Ellenanne says it right there, in black and white. You know far too much."

"I won't tell anyone. I swear. I would never do that to Ren."

"It doesn't matter. You stay here with him, and it's only a matter of time until the reporters come to write about the movie star and the sailor. And we both know they'll not be able to resist digging into the past. If you figured it out, one of them will, too. I can't allow that to happen. There's too much at stake."

She racked her brain in panic. "I'll . . . I'll leave. Tonight."

He laughed. "You've already left tonight. You're not the only one who got a note."

He slowly withdrew something from his jacket pocket.

A glint of metal.

A gun.

"I truly am sorry it's come to this," he said. "But you brought it all on yourself."

"You have to know you'll never get away with this. 'Young actress murdered on Martha's Vineyard'? You're worried about the press? They'll swamp this island once word gets out. It'll be just the thing you're trying to avoid."

He kicked at something metallic near his feet. She looked down. A rope of chain link. "Not if they don't find you."

So this was it. The end, here on the tranquil waters off Martha's Vineyard, the idyllic island she'd run to in order to figure out her life.

She heard the click of the hammer as he raised the gun toward her.

No.

In one nimble, superfast motion, she grabbed the thermos and flung it at his head, heard the crack of the metal against his skull as he stumbled backward.

Mercy leapt to her feet, kicked off her shoes, and dove over the side of the boat, plunging into the frigid blackness of the water.

August 21, 1959

Dearest Cass—

I'm scribbling this out to you as I wait for Ren. He's coming tonight to have our big talk. I am both nervous and also relieved. I feel like after everything we've been through we are finally going to jump over the final gulf and truly be with one another in the real sense. That I will have all of him, for the first time.

A lot has happened here since I last wrote you. The play was canceled due to a fire. It's a long story behind it, and I'll save that for another time. Suffice to say that everyone is fine, though I am so very disappointed for the playwright.

On a brighter note, Ren and I had a marvelous time today at the ag fair, which is what they call their county fair here. I secretly entered Ren's vanilla apple pie recipe and I won second prize! (I can't complain—the winning buttermilk pie, whose recipe I was told dates to old England, looked positively scrumptious.) It was really just an amazing day, the two of us wandering the fairgrounds like . . . just another couple in love.

And I do love him, Cass. So very much. In a way I never loved Louis. Underneath that scruffy exterior he is warm and funny and loving, and his heart is one of the biggest I have ever seen. It's all been so unexpected, and also so confusing. Because now it's almost time for me to come back, and somehow, after the mess in Boston with the writer, I don't want to. And yet I can't imagine staying, trying to be the oysterman's wife. I never wanted a life that small, which is how I ended up on a one-way trip to California. I wish he would leave, that we could go somewhere together, but where? He'd last three days in Hollywood. I don't know what I am going to do.

I suddenly have a terrible feeling of foreboding washing over me, and I am trying to fight it. Wish me luck, darling. I need it.

Fondly,
Mercy

Twenty-eight

OCTOBER 2018

It's a beautiful, crisp New England autumn morning, and Kit is just walking out of the Espresso Love coffee shop when her phone rings. She doesn't recognize the number but does recognize the area code: L.A.

"Hello?" she answers, balancing the bag with her bagel, nova, cream cheese, onion, and capers and her crimson berry iced tea with one hand as she cradles the phone with her shoulder. A frail, thin voice answers back.

"Hello, hello? Kit? This is Cass Goldman, in California."

Kit smiles. "Cass! How lovely to hear from you. How are you?"

"Oh, well, about as good as any woman as old as dirt can feel, I suppose. My mums are blooming nicely, so I suppose there's that. And you, dear? How are you? How are things in New York?"

"Actually," Kit says, plopping onto a wooden bench in front of the Old Whaling Church, "I'm on Martha's Vineyard. Still on the trail of Nan's missing summer, if you can believe it."

"Well, isn't that something," Cass replies faintly. Kit can almost see the look of surprise on the woman's face coming through the phone. "I suppose then that it's providence that I am calling you now. If ever there was a sign that it was meant to happen, the fact that you're there is it."

"Now I'm intrigued. Please, tell me more."

"Well, I suppose I should just come right out with it. I owe you an apology, Kit. I've been struggling with something ever since your visit. I have not been completely truthful with you."

Now Kit is most definitely intrigued. "I see" is all she can say.

Cass clears her throat—she's obviously rehearsed this. "I can only tell you that many, many years ago, your grandmother made me promise that I would keep what I knew to myself. It was important to her, that she be able to put that part of her life behind her. But then you showed up, and . . ." She trails off for a moment. "Well, you so remind me of her. Her vitality, her spirit. You know, I've carried a lot of guilt about your grandmother. It was my idea that she go to Martha's Vineyard, and then everything that happened . . ." Another long pause. "Anyway, I got to thinking about what you said, about Mercy saving those souvenirs, and whether that might have been a sign that perhaps she *did* want you to know. I have to tell you, it's caused me a good deal of lost sleep."

"You were a great friend, and you wanted to protect her," Kit says. "I understand that."

"I have to ask: How much have you learned from your travels?"

Kit exhales. "Not as much as I'd hoped. I talked to a man in New York, a musician who knew her that summer. His memory is pretty bad, but I got enough from him to know I had to come here. I managed to track down a woman named Vera who knew Nan back then, who says they were very close friends that summer, but I don't know—something in me says she's exaggerating the connection."

"Trust me, she is."

Kit is taken aback by Cass's bluntness. How did she know? "And I was able to identify the man in the photo—"

"Ren Sewards."

Kit almost drops the phone. So Cass *did* know what Nan was up to. A lot more than she told. Maybe everything. "Yes. Unfortunately, he passed away some years ago."

"I'm so sorry, Kit. I should have told you the truth when you were here. But I am going to try and make it up to you. I'm sending you a package. I was about to mail it to New York, but if you give me your address there I'll arrange to have it mailed there."

"A package? Of what?"

"Correspondence," Cass says. "I lied when I said that the letters Mercy had written me had been discarded. Your grandmother was a very loyal pen pal. She wrote me faithfully that summer, and I still have the letters. They should be able to fill in some of the blanks for you. Hopefully you'll walk away with a better understanding of what happened to her there, and why she made the decisions she did as a result."

The letters. Nan's own words, about her experiences the summer that changed her life. Part of Kit is ecstatic, part of her extremely annoyed—how much easier would this entire process have been if she'd had these from the start? It doesn't matter now. The key thing is to make sure she gets them, safe and sound. Kit wonders if Cass should just send them to her apartment in New York. But she doesn't have a doorman. What if they're lost? And if she can read them while she's still here, she might be able to track down other people mentioned in them, tie up the final threads.

Cass goes to retrieve a pen and paper; she will have one of the aides in the development post the package. Kit thinks quickly. She can't have them sent to her Airbnb, which she suspects does not even get mail service. Seth. She can have them sent to her in care of Seth, at the historical society.

They had dinner again last night. More seafood, another walk—this time to her cottage. Another languid kiss. Actually, several languid kisses, along with a fair amount of cuddling.

Having another excuse to see him wouldn't necessarily be the worst thing, either.

*

She knows she is being impatient, bordering on immature, but as Kit paces her rental cottage she feels like she's ready to jump out of her skin. It's two days after Cass's call, and Seth has promised to phone her the minute the padded envelope arrives from California. Now it's closing in on eleven in the morning and still no word. Kit paid for early morning shipping herself, walked through the address and all the details with the aide from Cass's community, made her repeat all of the information twice. The aide assured her she would hand them to the FedEx guy personally.

She texts Seth: *Any sign of the package?* As she stares at the screen, praying for three bubbles and a message saying, *Yes! Come get it!* the phone rings in her hand.

"Hey," she says to him. "Sorry, I know I am being so over-the-top here. I have a lot riding on this."

"I get it," Seth says. They'd had a drink late last night at Alchemy, and during two hours of arguing about the quality of television journalism (*Name me one documentary basic cable has ever produced that's worth watching. Go ahead. I'll wait,* he'd said smarmily) and a hilarious exchange of their most embarrassing childhood stories, she'd managed to get out of her head and stay there. There was even more kissing, and more . . . well. It had all felt good. Really good. In between there had been a few quiet moments just talking. She'd told him more about Cass's letters, how they could finally answer the riddle she'd come here to solve. She'd toyed, just for a minute, with the idea of asking him if he wanted to stay the night. But something told her to hold off, that better things might come if she didn't do her usual "disposable man" routine. And despite her adamant refusal to admit it to another human being, least of all the ever-inquisitive Priya, she had to admit to herself that she had, in fact, been thinking about better things with Seth.

"Still no delivery?" Kit asks.

"Not yet. I know it was already supposed to be here, but remember—"

"I know, I know: 'island time.'"

"I'm sure it will show up soon. I'll remind Bernard to text you immediately. But listen: I have to bolt. I'm sorry, I know the timing is terrible. But I have a meeting with my dissertation advisor that I completely screwed up the dates for—I thought it was next week, and it's this week. So I am driving to Providence now and staying over, but I'll be back early tomorrow. Can we meet for lunch?"

"Sure. Hopefully I'll have read the letters by then and can fill you in."

"Sounds like a plan. I'll text you tomorrow morning to confirm."

*

But the letters hadn't come.

Kit had called FedEx, which insisted that the package had been delivered to the historical society, though the representative—after a seventeen-minute hold during which she was continually reminded "your call is very important to us"—said that since the package had not been shipped "signature required," it was impossible to determine who had actually received the package, or whether it had been delivered inside the building or left on the porch. Kit had then called Cass's aide, grilling her as if the woman were a hostile witness, to the point where the aide was on the verge of tears. She swore she had done everything she'd been asked.

Kit had filed a claim, and FedEx was due to call her back with an update.

As she sits at a table on the porch of Lucky Hank's, not far from her rental, she feels like she is about to lose it. She takes another swig of Sauvignon Blanc. Kit never drinks at lunch—it makes her sluggish the rest of the afternoon—but today is an exception. She needs to calm the hell down. The letters are somewhere. They have to be.

Seth is due any minute. He'd texted early this morning, saying the trip had gone well and there was something important he needed to discuss with her. In her experience, that meant "the relationship talk." She likes him—a lot—and as recently as yesterday might have actually warmed to the topic. But she is not in the headspace for it right now.

Her phone buzzes and she flips it over. A text from Priya.

Hey. I need to talk to you. Call me

Kit sighs. No doubt another bad date story, which Priya seems to have in endless supply. She's so not in the mood.

The phone rings, the caller ID signaling FedEx, and Kit answers instantly. The woman on the other line begins, in a monotone fit for a burned-out high school chemistry teacher, reciting the steps they are taking to locate Cass's package. Kit feels the phone buzz again in her hand, briefly lifts it away from her ear to see another text from Priya.

Please call me it's important

OK, so maybe it's not a bad date. She'll ring her as soon as she gets off.

The bored woman is reciting the package's journey from Los Angeles to Memphis to Edgartown in excruciating detail when Seth walks up onto the porch of Lucky Hank's. Kit nods at him and holds up one finger. He's wearing his standard-issue "hot boy from Cape Cod" look: form-fitting maroon sweater, olive army jacket, jeans, and scuffed brown ankle boots. He's carrying a backpack, a strap lazily thrown over one shoulder. The phone buzzes again. Another text from Priya.

Why aren't you calling me? I have to talk to you. You're trusting the wrong guy

Kit is looking at Seth, about to tell the FedEx lady she's going to have to call her back, when Priya's next text comes in.

Seth Cabot is a Sewards

Twenty-nine

Kit stands, frozen, her eyes still locked with Seth's. She wonders if she's being at all successful in masking the body blow she is currently absorbing. His own eyes are squinting into a puzzled scowl, as if he's trying to decipher what's happening, when Kit hears the FedEx lady bleating into the phone.

"Ma'am? Ma'am? Are you still there?"

Kit swallows hard. "Yes, yes, sorry. Thank you for your help." She disconnects, shoves the phone back into her jeans pocket as she tries to adopt a look of nonchalance. "Hey," she says.

"Everything OK?"

"Yeah, yeah. I'm just stressed. Still trying to track down Cass's package." She tilts her head to the door. "Let's go in and get something to eat."

A few minutes later they're sitting at a table, Seth confessing he has been dreaming of a chicken BLT since he got on I-195 this morning, Kit looking at her menu and seeing nothing as she tries to calm the hurricane in her ears. In one of the worst acting performances ever, she looks at her watch and remarks, "Oh, I totally forgot I was supposed to call Claire. Do you mind? Order me the spring salad. I'll be back in five."

Seth nods wordlessly—he can tell she's acting strangely, but he's not pressing—as she dashes back out the front door onto the porch, frantically retrieving her phone.

"Oh my God!" Priya answers. "Where have you been?! I've been trying—"

"I know, I know! Later. I only have a few minutes. I'm out with him now."

"Seth?"

"Yes. Go."

"OK, OK. Well, as you know, I've been kind of obsessed with your new boy toy since I found his picture. So I did some more digging. He is a doctoral student at Brown, and he is writing his dissertation about the indigenous people of the Vineyard. But I found an interview with him in a history journal from two years ago where he talks about his responsibility as part of one of the island's founding families."

"That could be any of a half dozen families."

"I dug some more. His mother, Laura, is the daughter of Patrick Sewards, who was the brother of your mystery man Ren. Laura was married to an investment banker named John Cabot, and they had two children before they divorced. She was then remarried in 2007, to a lawyer named—"

"Mark Milleneux," Kit whispers.

Priya sighs. "Yes. So the woman you interviewed at Sycamore is—"

"Seth's mother." No wonder he'd been able to set up the meeting with Laura so effortlessly. *The Sewardses are notoriously private people.* If only she'd known how private. And secretive.

She'd walked right into a trap. Seth, Ren Sewards's great-nephew, had known everything she was after, every secret she was trying to uncover, and had relayed it all back to his family in a running commentary so they could thwart her at every turn. She thinks back to her visit with Vera Kolchak, how evasive the old woman had been. God knows what Laura Milleneux had coughed up to keep her quiet. It probably hadn't taken much. Pocket change for a family like that.

I've been so naive.

Two things are now perfectly clear. One is that, as she had suspected when she left Sycamore, Laura Sewards Cabot Milleneux is most definitely hiding something.

The other is even worse.

Seth has the letters.

She could kick herself. She'd had them *sent to him*. Yesterday, he'd simply waited for FedEx to show up at the historical society, swooped up Cass's envelope, and hightailed it down to Providence to pore over them himself. That's if he'd ever really gone to Providence at all. It was just as likely he'd gone to Sycamore, passing them back and forth to his mother. Where are the letters now? Are they embers in Laura's fireplace?

Kit shuts her eyes tightly, takes in a deep breath, slowly exhales. She needs to think carefully here. She has one card to play—Seth doesn't know that she knows.

"Kit? You there?" Priya asks.

"I'm here." She turns back toward the front windows of the restaurant, looks in and spies Seth scrolling through his phone at the table. "I have to get back inside," she says. "I don't want him getting suspicious. Email me any other details you can find out about him and his family: links, articles, blogs, whatever you can scrounge up. I'll call you later."

"On it," Priya says.

By the time she takes her seat back at the table, her salad is waiting for her. He starts digging into his chicken BLT. "Sorry, that took longer than I thought," she says.

They make idle chitchat, but she knows she's acting oddly because of course she's acting oddly—she's just been betrayed by the guy she was falling for. The first guy she'd perhaps truly started to fall for, ever.

"So I need to talk to you about something," he says, carefully folding his napkin next to his plate.

She keeps her eyes on her salad, stabbing the greens like she's knifing an attacker. "Mmm hmm."

"Kit."

"Yes?"

"Can you please look at me?"

She slowly raises her eyes, and in that moment she sees the realization dawn in his. He knows: the jig is up.

"I haven't been completely forthcoming with you," he says quietly.

"Though given how you've been acting since I showed up today I suspect you've become aware of that."

She can't answer. Her throat feels like it's stuffed with cotton. She just keeps staring at him, hardly blinking.

"Right," he says quietly. "So you have clearly discovered that I myself am part of the Sewards family. And I can only imagine how angry you must be. Actually, I don't have to imagine it, I can see it on your face. I don't have the words to express how sorry I am. It was the wrong decision—a really terrible decision—and I regret it bitterly. It's just—"

And then, like an eruption, "It's just what, exactly?" Her voice is low, harsh.

He closes his eyes. "You have to understand what it's like, growing up in a family like this. The Sewards thing . . . it's, it's like being the Kennedys in Hyannis. OK, so maybe not exactly. But you get the idea. It's a big legacy, and there are a lot of people who are interested in my family and its history, and particularly how my family acquired its wealth. And like any clan in America that has roots that go all the way back to the sixteen hundreds, there are going to be some skeletons rattling around in the closet. From what I know, my great-grandmother was crazy protective about that stuff, and she passed that sense of paranoia down to my grandfather, who passed it to my mother."

"And they say history doesn't repeat itself," Kit says. "I mean, you're the historian, right? Here you go—proof right here that it does."

"I don't understand."

"Sixty years ago, my grandmother came to this island for the summer looking for answers and got involved with a very dashing man from your family who ended up twisting her so badly that she literally vanished from her own life. And now here I am, and I come to this island looking for answers, and I get involved with a dashing man from your family, and it's also ending in complete ruin."

He impulsively darts his hand across the table, puts it atop her arm. "Kit, please don't say that."

She retracts her arm like she's been stung by a wasp. "Why? It's true."

"Look, I get why you're furious. I totally do. And I will do everything I can to make it right. But you're not seeing this from the full perspective. In the end, we're the same. We're both just trying to protect people we love."

"We are not at all the same," she hisses. "And no amount of your warped logic is going to change that."

Quiet descends on the table, him looking down, her looking away, as the server arrives to clear the plates. Reading the body chemistry between them, she quietly slips the leather sleeve with the check onto the table and whispers, "No rush. Whenever you're ready," and departs.

Finally, Seth says, "Can we please just go somewhere and talk?"

She shakes her head vigorously. "I know your mother and stepfather lied to me, just like you've been lying to me. I know someone got to Vera Kolchak and got her to clam up, too. But make no mistake, Seth—I am going to get to the bottom of what happened that summer if it kills me. And I don't care what it does to your screwed-up family and its closet full of secrets."

"Kit, please—"

She stands up and flings her bag onto her shoulder, grabs her jacket off the back of the chair. She walks around to where he sits, leans down, their faces now mere inches apart. He won't make eye contact. Which is better, she thinks.

"So here's how this is going to play out," she whispers, slowly and deliberately, to his profile. "You are going to meet me at Memorial Wharf at five P.M. today and you are going to hand over the letters from Cass Goldman that you stole. Every. Single. One. I am going to check with her on exactly how many she sent, and they better all be there. Because if they're not, I am going to start making calls. And I promise you that a camera crew and the nastiest New York cable news investigative reporter I can find will be here tomorrow, ripping through your sordid family history and how it made its money and plastering it all over the national airwaves. And then you truly *will* be the Kennedys."

She turns and strides out of the restaurant, Nan's words cresting in her brain.

You have no idea what I am capable of.

*

It's only a few minutes before five, but the sky is already darkening, the clouds above the harbor gray, dense, and swollen. Kit sits on a curved wooden bench, looking out at the water. Had Nan sat here all those years ago, a young woman taking stock of her life, wondering what to do?

It's a few minutes later when she feels more than sees him approaching, right on time, the backpack again slung over one shoulder. For a moment she wishes she'd put more effort into her own appearance. She'd gone back to the cottage and out of nowhere had dissolved into a raging cry that wiped her out so completely she'd collapsed into sleep. By the time she'd gotten up and ready she'd had no time to decently cover up her puffy eyes, never mind read any of the additional material Priya had emailed. Not that it mattered much now, anyway.

He slides onto the bench next to her, follows her sight line out over the water. "Hey."

"Hey," she says, her arms crossed in a defensive posture. She can't bring herself to loosen them, never mind make eye contact. "You brought them?" she asks.

He jostles the backpack. "Yes. They were in my backpack at lunch. I had been planning on giving them to you then."

She swivels to look at him. "Why didn't you?"

"You didn't really give me a chance."

You blew your chance, she thinks. She stands. "Whatever. Just hand them over and I'll be on my way."

He shakes his head. "Not so fast. Sit down."

"I don't think you understand—"

"Kit!" he says, loud enough to attract a glance from a woman walking an Irish setter nearby. He lowers his voice. "You had your say. Now I get to have mine. And then once you hear me out, I will hand over the letters and you never have to see me again. But you are going to hear me out. Ten minutes, tops. So, please. Sit down."

Her impulse is to argue, but she's tired. And it's ten minutes.

She slowly sits back down and takes out her phone, sets the timer. "Clock starts now."

"Then I guess I better talk fast." He smiles wryly. "I didn't have a ton of friends growing up. It's weird to grow up on an island, never mind one with a really harsh winter and not a lot of people on it in the offseason. The boys I went to school with were really athletic, sporty types. I was much happier sitting by the fireplace reading comic books or playing video games. When I was ten, my parents told my sister and me that they were getting divorced. I can't say it came as a total shock—I mean, they barely spoke the last two years they were together—but still, everything you've ever known goes upside down. I know you can relate, even if your world got flipped over before you can even remember.

"Anyway, my father moved off island to Brewster, and he started a new family and I didn't actually get to see him much, other than briefly after Christmas and for a week or so in the summer. I was really starved, I think, for that sort of adult male figure boys need to look up to. But I had an ace in the hole, a gift that got me through the worst of it. I had my great-uncle Ren."

For the first time she looks over at him, sees the misting of his eyes.

"My grandfather was a nice man, but he was stiff, formal," he continues. "Uncle Ren was old-school cool. I was in awe of him. He didn't say much, but he was the type of guy who, when he did talk, you listened, because anything he said was wise and worth hearing. He never treated me like a kid, but like a person. He assumed I was smart and mature, even when I wasn't particularly either. He taught me how to sail, how to shuck an oyster, how to tie a proper square knot. I could ask him anything, and he would answer, no bullshit. He was everything to me: father, grandfather, friend, confidante. I worried that he spent so much time alone, but I think he liked it that way. He was really that archetypal old man and the sea."

His voice is thick, and he pauses to collect himself. "As he got older, he needed more help—he developed arthritis, other things you get when you age. I wanted to make sure I was there for him the way he had been there for me. I wanted to make sure I took care of him."

Kit nods. If she swapped in Nan for Ren, she could tell an almost identical story. "And I'm sure you did."

Seth shrugs. "I tried. So when you showed up, and you showed me the picture of him and your grandmother, I don't know—I knew there was a story there, and I was fearful it could be a painful one. I looked at the man in that photo and there was this . . . *joy* on his face. I don't think I'd ever seen that look in all the time I spent with him. I wanted to be careful. I guess in a way I was trying to protect him, his meaning in my life, the way you're trying to protect your grandmother. So I went to the house and told my mother about your journey here. *That* was my big mistake. She went nuts, telling me I couldn't say anything, that 'we have to control the narrative here.' Whatever that meant. She wouldn't explain why. She just insisted she would handle it, and had me set up your visit with her. And yes, I mentioned you were going to see Vera Kolchak."

"So I was right," Kit says. "Your mother bought her off."

"She'd never admit that, even if I asked her. But I swear to you, I didn't know anything about it. If I had, I would have come to you right away."

"And yet that didn't stop you from stealing the letters."

"I didn't 'steal' them. I was always going to give them to you. I had planned on giving them to you today at lunch before you exploded."

"Don't blame me for that."

"I'm not. I deserved it. I own that. I just wanted the chance to explain why I did what I did. If it makes any difference, and I'm sure it doesn't, if I had to do it over I would do it all very differently. But I was only doing it for him. I swear. Look at me."

She slowly turns, meets his gaze.

"I never intended for any of this to happen," he says. "I screwed up, and I am so sorry, and I hope someday you'll be able to forgive me. Because I really, really care about you, Kit." Something catches in his throat. The emotion is blazing in his eyes. "Actually, that's a lie. It's way beyond that. I'm falling for you. And I realize I probably blew it, and I'll have to find a way to live with that. But I need you to know what an amazing, incredible person I think you are. And even if we never speak again, I will always, always be grateful I got to have you in my life, even for just a moment."

The timer on her phone goes off.

Seth reaches into his backpack, retrieves the faded stack of letters tied with a white ribbon. "Here."

Kit takes them, stares at the postcard on top, recognizes an early iteration of Nan's graceful cursive. "You've read them?" she asks.

"Yes."

She nods, then stands. "OK, then."

"They'll clear up some things," he says, looking up at her. "But I don't think they'll be able to give you the whole story."

"Do you *know* the whole story?"

"No. But I think I can help you finally get to the bottom of it. If you'll trust me."

"And why should I do that?"

"Because," he says, "my uncle Ren isn't dead."

Thirty

She sat, shivering. The water had been black and surprisingly cold, tap cold, and she hadn't expected the shock of it. Icy trickles from the sopping hair tangled around her neck seeped down her back. She spasmed involuntarily, tried to will the bitter chill away.

How had she not *seen*?

She had been stupid. So incredibly stupid.

No time for all of that now. Mercy inched closer to the wall, scurrying deeper into the shadows. The moon was full, luminous, enormous, the kind of harvest moon people write songs about. Tonight it was her enemy, washing the meadow in soft lavender.

She rubbed her arms vigorously, trying to get warm, thankful it was still late August and not November or, God forbid, February, when the combination of the plunge into the water and the New England frost might have already killed her. Still, it was too cool to try and wait out the night. Her teeth were chattering. She'd have to move at some point, figure out where to go and, more important, how to get there without getting caught. Because she knew he was still out there. Somewhere. Waiting to finish what he started.

What he'd planned all along.

A noise. Rustling. She whipped her head side to side, paranoia and fear filling her quickly, like water into a jug.

No, she thought. *I can't sit here, wait for him to find me. I'm not giving up like that. Not without a fight. I've come too far, found strength I didn't even know I had. I'm smart. I've figured out other things. I can figure this out, too.*

It was not lost on her that figuring out things is what had led her to this moment, trembling in the crisp night air, trying to survive.

Mercy inhaled, taking in a deep, steadying breath, and launched onto her feet. She placed her hands on the wall behind her to steady her legs, still tired and weak from the swim through the dark water. She was not familiar with Chappaquiddick, knew it only from the small arrowed wooden signs planted around Martha's Vineyard that vaguely pointed in its general direction. The ferry traveled here, five minutes over, five minutes back, every day, though she had no idea where the terminus was, or even where on this small patch of sandy, scratchy island she was. She only remembered hitting the water, the electric force of it enveloping her body, the survival instinct kicking in and her legs kicking with it, until she was once again above the surface, swimming, tentatively, clumsily at first, then smoother, calmer, talking to herself, remembering the lesson, commanding her limbs to move, right arm forward, slicing into the water, then left, turning her head to breathe, the familiarity of the strokes slowly returning to her muscle memory. She had occasionally heard the chugging of the motorboat nearby, but he'd had a hard time tracking her movements in the inky sea.

Impulsively she now bolted from the safety of the shadows and dashed through the meadow beyond, her clothes wet and heavy. It was like running underwater. *What time is it?* She almost laughed at the thought. *What possible difference could what time it is make in this moment? Is this how it is before you die—your mind crumbles into randomness to blunt the force of what's coming?*

She heard him.

Dennis was behind her, running, and she dared not look back. She could make out the tall grass whistling against his legs as he sprinted, trying to catch up to her. He was surprisingly agile for his age.

He was gaining.

She reached a worn white wooden fence and lunged across it, awkwardly tumbling onto a gravel road on the other side. Hands braced on the ground, she scrambled back up, but as she lifted her head, it was already too late. He was standing in front of her, chest heaving, eyes wild, the moonlight behind him giving a sinister glint to the gun he held in his right hand.

"I tried to tell you," he said, the anger raging in his low voice. "I tried to get you to leave it alone. That's all you had to do. Leave it alone, then go back where you came from. But you didn't."

No, she didn't.

She eyed him evenly. "I couldn't."

Her response seemed to catch him by surprise. And for a moment it was just the two of them, standing alone on a godforsaken road on a tiny, deserted stretch of tiny, deserted Chappaquiddick, staring into each other's eyes in the dim moonlight. She summoned the courage to speak again. "I had to know."

He shook his head, lifted the gun, and pointed it at her. "I hope it was worth it."

Then he pulled the trigger.

Her eyes were shut tight, waiting for the end, when she heard it. The bullet, whistling by her ear and ricocheting off the gravel. The thud of a body on the hard ground. Grunting. Cursing.

Mercy opened her eyes to see Ren, his body now on top of Dennis's thrashing form, his arms desperately trying to pin the older man's to the ground.

The two men writhed around like panthers, Ren continuing to pound Dennis's right wrist into the chalky stones, frantically trying to loosen his grip on the revolver. Finally, after one last brutal bang, Dennis's hand opened up. The revolver skittered out.

"Grab the gun!" Ren screamed.

Mercy scrambled after the weapon, scooping it up just as Dennis kneed Ren in the groin and kicked him over, deftly pulling him in front of him. Mercy leapt forward, the gun feeling like it weighed a hundred pounds as she pointed it shakily in his general direction. Only now she could see something else—something shiny, silver, in Dennis's hand. A switchblade, positioned right at the base of Ren's throat. For a moment there was just an eerie, malevolent silence, the pieces on the chessboard not moving, each taking careful stock of the other two.

"Well, well, dearie," Dennis finally said, digging the blade just a little into Ren's neck, breaking the skin. "It seems like you have a choice to make. How good a shot are you? I suspect not very. So you have a choice. You drop the gun, and kick it over there, or I cut your lover's carotid artery and you watch the life bleed out of him right here."

Ren said, "Don't do it, Mercy—"

"Quiet!" Dennis thundered. "This is between me and your girlfriend. She's the one who started all of this. She can be the one who ends it."

Mercy remained standing, trying to control the shivering, the result of both her clinging, damp clothes and her raw, frayed nerves. She kept the gun raised, ignoring the muscle pain shooting into her upper arm. The gun was getting heavier by the second.

Finally, she spoke. "How do I know you'll spare him?"

"This boy is like a son to me," Dennis said. "You know that. I don't want to hurt him. Or you. Just toss the gun and we'll all pretend none of this ever happened. And then you can go back to where you came from, and no one has to know anything."

Mercy stood for another few seconds, her eyes leaving Dennis's for only a few seconds to meet Ren's. *No*, they blared. *Don't trust him.*

She slowly began to lower the gun, Dennis's dead eyes fixed on hers. Then—

Ren's elbow slammed into Dennis's rib cage, causing him to drop the switchblade. Ren raised his hands and reached for the older man's neck, choking him, but Dennis kicked him in the stomach, sending both men careening back onto the ground.

Mercy found herself momentarily paralyzed, unable to move, unable to scream. She watched in horror as the men scraped and clawed at one another, until she saw Dennis retrieve the switchblade and raise it. She knew what he was about to do.

What she had to do.

She grabbed the grip of the gun with both hands, raised it, aimed, and fired, the blood exploding from his back like a geyser.

*

So much of it was still a blur. She sat on the front steps of the cottage, wrapped in a blanket, trying to put it all together.

Ren had hidden Dennis's body in some thick brush, then taken her in his boat for the quick trip across Katama Bay back to Edgartown. He'd given her the keys to his truck, with strict instructions to go straight back to the cottage and wait for him. He told her to take the back roads, just in case there was anyone still roaming the streets, though at that hour, the chances were slim.

Mercy had done everything he'd asked. She'd stripped off her damp clothes and put them in a trash bag, taken the hottest shower her aching body would endure, and then dressed and gone out onto the porch to wait for him. It was almost three hours later when she spied his figure approaching out of the overnight shadows, walking wearily toward the house. He eased down slowly next to her on the step and exhaled deeply. "It's all done. It's over now. We got lucky."

She couldn't process that. "Lucky?"

"Lucky that you ended up swimming to the most remote tip of Chappaquiddick. This all could have ended much differently if someone had seen us."

She looked at him tenderly. "Lucky you taught me how to swim."

He reached over, pulled her in to him.

"What did you do?" she asked. "Where—"

"The less you know, the better. No more questions. They've . . ." He trailed off. But he didn't need to finish, because she knew what he was saying. *They've caused enough damage already.*

"I'm so sorry," she said, gathering the blanket more tightly around her. She was suddenly freezing, as if she'd once again just emerged from the black water. "I . . . I don't know what else to say."

He began rubbing her back. "I know. Like I said, it's done now."

"How can it be done? We have to go to the police."

He pulled back a bit, looked at her as if she'd just suggested he burn down the cottage. "No. We cannot go to the police. We cannot tell anyone about this, do you hear me? No one."

"But what happens when they . . . find him?"

"They won't. At least not for a while."

"What did you—"

"Mercy, please. You have to trust me."

She fought back tears. Her voice was barely audible. "What about Bridie?"

He hung his head. "Bridie will find out soon enough." He rubbed his face. "It is well known around the island that Dennis gambles. And he sometimes loses. A lot. He often owes money to people who expect prompt payment. It will be entirely believable that things got out of hand with one of them. Eventually, that will be the theory people will go with."

"Because you'll make sure they do?"

"Because it's Occam's razor. It's the simplest explanation. The one that fits."

"Except it's a lie."

He looked at her gravely. "It's what we have."

They sat in silence for several minutes, the only sounds the gentle clicking of crickets, the faraway whoosh of the ocean. Overhead, the first streaks of dawn were appearing in the sky.

All of the emotion, pent up inside since she first stepped onto Dennis's boat, began to leak. In seconds she was sobbing uncontrollably. He took her more tightly into his arms, comforting her, whispering in her ear, assuring her it was all going to be all right.

Finally, after she'd calmed down and a few moments of soothing silence had passed, she said, "You knew."

"Not until it was almost too late. But once Vera gave me a note, allegedly from you, saying you'd left, I knew you had to be in trouble."

"Vera was in on this?"

"A delusional accomplice. Thank God she cracked quickly."

Panic filled her body. "She'll know, Ren. She sent me to the wharf to meet Dennis. She'll know I had something to do with his disappearance."

He brought her hand to his mouth, kissed her knuckles. "Let me handle Vera. You need to get some sleep. We both do."

"You have to tell me first."

"Tell you what?"

"How long have you known . . . what really happened to your father?"

He nodded slowly. "I've known a long time."

"And you never said anything? To anyone?"

"I couldn't."

She grabbed his arm. "Ren, that's crazy. This is all . . . crazy."

He simply stared ahead, his eyes fixed on the lone streetlamp, eerily glowing an orangey hue. Finally, he spoke again. "Do you know how they met? Mother and Dennis?"

Mercy recalled her talk with Ellenanne. She closed her eyes tightly. Another secret she was keeping. For every one exposed, there was always another one right behind it. "Not precisely."

"Mother came from nothing, you know. Her people were farm people, from New Hampshire. She didn't want anything to do with that life. So she went to Boston and went to work as a maid for a bank president and his wife. They had a summer house here, and the wife took Mother with her one summer to make sure the kids didn't drown at the beach while she drank and played cards. My guess is Mother targeted my father for capture the minute she saw him. I mean, I've seen pictures of her back then. She was a beautiful young woman. And clever. There was just one small problem. She'd left a suitor behind in Boston. Someone of her own station. Someone she'd agreed to marry."

Mercy flashed back to Ellenanne, sitting in her living room in the cottage, talking about Mint's journey to Martha's Vineyard more than thirty years ago. *She had evidently secretly been engaged to a working boy in Boston.* "Dennis."

Ren nodded. "Dennis. Poor slob. He never had a chance. When she stopped writing, he followed her here, determined to win her back. But he was no match for my father's money, the family lineage, the whole 'first family of Martha's Vineyard' bullshit. She and Dad were married in Boston that fall."

"That musn't have gone over well with your grandparents."

"It didn't. But Dad was always a rebel. And as the only son, he was given a lot of latitude. Too much latitude. Mother made a big effort to win them over, and she eventually did. She was like Eliza Doolittle in that play."

"*Pygmalion*."

He nodded. "She learned to dress, how to set a table, read important books, surrounded herself with the proper ladies. She had it all covered. Except one detail she didn't account for. Which was that my father was a violent, terrible man."

Mercy slipped her hand into his, gently caressed the rough texture of his skin with her thumb. "Tell me," she whispered.

He shook his head resignedly. "Years of abusive behavior. He drank. A lot. Hit her. A lot. Sent her to the hospital once. He could be incredibly nasty. It took a toll. On all of us. Especially Ellenanne."

The opening she needed. She took it. "I saw her, Ren," Mercy said. "She was here."

"I know."

Mercy's eyes opened wide. "You do?"

"She came to see me afterward. It's why I knew we really had to talk last night, to get it all out in the open, once and for all." He filled in more details of his going to the cottage, finding Vera and the forged note telling him she'd gone. How he'd shaken the truth out of Vera, immediately jumped in his boat to go find her.

"And you did," she said. "Just in time."

"No," he said. "Just a little too late."

She leaned a bit more into him. "Ren, we have to go to the police. I . . . I . . ." She almost couldn't get the words out. "I killed someone."

He whipped around, took her face gently in his hands. "You saved my life. That's it. That's all of it. You had a choice, and you chose to save me."

She shook her head, felt fresh tears running down her cheeks. "But the truth has to come out."

"The truth can never come out."

"But this has to stop. All of these years, Ren . . . your mother killed your father. And Dennis helped her cover it up."

"He was a young policeman, hopelessly devoted to a woman who was never going to love him back. But you only have half of it right. Dennis did help her cover it up. But that was all."

"What do you mean?"

"I mean, my mother didn't kill my father."

She pulled back slightly, perplexed. "How do you know?"

He looked her squarely in the eye. "Because I did."

Thirty-one

She is out of time.

It is the dominant thought running through her mind as she sits in the kitchen of the great house, staring out the window but seeing nothing. Jasper will be home from his latest trip to Boston tomorrow, no doubt well sated by the whore he keeps in Back Bay that he thinks she is too stupid to know about. But she is smarter, and more resourceful, than he suspects.

The dose of laudanum she took an hour ago has kicked in, and she finds herself slowly swimming in its powers. That's the good thing about a country doctor on a sleepy island—he doesn't argue as much, isn't as tied up in the "ethics" of things, especially if you have the money to make it worth his while. And especially if he has a wife desperate to climb into society, and you are able to grease the wheels for her.

She takes a long, deep breath, exhales. She has arranged for Ellenanne and Patrick to be taken out after school. That will give her time to talk to him. Convince him that this is the only way. For all of them.

She knows it is wildly unfair—how can she put this on the shoulders of a boy of fourteen? He is big for his age, strong, an outdoorsman, already quite adept as a sailor. But she has watched the last embers of his childhood innocence slowly flicker out. Each day the light inside him dims just a little more. She can see him becoming hardened and withdrawn due to Jasper's relentless tirades, the drunken slaps and punches. She knows what the receiving end of those feels like. Recently Jasper's begun being rough with Ellenanne. Patrick, her little ball of sunshine, will be next. Jasper will ruin all of them.

It all has to stop. Now.

She knows the truth: that Jasper is only months away, maybe even less, from divorcing her. When he is worse for the bourbon, which is most of the time, he jeers about it, threatens it, promises it. He has the money and power to ensure that she is left with nothing. She will be banished from the Vineyard, cast out without her children and with no recourse to see them, never mind get them back. And she cannot leave them with him, watch helplessly as he discards them, too, as he surely will. It would be better if they all were dead.

But it would be best if he were.

She knows that she has not been a good mother. She has not weathered the abuse well, has not protected Warren, has retreated into a fog of booze and medication to survive it. But she can see where the road is leading. She is out of options. Except this one. One that will leave a deep, bleeding scar on her eldest child but, just perhaps, save the other two. A Hobson's choice.

She hears him walk through the front door. "Warren? Is that you?"

"Yes."

"Come join me in the kitchen," she yells out.

And so he does. She has cookies waiting, which he now decries do not matter to him as a teenager but which he eyes hungrily and devours anyway. There is still the little boy inside him, the one who used to sit on her lap and read *The Story of Ferdinand* as she played with his sandy hair. They engage in idle chitchat about school and sailing this summer and Will Inbusch's birthday party next week. She sneaks in a question about Vera Harding, who is in the same grade as Ellenanne and clearly worships him and whom he most definitely does not want to talk about.

"When is he coming home?" he asks. "He." Not "Dad."

"Tomorrow. That's what I want to talk to you about."

He wolfs down the last cookie. "OK."

She scoots her chair closer to him, takes his hand in hers, pausing to brush the hair out of his eyes. She sees the scar of the hairline fracture he suffered last year after Jasper knocked him over the dining room table for laughing at his tie. A sign. A reminder she's doing the right thing.

"Warren, you're the oldest. You're not a child anymore. You're a young man now. A fine young man. And I need your help."

He looks at her warily, says nothing.

"We can't keep living like this. With Dad," she continues. "I think you know that. You'll be the head of this family one day. And so I need you to help me. Help all of us. To protect our family. To *preserve* it."

He clearly has no clue where she's going with this, a fact attested to by the look of bewilderment now on his face.

"I am going to tell you the truth, Warren. Dad is going to divorce me and send me away. And I am powerless to stop him. He knows the right lawyers, the right judges. He'll banish me and I will never see you or your sister or brother again."

Bull's-eye. She can see him fighting to retain his composure. His eyes are now pure alarm. She keeps rubbing his hand, maintaining eye contact, keeping her voice steady, soft, as she lowers the boom. "Once I'm gone it'll just be you three here with him, alone." It isn't really the truth. She knows that Jasper will have the children sent away to boarding schools, discarded like old clothing as he makes room for a new, younger Mrs. Sewards.

That does it. A tear rolls down her son's right cheek as he grips her hands in his. "No," he whispers. "No, Mother, no. He can't. Please. I can't—"

"I know. I know," she says in her most soothing, reassuring tone. "But there is a way out for us, Warren. But we need to summon the courage to take it, both of us. You and me. Because we're the only ones who can do it. Who can save our family from ruin. I can't do this alone. But *we* can. Together."

He looks at her, fearful and expectant, and in this moment she considers pulling the plug on all of it. How can she do this to him?

What choice does she have?

She speaks carefully, deliberately. "Tomorrow night, when Dad is back, after dinner, I am going to send you all upstairs, as always. But then you will come back down, quietly. And Dad will go out for his nightly cigar, standing at the cliffside out front. But tomorrow night, he will be a bit more woozy than usual." Woozy from the laudanum she will make sure is in every drink he consumes at dinner. "And then . . ." She swallows hard, and for a second thinks she will not be able to utter the words. But she must. She knows she must.

"And then you are going to get a running start, and run as fast and as hard as you can out the front, and all it is going to take is one hard shove from the back, Warren. Just one. And then it will all be over. We'll be safe. All of us. Forever. You can save our family."

She can't look at him, cannot bear to see whatever it is in his eyes, because how do you look at your son after you have just told him he needs to kill his father? Instead she keeps her eyes on her lap, slowly massaging the tops of his hands with her thumbs, choking back the sob of shame now caught in her throat.

It is a few minutes before he says anything, but then he says, calmly, dispassionately, as if remarking on the weather, "I'll go to jail."

"No," she says. "You will not. I promise. I have a very good friend who's a policeman here. He'll make sure that doesn't happen. He'll make sure it will all be seen as an accident. Which it is, Warren, when you think about it. This is all a terrible accident, us getting into a mess we didn't ask for. But we owe it to Ellenanne and Patrick. We have to save them. Only we can do it. You and me."

"You could do it."

She has prepared for this. "I would," she says clearly. "I would. But I am too slight. I wouldn't be able to summon the proper strength. But you . . . you can."

By the time she meets his eyes she can see the difference. The very last vestiges of his boyhood innocence, extinguished in one horrible conversation. There is only the smoke in his stare now. A look of disdain. Fear. Loathing. Resentment. And duty. It is this last that she hopes will win him over. That he will embrace being the man he is now being forced to be.

It's quiet for what seems like an eternity.

"All right then," he says finally, his voice barely a whisper. And with that he gets up from the table and walks calmly out of the room.

She throws her head into her hands and sobs.

*

"Another mediocre meal," Jasper is saying, unfolding the *Wall Street Journal* and beginning to idly flip through the pages at the dinner table. "The potatoes were all right, I suppose."

She's made his favorite—chicken cordon bleu—and watched him eat it hungrily, slovenly, as he always eats when he's had too much to drink. Not that tonight it's his fault. She has been liberal with the bourbon, even more liberal with the laudanum. She has to be careful—the last thing she needs is him skipping his evening cigar and heading straight to bed.

She clears his plate as he belches, tries to retain a look of impassivity as she strolls back into the kitchen. She places her palms firmly down on the counter and lets out a long, staccato breath. *Just a little longer, Margaret,* she tells herself. *Just a little longer and this will all be over.*

She is walking back out into the dining room when she spots him, lurking in the shadows of the dimly lit living room beyond.

Warren stands by the front hall closet, dressed in a T-shirt and pants and sneakers. She can barely make out his face. For this, she is thankful. Patrick is already asleep, a creature of habit and a strict schedule. She hopes to God Ellenanne is still firmly ensconced in a storybook in her room.

"Do you want some dessert, or are you going to go out for your cigar?" she asks blithely.

He doesn't bother looking up. "Just checking the market and then I'll go out." He pats his breast pocket. "Bill Carter gave me a little Partagas today. Should be a sweet smoke."

She thinks grimly, *You have no idea.*

The minutes tick by like hours. She clears the rest of the plates and serving dishes, begins running warm water. The housekeeper is away this week, visiting family in New Jersey. It's why she knew she had to get this done now. Tonight. No witnesses. Keep it neat.

She's standing at the sink when she hears the French doors of the dining room open, his footsteps fading as he walks down toward the cliff. She shuts her eyes tightly, picturing Jasper stopping, extracting the cigar, lighting it up—

Just as she turns toward the kitchen doorway she sees her son's athletic figure whiz by, the blur of his billowing shirt and charging legs. Then he's gone.

She turns back to the sink, holds on to the sides for support as her knees begin to buckle.

A minute passes. Then another. An eerie quiet settles over the house.

She turns off the faucet, mindlessly dumps the dishes into the hot, soapy water. She wipes her hands on the dish towel, then pivots and begins walking slowly toward the still-open doors, outside onto the portico.

He is sitting on the top step, his head in his hands, his body rock still. She looks past him, out toward the cliff, and sees . . . nothing. There is only the bright light of the nearly full moon, the sound of the crashing waves below.

She walks past him, out onto the lawn, and stares up at the heavens. *Please forgive me*, she prays. *Forgive me. I didn't know what else to do.*

A distant light to her left captures her attention. She can see the kitchen light of the Chadwick house, make out a small figure inside. John, or Grace? She can't tell. Adrenaline splashes into her veins. *Did they see? Do they know?*

She can't think about that now.

She turns back to Warren, sitting still as a statue, and walks toward him. She reaches out, leans down to hug him. "My brave boy—"

"Don't touch me!" he screams, flinching away as if she's on fire. His eyes seethe with hatred. She made him do this. She turned him into . . . this. It is in this moment that she realizes what a truly magnificent price has been paid.

He stands and bolts back into the house, until a few seconds later she hears the slamming of his bedroom door.

It takes a few minutes for her to gather herself, to walk calmly back inside. She goes to the living room, picks up the receiver from the telephone on the side table, and dials.

"Edgartown Police."

"Sergeant Dennis deCoursey, please," she says.

Thirty-two

Are you sure we should be here?" she asked flatly.

Mercy looked out the passenger side window of the truck. She still felt tired. So very tired. Will she ever sleep again? Will she ever outrun the image burned into her brain, lifting the gun, firing the gun, watching the violent result?

Ren had just pulled the truck up to Sycamore. "Yes, I'm sure," he said. "It's time we got to the bottom of the whole story. We're owed that."

"You told me the whole story." And he had, in excruciating detail. The only thing that had confused her was Grace Chadwick and Ellenanne, who had both said they'd witnessed Mint do the deed. Grace, Ren had told her, was too far away to discern who had actually perpetrated the crime. Ellenanne, on the other hand, knew it had been him. She had just insisted that the blame always be placed where she knew it belonged—with Mint.

Mercy was still trying to absorb it all, the horror of what Mint had coerced Ren into doing, the dark secret she had sentenced a fourteen-year-old boy to carry for the rest of his life. And now they were here, literally at the scene of the crime, trying to get to the truth about another murder.

The one she herself had committed.

It had been over a week since that ghastly night on Chappaquiddick. Sparsely populated or not, it had been nothing short of a miracle that no one had seen or heard anything that had occurred. Vera, Ren assured her, knew nothing and no doubt wanted to know even less, lest she be implicated in any malfeasance. That left only the issue of Bridie, who after two days had officially reported Dennis missing, and had been frantically calling anyone she could think of trying to find out what had happened to him. With a former police officer vanished, the Edgartown cops were in overdrive trying to get to the bottom of it. Ren had been right: the *Gazette* had published a story containing the theory linking Dennis's disappearance to gambling debts. Ren was convinced that by the time Dennis was found—if ever—there would be no way to connect his death to them.

Which only left one outstanding question: Why had Dennis done it?

The thought of having to face Mint again had Mercy visibly trembling. "I don't think I can do this, Ren," she said. "It's too much."

He reached across, placed a hand gently on her arm. "She'll shut down with me. But it will be much harder to do that with you there." He took her chin between his thumb and forefinger and kissed her softly. "Always be brave."

So up and in they went, the startled maid who answered the door giving a quick "I don't want any trouble" look as she scurried upstairs to retrieve the mistress of the house.

Five minutes later Mint walked into the sitting room, spine stiff and chin raised, surveying the two of them standing near the fireplace. She wore a lavender blouse and draping gray slacks. She sported matching lavender eye shadow that gave her the appearance of an evil queen in a Walt Disney cartoon.

"Where's Patrick?" Ren asked. No greeting, no attempt at even basic civil formalities.

Mint glanced from him to Mercy, lingering just a few seconds, and then back to him. "He's gone back to Dartmouth," she said. There was a few more seconds of engulfing silence, and then Mint tentatively waved them onto the sofa. "Please, sit down," she said. "May I offer you something?" The baroness of the estate to the last.

They dutifully sat as she gracefully sank into a chair opposite them, casually crossing her legs. "And to what, may I ask, do I owe this . . . impromptu visit from my eldest son and his consort?"

"We have a few questions for you," Ren said.

"I see. About what?"

"About Dennis deCoursey."

She scrutinized him. "What about him?"

"You know he's missing."

"Yes, I heard. I've sent a note to Bridie, offering any assistance she may need."

"How generous. Do you know what's happened to him?"

Mint's eyes fluttered with surprise. "No. How would I?"

"I figured that perhaps because you asked him to kill Mercy, you might have a clue."

Her eyes dropped in disdain. She shook her head vigorously. "The older you get, the more ridiculous you get, Warren. I worry about you. That comment is so ludicrous I find it impossible to gather the facility to dignify it with a reply."

"Well, let me fill you in on just how ludicrous it is, Mother." And then he did. He methodically relayed all of it: the forged notes, Dennis luring Mercy out on the boat, their confrontation on Chappy and its malevolent end, though in his retelling the identity of the shooter was implied to be him. At the denouement Mint turned ghostly pale. She began to visibly shake. "You're lying," she hissed. "To say such a thing . . . You're a monster."

"You forget, Mother," he replied flatly. "You created this monster."

It was almost too much for Mercy to endure, wallowing in this nightmare that had bonded mother and son for fifteen years. Ren continued, "Did you put him up to it? For once, tell the truth, Mother."

"How could you ask such a thing?"

"Because you've done it before." Mint's eyes flew wide open as they quickly met Mercy's. "Yes," Ren said. "She knows."

It was as if someone had punctured a balloon. Mint's entire appearance changed in an instant. The formidable, stony matriarch melted, like the witch after Dorothy's flung bucket of water, replaced by a shell of herself, suddenly looking small and fragile against the tapestry of the grand tufted chair. She shook her head. "Poor Dennis," she said softly. "He had one fatal weakness."

"You," Ren said.

She nodded. "Me." Mint trained her eyes back on Mercy, directly addressing her for the first time since they'd arrived. "I am sure he has filled your head with all sorts of stories about me, and that's fine. Some of them may even be true. As I am sure you've learned from him, as well as from Grace Chadwick and no doubt others, I was not exactly a model mother for my children. But I tried. Everything I ever did, then and now, I did to protect them. That's all I ever wanted. All any mother wants. To protect her children."

Mercy glanced over at Ren, who sported a look that combined pity and utter disdain. It was clear that no amount of time would ever repair the broken bond between mother and son. Especially not now, with so many more victims caught in the wake of the death of Jasper Sewards. Ellenanne. Staxx. Grace. Vera. Dennis. Bridie. Her and Ren. All of them collateral damage from a terrible decision made fifteen years earlier by a desperate, lonely, suffering wife afraid of losing everything.

"Did you put him up to the fire at the theater?" Ren asked.

"No. Though I take responsibility for that." She looked over at Mercy. "I did go to him, tell him I was concerned about your inquisition into our family. But I never told him to do that. And I certainly would never have encouraged what came after, had I known."

Ren scoffed. "That's you. Never leaving fingerprints." He stood, Mercy haltingly following suit. "We'll be going now," he said tersely. "I need to go and see Bridie."

Mint looked up at him plaintively. "What will you tell her?"

Ren eyed her dismissively. "Something she can live with."

"I'll have Patrick set up a trust," she said. "She'll be taken care of."

"I'm sure that will bring her great comfort." Ren took Mercy by the elbow and began to lead her out. "Goodbye, Mother."

*

They stood back on the beach at Great Rock Bight, the crossroads of their summer romance. How different it looked now from that first day they'd come, when he'd taken her out on the boat, only to have the two of them topple overboard. He'd taught her to swim, which would later, in the darkness off Chappaquiddick, save her life. And it had been here that they had made passionate love for the very first time, an image that would be forever seared into her memory. She wondered if the same thoughts were running through his mind.

"I guess you could call this 'our place,'" Mercy said.

Ren looked over at her on the blanket they'd spread on the sand. "Yes. Though there are several places I'll always think of as ours."

"It feels different this time."

"How?"

"It feels like goodbye."

He said nothing for a while, just kept looking out at the ocean. People were frolicking in the water, sitting under umbrellas. Everyone trying to wring out the last moments of summer before Labor Day in a few days. Finally, she couldn't take it anymore.

"Ren, look at me."

It took a few seconds—he clearly did not want to look at her in this moment—but he complied. His expression was inscrutable. "Please don't do this," she said.

"Do what?"

"Retreat."

"Is that what you think is happening? I'm retreating?"

"It certainly feels like that, yes."

He looked back to the ocean. "We've been through one hell of an adventure, you and I. And all because you didn't know what wine to order with oysters."

She laughed. "If I'm being honest, I'm still not sure." She threaded her arm around his. "That's why I need you. To keep me on the mark with my wine pairings. Among other things."

He turned to her. "Mercy—"

"Please don't say it, Ren. Please. I've been thinking. A lot. I'm not going back to Hollywood. There's nothing left for me there but empty glamour and people climbing over one another to get ahead. I've experienced what it means to really love someone, to want a life with them. I'll stay. We can be together. Here."

He looked deeply into her eyes, and she could see it again now. The love he couldn't hide, no matter how hard he tried. But something else, too. Melancholy. A deep, deep sadness.

"You're romanticizing too much," he said, and as she began to object he gently placed his fingers across her lips. "Please, baby. Let me talk. We both know I don't do a lot of talking. But let me say what I need to say."

She nodded meekly, afraid to utter a sound. Because she could feel the truth, welling up inside her body, slowly rising to the surface. The stark knowledge that, in this matter, she'd already lost.

"You are the most amazing woman I have ever met. Beautiful, kind, funny, smart, and a bit too inquisitive." They both smiled. "I have never been able to be my whole self with anyone before you, and I doubt I ever will again. And I thank you for that, from the bottom of my heart. You awoke something in me that I thought had died years ago, on that cliff in front of Sycamore. I will always be grateful to you for that.

"But we come from two very different worlds, Mercy. We can't stay here in this bubble forever. You have no idea how harsh the winter here can be. And in those bitter months I will be gone for long stretches out on the water, up in the middle of the night, exhausted and in bed by dinner. The winter population on this island can drop into the hundreds. You'll be horribly lonely here, and I cannot sentence you to that."

"I could try," she said meekly.

"That's not all of it, though, is it? Suppose you stay. Once the reporters find out you've abandoned your movie career to be an oysterman's wife, how long will it be before they show up, asking questions? All it will take is one nosy writer to ply Vera with too many glasses of wine at the Harborside and our entire lives could unravel. And it won't be just us they'll take down. I can't risk Ellenanne, or Patrick, being swept up in that. Or even my mother. And then there is Bridie to consider, and others like Mrs. Chadwick. It's a house of cards, Mercy. There's just too much at stake. Every day that we wander into town or sit at dinner we'd always be looking around, wondering who is watching, who might possibly know. Waiting for the day it all collapses. What we've done will always be there, between us, hovering over us like a shadow for the rest of our lives. We've each killed someone, Mercy. We can't tempt fate any more than we already have."

The irony was not lost on her that it was almost the exact argument Dennis himself had made. "But none of this is our fault," she pleaded. "Your mother—"

He shot his hand to her face, began caressing her cheek. "Sometimes, it doesn't matter whose fault it is, my love. It merely is what it is. You need to go back to California and find your life."

"I found it here."

"You found who you *are* here. But your life isn't here."

She felt her heart slowly breaking into pieces, fought to keep her voice from cracking. "You could come with me."

But his face told her what she already knew: He would never leave Martha's Vineyard. It was in his blood. And no amount of pleading or rationalizing from her was ever going to change that. The worst of it was that, deep down, she knew he was right. Going from being an actress to an oysterman's wife would be a jarring adjustment at best, particularly in the brutal throes of a New England winter. Never mind the constant company of the ghosts of Jasper Sewards and Dennis deCoursey. But she meant what she'd said. She didn't want to go back to show business. She would need instead to go somewhere big, a hive of activity, somewhere without eyes upon her. Where she could figure out what came next. Figure out who she had now become after this fateful summer.

She threaded her hand into his and rested her head on his arm as they looked out over the water, and into the future.

*

Martha's Vineyard Airport was bustling—or at least as bustling as an airfield that tiny could be—with post–Labor Day travelers heading out, many of whom, like her, had been on the island for the entire season. Looking around, Mercy was sure none of them had experienced the life-changing summer she just had.

"It feels odd to be back here," she said.

"Why?" Ren said.

"It seems like a lifetime ago when I first arrived here."

"It has been."

What more was there to say that had not been said? They both stood inside the small terminal, looking at the people around them and yet seeing nothing. "I feel like Ingrid Bergman in *Casablanca*," Mercy said finally.

He smiled wryly. "We'll always have Martha's Vineyard."

She felt the fresh tears coming and fought to keep them at bay. Because what she wanted to say in this moment was, *Come with me. Leave here. Let's go somewhere. Anywhere. Just us. We can be happy. I know we can.* But she knew what he'd say.

"I'm still surprised you're not going back to Hollywood," he said.

"There's nothing left for me there. Mercy Welles has been running the show and she's made sort of a mess." They both laughed softly. "Maybe it's time to let Edie Stoppelmoor take over for a while."

"I think that's a capital idea," Ren said. "Though, for the record: it wasn't *all* a mess."

Mercy stared deeply into his eyes. "No. It wasn't."

She opened her bag and retrieved a small parcel wrapped in brown paper and string and handed it to him. "This is for you." He was about to pull at the string when she darted her hand out to stop him. "Oh, no, not here. Open it later. Please."

He slid the package under his arm and retrieved a petite box of his own from the pocket of his jacket. It had a small envelope on top. "I suppose this is our 'Gift of the Magi' moment," he said, handing it to her. "This is for you."

She looked up at him with shining eyes and whispered, "Thank you," then added, "for everything." She reached up, cupped his cheek. "I'll never forget you."

He placed his hand atop hers. "Nor I you, my love."

The intercom crackled to life. The boarding call for the flight to Boston. Slowly, people around them began to file by.

They looked lovingly into one another's eyes. And then, with one last passionate kiss, one last soulful embrace, they parted.

Thirty minutes later Mercy sat on the tiny plane, fighting with every ounce of strength she could muster to retain her composure, fingering the small package on her lap. Finally, she carefully opened the envelope, extracting the heavy stock notecard with SYCAMORE emblazoned at the top, and laughed out loud at the irony. When had he purloined it from Mint's study? She read the inscription:

Nancy—Something to remember me by, or to stow away in the attic. R.

Mercy opened the lid of the small blue box, and found the stunning sapphire necklace looking back.

September 3, 1959

My dear friend—

I write this to you on the last morning here in my cozy little cottage in Edgartown. Ren is coming soon to pick me up to take me to the airport. I am filled with such wild emotions as I prepare to leave this island, which has proven to be both magical and tragic and often both. The only thing I know for sure is that this trip has truly changed my life forever.

I am not coming back to Hollywood. I know I mentioned this possibility in passing in my last letter, and no doubt you thought I was mad, and probably still do. And maybe I am. But I discovered something very real here, what it is like to experience real emotion, real joy, real love, none of which I ever felt during my years pursuing the empty dream of stardom. It's a fine and glamorous life for a lot of people, but I have discovered that it is not for me.

I won't go into everything that's happened since I last wrote you. It's extremely complicated and, frankly, some of it is quite painful and will be carried with me for the rest of my life. But suffice to say that Ren and I have determined that a future together is not possible for us. Although this realization pains me more than I can put into words, I have to trust that God has another path for me to follow, and that there will be happiness in it. I am going to go to New York, where I can take off the mask of Mercy Welles and try to rediscover the Edie underneath. I just want to spend some time anonymous, roaming the streets and drinking wine at a café and wandering through dusty bookstores. I still have some money left, and I am going to use it to attain a skill I can use to support myself while I am trying to figure out the most basic thing: who I am, and what I truly want out of life. It turns out, to my surprise, it's not an Oscar after all.

I cannot express what your encouragement and support have meant to me this summer by just being there, by listening, by being a witness to all of this. And although this journey is ending on a bittersweet note, I will always be thankful that you sent me here. You are cranky, irascible, blunt to a fault—and one of the best friends I have ever had and will ever have.

I'll call you from New York once I am settled. In the meantime, send your best hopes and wishes, as I do to you. And if I may impart one piece of wisdom I have gleaned from this experience, let it be this: never, ever order red wine with oysters.

With so much love,

Mercy

Thirty-three

Kit's heart is pounding so hard she's surprised Seth can't hear it. They're headed up the small stone path that leads to Ren Sewards's bungalow off Lucy Vincent Beach. It's an area that's now filled with pricey saltbox houses with flower boxes and lustrous shutters and manicured lawns comprised of soft white pebbles. Kit isn't surprised to find out that this is where Ren settled, and stayed, decades ago. It's one of the least crowded parts of the island.

Seth's mother, it turned out, had been telling the truth about one thing: Ren had never married. Seth had told her that while he had not lived a hermetic life, Ren had lived a solitary one, comprised mainly of his oystering business, his summer work as a handyman, and his occasional foray into genial unclehood with Ellenanne's and Patrick's kids. And she already knew about Seth's deep connection with him—it was clear from the way he talked about him that Seth had a very special place in his heart for his great-uncle.

After getting over her initial shock at finding out that Ren Sewards was, in fact, very much alive, Kit had experienced a wide range of emotions: anger that even more had been kept from her, but also, oddly, compassion that Seth had wanted to make sure Ren, a fiercely proud and private man, had been protected from abrasive intrusion into his past. He didn't welcome many visitors these days, other than the caretaker the family had in daily to do his laundry, make his meals, and generally make sure he wasn't lying in a hallway with a broken hip. He had steadfastly refused any overture to move into

Sycamore or housing for the elderly. At the age of eighty-eight he lived his own way, and he was going to die his own way, too.

As they stand before the front door, Kit lets out a deep breath. "You OK?" Seth asks.

"He knows, right? Who I am, what I'm here for? You're sure he's OK with this?"

He offers her a look of reassurance. "Yes. I promise. He wants to meet you. We wouldn't be here if he didn't."

They walk into the small house, and it is exactly what Kit expected: spartan, orderly, slightly musty, decorated with seafaring imagery and maps on the walls, and furnished with neat but worn uphol-stered pieces in heavy wood. There's a brick fireplace coated in soot, and a side table laden with books, mainly biographies and memoirs. To the left of the fireplace is a tidy bookcase holding a lamp. Next to the lamp sits a small silver picture frame. Kit forgets herself for a mo-ment and bolts toward it, impulsively picking it up. She looks down at the same yellowed photo she has in her own bag, of Mercy Welles and Ren Sewards looking so much in love.

"The ag fair in 1959," comes a gravelly voice from her right, and she looks up to see him, ambling toward her on a cane made of pine. His hair is shocking white, matched by a scruffy beard that gives him the look of a slightly macho Santa Claus. His skin is pocked with brown sunspots and deep creases, a testament to a life spent on the water. He wears a simple flannel shirt and baggy jeans, black sneakers on his feet. He's not quite as tall or imposing as she's imagined, but suspects he's lost more than a few inches as he's aged. He stops in front of her. He doesn't smile—it's more of an appraisal—but his eyes are warm, with a hint of mirth. He points down to the picture. "I made your grandmother take the original. I got a copy from the photographer."

Kit looks around quickly. There are no other photos on display anywhere else in the entire room. Only this one.

Seth sidles up next to her. "Uncle Ren, I'd like you to meet Miss Kit O'Neill," he says, "Mercy's granddaughter."

"It's so lovely to meet you," Kit says, taking his weathered hand in hers. "Thank you for agreeing to see me."

He nods in an almost courtly manner as Seth announces he's going into the kitchen to make some tea. Ren's eyes constrict, focused on the sapphire necklace around Kit's neck. "She kept it," he whispers.

"She wore it every day," Kit says, clutching the stone. "It obviously held great meaning for her." Kit recalls her conversation with Vera, the old woman's contention that Nan had finally succumbed and bought the necklace for herself. But Kit can see the truth in his eyes. "You," she says. "You gave this to her." She opens her bag, extracts the notecard. "You wrote this, and attached it to the box with the necklace."

His eyes widen slightly in astonishment to see the note, so carefully preserved. "That I did," he says quietly. "The day she left the island." He waves her into a chair. "Now, you must sit and tell me all about her."

Seth brings in the tea and Kit spends more than an hour filling Ren in on Nan's life: her marriage to Pop, losing her only son and his wife in a terrible accident, and raising two granddaughters. She edits her years of rebellion, saying only that Nan had shown immeasurable love and patience with her and Claire, and that they had grown up feeling loved and nurtured. His eyes mist a bit as she talks about her passing. Kit concludes with the discovery of Nan's former identity, the playbill and seashells and yellow prize ribbon in the attic, the letters to Cass, and her journey around the country to piece together Mercy Welles's missing summer.

"It seems you've had quite the escapade," Ren says finally. "Almost as wild as the one she had."

"I don't want to bring up painful memories for you," Kit says, "but I have so many questions. I'm trying to understand what could have happened that would have made her give up her career, literally her name, and go down a completely different path. Can you help me fill in the gaps?"

He's quiet for a bit, contemplative, and for a panicked moment Kit worries she's pushed him too far, that he's going to politely decline and send her on her way. But then he meets her eyes again and nods slightly. "It all started," he says, a slight dash of mischief in his voice, "because your grandmother had no idea how to properly order wine."

For the next two hours, he talks. It is, Kit somehow suspects, and the expression of wonder on Seth's face reflects, more than he's talked in a very long time. He walks her through the entire dramatic summer: their romance, including their tumble into the water at Great Rock Bight and how it proved to be the turning point in their relationship. When he gets to the part about telling Nan in the water, *Always be brave,* Kit must summon everything in her power to keep from bursting into tears.

It is a far more incredible tale than Kit could have ever imagined. Ren talks about Mercy's ill-fated trip to Boston, the fire at the theater, everything leading up to the night in Chappaquiddick. And it is here that he hesitates. "Are you sure you want to know it all?" he says, looking at her with grave seriousness. "Because once you learn the truth, it cannot be unlearned."

Kit doesn't hesitate. "Yes, I do."

And so he tells her—about Dennis's deception, the confrontation on the island and its deadly end. Kit tries valiantly to retain her composure, but inside her brain is on fire. Nan had taken someone's life.

You have no idea what I am capable of.

Just when she thinks the story has reached its climax, he then calmly tells his own part, reveals his own past, the details of the terrible night fifteen years earlier when everything that would happen that summer would be first set in motion. Kit looks over to Seth, sees his expression of unvarnished disbelief. She doesn't know if Laura knew the whole story. But it is clear Seth didn't.

She will need time later to properly process it all. But she can see Ren growing tired, the toll that reliving all of this has taken in one afternoon. She doesn't want to add to that. She looks back to Seth, who seems to be thinking the same thing, and then turns back to the old sailor. Kit leans across, places her hand atop his on his knee. "I want to express my gratitude to you, so much, for sharing all of that with me," she says. "I know how incredibly hard that must have been. Thank you for trusting me."

"You're so like her," he says, placing his other gnarled hand atop hers. "Beautiful, alive, relentlessly inquisitive." He glances over at Seth. "Clearly the Sewards men have a weakness for the Welles women."

Seth blushes and they all stand up, Ren gently complaining about his arthritic knees. Kit realizes she still has the framed photo on her lap, and walks back to the bookcase to replace it.

She's about to turn away when she spies it, lined up on the second shelf. Its beige spine stands out because, along with the title, it features a stencil of a girl detective holding a magnifying glass. She slowly slides the book off the shelf. *The Secret in the Old Attic.*

"Nancy Drew," Kit whispers. She flips it open, and a letter falls out onto the floor. Kit bends down to scoop it up, and as she does, she notices the inscription inside the book.

To my forever man of mystery– It's signed, simply, *Love, Mercy.*

She looks up at him. "That's why you addressed your note with the necklace to 'Nancy.'"

He smiles at her. "Yes. She was reading that book the first time I ever went to her cottage. Your grandmother gave that to me at the airport, the day she left." He turns to his great-nephew. "Seth, can you give me a moment alone with Kit, please?"

Seth looks to Kit and then back to Ren. "Of course. I'll be waiting outside."

After he leaves Ren turns back to Kit, who's still holding the book. "I want you to keep it," he says.

"Oh, I don't feel right about that. This was a very meaningful gift, from her to you."

"Please take it. I am an old man, and I won't be here much longer. No one will appreciate what that means as much as you will."

Kit looks down at the book, feels a tear drop down her cheek. "OK, then," she whispers, looking up at him with shining eyes. She holds out the letter. "Here is your letter."

"No, that goes with the book. You've told me about the letters your grandmother sent to her friend in California. This is the one letter she wrote to me. It might answer your last questions. Maybe it will help you understand the choices she made a little better."

Kit absorbs the enormity of the gesture, and a large lump catches in her throat. "Thank you," she says. "For everything."

He puts a gentle hand on her shoulder. "Will you take one piece of advice from an old soul?"

She smiles. "Of course."

"Seth is a good man with a good heart. I can tell there is clearly something between you. He told me what happened. His mother can be a formidable person, as my own mother was. Don't judge a man by the sins of his family. Your grandmother didn't."

Her chest is now heaving with emotion. She steps forward and closes her eyes as she envelops him in a tight embrace, feeling Nan's love coming through him, pouring out of him, and in this moment, it is everything she needs.

*

A cold wind whips around the beach. Kit shoves her hands deeper into her coat pockets as she and Seth stroll slowly along the shore-line. Save for the occasional jogger and two teenage boys tossing a football in the distance, there's no one here. The autumn sun provides inadequate defense against the chill but marvelous, shiny dappling on the water, which seems even bluer than usual, small waves cresting into foamy breakers on the sand.

She stops, marveling at the gigantic boulder plopped right in the middle of the rolling surf, and thinks, *This was their place. Right here. Almost sixty years ago, she stood here with Ren, trying to navigate life and love and loss. Trying to decide the right path forward. And now here I am, doing the same thing.*

"So," Seth asks, "did you get them?"

"Get what?"

"Answers."

She considers this for a bit. "Maybe," she says. "It's more like I came here looking for something specific, but I'm leaving with something else entirely. That doesn't even make any sense. I guess I'm still trying to wrap my head around it all." She looks up at him. "Thank you for taking me to see him. I realize you could have just kept that a secret, and you didn't."

"I'm just trying to make it right. To assure you I'm . . ." He trails off, looks away.

"To assure me you're what?"

He meets her eyes again. "That I'm not *them*. That I'm a man you can trust. Do you think that's possible? That I can earn back your trust?"

It's her turn to look away. She knows what the moment calls for her to say, but she can't bring herself to utter the words.

And then she thinks of Nan, all those summers ago, making mistakes, trying to make it all right. The irony is not lost on her that here she stands, two generations later, with a chance to create a different ending than her grandmother and Seth's great-uncle had. Perhaps second chances come in all sorts of ways. Because is there any real difference between Mercy then and Seth now? Mercy had kept things from Ren, and then had to earn back his trust. Wasn't it only fair that she manifest the same? And if she doesn't, what happens then? Is she really going to turn her back on the only man she's ever let in?

The man she now knows that she loves.

They stand in silence for a few minutes until he speaks again. "I'm going to leave you here for a bit so you can get some alone time to gather your thoughts. I'll go up and wait for you in the car."

He turns to walk away. She darts her hand out to grab his arm, spins him back toward her.

"Seth."

His eyes are as transparent as glass, filled with remorse and gratitude and hope. But most of all, filled with . . . love.

"I forgive you," Kit says.

Seth answers with a slight smile, as if he's trying to hold back something stronger. He takes her in his arms and kisses her, tenderly, meaningfully, a man not with something to say, but rather to prove. "You know," he says, still holding her, "once my dissertation defense is done, I'll need to find a full-time teaching gig."

"Is that so?"

"Yes. And I was thinking that maybe . . . New York would be a place where there are opportunities." He looks intensely into her eyes. "What do you think of that idea?"

"Is that the only reason you'd want to go to New York? 'Opportunities'?"

"Well, actually, there's this girl . . ."

She smiles. "She must be pretty awesome."

He nods emphatically. "She is."

Kit reaches up, gently strokes his cheek with the backs of her fingers. He squeezes his eyes shut, relishing the moment. And as she looks at him, sees the purity of his feelings on his face, she thinks that maybe history doesn't always have to repeat itself. Nan had left her great love behind. But perhaps, by doing so, she had paved the path for Kit to find hers.

"Look at me," she says. He opens his eyes. "I love you, Seth."

"I love you, too, Kit." This time the kiss is deeper, richer. The future is here; the past is fading. Except, perhaps, for one final moment.

"I'm going to go up," he says, nodding slightly toward the path back up to the road. "Take as much time as you need." He kisses the top of her forehead, then begins the trudge back up the twisting beach path and out of view.

She reaches into her coat pocket, extracts the letter. It feels like a violation, in a way, to read it, but inside her head she hears Nan telling her it's OK, nudging her along on her own journey to happiness.

Kit sits down on the sand, takes a deep breath, and opens the letter.

September 9, 1959

My dearest darling—

I sit here at the kitchen table in my cottage, my bags packed, wondering what awaits me when I board the plane and leave this island. I can't help but think of something I read years ago. There is a French philosopher named Albert Camus who wrote a book called 'The Myth of Sisyphus' in the early 1940s. I had a period early on in my adventures in Hollywood when I thought reading 'deep' books would make me appear worldly and sophisticated to casting directors, so I sought out stuff like that. Anyway, I was thinking today of something Camus penned that I have never forgotten. He wrote, 'Living an experience, a particular fate, is accepting fully.' I don't think it's an accident that popped into my head today. Because I am here, struggling with accepting my particular fate. Our fate.

Like you, I so wish things could have turned out differently. But I accept things for what they are, and I possess neither the strength nor the tenacity, I fear, to try to convince you there is another path available to us. But that does not mean I do not mourn what might have been. I suspect I always will. Because in you I found everything I had been looking for, and didn't even know I was looking for, in another person—someone kind and humane, who challenged me and treated me not as a 'movie star' or as a silly, naive girl, though in truth I came here as both and leave here as neither. You were, I think, perhaps the only person who saw the me inside, who brought her out, and in turn I saw the you inside, and I brought you out, and together we had a brief but glorious time together, feeling the sun on our faces, love in our hearts. I will always be so very deeply grateful to you for that, for giving me a season of love most people never get to experience in their lifetimes.

We will be bound forever by our secrets this summer, and while there is much pain in that, there is also joy. For I will stand in the shallow surf of the Atlantic somewhere far away and I will look across the wide ocean and I will see you somewhere across, smiling at me, and that will bring me comfort as I rebuild my life anew.

And I will bake vanilla apple pie until I die.

When the nights are windy and cold, and the chill off the water seeps into your bones, I hope you will sometimes think of me and what we shared, and that it will bring you some warmth and solace. I know it will for me.

I will never forget you, my love. Stay true. Be happy.

Always be brave.

All my love,
Mercy

———

Acknowledgments

In the early 1990s I was stuck in a life I didn't want. In an effort to gain some clarity, I took a trip to Martha's Vineyard. I don't recall how I had learned about the island, or why I was so intent on going there. I arrived in October, when the island was relatively deserted and in the crisp embrace of autumn.

Roaming around Edgartown I found a bookstore and bought an old secondhand mystery set on the island. That afternoon, as the skies opened and it poured rain, I sat on the porch of the inn where I was staying and immersed myself in the novel. The proprietor came out and served me tea. To say the entire tableau was a desperately needed tonic would be an understatement. My love affair with Martha's Vineyard had commenced.

There is something uniquely curative about the place—a particular mystique—that, despite traveling pretty far and wide around the world, I have never found anywhere else. I was extremely fortunate when I was accepted into the Martha's Vineyard Writers Residency at the Noepe Center for the Literary Arts in 2015. I wrote a chunk of my second book there, and—exploring the tranquil idyll by car, bicycle, and foot—came up with the idea for this one there, too.

I kept returning to do research, and as the story came together, I knew I would need help to bring the Martha's Vineyard of 1959 properly to life. First and foremost, I owe enormous gratitude to Justen Ahren, the winsome director of the Noepe Center and a proud island native, who not only welcomed me into his writing fold but connected me with sources, beta-read the book, and most of all, encouraged me to tackle the project. I will forever be indebted to all of the writing fellows I have befriended at the Noepe colony, which will always be a magical place for me.

My deep thanks to Bo Van Riper, research librarian at the Gale Huntington Library at the Martha's Vineyard Museum, who braved a mountain of dust unearthing archival newspapers, photographs, postcards, advertisements, and random other ephemera from 1959 that allowed me to build an accurate historical setting. Eric Alexander, librarian at the Edgartown Public Library, directed me to additional books, articles, and records. And I carry deep affection for the late Shirley W. Mayhew, who herself married into one of the founding families of Martha's Vineyard and spent an entire afternoon with me at her home in West Tisbury regaling me with stories of life on the island in the 1950s. She died in 2020 and left an incredible legacy behind.

Several books provided key background details past and present to bring authenticity to the story, among them *Vineyard Voices: Words, Faces, and Voices of Island People*, by Linsey Lee; *Island Stories: Highlights from the Martha's Vineyard Museum*, by Bonnie Stacy; *African Americans on Martha's Vineyard: From Enslavement to Presidential Visit*, by Thomas Dresser; and *Shucked: Life on a New England Oyster Farm*, by Erin Byers Murray. Additionally, a word of thanks to all the unsung writers who have spent their careers chronicling life for the *Vineyard Gazette*, the island's paper of record, whose archives proved an incredible historical resource.

Though several key locations in the novel—most notably, the White Whale, Sycamore, and this iteration of the Martha's Vineyard Playhouse—are completely fictitious, I have attempted to otherwise re-create life on the island in 1959 as accurately as possible. Any mistakes are entirely my own.

To my agent, the legend that is Jane Dystel, my continued gratitude for always being the voice of encouragement and reason. This is my third novel with my editor, Nicole Angeloro, who has believed in my storytelling from the beginning and whose insightful queries and nimble editing proved, as always, to be invaluable in polishing the story. To her and everyone on the team at HarperCollins, my heartfelt thanks.

Writing is done alone, but shaping a narrative truly takes a village. I am so grateful to have had the amazing members of my writing group—Cheryl Della Pietra, David Williams, Malcolm Burnley, Jordan Heil, and Joseph Earl Thomas—to help me stay focused and sane as they asked probing questions and delivered invaluable feedback. And to Brent Baker, who not only beta-read the entire book in a fortnight but also allowed me to name a villain after him, my deepest thanks for your trenchant analysis, and even more so for your incredible and generous friendship.

To my California crew—Dan Hess, Brian Dent, Mark Campbell and Robert Gibson, Stan Scoggins and Nelson Sanchez, Justin Pizzi, Courtney Kemp, Bill Salada and Cory Preston, Will Inbusch and Anu Devabhaktuni, Ed and Perrine Mann, Shanti Hinojos and Jonathan Kappelman, Duane and Meredith Swierczynski, and the whole gang in StratComm at UCLA—thank you for supporting me in my new L.A. home these first few years with your goodwill, your laughter, and your loving support. I am so blessed to live the life that I do.

And finally, to the people of Martha's Vineyard, thank you for always welcoming me and every other interloper who washes up on your shores with your hospitality, your warmth, and your endless patience at our regular intrusion into your lives. The island's charm comes from its environs, but its convivial spirit comes from its people.

I'll be back.

ABOUT

MARINER BOOKS

Mariner Books traces its beginnings to 1832 when William Ticknor co-founded the Old Corner Bookstore in Boston, from which he would run the legendary firm Ticknor and Fields, publisher of Ralph Waldo Emerson, Harriet Beecher Stowe, Nathaniel Hawthorne, and Henry David Thoreau. Following Ticknor's death, Henry Oscar Houghton acquired Ticknor and Fields and, in 1880, formed Houghton Mifflin, which later merged with venerable Harcourt Publishing to form Houghton Mifflin Harcourt. HarperCollins purchased HMH's trade publishing business in 2021 and reestablished their storied lists and editorial team under the name Mariner Books.

Uniting the legacies of Houghton Mifflin, Harcourt Brace, and Ticknor and Fields, Mariner Books continues one of the great traditions in American bookselling. Our imprints have introduced an incomparable roster of enduring classics, including Hawthorne's *The Scarlet Letter*, Thoreau's *Walden*, Willa Cather's *O Pioneers!*, Virginia Woolf's *To the Lighthouse*, W.E.B. Du Bois's *Black Reconstruction*, J.R.R. Tolkien's *The Lord of the Rings*, Carson McCullers's *The Heart Is a Lonely Hunter*, Ann Petry's *The Narrows*, George Orwell's *Animal Farm* and *Nineteen Eighty-Four*, Rachel Carson's *Silent Spring*, Margaret Walker's *Jubilee*, Italo Calvino's *Invisible Cities*, Alice Walker's *The Color Purple*, Margaret Atwood's *The Handmaid's Tale*, Tim O'Brien's *The Things They Carried*, Philip Roth's *The Plot Against America*, Jhumpa Lahiri's *Interpreter of Maladies*, and many others. Today Mariner Books remains proudly committed to the craft of fine publishing established nearly two centuries ago at the Old Corner Bookstore.